WEAPONS

OF

OPPORTUNITY

BOOKS BY DALE BROWN

WEAPONS

OF

OPPORTUNITY

A NOVEL

DALE
BROWN

**BLACK
STONE**
PUBLISHING

Printed in the United States of America
Originally published in hardcover by Blackstone Publishing in 2023

First paperback edition: 2024
ISBN 979-8-212-18839-5
Fiction / Thrillers / Military

Version 1

Blackstone Publishing
31 Mistletoe Rd.
Ashland, OR 97520

www.BlackstonePublishing.com

*This novel is dedicated
to the ones who keep watching to keep us safe . . .
around the corner or around the world.*

"To surprise the enemy is to defeat him."
—Alexander Suvorov,
eighteenth-century Russian general

"Madness is however an affliction which
in war carries with it the advantage of
SURPRISE."
—Winston Churchill

PROLOGUE

TAMBOV MILITARY AIRFIELD, RUSSIA

NOVEMBER

Winter had come early to this part of Russia, four hundred kilometers southeast of Moscow. Snow drifted down out of the cloudy night sky, becoming a swirling curtain of dazzling white where it fell into the beams of the powerful lights ringing the airfield. Along the base's western perimeter, a stand of bare-limbed birch trees faded from sight—obscured by the steadily increasing snowfall.

Several narrow-body jets were parked out on a wide apron just off the concrete runway. Fitted with the needle-shaped nose of the much-larger Tupolev Tu-160 sweptwing supersonic bomber, they were Tu-134UBLs—models of a 1960s-vintage civilian passenger plane converted to train bomber crews rotating through Tambov's 1,449th Air Base. But these specialized training aircraft were dwarfed by the single enormous, four-engine airliner sitting on a taxiway not far away. Comparable to America's Air Force One, this Ilyushin-96-300PU was Russian president Piotr Zhdanov's personal transport.

Outside near the flight line, a handful of stern-faced body-guards surrounded Zhdanov. He took a long drag from his cigarette and then irritably pitched it away across the tarmac. Its lit end glowed orange in the darkness for a brief moment before vanishing, extinguished by the falling snow. *Much like any man's life, in the end*, he thought dourly. One brief flash of light and warmth and then oblivion for all eternity. His hard mouth tightened in a grimace. Despite his thick black coat and fur hat, he could feel the cold gnawing at his bones. The glory days when he could strut bare chested through freezing temperatures for propaganda videos were long gone. More and more, age and ill health were catching up to him.

Impatiently, Zhdanov turned to the much younger, immaculately dressed man at his side. "Well, Voronin?" he demanded. "Now can you tell me what's so important that you've dragged me out here to the ass end of nowhere?"

In answer, Pavel Voronin first checked his watch before looking back down at Russia's autocratic ruler. His well-mannered smile never reached his pale-gray eyes. "I've invited you here for a demonstration, Mr. President," he said evenly.

Zhdanov snorted. "A demonstration of what? Frostbite?"

"The future," Voronin answered, ignoring the older man's show of ill temper. Although it was not widely known outside Russia, his shadowy company—Sindikat Vorona, the Raven Syndicate—supplied military and intelligence services, equipment, and expertise to the highest bidders among Moscow's allies around the world. Aided by enormous wealth and utter ruthlessness, Voronin himself had risen through the ruling elite to become the president's closest strategic adviser. Although he was nominally still only a private citizen, his influence over Zhdanov effectively made him the second-most-powerful man in the Russian state.

Zhdanov frowned. "Pavel, I'm in no mood for riddles—"

Suddenly, one of his bodyguards broke in. "Sir, we have to get you into cover! Right now!" He tapped at his radio earpiece. "The Tambov control tower reports defense radars have just picked up an unidentified aircraft at close range!"

Voronin's smile widened a bit. "Relax," he said. "This new arrival is no threat. Not to us, at least." He nodded toward the southern end of the runway. "You see?" And as if in response, a pale-gray shape materialized out of the darkness—gliding downward through a vortex of whirling snow. Batwing configured, the mystery aircraft was roughly seven meters long, with a similar wingspan. That made it significantly smaller than most modern combat planes, considerably less than half the size of Russia's Su-35 air superiority fighter, as an example.

The wheels of its retractable landing gear were already lowered and locked in place. The aircraft touched down gently and rolled toward them along the runway, slowing fast until it came to a full stop only meters away. Its single wing-buried turbofan spooled down with a muted, remarkably quiet whine.

Zhdanov stared at the mystery plane for a moment. Then he swung back to Voronin. "Where the devil did that *thing* come from?" he snapped, not bothering to hide his irritation at being kept both literally and figuratively in the dark about this surprise landing.

"This prototype aircraft took off two thousand kilometers to the east," the younger man told him. "At a small airfield near Omsk."

Zhdanov raised an eyebrow. "Omsk? Our armed forces don't have a base there."

"They do not," Voronin agreed with a shrug. "But I do." He nodded at the gray, batwing-shaped plane. "This new aircraft is the product of an intense development effort funded by my Raven Syndicate." He smiled again. "Aided, of course, by advanced scientific and engineering research data obtained through other . . . less conventional . . . means."

"Through espionage," Zhdanov realized.

"Why spend years and hundreds of billions of rubles to reinvent what our enemies already have in their possession?" Voronin asked.

The president matched his wry expression. "Why, indeed." His eyes narrowed. "And the point of all this effort and expense? What's so special about this new plane of yours?"

"Among other things, the fact that it flew all the way here without being detected by a single one of our vaunted air defense radar systems," Voronin answered. "Not, in fact, until the moment it lowered its gear for landing."

Zhdanov nodded his understanding. "You've built a new stealth aircraft," he said appreciatively, eyeing the lines of the aircraft's carefully designed configuration. "Introduce me to your test pilot, Pavel. I will congratulate him."

"There is no pilot," Voronin said.

The older man stared at him. "This is a drone?"

"What our military calls an unmanned combat aerial vehicle," Voronin agreed. "A UCAV."

Zhdanov snorted. "Ah, where would our generals be without their bullshit jargon?" He jerked a thumb at the plane. "So, does this new robotic flying machine of yours have a name? Or only a number?"

"We call it a Mora," Voronin told him.

Studying the aircraft now flecked here and there by clumps of accumulating snow, Russia's leader bared his teeth in an icy, predatory smile of his own. The name the younger man had given to his new weapon was highly appropriate. In Slavic mythology, a Mora was a night demon. Transforming itself into the thin, almost invisible shape of a piece of hair or straw, the demon could flit unnoticed through locked doors—and then drain the blood of its chosen victims.

———

Later, during the flight back to Moscow on Zhdanov's plane, Voronin allowed himself a moment to savor the remarkable success of his bit of theater with the Mora drone. The serious risks he'd taken by approving this prototype's first long-range, cross-country flight had paid off handsomely, greatly strengthening his clout. It was, he admitted inwardly, a triumph he had very badly needed. Months before, the unexpected and still-unexplained failure of a Raven Syndicate operation code-named MIDNIGHT had infuriated the president, leaving Voronin momentarily vulnerable. Among Zhdanov's inner circle, there were many old military men and politicians—cautious and cowardly relics of an earlier age—who envied and resented Voronin's swift rise to power. Only the president's awareness that none of them had even a fraction of Voronin's aggressiveness, imagination, or daring had saved him from being cast aside. At the time, he'd assured Zhdanov that he had other weapons to use against the Americans. Tonight, he had made good on that promise.

His smartphone vibrated softly, alerting him to an urgent message from his top deputy, Vasily Kondakov, a former colonel in the GRU, Russia's military intelligence service. He checked the screen. *Ferrets report small signs of prey*, Kondakov had written. *Possible Langley connection makes endeavor highly risky. Request authorization to pursue further.*

Voronin sat back in his seat to consider his response. Within days of MIDNIGHT's disastrous end, he had set agents in motion with orders to identify those responsible. Now, at last, after months wasted prowling down blind alleys, it seemed that his operatives had a solid lead, however tentative. *And high time, too*, he thought coldly. With the planning for another covert large-scale attack against the United States already underway, the Raven Syndicate could not afford to give its unknown enemies free rein. They must be tracked down, pinned, and marked for destruction with all possible speed.

Still, he thought uneasily, there was no denying that the possibility of CIA involvement came as an unpleasant surprise. Early on, he had firmly ruled out any idea that the bloated, risk-averse American intelligence organization headquartered in Langley, Virginia, could have played an active part in thwarting his previous operation. His mouth curled into a slight frown. Taking direct action against anyone connected to the CIA would not be at all popular with Moscow's own official spy services, the SVR and the GRU. In general, they preferred waging their clandestine war with the West through proxies . . . leaving most of the real dirty work to other, deniable hands. That would go double for any potential "wet work"—killing—within the precincts of the US capital region.

Voronin's smile returned. So be it. If it proved necessary, he would show the hidebound men who ran the SVR and GRU the value of swift, decisive action—even right in the enemy's backyard. Swiftly, he typed in a single-word reply to Kondakov: *Proceed.*

ONE

SOUTHWESTERN VIRGINIA

SOME WEEKS LATER

Nick Flynn crouched low behind the thick trunk of an old oak. His breath steamed in the air, visible in the wan winter sunlight filtering down through the trees carpeting this steep Appalachian hillside. Quickly, he checked the fire-mode selector on the short-barreled HK417 carbine he carried, making doubly sure it was set on semiauto. His Quartet Directorate action team had chosen the German-designed weapon because its 7.62mm rounds had better stopping power and armor penetration than NATO-standard 5.56mm bullets. But those same rounds were also bigger and heavier, so each rifle's standard magazine only held twenty rounds instead of thirty. Going full auto could empty a whole magazine in seconds. *And running low on ammo is not exactly a great plan in a combat situation*, he thought wryly. Unless, of course, he intended to try beating an enemy to death with the HK's polymer stock.

Flynn glanced right and saw a short, compact man wearing

a mottled white-and-brown winter camouflage smock settle into
cover behind a boulder roughly twenty yards away. Shannon
Cooke, a tough, forceful ex–US Special Forces operator, was
in position. Flynn held out an open palm, signaling Cooke to
hold in place for now.

With a tight grin, the other man flashed him the OK sign.

Looking left, Flynn spotted Wade Vucovich, the second
member of his team, going prone behind a tree trunk of his
own. Vucovich, a former US Army soldier, acknowledged the
hand signal and then sighted through the optic fitted to his own
HK carbine—scanning the snowy, tree-studded slope rising
above them.

A final quick check backward showed Cole Hynes in his assigned slot about twenty yards downhill. The broad-shouldered
ex-soldier was ready to maneuver to either flank if they ran into
trouble.

That left only the action team's fifth man, Tadeusz Kossak.
The Pole, a veteran of his own country's elite Special Troops
Command, was not anywhere in sight—exactly as planned.
Flynn nodded to himself. So far, so good. They'd cleared the
wooded valley behind them without taking any casualties, but
it was high time they got moving again. While rushing headlong into a possible enemy ambush would be dumb, there was
no way to complete this mission without pushing deeper into
hostile country. Their final objective lay at the very top of this
next piece of high ground.

He shot a quick flurry of hand signals to the others, alerting them to what he intended. Then, cautiously, he climbed
back to his feet and moved forward with his HK carbine at the
ready. On the left and right, Vucovich and Cooke did the same,
paralleling his steady advance up the slope.

Snow crunched softly under Flynn's boots. He winced a

little at the noise. It sounded much louder against the hushed, frozen silence of these wooded hills and valleys. Growing up in sunny Central Texas, where serious winter weather was a rare event, wasn't exactly the best training for sneaking around on icy ground. Then again, before he'd joined the highly secret Quartet Directorate, his last assignment as a captain in the US Air Force had been to a remote radar outpost above the Arctic Circle. And compared to the howling winds and subzero perpetual dark he'd fought through up there, this brisk trek through southwestern Virginia's rugged backcountry was practically a stroll on some idyllic Caribbean beach.

With the HK tucked firmly against his shoulder, he swiveled from side to side as he climbed steadily, hunting for the slightest sign of movement or anything that looked at all out of place among the trees and snow-covered rock ledges ahead of him. He controlled his breathing. He needed to be able to hear even the tiniest sounds.

Twang.

Flynn spun left toward the noise and saw a man-sized shape bounce upward from behind a ledge less than ten yards away. He squeezed off two quick shots. *Crack-crack.* Two holes appeared dead center in the plywood target. The suppressor threaded to the end of his carbine dropped the sound of his shots to a decibel level his ears could handle without damage. Off to either flank, he could hear more gunfire as Cooke and Vucovich engaged pop-up targets of their own.

Suddenly, something flickered at the very outside edge of his peripheral vision. *Holy shit.* A target had remotely triggered up in one of the tall trees to his right rear, mimicking an enemy sniper concealed high among the thick, bare branches. Desperately, he swung around—knowing he wasn't going to make it in time. If this were real, he would be dead.

Whaaap. The target shuddered, hit straight on by a high-powered .338 Lapua Magnum rifle round. A fraction of a second later, the distant sound of the shot echoed across the surrounding hills.

"*Hostile down,*" Flynn heard Kossak report coolly through his headset. He breathed out.

"*Dzięki, Tadeuszu.* Thanks, Tadeusz," he radioed.

"*Just doing my job, Nick,*" Kossak replied. "*But you are welcome, anyway.*"

Flynn could imagine the satisfied smile on the Polish sniper's face. Long-range precision shooting was the other man's passion, and that had been a difficult shot through all the intervening trees. Kossak was on overwatch, assigned to cover them as they advanced toward the crest. He was in a concealed position on the other side of the valley they'd crossed—close to four hundred yards behind them now. *The seasons giveth and they taketh away,* Flynn thought with a grin of his own. Training in this cold weather might be a bitch, but at least it let them make full use of their best marksman's specialized skills. In summer or spring, with all the leaves still on the forest's stands of oak and hickory, the Pole would have had a very hard time keeping them in sight from any real distance.

"Lead to Posse," Flynn radioed to the rest of the team. "Push on for the crest. Same formation. Stay sharp. There are bound to be a few more surprises up ahead." Acknowledgments crackled through his headset. He readied his HK again and moved onward.

The next minutes proved his point. Time and again, they encountered expertly hidden pop-up targets. Or needed to safely navigate mazes of trip-wire pyrotechnics that simulated more lethal, real-world land mines and improvised booby traps. When he finally made it all the way to the top of the hill without being "killed," Flynn breathed out. He rolled his tight shoulders and neck, hearing the joints crack and pop. Then he put his carbine on safe and turned to observe the others as they joined him on the summit.

He was glad to see that they were all moving easily, without even the slightest sign of exhaustion or undue strain. Three of them—Cooke, Vucovich, and Kossak—had been badly wounded on their last major mission together. Between the necessary hospital stays and the long slog of arduous physical therapy required to mend broken bones and rebuild damaged muscles, each man had been out of the field for months. These weeklong tactical exercises were intended to prove that they really were fully fit. And so far, at least, they'd met and overcome every physical and mental challenge presented to them.

Assuming they could keep it up over the next couple of days, Flynn would be hugely relieved to have Tad Kossak and the others back at his side. Finding people with the sort of highly specialized skills needed by the Quartet Directorate was a tough task. Finding those who could be trusted to keep the organization's very existence absolutely secret was even tougher. Back at the beginning of the Cold War against the Soviet Union, veterans of America's OSS (the Office of Strategic Services, a forerunner to the CIA); Britain's SOE (the Special Operations Executive); and the anti-Nazi resistance movements of France, Norway, Poland, and other allied countries had seen the need for a covert private force able to act decisively against serious threats to the free world. Even then, it was already clear that the West's official intelligence agencies were both deeply penetrated by Soviet spies and increasingly mired in politics and bureaucratic caution.

The Quartet Directorate—usually referred to as Four by those in the know—was their answer. For decades now, Four's operatives had fought the free world's enemies—waging war from the shadows outside the control of risk-averse officials and politicians. As a result, the slightest breach of the secrecy shielding their activities would be catastrophic. Given the odds they faced, they needed to stay completely off the radar of both their foes and their own governments' regular spy services.

Nick Flynn himself had been recruited into Four after a pair of sketchy, poorly planned CIA covert operations blew up in Langley's face a couple of years before. Since he was just a lowly Air Force intelligence officer without the slightest ounce of political pull, the agency had tapped him as a convenient scapegoat for its own screw-ups—despite the fact that he'd risked his life to prevent even greater disasters. If anything, he realized, he'd probably been targeted precisely *because* he'd succeeded where the CIA's own people had fucked up. Gratitude was an alien concept in the ruling circles of Washington, DC, especially when there was blame to be shifted.

Compared to him, Cooke and Kossak were old Four hands. The two remaining members of his team, Cole Hynes and Wade Vucovich, were other survivors of the same debacle in Alaska that had ended Flynn's Air Force career. They'd tracked him down and finagled their own way into the Quartet Directorate some months back. And while the two former GIs were a little rougher around the edges than the organization's usual recruits, they'd already proved themselves in unconventional combat when it counted.

Flynn waited until the four men were gathered around him in a half circle. "Comments?" he asked.

"Our time was decent," Cooke allowed. "But we could probably shave a couple of minutes off on the next go-around."

Flynn nodded. He'd kept the pace a little slower this time to avoid overtaxing those who'd been wounded. Now that he'd seen them all in action, he could step it up. He turned to Kossak. "Tad?"

The Pole patted his Finnish-made TRG-42 bolt-action sniper rifle with a pleased look. "Any chance to shoot this nice little weapon is welcome," he said with a shrug. "Even if it is just at harmless paper or wood targets."

"Give me a little while, and I'll do my level best to find you something that shoots back," Flynn promised with a smile. He turned to the last two. "You guys?"

Quiet as usual, Vucovich only shook his head.

Hynes, typically irrepressible, showed his teeth. "Well, I thought we kicked some serious simulated ass, sir." He clapped Cooke on the shoulder. "Hey, that was a pretty sweet little assault course your cousins put together," he said. "Fixing pop-ups high in the trees like that? That's some intense grade-A-level evil nastiness right there."

"The boys certainly *do* enjoy their work, whether it's for us or the weekend warrior wannabes and paintball shooters they also run through these hills. Keeps 'em out of trouble," the other man agreed, with the hint of a smile. "Well, mostly, anyway."

Hynes grinned. "Trouble, huh? Like what? Revenuers hunting for their white lightning still? Or blood feuds with the neighboring clans? That kind of hillbilly shit?"

Cooke shook his head. "Now, Cole," he said kindly, "you've been watching way too much TV. We're all genteel, law-abiding folks around here." His Virginia drawl thickened slightly. "But if you do hear banjos off in the distance, my advice is to run while you can."

Flynn stifled a laugh. Like many of Four's original founders, the native Virginian came from a wealthy family. Much of the surrounding countryside belonged to them, and they had roots here dating back to the American Revolution. Cooke himself had chosen service to his country over more lucrative private pursuits like lawyering and managing money. He'd ended up

with the Army's ultrasecret Task Force Orange. As a conse-
quence, he'd spent a lot of time deployed covertly in extremely
unfriendly parts of the world, collecting crucial intelligence
needed for various high-risk US special forces operations. And
after leaving the armed forces, he'd been recruited to handle the
same kind of work for the Quartet Directorate. So when Flynn
had started planning these live-fire training exercises, Cooke
had gladly volunteered both the use of this private land and his
old family home as their base for the duration.

"Okay, guys," Flynn said briskly. "We'll head on over to
the house and grab some hot food. After that, my advice is to
rest up while you can. Because we're coming back at zero dark
thirty to run the course using night vision gear." He nodded
back down the slope. "And just to make it fair, that range is
going to be reset while we're gone—with a whole new slew of
obstacles and targets."

The others nodded their approval. No matter how good
your intel was, it was never perfect. There were always unpleasant surprises, and the only certainty in battle was uncertainty.
Anyone who wanted to come out alive at the other end of a
fight kept that firmly in mind.

TWO

COOKE MANOR

A SHORT TIME LATER

The large, elegant house that Cooke called the Manor, only partly in jest, lay at the end of a long, curving drive. Set high up on a ridge, the property offered sweeping views over the neighboring valleys and wooded ridges. The house itself had been built after the Second World War by Cooke's grandfather—as an homage to the beautiful châteaus the older man had admired while blasting his way across German-occupied France with the rest of Patton's Third Army. Its steep, mansard-style roof, wood-shutter-bracketed windows, arched stone front doorway, and cream-colored brick exterior above a layer of native rock enhanced the resemblance.

Already shrugging out of his camouflage smock, Nick Flynn took the stairs to the upper floor two at a time. The guest room he'd been assigned was down a hall leading to the back of the big house. And the luxury of luxuries, it came with its own attached bathroom. After a long, cold day spent trekking through snow-covered woods and up and down steep hills, he was more than ready for a hot shower—with an emphasis on *hot*. As in practically scalding.

He reached for the door handle and froze, suddenly aware of something hard prodding him in the back.

"Reach for the sky, pardner," a familiar, husky voice breathed into his ear. "And don't make any sudden moves."

Slowly, Flynn raised his hands. "Well, ma'am, you've sure as all get-out got me dead to rights," he drawled, glancing back over his shoulder with a lopsided smile. "But in my own defense, I wasn't expecting any special visitors today."

"That's kind of obvious, Nick," Laura Van Horn said with a grin of her own. The attractive dark-haired woman slid the smartphone she'd used to mimic a pistol back into the pocket of her stylish winter coat. She shook her head in mock disapproval. "Seems a little careless of you, doesn't it?"

Flynn lowered his arms and turned to face her. "Maybe a bit," he admitted. "Since you do have a certain knack for turning up unexpectedly . . . right out of the blue."

They'd first met when the damaged Air National Guard C-130J she'd been copiloting came in for an emergency landing near his last duty station in Alaska's frozen wilds. At the time, he'd thought that was sheer coincidence. Only later did he learn that she was also one of the Quartet Directorate's top field agents—and that it was at her urging he'd been recruited into Four.

He eyed her hopefully. "I don't suppose this is a social call?"

"No such luck," Van Horn said with regret. She looked him up and down with a wicked gleam in her eyes. "Which is too bad because some 'just us' time would have been a lot of fun. Though I guess possibly a little hard on that weak heart of yours."

"Hey, my heart's just fine," Flynn retorted.

If anything, her expression grew even more mischievous.

"Maybe *now* it is." Her generous mouth curved upward. "But later? Well, that might be a different story, cowboy."

He had a sudden, very vivid mental image of Laura wearing a lot less and in far more private circumstances. *Down, boy*, he thought desperately. He cleared his throat, trying mightily to rein in his freewheeling imagination and focus on business. "So why *are* you here, then?"

"Br'er Fox asked me to fly him up. We just got in, and he's downstairs waiting for us now."

Flynn felt his eyebrows go up. Carleton Frederick Fox was the head of Four's American station, which made him their boss. In practice, he gave his subordinates a lot of room to run training ops and even missions in their individual ways. So his sudden decision to come here in person could only mean one thing. "There's trouble brewing?"

Van Horn nodded. "Yep. And I'm guessing it's the kind Four pays us the big bucks to handle."

He considered the state of his bank account and started to open his mouth in protest.

"Okay," she amended. "Make that 'barely adequate bucks.' But you get the drift."

"That I do," Flynn allowed. Money wasn't a motivation for anyone in the Quartet Directorate. He'd joined up because Fox had promised him opportunities for independent action in a good cause, without being second-guessed or held back by careerist senior officers and cowardly politicos. The fact that those opportunities usually came with a significant risk of death or injury was understood. He gestured politely toward the stairs. "Well, ma'am, after you, then. Because I guess it wouldn't do to keep our fearless leader waiting long."

———

Cooke Manor's library took up a significant portion of the ground floor. Several large windows set into one wall offered plenty of natural light. Except for a door out into the main hall, the other walls were lined with floor-to-ceiling cases crammed full of hardcover books, a mix of military history, mysteries, and classic Golden Age science fiction. Comfortable leather-backed chairs surrounded a table placed in the very center of the room.

Fox, a thin, middle-aged man with graying hair, rose from the table when Flynn and Van Horn appeared. His pale eyes studied them from behind a pair of wire-rimmed glasses. "I'm sorry to break in on your training cycle like this, Nick," he said quietly, waving them into seats and then sitting back down himself. "But we've got something of a situation developing."

For *situation*, read *something wicked this way comes*, Flynn realized. Over the past year or so, he'd learned that the head of Four's American station had a remarkable gift for understatement.

"It concerns my top contact at the CIA," Fox went on. His mouth twisted slightly. "Or more accurately, someone who *was* my most significant source inside Langley . . . right up until a few months ago."

"Who?" Van Horn asked.

"Philip Demopoulos."

Flynn whistled softly. Like the other Quartet Directorate heads of station, Fox kept up a series of discreet, arm's-length relationships with people in the official military and intelligence services. All of these contacts were painstakingly screened, and as an added precaution, none of them were given the full picture of Four's real aims or capabilities. But Demopoulos had been the head of the CIA's Directorate of Analysis—one of its most senior executives. Learning that the fourth- or fifth-highest-ranking person in the CIA, depending on the current state of its torturous office politics, had been one of Four's backdoor "friends" came as a real surprise.

Fox nodded at his reaction. "Philip was extremely useful," he said. "He was in an excellent position to funnel classified intelligence to us when we needed it. Just as important, he sometimes served as a conduit of vital information we collected to the powers that be in the US national security apparatus."

"Passing it off as a product of the CIA's own work," Van Horn realized.

Fox nodded. "Or as material from other confidential intelligence sources."

"So what happened to him?" Flynn asked the older man.

"Unfortunately, *we* happened," Fox answered. "Last year, I passed him the intel your team gathered on that Russian and Iranian plan to hit us with a concealed, sea-launched ICBM."

"That sick son of a bitch Pavel Voronin's Operation MID-NIGHT," Flynn realized. The code name their enemies had selected had been apt, given their intention to hurl the United States into a new Dark Age—murdering hundreds of millions of innocents through starvation and disease.

Fox nodded. "I'd hoped Demopoulos could persuade his agency superiors to act directly to eliminate the threat. Either by using the CIA's own covert operations capabilities or those of our regular armed forces."

"But instead they all sat on their fat asses and did nothing," Van Horn said bluntly.

Flynn gritted his teeth. Navy or Air Force bombers could easily have sunk the ship ferrying that deadly nuclear-tipped missile into striking range of America's heartland. Instead, he'd been forced to lead a desperate, rapidly improvised assault to take it out—with more than half his team killed or seriously wounded in the process.

"A sadly accurate assessment," Fox said evenly. "Apparently, the intelligence we provided was discounted as insufficient to justify risking the current administration's high-level diplomatic push for closer, friendlier ties with Iran." He shrugged. "If nothing else, the current director of the CIA is a consummate political animal, with a time-honed ability to sense which way the winds inside the White House are blowing."

"And when Demopoulos turned out to be right after all?" Van Horn prompted. "He got the chop?"

Fox nodded again. "The DCI pushed him into taking early retirement." He shook his head. "It's an old story inside the CIA and the military alike. No good deed goes unpunished, if you make the upper echelons look foolish." He glanced across the table at Flynn. "As you know all too well."

One side of Van Horn's mouth quirked upward in a crooked grin. "Of course, Nick's natural orneriness probably didn't help him there much either. Guys with stars on their shoulders really hate it when someone tells them they're full of shit."

Flynn spread his hands modestly. "What can I say? It's a gift." His eyes narrowed as he turned back to Fox. "Okay, this Demopoulos character got canned unfairly. But if he's out of the CIA, he's out of the intel game. End of story. So what's our angle here?"

"Our angle is that he sent me a coded email a few hours ago seeking our assistance," the older man replied. "He's convinced that he's currently under close physical and electronic surveillance by someone."

"Yeah, but that might just be some of the CIA's internal-security types. Or maybe FBI agents, acting on Langley's behalf," Van Horn suggested. She shrugged her shoulders. "Nothing weird about the agency wanting to keep tabs on one of their top people who got forced out in a power struggle.

Demopoulos has to know where enough bodies are buried to raise a big stink with the press or on Capitol Hill."

Fox shook his head. "I still have a few other lower-level sources in both the CIA and the FBI. Enough to be sure that whoever's watching him, it's not someone from our own government."

"You think these are hostiles?" Flynn asked carefully, using the common Four shorthand for agents of an enemy intelligence service.

"It's possible," the other man said. "Perhaps even likely." His tone was serious. "As a precaution, I had one of our local part-timers in the DC area make a quick pass by his northern-Virginia home earlier this afternoon. Nothing looked out of place then, but now Demopoulos has gone completely silent."

Flynn felt the nerves at the back of his neck twitch a little. In ordinary circumstances, the fact that the retired CIA executive wasn't answering his phone or emails wouldn't arouse concern. However, the circumstances weren't ordinary. Sure, maybe Demopoulos was just seeing ghosts, watchers who weren't there. But, Flynn thought, even paranoids could have real enemies. He looked at Fox. "Let me guess: You want my team and me to go and take a look, up close and in person?"

The older man nodded.

"Even though this could be a trap of some sort?" Flynn pressed. "Laid by some very nasty types who've deliberately spooked Demopoulos precisely to find out who comes running when he screams for help?"

"*Especially* in that case," Fox said calmly. "Personally, I much prefer the idea of being the hunter to being the hunted."

Van Horn smiled. "Amen to that," she murmured, then leaned forward. "Worst case, Br'er Fox: How much does this guy really know about Four?"

"Very little," Fox said with a slight shrug. "We haven't met in person for years, and I wasn't using this name then. Our communications were solely by email through a covert server that can't be traced back to us."

Flynn considered that. Put bluntly, they could probably sit tight and do nothing without running a serious risk of compromising the Quartet Directorate. Cutting distant assets like Demopoulos loose when they became dangers or embarrassments was common practice for the CIA, the UK's MI6, and other government-run spy outfits. Pulling the whole "the secretary will disavow any knowledge of your actions" stunt wasn't heroic or honorable, but it was often both the smart play and the safest political option. The men and women in Four, though, operated on very different principles: they did not lightly throw people who'd helped them to the wolves. Demopoulos apparently had done his best for the Quartet Directorate, so now it was up to them to do their best for him.

THREE

A FEW HOURS LATER

Nick Flynn went prone at the edge of the trees and scanned the wide lawn ahead of him through his night vision goggles. This close to midnight, under a moonless, cloud-covered sky, there was little ambient light apart from a few distant streetlamps glowing in the distance. Fortunately, the image intensifiers in his goggles were powerful enough to turn the surrounding darkness into a monochrome vista almost as bright as natural daylight.

Directly ahead, he could make out the rear of Philip Demopoulos's large, two-story colonial-style home, which backed onto this wooded nature preserve. From what Flynn could see, there were no lights on inside. The other expensive-looking houses set around the quiet cul-de-sac were equally dark. This part of McLean—one of the wealthiest and most desirable suburbs in Washington, DC—was home to a host of high-ranking US government officials and foreign diplomats. The CIA's Langley headquarters was less than four miles away.

"Hell of a big place for just one guy," Cole Hynes murmured from beside Flynn.

Flynn nodded. According to his intel, Demopoulos had been divorced for some years and both of his children were grown and flown, leading their own adult lives in different parts of the country. Unlike some in the political and national security establishment, the retired CIA executive wasn't independently wealthy, so his house, bought years before the rapid escalation in local real estate prices, probably represented the bulk of his assets. Whether from pride or a preference for plenty of elbow room, he obviously hadn't been willing to downsize to a smaller townhouse or apartment.

Flynn keyed his tactical radio. "Prowler Eyes, this is Prowler Lead. What's the bigger picture?"

"*No signs of movement, Nick*," Laura Van Horn replied. "*All the virtuous folks seem to be safely in bed.*" She was posted a couple of miles away. From there, she was remotely piloting an ultraquiet quadcopter drone equipped with a night vision camera of its own. It was currently orbiting low overhead, giving her a bird's-eye view of the neighboring streets. Since McLean was well within the national capital's restricted airspace, a piloted plane providing aerial surveillance for them would have been immediately detected on radar, intercepted, and forced down. However, with a bit of luck, her battery-powered drone, though equally illegal, would be much harder to spot or to hear and would go unnoticed.

"Copy that," Flynn acknowledged. He motioned to the three other men with him at the tree line, Hynes, Vucovich, and Cooke. "Okay, let's move."

Together, they drifted silently out of the woods and headed toward the back of the darkened house, following a line of approach that kept them out of sight from the nearby homes. Their boots scuffed lightly across the dormant brown grass.

Besides the rucksacks slung across their backs, each man carried his compact HK417 carbine at the ready and wore gray-pattern camouflage and body armor. Deciding that they were screwed anyway if they were caught by the police or other authorities, Flynn had opted for firepower and protection over inconspicuous civilian clothing and concealed sidearms.

A few yards from the house, he signaled another quick halt. They all dropped to one knee and froze in place. At a nod from him, Wade Vucovich tugged a handheld electromagnetic- and radio-frequency detector out of one of the accessory pouches attached to his armor. The tall, wiry former soldier switched it on and carefully swept the attached probe through arcs that covered the house from side to side and top to bottom. His eyes were fixed on the device's display as he cycled through checks for the EMF and RF signatures typically emitted by active security systems.

Watching him, Flynn tamped down a sudden grin. Shortly after Vucovich joined Four, Fox had sent him for intensive training in surveillance and countersurveillance technologies and techniques. The older man had decided that the ex-Army-enlisted man's natural flair for engineering field expedients—like building stills to produce moonshine whenever he'd been stationed in a dry town or county—should be turned to more productive, if still technically illegal, uses.

Vucovich studied the results of his scans intently. "It's like we figured, sir," he murmured to Flynn. "That place is crawling with cameras and other sensors and alarms."

Flynn nodded. Any CIA senior executive was bound to have top-notch security for his home. "Think you can bypass some of them so we can get inside?"

"Yeah, if I had to," Vucovich said, sounding slightly disgusted. "But it's not necessary. That whole system's been turned off."

Flynn felt one of his eyebrows go up. "Turned off? You sure about that?"

Vucovich nodded. "Completely sure, sir." He tapped at the small screen on his detector. "An active security system with that many separate components should be blasting multiple signals in the EMF and RF bands. But all I'm picking up are really low levels of background noise—about on the order of what I'd expect from TV and stereo remote controls and a wireless network for computers and other home electronics."

"Gee, how very . . . convenient," Flynn said. "Nothing so inviting as an open front door, right?" It was looking more and more likely that Demopoulos's fears had been justified. There was no logical reason for a man afraid he was being watched by enemy agents to shut down his home alarms and other security systems. Something was very wrong here.

"'Come into my parlor,' said the spider to the fly," Cooke ventured from his position.

Flynn grinned back at him. "Which is why I think we should set our sights a little higher." With the rest of his team in tow, he covered the short distance to the back of Demopoulos's house, near its northeast corner. Directly above them, on the second story, a sash window opened into what he hoped was a spare bedroom or maybe a home office. Another set of upper-level windows on the southeast corner marked a likely larger master suite.

Hynes slid the rucksack off his back, unzipped it quietly, and took out a collapsible tactical assault ladder. Basically a long, folding pole with dual rungs and made out of black anodized aluminum, it weighed less than twelve pounds. Working quickly, he assembled the ladder and then meticulously placed its hooked upper end over the windowsill above them. Satisfied that it was firmly set, he flashed a thumbs-up.

My turn, Flynn thought coolly. Time to become Nick Flynn,

Cat Burglar. He was well aware that as soon as he tried opening the window, this whole covert reconnaissance operation moved from simple trespassing to a prison-grade felony offense. But only if they got caught.

He slung his HK carbine and climbed up the ladder to the very top. Swift examination showed that the window was fastened shut with a pair of simple latches. That was good luck but no real surprise, since like many people, Demopoulos apparently put more faith in his elaborate, high-tech security systems than in lower-end mechanical locks and bolts. Flynn pulled a thin-bladed knife from a sheath on his chest rig.

Gingerly, he slid the tip of the knife between the upper and lower sashes and popped the first window latch open before moving to the second. The whole process took him less than twenty seconds. It was a method that left some traces, but at least it was quieter than smashing the glass. Sheathing the knife, he took out a small piece of plastic card and a roll of duct tape. Then, with one hand, he slowly levered up the bottom sash in tiny increments, while at the same time moving the plastic card up the inside of the window frame—pressing it firmly against the surface. When he reached a small alarm button built into the frame, he stopped and held the card against it while duct-taping it in place. Even if this component of Demopoulos's home security system activated later, this trick should spoof it into thinking the window was still safely closed.

Breathing out, he slid the sash all the way up and dropped quietly into the darkened room beyond. A twin bed against one wall, a small desk, and old pop-band posters on the walls confirmed this had once been a teenager's room. "First room, clear," he murmured into his mike, unslinging his carbine and moving toward the only door. "Come ahead."

One by one, the other three men climbed up the pole ladder

and clambered in through the open window. Preparing their own weapons, they formed up behind Flynn. Terse nods confirmed that they were set.

Slowly, he eased the door open, listening keenly for the faintest sounds. The brush of cloth against a surface. An indrawn breath. The metallic click of a safety being released. Anything that might signal the presence of someone waiting beyond this door with a gun aimed and ready to fire. But there was nothing, only silence.

Carefully, Flynn slid through the opening and ghosted to the right along a curving wall with his HK tucked into his shoulder. The others followed, moving in different directions to cover their own sectors. They had emerged onto an open circular landing at the center of the second story. An interior balcony looked down into a ground-floor foyer. Off to the left, a carpeted switchback staircase led downward to that level of the house. To the right, more closed doors marked other rooms. And directly ahead, around the railed balcony, Flynn could make out a pair of double doors. He judged those probably opened into the home's second-story master suite.

Hand signals sent Cooke and Hynes prowling down the stairs to search the lower level. As they moved out, Flynn headed around the landing toward the suite. Behind him, Vucovich went to one knee, covering the other closed doors with his raised carbine. From there, almost at the dead center of the building, he was also in a good position to monitor any sudden changes in interior RF signals.

"*Family room and kitchen clear,*" Cooke radioed quietly from below. "*We're moving on toward the front of the house.*"

"Understood," Flynn acknowledged. Gently, he pushed one of the double doors open and slipped through the narrow gap into a much bigger chamber beyond. He'd been right. This was Demopoulos's master suite. And there were definite signs of occupancy here, with books and magazines stacked up on a nightstand next to an unmade king-size bed. A faint hint of aftershave or deodorant hung in the air. The blinds were drawn across the windows, closing off any view of the woods behind the house.

Sighting down the barrel of his HK, he moved warily toward another pair of double doors on the far wall. Carefully, he turned a knob and used the tip of a boot to prod one of them open. It swung back—revealing a sizable bathroom with a pair of sinks, large mirrors, and a walk-in shower set in the very middle of the room.

Flynn froze, making out an indistinct figure curled up on the floor of the shower. Through the lightly frosted glass and with almost zero ambient light this deep inside the house, it was impossible to make out any real details with his night vision gear. He risked lowering his carbine slightly and pushed the goggles up off his eyes. Then he flicked on the compact tactical flashlight mounted on the HK's short barrel.

"Ah, hell," he muttered.

In the thin beam of light, Flynn could see the naked body of a man wrapped tightly in clear plastic—a man whose wavy gray hair and stylish goatee matched the pictures of Philip Demopoulos. Flynn felt suddenly nauseous, seeing the multiple lacerations, burn marks, and other injuries plainly visible on the corpse. It was all too obvious that the ex–CIA executive had been brutally tortured before being killed.

"*Sir!*" Vucovich snapped over the radio. "*Some alarm just triggered. I've got a powerful RF spike somewhere overhead in the attic!*"

And then Flynn saw what he'd missed earlier. A tiny oval device, less than a quarter of an inch wide, was fastened to the outside of the plastic sheeting swaddling the dead man. Wavy red lines across its face marked it as a photoconductive cell. A thin, almost invisible wire ran from it up the side of the shower and into the ceiling above, where it undoubtedly connected to a wireless alarm unit. He'd tripped that alarm the moment his flashlight beam hit the photocell. Which meant that whoever had tortured and then murdered Demopoulos had wanted to know the moment his body was discovered. And that was double-plus, seriously *not* good.

Just great, he thought. Their still-unknown enemy was both extremely clever and vicious . . . his least favorite combination in an opponent. "Warning Red!" Flynn barked over the team circuit, alerting everyone that they were blown and under imminent threat.

"*Lead, this is Eyes. Movement alert,*" he heard Van Horn say through his earpiece, relaying what the camera on her orbiting quadcopter was seeing. "*Two vehicles just started their engines and pulled out a couple of streets west of you. They're heading your way. ETA to your location is roughly ninety seconds.*"

Another voice came over the radio. "*Two more armed hostiles approaching on foot,*" Tadeusz Kossak reported. The Polish sniper was deployed in a concealed position outside. "*They're coming through the woods toward the back of the house.*"

Flynn's jaw tightened. They were in a neat little trap, about to be boxed in from front and back.

"*Could be FBI or CIA guys, sir,*" he heard Hynes suggest.

Flynn shook his head, staring at Demopoulos's mangled corpse. "Negative on that, Cole," he said. "Or if they are FBI or CIA, they're dirty as hell and I'm not inclined to sit tight and hope for the best." He switched off his flashlight and donned his night vision gear again. Twenty seconds had elapsed since he'd tripped that alarm. It was high time they got moving.

He snapped out a string of orders as he headed back out to the landing. "All Prowlers indoors, bug out as briefed. Prowler Two, bar the door."

"*Roger that, Lead,*" Cooke replied. "*On the way.*"

Together with Vucovich, Flynn darted down the main staircase, taking the steps two at a time. Reaching the bottom, they spun left in the foyer and moved fast into a breakfast nook directly below the master bedroom. Hynes was there ahead of them, poised at a back door that led outside.

Cooke barreled in seconds later. He nodded tightly to Flynn. "All set."

"*Those vehicles are pulling up outside,*" Van Horn radioed. "*Six armed hostiles have exited, and they're headed toward the front door. They're moving tactically, Nick. These guys are pros.*"

Flynn nodded. "Copy that, Eyes. Listen up, all Prowlers outside: execute Omega."

"*On the way,*" Van Horn said crisply. "*Affirmative.*"

Kossak radioed a beat later, acknowledging the order.

At the same time, Flynn and the others inside the house dropped prone, pressing their faces tight against the tile floor. This was going to be messy.

IN THE WOODS
THAT SAME TIME

One hundred yards north of Demopoulos's house and nestled invisibly in a camouflaged ghillie suit that made him appear to be nothing more than a low, hummocky mound of dried brush, Tadeusz Kossak sighted through the scope of his TRG-42 sniper rifle. His crosshairs settled on the chest of a black-clad gunman taking up a position behind one of the trees that marked the back of the ex–CIA executive's property.

"*Execute Omega,*" Flynn's calm voice said in his earpiece.

"Affirmative," Kossak breathed out. He squeezed the trigger gently.

Crack.

A dark puff of blood and pulverized bone erupted high on the distant gunman's chest. He crumpled without a sound.

One down, Kossak thought with satisfaction. Without hesitating, the Polish marksman swiveled slightly, bringing his high-caliber rifle to bear on his next target. This man had thrown himself flat and was desperately swinging his own weapon—some kind of submachine gun—around in the direction from which the sound of that first shot seemed to have come.

Kossak squeezed the trigger a second time.

Crack.

Hit squarely by a .338 Lapua Magnum round moving at more than three thousand feet per second, the hostile gunman's head simply exploded.

"All hostiles at the rear are down," the Pole reported matter-of-factly.

A MILE EAST
THAT SAME TIME

Seated behind the wheel of the delivery van one of Four's part-timers had rented for the Prowler team, Laura Van Horn carefully tweaked the twin sticks on her remote control panel, maneuvering the distant drone into position. She had the onboard camera angled to see both the SUVs now parked right outside Demopoulos's house and the gunmen getting ready to execute a forced entry through the front door. They were in a tactical stack, lined up along the front of the two-story building. Her eyes gleamed. Any second now.

In the green-tinged light of her controller's small screen, she saw the lead gunman slam a battering ram into the door—smashing it wide open. He spun off to the side, clearing the way for his comrades to charge in with their weapons up and ready.

WHAMM.

The first man through the door tripped an antipersonnel charge wired there by Shannon Cooke moments before. In a blinding orange-red flash, razor-sharp fléchettes sleeted outward in a fan-shaped arc—instantly ripping every single one of the attackers to shreds. Simultaneously, every ground-floor window at the back of the house blew out in a tinkling spray of shards.

"Boy, I bet that hurt," Van Horn said conversationally to herself. Concentrating hard, she flew the quadcopter sideways. She tapped a control. On her screen, a crosshair suddenly appeared—centered on the first SUV. Her finger tapped the control a second time.

Released from its position dangling below the drone, a foot-long, French-made APAV40 (antipersonnel/antivehicle) grenade whistled down out of the sky, slammed into the roof of the SUV, and detonated. The vehicle disappeared in a ball of smoke and fire, only to reemerge a moment later as a crumpled mass of burning wreckage. The second SUV, caught in the blast, was also ablaze.

"Bull's-eye, Lead. Scratch two enemy gas guzzlers," Van Horn reported cheerfully.

INSIDE THE HOUSE
THAT SAME TIME

With his ears still ringing from the blast that had torn outward through the open front door, Flynn raised his head and spat out a mouthful of plaster grit. *Maybe rigging that charge wasn't exactly subtle*, he thought with a twisted, inward grin—but it had been hellishly effective all the same. Quick glances to either side showed that Cooke, Hynes, and Vucovich were all okay. Distantly, as though he were deep underwater, he heard Van Horn's and Kossak's radioed reports. Their way out was clear.

"Okay, guys," he ordered. "Let's vamoose. Time's not a friend now." Followed by the others, he scrambled upright, slammed the back door wide open, and sprinted out across the back lawn and into the cover of the woods. Red light flickered from the front of the house as the fires their explosives and Van Horn's air-dropped grenade had set took hold. In the distance, they could hear police and fire sirens starting to wail.

A couple of minutes later, joined now by Kossak, the Quartet Directorate agents hopped aboard the five whisper-quiet electric motorbikes they'd used for the initial approach to Demopoulos's home. With Flynn in the lead, they sped deeper into the nature preserve—along a winding trail that would take them to the rendezvous with Van Horn and the rented delivery truck. Once they'd stowed their gear aboard, back roads would take them the sixty-six miles to the Winchester Regional Airport . . . and a waiting executive jet. By the time anyone in law enforcement started to figure out that people had gotten out of that burning, bomb-gutted home alive, Flynn and his team would be long gone.

And on the way, Flynn decided grimly, leaning over the handlebars to clear some low, overhanging branches, he was going to devote some quality thinking time to figuring out just what the hell was going on here. What was supposed to have been a quiet snoop around had just turned into a full-scale pitched battle. Sure, he'd wondered if they were likely to run into some trouble—but not to the point of setting off their own miniature version of World War III in the CIA's own backyard.

FOUR

OUTSIDE MOSCOW

THE NEXT DAY

Ninety kilometers southeast of Moscow, Pavel Voronin's palatial country home occupied the summit of a hill enclosed by his own private pine forest. This woodland stretched for more than two kilometers in every direction. And in among those trees, invisible from the main house, was layer upon layer of defenses—razor-wire perimeter fences topped by cameras and motion sensors, prowling dog patrols, and armed sentries. Their presence guaranteed his privacy and promised uninvited guests an inevitable, messy, and intensely unpleasant end.

Constructed with steel and glass, Voronin's villa itself had wall-length, floor-to-ceiling windows that looked out across the snow-dusted woods and the silver-gray ribbon of the iced-over Moskva River. Original paintings and sculptures by some of the world's most famous abstract artists—Kandinsky, Rothko, and others—lined the interior walls and spaces, intermingled with modernist furniture from the best designers. Everything had been carefully selected to exhibit both his enormous personal wealth and his utter disdain for anything traditional or conventional.

His private office on the second floor, however, was distinct from the rest of the house. Containing only a couple of purely functional chairs and a large desk topped by several computer monitors, it was empty of any ostentatious display. Luxury had no place here. This was a room dedicated entirely to work.

Seated behind that desk now, Voronin kept a tight rein on his expression as he listened to the report from his senior deputy, former GRU colonel Vasily Kondakov. The older man seated across from him knew full well how unwelcome his urgent news was. They had lost contact with the Raven Syndicate's elite covert operations squad operating in the area of Washington, DC. The eight-man group had been made up of a mix of former Spetsnaz and SVR officers, along with two experienced Syrian assassins recruited from Bashar al-Assad's brutal military intelligence service, the Mukhabarat. The last report received from them had confirmed that they were springing the trap so carefully laid in McLean. Since then, however, there had been only silence. But now an analysis of intercepted police, fire, and ambulance emergency calls indicated that all eight members of the squad were dead, either blown apart by the detonation of an antipersonnel booby trap or eliminated by rifle fire.

By the time Kondakov finished, Voronin had a small scowl on his face. "There's no doubt about this?"

"None, I'm afraid," the other man said. "The location, equipment, and weapons found, and the physical descriptions of the bodies, what was left of them at least, all match. Besides, if any of our people had survived, we would have heard from them by now."

Voronin's frown deepened. "Unless the Americans have

taken a survivor or two as prisoners," he pointed out, "and are keeping them under wraps while they're interrogated. In which case, we're fucked—"

Behind his horn-rimmed spectacles, Kondakov's brown eyes were watchful. Operating a Syndicate assassination squad in the DC area had been a high-risk enterprise from the outset . . . something he had taken great pains to make clear to his superior. "Our analysts have ruled out such a possibility," he said carefully. "They assess the emergency radio calls we picked up as genuine, and from the carnage reported at the scene, there were definitely no survivors."

"Then there's one piece of good news, at least," Voronin retorted. The covert ops team they'd just lost had been thoroughly sanitized before being infiltrated into American territory. None of the false identities, weapons, or other gear its members were using could be traced back to Russia or to the Raven Syndicate. Dead, those operatives were far less dangerous than they would have been if captured alive. And while some of the brighter, more imaginative Americans might have their suspicions about who the unit had been working for, there would be no proof to trigger an embarrassing diplomatic incident. "That ought to keep the jealous wolves whining outside our door at bay for a while longer."

Kondakov nodded his understanding. Over the past couple of years, Voronin had made serious enemies among the ranking members of Moscow's defense and intelligence establishments— both by poaching so many of their best-trained special forces soldiers and spies and by insinuating himself so deeply into the confidence of Russia's autocratic president, Piotr Zhdanov. Being tied directly to a disaster like this would have given those bureaucratic rivals plenty of ammunition to use against him.

"But that isn't much consolation, considering everything else we've failed to achieve in this complete mess," Voronin ground out. His pale-gray eyes hardened. A tip from a Raven Syndicate–run informant inside the CIA had fed them the name of Philip Demopoulos as a possible link to whoever had wrecked MID-NIGHT. But even under torture, the former CIA official had failed to provide them with significant, actionable intelligence.

Apparently, Demopoulos had no direct contact with the mysterious group ultimately responsible for sabotaging the joint Russian-Iranian plan. Pretty much all that Voronin's agents had managed to bludgeon and burn out of the American was a code name—GLASS ISLE—for the anonymous intelligence source that had originally tipped the CIA to MIDNIGHT. But that was something Voronin had already known, thanks to his own paid agent inside Langley.

Unfortunately, apart from that bit of unimportant trivia, every other piece of information they'd pried out of Demopou-los before he died was useless. The American's association with these GLASS ISLE people seemed to have begun years before, back when he was still just a junior officer on the rise inside the CIA. At the recommendation of other, older agency officials he'd trusted, Demopoulos claimed to have met several times with a man who'd called himself Martin Finlay in order to establish those ties. But since none of those older CIA pros were still alive to be interrogated themselves, that was ultimately a literal dead end. Nor would the physical description of this so-called Finlay they'd ripped out of Demopoulos be of any real use. It was years out of date . . . and so vague in any case that it could have matched any one of millions of people.

The plan to ambush and capture anyone coming to De-mopoulos's aid had been a last resort. And now even that had blown up in their faces.

Wisely, Kondakov stayed silent.

With an effort, Voronin mastered his frustration and anger. If nothing else, this episode confirmed that those who had been pulling Demopoulos's strings would react quickly, violently, and efficiently to any threat to their people—even to one so far removed from the core of their organization. Despite undoubtedly realizing the ex–CIA official knew nothing of value, they had still risked other agents' lives in a vain effort to rescue him. And that, in turn, suggested they were a clandestine group that prized loyalty to its members above other, more rational considerations.

His mouth curled into a small sneer. For all the apparent skill of these people, that was a mark of amateurs, not true professionals. In his judgment, such sentimentality was a weakness, one that might someday be usefully exploited. Thinking it through, Voronin realized this encounter had been much like the first touch of blades in a duel—that fleeting moment when an experienced swordsman could begin to read his opponent's skill and likely aggressiveness from the tiny, almost imperceptible movements of the other man's eyes in those last milliseconds of calm before everything exploded into a whirlwind of clashing steel and spattering blood. So he would remember what he had learned about these mysterious, unseen enemies—and somehow, someday, he would find a way to turn their very loyalty to one another into a weapon . . . a weapon he could wield with deadly effect the next moment their paths crossed.

In the meantime, Voronin thought icily, he needed to refocus his energies and efforts on the intricate preparations necessary to set the Raven Syndicate's next major operation fully in motion. He said as much aloud.

Kondakov whistled quietly. "The president has approved your proposal to move ahead with GLAVNAYA BASHNYA ZAMKA, CASTLE KEEP?"

Voronin nodded. "You seem surprised, Vasily."

"I am," the older man admitted. "Brilliant as your concept is, the risks involved are uncomfortably high—at least from a political perspective." CASTLE KEEP was a high-stakes gamble designed to vault Russia to the height of world power. But if the operation was blown before its final stages, the best possible result would be a political and diplomatic disaster . . . and at worst, perhaps even open conflict with a prepared and fully alert United States.

Cynically, Voronin shrugged. "Well, I'm sure the president is confident that he will be the one holding the reins. If anything significant starts to go wrong, or if his fears about the possible consequences begin to overwhelm the advantage he sees in going forward, no doubt he believes that it will be possible to abort the operation—even right up to the last possible moment. Naturally so, since he is our nation's commander in chief."

"Naturally," Kondakov agreed slowly. The other man's real meaning was plain. Voronin intended to push CASTLE KEEP to completion whether Zhdanov got cold feet or not.

Voronin's expression softened slightly into a reflective smile. When his new operation's full scope was finally revealed, it would terrify the old, cautious counselors who clustered around the president. Like most of Russia's aging elites, they were small and petty men—cowards who were only comfortable playing for small and petty stakes. While it was true Zhdanov was a man of somewhat wider vision than his advisers, that was a remarkably low bar to clear.

What everyone else now in power in Moscow failed to realize was that there was no longer any time for mere half measures. The tools of conventional geopolitical strategy—economic and military power, arms treaties, and foreign alliances—had mired the Motherland in a bog from which there was no escape, only inexorable decline and decay. He alone saw the only clear path forward out of this swamp. Yes, CASTLE KEEP was filled with risk, but it was also the best way to claw down Russia's most dangerous enemy: the United States. And when Russia emerged triumphant as the world's greatest power, Pavel Voronin would stand ready to reap the rewards due to the savior of the state. Nothing would be beyond his grasp. Nothing at all.

FIVE

WINTER PARK, NEAR ORLANDO, FLORIDA

TWO DAYS LATER

Avalon House lay at the end of a long, looping private drive bordered by tall palm trees. Extensive gardens and wide lawns ran from the two-story mansion down to the shores of a small, almost circular lake. Between its red roof tiles, stucco walls painted a subdued yellow, wrought-iron entry gate, and high, arched windows, the building's architecture was a perfect match for that of classical Spain.

Originally built in the 1920s, it had once belonged to a wealthy banking family—and served as their welcome refuge from frigid New York City winters. But then, during World War II, one of the family's sons had served in the OSS. When the war came to an end, he'd seen the dangers looming and helped found the Quartet Directorate. Eventually, he'd handed over the mansion to Four as a headquarters for its fledgling American station.

To outsiders, however, Avalon House seemed only another

old, overly large private home converted into offices for a handful of small nonprofit and commercial enterprises. Weathered bronze plaques near the main door identified its long-standing tenants as the Sobieski Charitable Foundation, Sykes-Fairbairn Strategic Investments, and the Concannon Language Institute. On the surface, they were dull, eminently respectable organizations of the sort that never made the headlines or generated much public interest.

In reality, nothing could be further from the truth, Nick Flynn thought with a quick, slashing smile as he crossed through the gate and headed for the front door. All three entities were actually fronts created by the Quartet Directorate to mask its clandestine work.

He pressed the buzzer and turned his face upward, waiting patiently for the biometric sensors inside the camera mounted over the heavy dark-wood door to scan his features. Those unaffiliated with Four were almost never admitted inside.

The door opened onto a large, brown-tiled foyer presided over by a reception desk. Off to the right and left, other doors closed off the rest of the building. At the far end, a wide, elegant staircase curved up to the top floor.

"Welcome back to Avalon House, Mr. Flynn," the petite Korean American woman sitting behind the desk said briskly as he entered. Anyone who didn't know her well would have written off Gwen Park as a fashionably dressed, middle-aged receptionist or executive secretary. But appearances were, as so often with some of those in Four, deceiving. She was both an expert in hand-to-hand fighting and a crack shot. And before taking over as the American station's chief of security, she had put in years masterminding intelligence and counterterrorist operations deep in Southeast Asia's dangerous Golden Triangle. Her teeth gleamed in a bright smile. "I see that you've managed to stay in one piece again. Despite wreaking havoc across a very tony DC suburb."

"*Havoc* is putting it a little strongly," Flynn pointed out. "After all, we only wrecked one house." She raised an eyebrow. He capitulated. "Okay, we also blew up a couple of vehicles. And killed a few bad guys, too, I guess."

"Somewhat below your usual standards," Park said with mock severity. "No sunken ships this time? No underwater nuclear blasts? You're slipping, Mr. Flynn."

"Yes, ma'am," he agreed. "I guess I must be getting more prudent in my old age." He shrugged. "Which is why I just spent the past couple of days on the move before I headed this way, doubling back a few times to make sure no one picked up my trail." That was standard practice for any Four agents who'd had a brush with hostile forces. The Quartet Directorate had kept its existence secret for decades by exercising caution whenever possible. And one of the benefits of siting Four's American station here—so far from DC's swarming hive of federal intelligence agencies, foreign operatives, snooping journalists, and busybody politicians—was that no one would expect to find a private intelligence organization operating in a part of the country known for major theme parks and vacation resorts.

Her eyes crinkled with amusement. "A sensible precaution. Wisdom comes to us all, I suppose. Eventually."

Flynn yielded gracefully. "I may be a little slow, but I do get there in the end."

Park chuckled. "*Slow* is not really a word I would ever apply to you, Nick." She half turned and waved a hand at the staircase behind her. "And in this case, as it happens, you're right on time. You can go on up."

"Thanks, Gwen." With a final nod to her, Flynn headed up the stairs at a rapid clip. Most of the mansion's upper floor was set aside as temporary living quarters for Quartet Directorate agents needing rest and recuperation between difficult field assignments. One of the remaining rooms was a private study reserved for briefings and planning sessions. Once the inner sanctum of the prominent New York banker who'd built Avalon House, it was full of somewhat worn, though still comfortable furniture.

Fox and Laura Van Horn were there waiting for him. They occupied a couple of the high-backed leather chairs set around a small coffee table. The older man motioned him into a remaining seat. "Any trouble on the way, Nick?"

Flynn shook his head as he sat down. "Nope. Cooke and the others are back at the Manor, finishing up the last batch of live-fire training exercises I had planned. I didn't want any of the locals up there wondering why everything had suddenly gone quiet. Just in case a couple of them have friends in the FBI who're trying to put two and two together about guys who could have the wherewithal to blow the shit out of a house in McLean."

The other two nodded. The FBI relied heavily on paid informants for its investigative work. And it was a safe bet now that its agents were putting out the word to all their sources, telling them to be on the lookout for anything that smacked of suspicious behavior. The sudden disappearance of a group of gun enthusiasts who'd been in the middle of a booked week at a very expensive private firing range in Virginia would certainly have qualified. Especially if they vanished right after the shoot-out near the nation's capital.

"An excellent idea," Fox said in approval. He leaned forward. "Though I do assume you've noticed the surprising absence of hysteria over this incident by the media?"

"Meaning that film footage of a bombed-out house, burning vehicles, and eight dead guys all practically within earshot of CIA headquarters *isn't* running nonstop day and night on every cable news channel?" Flynn guessed.

"Or anywhere else, for that matter," Fox replied. He passed over a single newspaper clipping. "In fact, this seems to be the extent of the media coverage."

Flynn scanned it quickly. It was a short article from the metro-news section of the *Washington Post*. According to the reporter, Philip Demopoulos, a retired senior government official, had been found dead in the tragic aftermath of an accidental house fire. Unnamed authorities were said to be attributing his death to "smoke inhalation." Flynn's forehead wrinkled in disbelief. "That's it?"

This time it was Laura Van Horn who nodded. "Classic black-ops bullshit," she said. "The old 'You didn't see me. I was never here. And neither were you' crap."

Flynn suddenly felt cold. "Are you telling me the guys we killed were our own people after all?" he said slowly. "CIA covert operators or deep-cover Special Forces, I mean?"

"Not in the least," Fox assured him. "I still have enough reliable sources in relevant sectors of the government to be sure of that."

Relieved, Flynn nodded. Whether they were dirty or not, he hadn't relished the possibility they might have killed fellow Americans—even ones who'd seemed pretty determined to kill him and the rest of his team first. He tapped the newspaper cutting. "So why the blackout?"

"Political expediency is my guess," Fox said. "Answering questions from the press—and up on Capitol Hill—about exactly how and why Demopoulos was murdered and eight other men ended up shot or blown to pieces in and around his house would not be a very comfortable experience for those in charge of the CIA."

Van Horn signaled her agreement. "Lot of loose ends there that could prove embarrassing as hell to those clowns at Langley," she said. "Like, why was the agency's top analyst pushed into early retirement? And what do you mean, it was because he tried unsuccessfully to warn you about a nuclear-tipped missile being smuggled toward the United States? One that was going to knock us back to the Stone Age by taking out the entire electrical grid? And oh, by the way, who actually blew up that missile before it could be fired? Seriously inconvenient questions like that."

"I get your point," Flynn said with a tight grin. He turned back to Fox. "So if the people we nailed weren't US government, who were they?"

The older man spread his hands. "That's still unclear." He slid more documents across the coffee table—a pair of Virginia driver's licenses and a handful of credit and debit cards. "Kossak retrieved these from the two men he shot."

Flynn examined them. "Are these legit?" he asked.

Fox shook his head. "Not at all. But they are high-grade forgeries."

"How high grade?"

"As good as anything produced by the CIA. Or by us," Fox replied. "Or by the SVR or the GRU."

Flynn stared down at the forged IDs. Speculation suddenly solidified into certainty. "My bet is those guys were Raven Syndicate," he said.

"Explain," Fox said, not sounding at all surprised.

Flynn held up a finger. "One: Kidnapping, torturing, and then murdering a senior CIA exec? In his own home, no less? That's a seriously risky move. Even at the height of the Cold War, the KGB would have hesitated to pull a stunt like that—at least not unless they could use a deniable terrorist group as a proxy. I strongly doubt either the SVR or the GRU have the balls to try this kind of 'wet work' crap now. I don't care how carefully sanitized that kill team was; the odds of triggering serious blowback are way too high for any kind of official government involvement."

"Go on," Fox said.

"But we do know that Voronin's a stone-cold psychopath . . . and incredibly aggressive," Flynn continued, thinking it through out loud. "After the black eye we gave him by smashing MID-NIGHT, he's got to be out for blood. What I figure is that when the CIA tried to claim credit for stopping his missile launch, the news got back to him. And from there it would be a pretty short step to Demopoulos, the only senior executive at Langley who had any real inkling of the threat."

Fox pulled at his chin. "That's logical," he admitted. But then he shook his head. "Except that the information on Demopoulos's unsuccessful efforts to push the agency to act has been very tightly held inside the CIA to blunt any possible scandal. That's exactly why the director booted him in the first place."

From the chair next to him, Van Horn snorted. "Yeah, but I bet that whatever we know, Moscow already knows it, too. What are the odds that either the Russian government or the Raven Syndicate itself has someone inside the CIA on their payroll? And probably the Defense Intelligence Agency, NSA, and the rest, too."

"I won't take that bet," Flynn said.

"Nor will I," Fox agreed, with a sour look on his face.

Voronin had personal control over billions of dollars, and he'd already demonstrated a willingness to spend freely to get whatever he wanted. The unhappy reality was that, in the shadowy world of espionage, money was a weapon all on its own. Some people, no matter how carefully screened and monitored, were always for sale—if the price was right. In fact, throughout the decades-long history of the CIA and the FBI alike, some men and women had proved willing to betray their nation's trust, often for surprisingly small sums.

Flynn felt a shiver run down his spine. While it was true that Voronin was vicious, he was also not stupid. In fact, all the available evidence indicated that he was almost inhumanly brilliant. Which meant Flynn's first assumption had been partly wrong. The Russian's willingness to take so many chances to go after Demopoulos couldn't be attributed solely to a desire for revenge. Instead, it strongly suggested that Voronin had something else in mind—something so important that it justified all the risks involved in carrying out a hit right in Langley's backyard.

"Voronin is clearing the battlefield," Flynn realized abruptly. "He's got another large-scale op in mind—or, more likely, already underway. That's got to be why he's so determined to figure out who beat him last time . . . and to wipe us off the map before we can interfere in his plans again."

Van Horn's generous mouth turned downward. "Damn," she said. "Nick's right."

"Indeed," Fox concurred. His own expression was bleak. "Unfortunately, it is the answer that best fits all the fragments of information we possess." He sighed. "But even knowing that is no real help."

Flynn nodded. If he was correct and the Raven Syndicate was in the process of organizing some new attack aimed at the United States or its allies, all they currently had was the unwelcome sense that a fuse had been lit—but where and to what ultimate end was still a complete mystery. "And we can't go poking around for new intelligence," he realized. "Not from anyone inside the government anyway. Not even from our other sources inside the CIA."

"It would be far too dangerous," Fox agreed. His face was

grim. "If Voronin or his masters in Moscow do have moles inside Langley or the other government intelligence outfits, any contact by us only increases the chance of giving the enemy clues that could lead them back here, to Avalon House. And ultimately, to Four itself."

Which was a risk they could not take, Flynn understood. At least not as long as they had any other options. The secrecy surrounding the Quartet Directorate was its surest shield and the best guarantee that it could continue to act freely against threats to the West and the whole free world.

"So what can we do?" Van Horn demanded. "Sitting on our hands and hoping for the best seems like a really bad idea."

"Aptly put, Laura," Fox acknowledged with a slight smile. His fingers tapped lightly on the coffee table. "For now, however, I think our best move is to pass on our suspicions to the rest of Four's national stations. If our colleagues around the world are on the alert for evidence of new Raven Syndicate activity in their areas of operations, we might pick up those signs in time to act."

Flynn stared at him. "That's one boatload of nasty *if*s hanging out there in thin air, Br'er Fox. *If* someone sees something. *If* they realize what they've seen is significant. And *if* it's anything we can handle . . ." His voice trailed off.

"Quite so," the older man said seriously. "Unfortunately, for now, we are in the unwelcome position of being forced to hope that our enemies will make some small error. Any error."

"Or that we get lucky," Van Horn added. "As in maybe the bigwigs at the top of the CIA food chain start asking hard questions of their own about who killed Demopoulos and why. House fire or not, they must have enough forensic evidence to realize that he'd been tortured to death. Something like that should be pretty hard to just wave away."

Fox nodded. "True. Perhaps the current leadership at Langley will surprise me and look beyond the easiest answers—for once." Then he shook his head darkly. "Unfortunately, the odds of that happening aren't especially high."

Flynn knew he was right. Like most DC insiders, the director of the CIA and his top subordinates prided themselves on their brilliant intellects . . . and yet somehow they always seemed to gravitate toward the blandest forms of conventional wisdom. Considering more complicated and less politically palatable scenarios was usually their last resort.

SIX

CIA HEADQUARTERS, NEAR LANGLEY, VIRGINIA

THAT SAME TIME

There were days when Miranda Reynolds, the head of the CIA's Directorate of Operations, found it difficult to conceal her disdain for those above her in the agency's pecking order. That was especially so in the case of Charles Horne, the director of Central Intelligence. Overweight, with a face that flushed bright red whenever he was annoyed, Horne was not an intelligence professional in any sense of the term. By inclination and experience, he was a thoroughly political animal—appointed to head the CIA because the current White House team counted on him to avoid entangling the administration in unwanted controversies. From the first day on the job, he'd made it plain that Langley's intelligence analysis and activities should be designed to please the president and the rest of his national security team whenever humanly possible.

In that light, there had never been any doubt about Horne's attitude toward the unexplained deaths of Philip Demopoulos and eight other, as-yet-unidentified men at the former CIA official's home. Although the unexpected violence had unnerved him to the extent of ordering additional armed security for himself and other senior agency heads, an in-depth investigation was the last thing he wanted. Instead, his priority was to see this entire grotesque affair buried, quickly, cleanly, and with an absolute minimum of fuss or political fallout. And he'd assigned her to the task of getting that done.

As someone who'd come up through the ranks, Reynolds instinctively disliked her superior's willingness to shade the facts to curry favor. But she hadn't survived the CIA's brutal maelstrom of internecine office politics by ignoring hard realities. Two relatively recent agency fiascoes—a botched bit of arms smuggling in Libya and the destruction of a stolen Russian stealth bomber the US government had paid billions to acquire—could be blamed, however unfairly, on her. That made staying on Horne's good side imperative if she wanted to hold on to her job as head of Operations. Might made right inside the agency, and someone like Demopoulos who forgot that and tried to force the DCI to confront uncomfortable truths quickly found himself on the outside looking in.

And now dead, she reminded herself grimly.

"What's the state of play?" Horne growled at her from across his desk. They were alone in his private office. Given the situation, he had decided the fewer witnesses there were to this conversation, the less likely it would be to leak out. He definitely did not want any official record kept of what passed between them. "Can we keep this situation locked down tight?"

"Yes, sir," Reynolds told him, mentally crossing her fingers that she was right about that. "The FBI has taken complete control over the investigation and seized all the physical evidence—all the bodies, weapons, and other bits and pieces retrieved from the scene. The local police may not be too happy, but the moment we labeled this a case of possible terrorism with major national security implications, they lost their jurisdiction."

Horne's thick lips pursed in thought. "Getting the matter away from the local yokels is all well and good, but how far can we really trust the bureau on this one?"

"Far enough," Reynolds said. "I briefed my counterparts at the Hoover Building. They understand just how bad this would be—for all of us, including them—if the media or Congress pick anything up on what really happened. Nobody in the FBI wants the White House on the warpath against them for screwing this up."

Horne nodded. That was language he fully understood. Then a faint frown crossed his jowly face. "What about Demopoulos's neighbors? Can we rely on them not to blab to some damned reporter or another?"

"We got lucky there," Reynolds said. "They're all senior government executives, some of them near retirement. Our security personnel and the FBI have both put the fear of God and the loss of pension benefits into them. They'll keep their mouths shut. Especially since we dropped hints we might not be able to protect them if the vicious bastards responsible for piling up all those corpses decide to eliminate possible witnesses. Something that would become far more likely if this mess turns into a public spectacle."

Horne looked pleased at that. Self-interest and self-preservation were two of the salient characteristics of those who reached the topmost positions in the federal bureaucracy. "Excellent work," he commented.

"I've also had my team take one other precaution," Reynolds continued. She leaned forward a little in her chair. "We've planted rumors on the most extreme right- and left-wing internet conspiracy theory sites. Rumors that pretty much match exactly what we think went down at Demopoulos's home."

Horne stared at her in obvious surprise. "For what possible reason?" he demanded.

She smiled thinly. Subtle thinking was definitely not the director's forte. "Because," she explained patiently, "it virtually guarantees that no 'reputable' journalist will go anywhere near the true story. The moment anyone does is the moment we can believably tag them as nutcases parroting other obvious lunatics from the so-called dark web."

Horne's heavy-lidded eyes brightened in understanding and appreciation. "Deft, very deft," he murmured. "Quite a nice smoke screen to baffle those seeking the facts we don't want anyone else to have." He paused briefly, almost hesitantly, and then carefully asked, "And what are those facts, Miranda? As you assess them, I mean. What in God's name is actually going on?"

Reynolds hid her amusement. What the director really meant was: *Do I need to worry that the same assassins who tortured and then killed Philip Demopoulos in his own home might come after me? Has someone in a rival government or a terrorist group put a price on the heads of current and former CIA officials?* Horne might be a skilled political infighter, but no one had ever accused him of possessing physical courage.

"I think what happened confirms that you were absolutely right to bounce Demopoulos out of the agency on his ass," she said. "As you know, starting last year with that whole Iranian-oil-tanker episode, we began to suspect that he was in covert contact with multiple political factions and different espionage outfits around the world. And that he was both feeding and receiving information . . . and disinformation . . . to and from these various groups."

Horne nodded. He'd read the eyes-only reports she'd supplied—reports that had cut Demopoulos off at the knees by revealing his secret connection to an anonymous intelligence source he'd code-named GLASS ISLE. She'd obtained that information by using some of her own operations officers to investigate him when he still headed the Directorate of Analysis. Doing so was a complete violation of CIA internal protocol, but the DCI had been happy to overlook that since it gave him the ammo he'd needed to force Demopoulos out. "Was he feeding them information for pay?"

Reynolds shrugged. "Probably. It's the most logical motive. And while the Office of Security hasn't yet turned up hard evidence that he was getting money under the table, I'm pretty confident they'll eventually track down his secret bank accounts."

"So when we canned him, his paymasters must have decided that he wasn't of any further use to them—" Horne realized.

"Correct," she agreed. "Pretty clearly someone he was working with, or for, wanted to shut his mouth. And quite permanently at that." She frowned. "But some other group he was also in bed with had very different ideas. Hence the shoot-out at his home."

The DCI frowned. "Who are we talking about?"

"There are a number of possible players here," Reynolds said. "Everyone from the Saudi General Intelligence Directorate to Israel's Mossad or any one of several rival Iranian revolutionary groups opposed to the mullahs in Tehran. Although we haven't been able to positively identify any of the dead men found on the scene, two of them definitely appear to have Middle Eastern origins."

Horne frowned. "And the other six?"

"They could easily be mercenaries hired to facilitate covert operations here or in Europe," she said. "There are a lot of out-of-work soldiers, former intelligence operatives, and other hard cases drifting around the world at the moment."

The DCI nodded heavily with a look of distaste on his broad face. "So, in your judgment, Demopoulos was playing with fire . . . and he got burnt."

"That's how I see it," Reynolds confirmed. "When you sup with the devil, you should use a long spoon," she continued, quoting the old proverb. "His spoon was too short. And his luck finally ran out."

Horne sat back, looking calmer. "Which means the agency as a whole is in the clear with regards to this mess?"

"Almost certainly, sir," Reynolds said. "Unless, of course, our cover story springs a leak."

"See that it doesn't," the DCI said bluntly. "I'm counting on you to bury this unpleasant episode and bury it deep. Don't fail me, Miranda."

SEVEN

GENERAL GUADALUPE VICTORIA INTERNATIONAL
AIRPORT, DURANGO, MEXICO

EARLY SPRING, SOME WEEKS LATER

A sleek executive jet—a twin-engine Bombardier Global
7500—touched down on runway 21 with a fleeting puff
of black-tinged gray smoke from its landing gear, braked
smoothly, and then slowly taxied on past the main terminal
building. Off to the west, the rolling foothills of the Sierra
Madre lined the distant horizon. Turbofans whining down,
the Bombardier jet swung onto another taxiway at the far
end of the field and rolled into a large hangar before coming
to a full stop.

The doors of three Mercedes sedans parked along one side
of the hangar popped open, and several men climbed out. All
but one were obvious bodyguards, openly carrying compact
Mendoza HM-3 .380-caliber submachine guns. The man they
surrounded, dark haired, lean, and hawk faced, wore a perfectly
tailored Italian-made suit. Only the intricate neck and facial

tattoos visible above his collar line distracted from an overall impression of urbane elegance. He strode confidently toward the newly arrived plane.

Once its engines fell silent, the executive jet's forward cabin stairs unfolded. Several hard-faced men in business suits emerged from the aircraft and fanned out in a protective perimeter. Slight bulges marked the holstered sidearms concealed beneath their jackets. As soon as they were in position, Pavel Voronin came down the steps to greet his smiling host.

"Welcome to Durango, señor Jones," Joaquin Lopez said amiably, deliberately emphasizing the name on the forged British passport Voronin carried for this leg of his journey. His geniality did not reach his eyes, which remained coldly wary. Despite his outwardly polished appearance, Lopez retained the instincts and habits of a hardened killer—as was natural for the acknowledged second-in-command of La Hermandad de la Sangre, the Brotherhood of Blood. The Brotherhood, one of the most powerful and violent drug cartels, was virtually a law unto itself in this region of Mexico, and its tentacles ran far across the northern border, extending deep into the United States itself. "My *patrón* and I are looking forward to hearing the details of your most interesting proposal."

Lopez waved a manicured hand toward the line of waiting sedans. "But for now, I'm sure you wish to rest and refresh yourself after what must have been a very long flight. We have rooms up at the hacienda ready for you and your security men."

Voronin nodded in thanks. The last leg of his trip had covered over ten thousand kilometers and required more than eleven hours of total flight time—despite the Bombardier 7500's status as one of the world's fastest civilian jets. And luxurious as the aircraft's interior fittings were, he never slept especially soundly in the air. He glanced around as they strolled toward the cars,

noting the tractor-towed baggage-handling cart already trun-
dling across the tarmac directly toward this hangar, no doubt en
route to retrieve luggage from the jet. "And the other arrange-
ments here?" he asked quietly. "As you know, a certain amount
of . . . *discretion* . . . is vital."

"Do not worry, señor *Voronin*," Lopez said with a somewhat more genuine smile. "Our people control all aspects of
this airport's operations. There will be no official record of your
arrival. Or your departure, of course."

With some amusement, Voronin noted the carefully implied
threat hidden in the other man's reassuring words. Clearly, Lopez
wanted his "guest" to understand exactly who held the balance
of power in this situation. Within the bounds of its territory,
the cartel reigned supreme. No matter how much wealth and
political influence the Russian oligarch possessed in his own
country, here in Mexico he remained an outsider—one subject
to the murderous whims of the Brotherhood's leaders if they
judged him unworthy of an alliance. He shrugged inwardly.
All predators are alike in seeking dominance, he thought. What
remained to be determined, however, was which of them—the
Brotherhood or his own Raven Syndicate—would ultimately
emerge with the whip hand.

Calmly, he followed Lopez over to the middle Mercedes, slid
into one of the rear seats beside him, and leaned back against
the comfortable headrest. He closed his eyes as it pulled away
from the hangar—heading for the highway that would take
them deeper into the rugged Sierra Madre. The first sedan full
of cartel bodyguards swung in ahead, while Voronin's security
team followed in the third car.

Out on the airport tarmac, the baggage handler whistled a quiet tune of his own as he drove steadily over to the
now-empty hangar and the large business jet parked inside.

The high-powered digital camera hidden behind the grille of his little four-wheeled tractor should have captured some excellent close-up images of the two men who'd just met there. He strongly suspected those pictures would make very interesting viewing for his superior officer.

S-2 SECOND SECTION (MILITARY INTELLIGENCE), SECRETARIAT OF NATIONAL DEFENSE, MEXICO CITY
A SHORT TIME LATER

Colonel Antonio Maria Herrera heard the soft ping of a message arriving on his personal smartphone. Swiveling around in his office chair, he pulled the device out of his uniform jacket and glanced idly at the header displayed on the screen: *Colibrí*, or in English, *Hummingbird*. His pulse quickened a bit, not much . . . only a few heartbeats per minute. Just enough to register in the back of his mind.

"Got something important?" his deputy asked curiously from his place over at the only other desk in the secure office they shared.

Herrera shook his head. "Just a text from my wife reminding me to pick up her dry cleaning before the shop closes this evening," he told the younger major with a shrug. He raised a single graying eyebrow. "I don't suppose you'd be willing—"

The other man laughed. "Not I, Colonel. I have my own list of domestic errands to run this evening. And I'm pretty sure Elena would kill me if I put myself at the beck and call of another woman, especially one as charming and beautiful as the wife of my esteemed commanding officer."

"There are fates from which even obeying a direct order

cannot save you," Herrera acknowledged gravely. He forced himself to yawn, before glancing idly at the wall clock. "Well then, at least go grab us a couple of coffees from the canteen, okay, Roberto? Because without some caffeine, I swear I'm going to wind up facedown and snoring on this desk of mine."

"Now that I can do," the major promised, standing up and pulling on his own uniform jacket. "In the interest of increasing our military efficiency, of course." With a cheerful wave, he left the office. The door closed and automatically locked behind him with an audible click.

Safely alone now, Herrera swiped his fingers across the screen of his phone to unlock it and then opened the encrypted message he'd been sent. Studying the pictures attached to the file, he rubbed thoughtfully at his jaw. Well aware that officials at Durango's airport were completely compromised by the Brotherhood—partly through fear and partly through bribery—he'd managed to insert one of his own deep-cover agents into a menial job there. The cartel's ties to other criminal organizations, terrorist groups, and unsavory, hostile governments throughout Central and South America ran deep. Having the undercover intelligence operative he'd code-named Hummingbird keep tabs on unusual activity at the airport had yielded useful information on those various international connections as they ebbed and flowed over the past couple of years.

Now, though, Herrera wondered, what should he make of this most recent report? A meeting between that nasty drug-lord piece of shit Lopez and an obvious foreigner? A man whose facial features seemed somehow more European or American than those of the cartel's usual associates and clients? Moreover, a foreigner with extraordinary wealth at his disposal, judging by the large, expensive-looking private jet he'd flown in on. He frowned. Whatever was going on seemed likely to be far out of the

Brotherhood's run-of-the-mill business endeavors—which generally ranged from smuggling fentanyl, cocaine, heroin, and other illegal drugs to murder and extortion. Offhand, he couldn't imagine what such a meeting might portend, but given the horrors already unleashed by these powerful criminal gangs, the prospect of seeing one of them grow even stronger was grim indeed.

Forehead wrinkled in thought, the colonel closed his phone and sat back to ponder the situation. It was an open secret that Mexico's drug cartels had penetrated deep into the upper echelons of the Mexican government. Corruption and subversion were constant threats, with the vast riches produced by international drug trafficking available to purchase the allegiance of officials whose morals were *flexible*. And the readiness of the cartels to employ extreme violence often broke the resistance of those who could not be bought. Could anyone blame men or women who yielded in the face of genuine threats of death or torture—threats that often included their entire families?

That was why Herrera was the only one who knew he had an informant in Durango. It was the surest way to keep Hummingbird safe from exposure. Unfortunately, it also meant that passing this new intelligence through conventional channels would quite likely be signing his agent's death warrant . . . and possibly his own as well. Word that the government had a spy at the airport would be bound to leak back to the Brotherhood—and if Herrera was right about the significance of this unknown foreigner's contact with the cartel, they were sure to react with lethal speed . . . moving to seal the breach in their security with absolute finality. Like venomous snakes and scorpions, the drug lords never hesitated to strike at anyone who posed the slightest threat.

Herrera scowled. He seemed to be faced with two unpalatable alternatives: Do nothing for now, and hope that his instincts were wrong. Or doggedly put his government's available investigative resources to work on the problem, and risk betrayal and death.

Reyes. The name popped into his mind and stuck there.

Slowly, he nodded. This might well be a situation where his longtime friend and colleague Miguel Esteban Reyes could prove helpful. Very helpful.

The other man had once headed the federal police unit responsible for covert operations and infiltration. But he'd proved to be far too good at his job for those who ran the drug cartels—and for their paid underlings in the government. Too canny to allow himself to be assassinated and too honest to be easily trapped in a corruption sting, Reyes had finally been forced into retirement on direct orders from the very top of the Mexican political establishment.

Since then, Reyes had apparently found gainful employment as a security consultant for various international corporations interested in doing business in Mexico—advising them on the best ways to minimize cartel interference in their operations. And from careful conversations during their occasional meetings for dinner or drinks, Herrera knew the other man still kept in touch with many of the foreign law enforcement and intelligence contacts he'd made throughout his long career. If anyone could pin down the identity of this wealthy, unknown foreigner meeting with the leaders of the Brotherhood of Blood—and what they were planning together—it might be Reyes. If nothing else, the colonel knew, he could at least count on Miguel Reyes's absolute discretion and shrewd common sense. That alone would make it worth reaching out to him for help.

He swiped at the screen of his smartphone again and opened his personal email account. It was time, he decided, to invite the former federal lawman over to his home for a very discreet discussion and a top-secret slideshow.

EIGHT

AVALON HOUSE, WINTER PARK, FLORIDA

THAT NEXT DAY

Nick Flynn stepped out onto a tiled veranda that ran the whole length of the Spanish-style mansion's lakeside. He narrowed his eyes a little against the glare of bright morning sunlight reflecting off the water and saw Laura Van Horn already out there ahead of him. Looking cool and lovely in a cream-colored linen blouse and a tight pair of blue, straight-legged jeans, she sat pensively in one of the battered rattan chairs scattered along the veranda. Overhead, ceiling fans turned slowly under a wood-beamed roof.

A smile tugged at the corners of her mouth when she saw him. "Tardy for an urgent briefing? Shocking."

He grinned back at her. "No one's tardy until the professor sits down, ma'am," he said with a lazy Texas drawl. Abruptly, the door opened right behind him, and Fox came hurrying through. "Though I reckon that would be just about now." He quickly dropped into the chair beside her.

"Saved in the very nick of time . . . Nick," Van Horn murmured.

Resolutely ignoring their teasing banter, Fox took his seat. He placed a manila folder on the small round table between them, flipped it open, and pulled out a series of photos. "We've finally got a bite," he said briskly. "The head of Four's station in Mexico forwarded these surveillance pictures a short time ago. They were handed to him last night by a high-ranking contact in his country's military intelligence service."

Flynn fanned the handful of photos across the table and looked them over closely. "That's Voronin, all right," he said, tapping one of the two men greeting each other in the first picture. The color photograph was crystal clear. Up to now, their most recent available depiction of the head of the Raven Syndicate had been a single blurry black-and-white image. Every other photo in the Quartet Directorate's files showed the Russian as a much younger man—in formal school portraits taken during his education at the elite Phillips Exeter Academy in New Hampshire, as an undergraduate at Oxford, and while studying for an MBA at Harvard Business School. Voronin obviously preferred keeping a low profile.

Fox nodded.

Van Horn leaned over. "Who's the guy with him?" she asked. "The one with the fancy suit and the neck and face tats."

"Joaquin Luis Lopez Moreno, more commonly known as Joaquin Lopez," Fox answered. "He's the number two man in La Hermandad de la Sangre, the Brotherhood of Blood."

Flynn's mouth tightened. "Which just happens to be Mexico's most powerful drug cartel," he said, sitting back in his chair. "Our boy Pavel really does mix with all the best people, doesn't he?"

"So it seems," Fox said with a slight nod. "The Brotherhood

is aptly named. It's been responsible for the deaths of thousands of innocent civilians throughout the territory it claims inside Mexico."

"And also for the deaths of tens of thousands of Americans from overdoses caused by the drugs those bastards peddle here," Van Horn interjected. Her eyes were ice cold. She was focused intently on the image of the Mexican drug lord, almost as though she were seeing him through the telescopic sights of a high-powered rifle. After a moment, she shook herself and looked back up. "Okay, Br'er Fox, what's the bigger context here?"

"That's not yet clear," the older man admitted. "We know this meeting between Voronin and Lopez took place in a hangar at Durango's international airport. And we also know that, shortly thereafter, the two men left together by car. Beyond that, we don't have data from which to draw any solid conclusions."

"Could the Raven Syndicate be peddling weapons to the Brotherhood?" Van Horn wondered aloud. "Based on what we know from firsthand experience, Voronin's guys have access to just about everything in the Russian arsenal. For the right amount of cash, they could supply anything from small arms to handheld SAMs."

Fox shook his head. "I think that's unlikely." He shrugged his narrow shoulders. "The cartel's 'soldiers' are extremely well armed. I can't see any urgent need for them to acquire Russian-made weapons in addition to their own existing stockpiles."

Flynn suspected the older man's assessment was probably accurate. Decades of fighting among themselves and against Mexico's police and military had motivated the drug lords, the narcos, to recruit and arm their own private armies. In recent years, they'd even gone into combat using improvised armored vehicles mounting everything from heavy machine guns to recoilless rifles. All too often, the police commandos and even regular soldiers sent in to confront them had been badly out-gunned.

He leaned forward again, studying the photos on the table. In one of them, surrounding Voronin and Lopez, he could make out a number of very tough-looking men toting subma-chine guns. "Maybe the Raven Syndicate is recruiting more personnel," he said, tapping the image. "Voronin hires covert ops specialists and assassins, right? Could be he wants to add people who aren't so conspicuously Russian to his roster. Having Spanish speakers on the Syndicate payroll might come in handy for running deniable operations in certain parts of the world."

"Not a bad theory, Nick," Fox said, examining the same picture. But then he shook his head. "Except there's one big hitch. All our intelligence indicates that the Brotherhood has one overriding rule: It never hires out its sworn members. Not to anyone. Neither Lopez nor his *patrón*, Diego Barros, want to run the risk of their people transferring their loyalty to a new employer. Their rules are clear. Once someone has vowed his or her allegiance to the cartel, there's no way out—except through death."

"Servitude for life? Gee, how remarkably . . . feudal," Van Horn commented. "These narco assholes act like they're living back in the Dark Ages."

Fox nodded. "Quite so. At least as far as all of that era's nas-tiest and most brutish aspects are concerned."

"Then turn it around," Flynn argued. "Maybe the Raven Syndicate is offering the Brotherhood the sort of elite military and intelligence specialists it can't find in its own ranks. Even a handful of trained ex-Spetsnaz officers or GRU types could make a big difference in a throwdown against some rival gang whose gunmen are mostly illiterate peasant types." The Mexi-can cartels periodically fought bloody wars among themselves for control over territory and resources. Alliances between them were always alliances of convenience—honored only until one side or the other saw an advantage in murdering its rivals.

Fox considered that. "Perhaps so," he said slowly. "But I can't see why Voronin himself would fly into the Brotherhood's territory to make such an arrangement. It's an unnecessary risk, given the cartel's hard-earned reputation for treachery and deceit."

"Meaning he'd be more likely to delegate the task to some expendable underling?" Van Horn said with a twisted smile. "Just in case those kill-crazy cartel bosses get pissed off during the negotiations and suddenly decide they want a Russian head for their trophy wall?"

"Something along those lines."

"Then Voronin has to be there because *he's* the one who wants something from the Brotherhood," Van Horn reasoned. "Something very important to him. Something no one else can provide."

"Makes sense," Flynn agreed. Then he shook his head. "But it can't be narcotics, even though that's their main stock in trade."

Both Fox and Van Horn nodded. With the world awash in illegal drugs produced everywhere from Asia to the Middle East and South and Central America, Voronin could easily obtain whatever addictive and deadly substances he desired elsewhere. And do so without risking his own precious hide to the not-so-tender mercies of the Brotherhood of Blood.

And then Flynn saw the answer they'd been missing. It was as though a map had suddenly flashed into existence inside his head. "Their smuggling routes into the US," he said abruptly. "That's what Voronin is after." Mules and gang members working for the Brotherhood and the other cartels routinely slipped undetected across the porous US-Mexico border. But to move anything else, materiel or agents, safely by those routes, the Russian would need both the permission of and aid from the cartel's leaders.

Fox leaned back with his eyes half-closed, considering the idea. Then he nodded. "I think you're right. It's the closest fit for what little we know now." His mouth thinned. "Which leads to the next obvious question: Who or what is Voronin so eager to smuggle into our national territory?"

"I've got a bunch of guesses," Flynn told him. "But there's no way to know for sure. Not without a hell of a lot more information."

Van Horn frowned. "I say we don't wait to find out."

"Meaning what, Laura?" Fox asked carefully.

"Meaning now that we've finally picked up Voronin's trail, our next move is pretty clear," she told him. "We kill the son of a bitch."

Flynn hid a grin. Trust her to go straight for the throat. For someone who'd mostly flown cargo and search-and-rescue aircraft during her Air National Guard service, she had a fighter pilot's aggressive instincts. And as it happened, she was right. Throughout the Quartet Directorate's history, assassination had been a very rarely used tool, but if there were ever a textbook case of someone who needed killing, it was Pavel Voronin. In a real sense, this would be no different than the British SOE or the American OSS orchestrating the elimination of Reinhard Heydrich and other high-ranking Nazi officials during World War II.

True, the war they were in right now was undeclared, but that didn't make it any less real or deadly. Sitting idly by waiting for Voronin to carry out his current plan—whatever it was—was not an option. The Russian had come much too close to success the last time out. And while Flynn and his team had managed to stop him in the end, the effort had been enormously costly. It also relied on a huge helping of good fortune. Four could not count on being so lucky again.

Fox nodded. "I agree." But then he shrugged ruefully. "Unfortunately, we can't plan on getting a decent shot at Voronin while he's still in Mexico."

Flynn saw what the other man was driving at. The Brotherhood of Blood exercised almost total control over its home territory. Punching a team through that level of security to take out Voronin would require an all-out assault. And even the thumb-suckers at Langley might notice someone blowing the hell out of a bunch of Mexican narcos and a Russian oligarch . . . which could lead them to start asking some very inconvenient questions Four would rather not have answered.

Which meant, he realized, that they needed to figure out where Voronin might go when he left Mexico. It was unlikely to be anywhere he would be more vulnerable, but they couldn't ignore the possibility. Maybe it was clutching at straws, but they weren't exactly flush with other good options at the moment.

Flynn paged through the photos on the table until he found one that clearly showed the large private plane Voronin had arrived on. He showed it to Van Horn.

"A Bombardier Global 7500 executive jet," she confirmed. "Top of the line in its class. And one hell of a nice ride from what I hear."

"Ever flown one?"

She snorted. "Not hardly, Nick. The bottom-line cost on a bird like that was somewhere north of eighty million dollars last time I checked." She shrugged. "Which is way above our equipment budget."

Flynn turned to Fox. "Filed flight plans can be checked, right?"

"They can," the older man confirmed with a slight smile.

Meaning that he'd already done so, Flynn realized. He should have guessed. The head of Four's American station rarely missed an obvious avenue of approach to any problem. "So did our least favorite psychopath fly straight to Mexico from Moscow?" he asked.

"From what we can tell, Voronin didn't fly out of Moscow at all," Fox answered. "That plane took off from Dubai."

Perplexed, Van Horn stared at him. "Say again?" She shook her head. "The Bombardier's a sweet, fast-flying machine, but there's no way it has the range to make it so far in a single hop."

"Nor did it," Fox assured her. "Records show that the jet made a very short refueling stop in Minsk on the way."

"Nice dodge to avoid inconvenient passport checks," Flynn commented with a wry smile. Minsk was the capital of Belarus. And Belarus, closely aligned with Russia's authoritarian regime, was almost a client state of the larger country. Its border-control officials would never dare interfere with the activities of one of Piotr Zhdanov's closest associates. "I suppose Voronin boarded the Bombardier there. After all, it's only a short hop from Moscow."

Fox gave him a noncommittal look. "That is where the story gets interesting," he said. "Before coming here, I reached out to certain . . . friends . . . in various places in the Middle East, including the United Arab Emirates. They confirm that a man named Simon Jones, supposedly an expatriate British citizen living in the UAE, originally boarded the aircraft in Dubai."

"And you think Voronin is traveling as this guy Jones, using a false passport?" Flynn asked.

"It's a logical assumption, though admittedly one I cannot prove," Fox said. "But it seems probable, especially given the corporate ownership of the Bombardier 7500. That singularly expensive aircraft is registered as the property of a commercial company based in Dubai, a company named Wickham Imports and Exports," Fox went on. A half smile sleeted across his thin face before vanishing. "And the chief executive officer of Wickham Imports is listed as one Simon Jones."

Flynn nodded. There were times in the murky world of spies and counterspies when two plus two actually *didn't* add up to four. But this particular situation wasn't looking all that complicated. "What does this Wickham Imports do, exactly?"

"That is the prizewinning question, Nick. Unfortunately, no one seems very sure," Fox said with a slight shrug. "Ostensibly, the company resells low-end consumer electronics to middlemen in developing nations across Africa, the Middle East, and parts of Asia."

"Which is bound to be a cover for something else," Van Horn said.

"Almost certainly," Fox agreed. "There are persistent rumors that Wickham Imports trades in weapons and stolen advanced military technology. But there's no real evidence one way or another." He spread his hands. "Nor are we likely to find any, at least not through ordinary channels. Their corporate records are completely off limits. Much like Switzerland in the old days, the UAE guarantees its wealthy foreign residents absolute privacy in certain financial matters."

Flynn frowned, thinking it over. "Weapons and hijacked military-grade tech sure ties in with the Raven Syndicate, all right. The trouble is I just can't see Voronin pissing around with some arms-smuggling business in the Middle East. Not when everything else we know about him suggests he's angling to become the gray eminence behind Zhdanov's throne in Moscow."

"Nor can I," Fox admitted. "Which certainly implies that we're still missing a rather large piece of this particular puzzle."

Absently, he pushed his glasses a little higher on the bridge of his nose. "On the other hand, whatever part this Wickham Imports plays in Voronin's plans, it's important enough to assign a very expensive corporate jet to the firm. And that justifies further investigation."

"Plus this is the only serious lead we actually have right now," Flynn realized. "So we either chase this down or sit back waiting for some other lucky break."

"Regrettably, luck has been in rather short supply lately," Fox said. "Which is why I want you to put together a team to dig deeper into this mysterious import-export company in Dubai ASAP. And, naturally, take a shot at Voronin if he actually is operating there in person."

Van Horn frowned. "He might just fly straight back to Russia when he finishes his business with the Brotherhood," she warned. "And we can't touch him there. Not without rustling up a cruise missile somehow."

"That is true," Fox conceded. "But even so we are still left with the various tantalizing questions surrounding Wickham Imports." He turned toward Flynn. "I would infinitely prefer our friend Pavel with a bullet in his brain, Nick. Death has a useful finality all of its own, especially for an exceedingly dangerous man like Voronin. But if wiping him off the board proves impossible, I would settle—however reluctantly—for concrete, verifiable intelligence on his current operations."

NINE

HEADQUARTERS OF LA HERMANDAD
DE LA SANGRE,
IN THE SIERRA MADRE,
WEST OF DURANGO, MEXICO

THAT SAME TIME

Pavel Voronin followed a silent, unsmiling servant down a long, whitewashed corridor and out into a sunlit interior courtyard surrounded on all sides by the hacienda's main building. A single table and three chairs were set out in the middle of the square, paved expanse, shaded by a few potted fig trees. His gaze flicked upward, toward the low, flat roof. Armed sentries were visible there. Other gunmen loitered in the shadows of the arched arcades running around the courtyard.

This is a fortress, he thought. Originally the property of a prosperous, landowning family, the estate now served as the nerve center of the cartel. What had once been the social hub of the district's landed elite was now a place the locals avoided if at all possible. A thick wall surrounded the central buildings, topped by additional armed guards, cameras, and other electronic sensors. And for tens of kilometers in every direction, the Brotherhood maintained a tight grip over all of the surrounding villages—enforcing its will through a calculated blend of raw terror and cash payoffs. Those who crossed the cartel ended up dead, usually in gruesome and painful ways. Those who submitted received small monetary gifts that were designed to make them dependent on the whims of the Brotherhood's bosses.

Joaquin Lopez, now more casually attired in an open-necked polo shirt and khaki designer slacks, looked up from his earnest conversation with a much shorter, broader-chested man—Diego Barros, the cartel's unchallenged supreme leader. In sharp contrast to his chief lieutenant, the drug lord showed no trace of style or sophistication whatsoever. Dressed in a sleeveless white T-shirt and jeans, he was completely bald and bullnecked. His small, hard, close-set eyes glared out on the world with a mixture of native cunning and unrelenting suspicion. At first sight, Barros reminded Voronin unpleasantly of his rivals in Russia—the jumped-up peasant generals and politicians who made up President Zhdanov's inner circle. Everything about Barros, from his speech to his manners, was coarse and crude.

"Come sit down, señor Voronin," Lopez said, indicating the sole empty seat. His teeth flashed in an insincere smile. "I trust you slept well?" He pushed across a steaming cup. "Coffee?"

Voronin nodded politely. "Thank you." He took a cautious sip of the dark-brown liquid. It was bitter and remarkably strong.

Watching him, Barros snorted. "At least Joaquin here knows how to make such a pussy drink with a little bit of machismo, eh?" He poured a liberal splash of tequila into his glass of orange juice. "As for me, I like something with more kick in the morning." He took a puff from a cigar smoldering in an ashtray and set it back down. "So, to business."

Voronin put his coffee back down. "Of course, *Patrón*."

"Joaquin has run the outlines of your plan past me," Barros rasped.

Or at least as much of it as you are entitled to know, Voronin thought with a tinge of amusement. He kept close control over his features. These were extremely dangerous, untrustworthy men, and it would not do at all for them to comprehend his real intentions. "I hope we can come to an amicable arrangement," he said smoothly.

"That remains to be seen," Barros said. His mouth compressed. "As I understand your idea, your people will plant their asses here, on my turf. In one of my safest production facilities." The cartel leader poured more tequila into his juice glass and bolted it down. "And you want my soldiers to help keep them safe from the *federales* and the *gringos*, while they work their little schemes?"

Voronin nodded coolly. "Correct."

"And for taking the risk of calling even more heat down on my head, maybe from the CIA, maybe from the American Pentagon, I get what? Money?" Barros continued, not hiding his contempt. He laughed hoarsely, nodding at the hacienda around them. "Money I have already. More than you, I think."

Voronin forced down a grimace. That much was true. And it grated on him. His Raven Syndicate controlled something on the order of three billion US dollars at any given moment, depending on the current state of the world's investment markets. But according to his analysts, the Brotherhood's accumulated wealth was more than three times higher.

Barros shrugged. "Your money means nothing here, Russian. Not in my backyard."

"I did not expect that it would, señor Barros," Voronin replied easily. "Which is why I am offering something far more valuable."

The cartel leader's eyes narrowed dangerously. "Like what?"

"The ability to move at least ten times your current deliveries of fentanyl and other drugs into the United States," Voronin told him flatly. "Without the slightest chance of the Americans seizing any of your product . . . or even realizing how the drugs are crossing their border."

Lopez whistled under his breath, greed obvious in his eyes. Fentanyl, fifty times more potent than heroin, was worth enormous sums of money on the street. And while most of the Brotherhood's drug mules made it across the border without being arrested, even the limited amounts of narcotics American law enforcement managed to intercept still cost the cartel hundreds of millions of dollars a year.

Barros stared hard at Voronin. "And how much will you charge to work this miracle?" he demanded, sarcasm thick in his guttural voice.

"Not a single centavo," Voronin said. "Your shipments will move with my own." He shrugged. "What is more, my people will deliver your drugs to your wholesalers in America at a safe location of your choice. And again, wholly without charge."

Lopez and Barros exchanged glances. "And if the Americans do capture one of our shipments?" the younger man asked. "Despite your bold assurances?"

Voronin shrugged. "Then we pay you double its market value." He eyed the cartel boss and his lieutenant closely, knowing he had them. For all of Barros's macho posturing, greed was the principal force driving the Brotherhood of Blood. In the end, he knew, the two Mexican drug lords would swallow his bait—too blinded by profit to sense the hook it secretly contained.

And CASTLE KEEP would move into its next operational phase, steadily unfolding in scope and complexity as it drew nearer and nearer to its devastating fruition.

TEN

ABU DHABI INTERNATIONAL AIRPORT,
UNITED ARAB EMIRATES

TWO DAYS LATER

Nick Flynn towed his rolling carry-on bag out through the sliding glass doors of the airport's newly completed, ultramodern terminal building. Behind him, its soaring roof rose and fell in blinding white curves that echoed those of the desert's rolling sand dunes. The late-afternoon sun reflected off massive windows. He donned his sunglasses and inhaled deeply, catching the faint traces of diesel fumes and salt water borne inland by a light breeze off the nearby Persian Gulf.

Shannon Cooke and Cole Hynes came up on either side, pulling their own luggage. Like him, they were traveling under false passports and carrying documents that identified them as employees of Sykes-Fairbairn Strategic Investments, one of the Quartet Directorate's front companies. The fact that Sykes-Fairbairn maintained a small office as an accommodation address in Dubai, sixty miles to the north, helped lend credibility to their cover. As far as Abu Dhabi's customs officials knew, Flynn and his two colleagues were here on a whirlwind trip to meet potential clients and indulge in some company-paid sightseeing.

Though they weren't particularly happy about it, Laura Van Horn, Tadeusz Kossak, and Wade Vucovich had all been left behind in the United States. The UAE was far more liberal than many countries in the Middle East, but the presence of a woman in their little group would still have drawn unnecessary attention. Nor did the rough ideas Flynn had sketched out for this operation seem likely to require Kossak's skills as a long-range marksman or Vucovich's expertise in electronic surveillance and alarm systems. However this played out, Flynn thought, it was probably going to go down fast and hard—with a premium on speed and not finesse. The fewer of Four's people he put at risk in this hurriedly planned action, the better.

"Ride's here, Nick," Cooke said, nodding toward the curb ahead of them.

A dark-suited man in a chauffeur's cap and sunglasses stood next to a large silver-gray Infiniti QX80 SUV. He was holding up a sign with the name GRANT scrawled across it in black marker. "Mr. John Grant and company?" he asked politely, seeing them approach.

Flynn nodded. That was the name on his fake passport.

The driver stowed their carry-on bags in the space behind the SUV's third row of seats and opened the doors for them. Once they were inside, he slid behind the steering wheel, doffed his sunglasses, and glanced back over the seat with a toothy grin. "Where to, guv?" he asked cheerily, in a horribly exaggerated Cockney accent.

It was Tony McGill. Based out of Four's UK station, the former SAS sergeant had joined Flynn's ad hoc strike force for their daring midocean assault on the Raven Syndicate's missile-carrying oil tanker. He was also one of the few men involved who'd emerged alive and unwounded. Since then, he'd been working to form a European action unit for the Quartet Directorate, a counterpart to the team already assembled by the Americans. At Flynn's urgent request, he'd flown in ahead to organize some of the necessary logistics before joining them for the mission itself.

"Nice to see you, too, Tony," Flynn said. He shook his head sadly. "You Brits are never going to forgive us for Dick Van Dyke hamming it up so much in *Mary Poppins*, are you?"

"Not easily, Nick," McGill admitted. "The world's all-time, absolute worst attempt to sound like a real working Londoner? You have to agree that was practically a bloody war crime."

From the seat behind Flynn, Hynes said unrepentantly, "Hey, I didn't think the movie was so bad when I saw it on DVD as a kid. Except for all the singing and dancing crap, I guess."

"Um, Cole," Cooke hissed. "That movie was all singing and dancing. And clunky animation."

"Yeah, but it starred Julie Andrews. And man, I thought she was *hot*."

McGill yielded generously. "Fair point, mate." Starting the engine, he checked his mirrors, pulled out smoothly around an airport bus, and took the loop road that would deposit them on a highway heading west toward the city itself. A few minutes of driving took them across a bridge and onto Abu Dhabi's main island. Palm trees and low-rise buildings lined the crowded streets. On one side, a vista of beaches and tree-shaded resorts slid by outside the SUV's tinted windows. In the other direction, gleaming office and apartment towers spiked along the horizon.

Another bridge took them out onto a much smaller island right on the edge of the gulf. McGill swung to the left, turning in to a residential neighborhood that curved around its southern and western shores. Modern villas with walled courtyards ran along both sides of a quiet, palm-tree-bordered street. Many of the houses had a dock for private motorboats and yachts. He pulled into a spacious parking spot in front of one of these villas and switched off the engine. "Welcome to our temporary quarters, lads. Some of the comforts of home included."

Once inside the door, Hynes set his bag down with a huge grin. "*Some* of the comforts?" he said incredulously. Elegant furniture that wouldn't have seemed out of place in a millionaire's Manhattan penthouse graced the villa's large, open-plan living and sitting areas. Beyond a highly polished sandalwood dining table easily big enough to seat a dozen people, they could see a fully equipped kitchen, complete with high-end, stainless-steel appliances. Picture windows at the far end offered a view outside over an attached L-shaped infinity swimming pool, fountains, walled garden, and private dock. "Man, I could sure get used to living like this. It beats US Army enlisted quarters by about a bazillion miles."

"It is a bit of all right," McGill said smugly. "Not cheap, but the best location for our purposes I could arrange on such short notice."

"Sadly, however, I'm afraid you won't be here long enough to fully enjoy all the amenities," a deep voice said, sounding faintly amused.

They all turned to see an older man emerge from one of the adjoining bedrooms. Strongly built for his age, he was shorter than any of them, with a high forehead and wispy tufts of bright-white hair.

"Let me guess," Hynes muttered to Flynn. "This guy ain't a rent-a-butler, is he?"

"Not exactly, Cole," Flynn told him, suppressing a laugh.

He moved forward to shake hands with the newcomer. "This is Professor Gideon Ayish," he told the others. "Four's head of station in Jerusalem. His people on the ground here have been doing some legwork on our possible target." After long combat service with the Israeli Defense Forces' most elite and effective special operations units, Ayish had supposedly retired to become a research fellow at an international think tank monitoring global terrorism. In reality, he'd been recruited into the Quartet Directorate and now ran a remarkably effective network of agents—Israelis and friendly Arabs alike—operating throughout the Middle East.

Flynn turned back to Ayish. "Since you've decided to come meet us in person, Gideon, I'm betting there were some significant developments while we were in the air?"

"There have indeed," the older man agreed somberly. "First and foremost, Nick, your primary objective has now been confirmed. Your orders are to take Pavel Voronin out—by any means necessary."

Flynn felt a surge of excitement. It was tempered by a realization that this mission had suddenly become far more dangerous than if it had remained a simple sneak-and-peek endeavor. "Voronin's already flown back to Dubai?"

Ayish nodded. "So it appears." He waited until they'd all taken seats around the living room before starting to brief them on what was currently known. Intelligence relayed from the Quartet Directorate's Mexico City station indicated that Voronin had departed from Durango aboard the Bombardier Global 7500 executive jet at around the same time their own commercial airline flight left Miami. Internet-based flight trackers had shown the aircraft making a very short stop in Havana before taking off again, this time on a direct return leg to Dubai's international airport.

"Cuba?" Flynn wondered aloud. "Why the hell would he land in Cuba?"

Ayish shrugged. "We have insufficient data to answer that question. Given the aircraft's total elapsed time on the ground in Havana of somewhat less than thirty minutes total, there seems no immediately obvious explanation."

"They could have been dropping someone off. Or maybe picking someone else up," Cooke commented. "Plus topping off fuel, I guess. But I doubt it was offloading any real amount of cargo. Thirty minutes is practically a touch-and-go for a civilian jet. Even with a highly trained crew on standby, there wouldn't be time to pull much out of the hold."

Flynn nodded. US Air Force C-130s and other dedicated cargo aircraft could unload tons of palletized freight within mere minutes. A civilian passenger jet with a standard baggage compartment didn't have anywhere near that same capability. "And I suppose we don't have any reliable HUMINT sources based at the Havana airport who could clear up that little mystery for us?"

"Unfortunately, none at the moment," Ayish confirmed, with a rueful shake of his head.

It figured, Flynn realized. Cuba's communist government might not be able to feed or clothe its own people, but it had dedicated more than sixty years to building one of the world's most oppressive and ruthless internal-security states. Like the old Soviet Union and East Germany, the regime dedicated enormous resources to surveilling anyone who might be tempted to oppose its rule—whether openly or covertly. Under those circumstances, the lifespan of agents recruited by Western intelligence services was often measured in weeks or months at most . . . except perhaps for those who were caught alive and then run by Cuban counterintelligence as double agents.

"What we do know, according to my sources inside the UAE government," Ayish continued, "is that the foreign resident calling himself Simon Jones did, in fact, disembark from that plane when it landed in Dubai earlier today. He was accompanied by three other European-looking men whose identity papers list them as employees of Wickham Imports."

Flynn leaned forward. "Well, there's one piece of good news," he said with a tight, predatory grin. "Sure, maybe Voronin got back here ahead of us, but at least now we know he's definitely in Dubai. Which means we'll get to take our shot at the bastard."

Cooke and Hynes nodded in eager agreement. In their judgment, the head of Russia's Raven Syndicate had earned death a hundred times over.

"Which still leaves us with the most pressing question," McGill pointed out. "Where's the best place to make the hit? We'll only get one bite at this apple."

"Yeah," Flynn said slowly. The ex–SAS sergeant had put his finger squarely on their biggest challenge. It was a sad truth that simply killing someone wasn't all that hard. The really difficult trick was doing the job and getting away scot-free. Unlike its official counterparts—the CIA, the UK's MI6, France's DGSE, and others—the Quartet Directorate couldn't offer any kind of legal protection . . . and certainly no James Bond–style "license to kill." He turned to Ayish. "What more can you tell us about this Wickham Imports?"

The Israeli replied, "Not a great deal, I'm afraid, except that it is profitable enough so that the relevant authorities are more than willing to overlook its more questionable activities. Which convinces me that the rumors of its involvement in illegal arms dealing and weapons-technology thefts are quite true."

"How about its facilities? Offices? That kind of thing?" Flynn pressed.

"Apart from leasing occasional warehouse space, this trading company maintains only a single rented office room on one floor of an older commercial building in Dubai's Al Garhoud district—which is conveniently close to the airport," Ayish told him.

Flynn didn't try to hide his surprise. "That's it? No fancy digs in one of the big skyscrapers downtown?" Dubai's skyline was packed with over two hundred enormous high-rises, including the Burj Khalifa—the tallest building in the world, soaring 2,700 feet into thin air.

"Those modern luxury office towers all have elaborate security systems that constantly monitor all visitors and employees coming and going," Ayish reminded him. "Short of owning the whole building from top to bottom, our Mr. Jones would be unable to assure the necessary *discretion* in his more private business dealings."

Flynn saw what the older man meant. If, as seemed almost certain, Voronin *was* using Wickham Imports to buy and sell stolen tech and weapons, the last thing he'd want would be digital video records of his black-market clients and sellers. Or, at least, records that were not in his sole control. He could see the Russian indulging in a spot of less-than-genteel extortion of those foolish enough to give him power over them. He could not see the other man allowing himself to be vulnerable to potential blackmail in return.

Ayish picked up on his thoughts and nodded. "Exactly, Nick. The Garhoud district, while older and much less fashionable, is considerably more . . . relaxed . . . about the less rule-abiding sectors of the commercial world."

"Okay," Flynn said, working through the problem out loud. "So what's the area right around that leased office look like?"

In answer, the older man picked up a remote control and turned on the villa's wall-sized smart TV. The detailed street maps and satellite views he'd loaded into the system earlier flashed onto the screen.

The other men studied those images in silence for several long minutes. Most of the other low-rise buildings near Wickham Imports' office were occupied by a wide range of small to middling businesses on their lower floors, with private apartments above.

Cooke stood up and moved closer to the television screen to focus on a square-built, concrete-block structure just a few doors up the street from the import office. "Well, shit," he said with a deep frown. "That's a goddamned bank." He tapped the screen. "And if there was one thing my granddaddy always cautioned against, it was committing mayhem close to where folks keep a lot of money. It tends to draw attention from ornery types, like very unsympathetic men with badges and big guns."

Flynn nodded reflectively. Financial institutions meant armed guards. And very loud alarms. Not to mention the likelihood of a rapid police response in the event of the slightest disturbance nearby. He glanced over at Ayish. "How about going after Voronin where he lives while he's here, instead?"

"Not practical, I'm afraid," the older man replied. "This man 'Jones' resides in a luxury high-rise, one with top-notch private security. Getting in past all those guards would be difficult. Getting out would be impossible." He pointed at the screen, now zoomed in to show only the five-story building containing Wickham Imports' rented office. "In contrast, this place apparently relies on a single security officer, more of a glorified concierge, really, manning a desk on its ground floor. Fairly typical for businesses in this area."

"What about cameras?" McGill asked.

Ayish shrugged. "A handful, all set only to monitor the main entrance and the rear service doors."

Flynn's eyes narrowed as he ran through their options. They were far fewer than he would have preferred. On the other hand, he hadn't signed on with the Quartet Directorate because it promised a cushy, safe life. "What if this is just an accommodation address?" he asked, finally. "Like the place we're renting as Sykes-Fairbairn?" He frowned. "I'd sure as shit hate to bust in there and find only a couple of empty desks and an answering machine. Embarrassing, I don't mind so much. Ineffectual and stupid is a whole different picture."

Ayish shook his head. "My agents have questioned some of the locals carefully," he reported. "They insist they've seen the 'Englishman' and his subordinates coming and going regularly— and even having lunch delivered from nearby restaurants."

"Okay, that's promising," Flynn agreed. He rubbed his hand across his chin while thinking, feeling the rough whiskers starting to sprout there. Their trip out from Florida to Abu Dhabi had taken more than twenty hours, and he was long overdue for a shave . . . and some sleep, for that matter. Fighting down a sudden urge to yawn deeply, he slowly straightened up. "But it still brings us back to the problem of pulling this off without experiencing a close encounter with Dubai's law enforcement. Personally, I'd really appreciate avoiding the opportunity of writing Tripadvisor reviews of the UAE prison system."

Ayish nodded. "A very sensible desire, Nick." He motioned toward the guest bedroom he'd come out of earlier. "And one I have already given some thought to."

Flynn and the others climbed to their feet and followed Ayish through the door. Seeing the items of clothing and other specialized equipment laid out there, they crowded closer.

After a moment, McGill turned to Ayish with a grin. "You've got a mind like a corkscrew, Professor. Crooked and twisty as hell. It's a bloody honor to work with you."

"Sometimes it is better to be so visible in such a particular way that prospective witnesses really, honestly do not *want* to see you," the older man acknowledged with a wry look of his own.

After a quick consideration of the available options, Flynn made up his mind and turned to face the others. "Okay, guys. Listen up. If the professor's men confirm Voronin slash Jones is in place tomorrow, this operation is a go." He bared his teeth. "Which means we're going to put this Russian motherfucker down hard and fast. Once and for all." He stared around the circle of faces. "Any questions right now?"

"No, sir," they chorused.

He nodded. "All right, then. We'll work through the final details later tonight. In the meantime, I suggest y'all grab some food and much-needed shut-eye while you can. Because I can promise you that the morning's going to be on us before too long."

ELEVEN

AL GARHOUD DISTRICT, DUBAI, UNITED ARAB EMIRATES

THE NEXT DAY

An older white Nissan NV350 panel Urvan drove sedately down an exit ramp off the E 11 highway, more commonly known as the Sheikh Zayed Road. Dents and scraped paint hinted that it had seen hard use as a delivery vehicle in the less prosperous sections of Dubai. At the foot of the ramp, the van turned south onto a narrow two-way street. Moving through moderate traffic, it passed a series of commercial and residential buildings on both sides. Signs over doors advertised restaurants, coffee shops, travel agents, and other retailers.

Cole Hynes was driving. He wore faded jeans and a dingy black T-shirt. Although the former soldier would much rather have been a shooter on this mission, his Arabic wasn't fluent enough to fool any locals who tried to engage him in conversation. That made the risk of using him outside the vehicle too high. But to appear less obviously American, he'd darkened his hair and skin tone. A false beard and mustache, along with cheek pad inserts that made his face look fuller, completed his disguise.

Nick Flynn, Cooke, and McGill, crouching behind him in the van's cargo area, had similarly disguised themselves—with one major exception. Instead of civilian clothes, they wore desert-camouflage fatigues and maroon berets. Their attire, plus their tan dagger-and-falcon shoulder flashes, marked them as soldiers of the UAE's elite Presidential Guard special forces unit. Flynn's shoulder boards carried the three stars of a *naquib*, a captain, while the other two Quartet Directorate agents had sergeants' stripes on their sleeves. All three men carried holstered 9mm SIG Sauer P320 pistols.

Gideon Ayish had also provided them with forged military identity cards. Authentic as they seemed, however, he'd warned that they wouldn't stand up to close scrutiny. "With a few more days to work, my guys could have produced masterpieces," the Israeli had told them apologetically as he handed over the IDs. "But these aren't exactly Rembrandts. They're more like my granddaughter's finger paintings."

Flynn had glanced down at the card made for him and flashed the older man an amused look. "Rembrandt or not, I'd guess your granddaughter's one hell of an artist, Gideon. Because for a rush job, these are pretty damned good." Then he'd shrugged. "Anyhow, if we do run into someone with the smarts to pick out their flaws, we're already screwed so badly that it won't matter."

He came back to the present when Hynes muttered, "We're just passing the bank on the right, sir. No guards posted outside. It looks real quiet." He braked slightly and then said, "Coming up on the target now."

Flynn leaned forward to peer through the Nissan's tinted windshield. Made of steel and glass instead of white or tan concrete blocks, the building that housed Wickham Imports' office on its third floor was much newer and looked more modern than the neighboring structures. "I see it, Cole," he confirmed.

He glanced back over his shoulder at Cooke and McGill. "All set?" he asked.

They both nodded, eyes and mouths narrowed in concentration.

Hynes turned in to a parking place right in front of the building, pulling in between a black Mitsubishi SUV and a pearl-gray Toyota sedan. He kept the engine running.

In one smooth motion, McGill yanked the van's passenger-side sliding door all the way open. He dropped lightly out onto the pavement. Flynn and Cooke were right behind him. They took a brief moment to straighten their berets, all the while haughtily scanning their surroundings.

At this time of day, there weren't many pedestrians in sight, but Flynn still noted that even the relative handful who were out and about carefully avoided making any eye contact with them. Ayish had been right, he decided. For all intents and purposes, their uniforms acted as a sort of cloak of invisibility. More than 90 percent of the UAE's inhabitants were noncitizens without any political rights and with very few legal protections. And since the security forces, especially the army's counterterrorist units, operated under their own set of arbitrary rules, none of these people wanted to draw unnecessary attention to themselves.

With a sharp nod, Flynn led Cooke and McGill directly across the pavement. A pair of sliding glass doors whooshed aside at their approach, admitting them into the office building's ground-floor lobby. Apart from a handful of rather withered-looking potted plants scattered around the tiled floor, a bank of elevators, and a fire door marked *Stairs* in both English and Arabic, there was just a single desk off to one side, under a signboard listing the names, room numbers, and floors of the building's tenants.

A bearded, heavyset security guard with a name tag fixed to his unbuttoned uniform coat lounged behind the desk. From the crumpled, grease-stained paper bag in front of him, it was clear he'd just finished eating lunch. The guard's eyes widened in surprise at their sudden appearance—and at the sight of their berets and shoulder flashes. He swallowed hard and sat bolt upright, almost as though he were coming to attention.

Scowling, Flynn flashed his forged military identity card. "*'Amn Aldawlati! La taqulu shaya'. La tafaal shaya',*" he snapped. "State Security! Say nothing. Do nothing."

Plainly shaken, the security man nodded quickly. Ashen faced now, he carefully laid both of his hands flat on the desk before him.

Ignoring him, Flynn pushed through the stairwell door with Cooke and McGill right on his heels. They took the stairs upward at a rapid pace. Their time to pull this off without interference was short and getting shorter fast. On the way, each man drew his own pistol and threaded a sound suppressor to its muzzle. Next, they pulled on tactical radio headsets and gloves. "Falcon Four, this is Lead," Flynn murmured over his mike to Hynes, waiting for them outside in the van. "Com check, over."

"*Falcon Lead, this is Four, roger, over,*" he heard the other man reply quietly. Cooke and McGill gave him thumbs-up signals. Their communications channel was clear.

Still moving fast, he reached the third-floor landing, yanked the stairwell door open, and went through. They were in a wide, tiled hallway that ran the length of the entire building. Tinted glass doors lined both sides of the corridor. According to Ayish's intel, Wickham Imports occupied a single large office at the far end, one that looked out over the nearby Dubai Creek golf course and yacht marina. At his silent hand signal, they headed down the hallway, with Flynn still in the lead. Cooke

and McGill flanked him on either side, following just a couple
of paces behind.

Ahead of them, a neatly dressed young woman wearing a
patterned silk headscarf left one of the nearest offices but froze,
seeing three uniformed and armed men coming straight at her.
Her face whitened in fear. Arrogantly, Flynn silently waved her
back inside. Obeying immediately, she scooted through the door
and hurriedly pulled it closed behind her.

"Jeez, Nick, Intimidation R Us," Cooke muttered.

Tamping down a reluctant grin, Flynn kept moving. So
far, so good, he thought calmly. But then, when they were only
a few yards from the entrance to the import-export company,
their luck ran out.

A stocky, broad-shouldered man in a sports coat stepped out
of the Wickham Imports office and into the hallway, turning
toward them. His dark-brown eyes, short-cropped straw-blond
hair, and high cheekbones all spelled *Russian* to Flynn. Which
almost certainly made him one of the Raven Syndicate agents
operating here in Dubai. Wide eyed, he gawked at the Four
agents for what seemed forever but couldn't really have been
more than just a second or two. As his eyes moved from their
uniforms down to the suppressed pistols they were carrying,
his gaze sharpened.

Well, shit, Flynn thought, *we're made*. "Hold it right there!
Hands up!" he ordered in Arabic-accented English.

"*Khuy tebe*! Fuck you!" the Russian snarled. His hand darted
inside his jacket to draw his own concealed weapon.

Without conscious thought and before the other man's gun
could clear his shoulder holster, Flynn raised his own pistol
and squeezed off two fast shots, aware immediately that Cooke
and McGill were both doing the same thing. Their suppressors turned what would have been the earsplitting crack of

high-powered pistol fire into moderately loud *cough-pop*s that were followed by a ringing tinkle as spent cartridges bounced away across the tiled hallway.

Hit by all six rounds at near-point-blank range, the Raven Syndicate operative crumpled, his blood splashing across the floor and walls.

Immediately, however, the half-opened door he'd come through slammed shut. There was a loud buzz as an electronically triggered lock activated, sealing it against unauthorized entry.

Damn it, Flynn thought angrily. He radioed Hynes. "Falcon Lead to Four. Buzzkill. Repeat, Buzzkill."

"*Copy that*," Hynes acknowledged from the van, aware now that the team had set off enemy action—enough, in all likelihood, to provoke intervention by the local authorities. "*The clock is running. Ten seconds down.*"

Flynn nodded tightly, hearing the count begin. At best, they would have just a few minutes before Dubai's police showed up in force. He spun around toward Cooke and McGill. "Let's move! Get that fucking door open!"

Reacting fast and following tactical patterns drilled into muscle memory through intensive, repetitive combat training, they all exploded into action. McGill unzipped the equipment bag slung over one shoulder, yanked out a short, two-handled battering ram, and sprinted down the hall to take position against the wall, just out of sight of the office door. Cooke slotted in right behind him. Flynn took the tail-end Charlie position. "Go!" he ordered.

Without a moment's hesitation, McGill stepped in front of the door and slammed his ram into the door latch with shattering force. It flew open in a welter of broken safety glass and splintered wood. Instantly, the ex–SAS noncom rolled away toward the other side of the doorway. The moment he was clear, Cooke leaned out and lobbed a flash-bang grenade into the room beyond.

WHAAMM.

The grenade detonated with a deafening roar and a dazzling burst of pyrotechnics. The whole building seemed to rock on its foundations. Swirls of dust and debris eddied down out of the ceiling above them. Sparks showered out through the doorway.

Right on the heels of the shattering blast, Cooke slid in past the broken, smoldering door hanging off its hinges. With his SIG Sauer 9mm up, he moved right to clear the room's most dangerous blind spot. Flynn followed him into the smoke-filled office, angling to the left. McGill came last, taking the central sector.

Thanks to the adrenaline flooding his bloodstream, everything seemed to blur into slow motion for Flynn. Milliseconds stretched into what felt like minutes as his brain fought to make sense out of near-total chaos.

There were three Russians still inside the room. And though they seemed dazed by the point-blank grenade blast, they all looked determined to fight back. No matter what the cost. Across the office, one tried desperately to raise his own pistol . . . and then slumped forward across a desk—hit twice in the chest by 9mm rounds fired by Cooke.

Scanning his own sector through the haze of gray smoke, Flynn saw a grim-faced man in an expensive-looking suit pulling out a compact submachine gun, a Russian-made PP-90, from a desk drawer. A nameplate on the desk read *Simon R. Jones.*

Got you, Flynn thought coldly. He squeezed off two shots from his own 9mm pistol. Both slammed home. In a welter of blood, the man slid out of his chair and sprawled onto the floor.

Flynn breathed out in relief. If they were lucky, Voronin's new plan wouldn't long survive its creator's sudden, violent death.

Just then, next to him, McGill fired, killing the last of their enemies.

Silence fell suddenly across the bullet-torn space. From start to finish, the fusillade of shots had lasted only moments.

"*Falcon Four to Lead, thirty seconds elapsed time,*" Hynes reported through his headset. "*No close sirens yet.*"

Not yet, maybe. But their luck wouldn't hold for long, not after they'd turned this office building into a war zone, Flynn knew. Acting quickly, he unscrewed the smoking suppressor from his pistol, dropped it onto the carpeted floor, and then slid the SIG Sauer back into its holster. Beside him, Cooke and McGill did the same with their own weapons. The suppressors were untraceable. And men carrying guns in their hands tended to draw unwanted attention.

Aware of the timer ticking down until the authorities arrived, they started searching the room at high speed. Everything easily portable—smartphones and wallets, for example—went into McGill's now-empty equipment bag. Filing cabinets lining one wall turned out to be empty, obviously just for show to create the appearance of a busy import-export company.

Flynn grabbed the laptop off "Jones's" desk and tossed it over to McGill, then knelt down to dig through the dead man's suit pockets. He glanced up at the slack-jawed face . . . and froze suddenly. "Damn it," he said, in utter disbelief.

Close by, Cooke turned toward him in surprise. "We've got a problem, Nick?"

Still staring at the body of the man he'd just killed, Flynn nodded tightly. "Yeah, we do." He looked up at the others. "Because while I don't know who this son of a bitch really is . . . he's sure as hell *not* Pavel Voronin."

TWELVE

DUBAI

A SHORT TIME LATER

Still playing the role of a cocksure UAE Army special forces officer, Flynn shoved the fire door open and arrogantly swaggered out into the lobby. He glanced at the trembling security guard still seated behind his desk. The sudden volley of shots and thundering explosion from upstairs seemed to have completely unnerved the man, whose normal duties probably involved nothing more dangerous than holding the elevator doors open for deliverymen. "*Kun hakiman. Kun samitan,*" Flynn said curtly. "Be wise. Be silent."

The guard nodded fearfully. He'd undoubtedly spill his guts quickly enough once the real authorities started questioning him, but any directive that might buy them time now, even if it was only a couple of minutes, was useful.

Not looking to the left or right, Flynn and the others strode out of the building, heading straight for their parked Nissan van. Now they could hear sirens wailing in the distance. They piled inside through both open side doors and slammed them shut.

"You guys in a hurry?" Hynes asked as he backed quickly out onto the street and headed south, carefully staying at the posted speed limit. He glanced briefly back over his shoulder with a shit-eating grin. "Hey, sir, I thought we were aiming for something a little more discreet this time? As opposed to blowing the crap out of that place? I'm only asking because I'm new to all this covert stuff and I figure I need to get trained up."

"Sadly, our brilliant plan didn't survive contact with the enemy, Cole," Flynn replied.

"Oh," Hynes said. "As per usual?"

"Roger that," Flynn acknowledged as he started stripping off his Presidential Guard uniform. McGill and Cooke were doing the same thing. Their desert-camouflage fatigues, maroon berets, sidearms, and other equipment were bundled into weighted plastic shopping bags. Underneath the uniforms, they were all wearing work-stained jeans and old T-shirts. The laptop and other materials they'd retrieved from the Wickham Imports office went into a separate, worn-looking duffel bag.

Hynes swung left onto a different street. On their right, they drove past a low, white arch emblazoned with green lettering that spelled out *The Irish Village*. This was one of Al Garhoud's major tourist attractions, with a lush garden plaza fronting its own small lake. The restaurants and pubs had been built with authentic Irish stone. In addition to showcasing handcrafted wood furniture and carvings, they served genuine Irish food . . . and beer.

"Ah," McGill said wistfully, watching the arch vanish behind them. "I could do with a pint right about now."

Flynn frowned. "Yeah, me too. And more than one." He shook his head, still wrestling with the horrifying reality that somehow they'd missed Voronin. He didn't doubt that the men they'd killed were Raven Syndicate operatives, but that was cold comfort. What mattered was that they'd failed to eliminate their primary target. And that, in turn, meant that whatever malevolence the Russian planned to unleash on the United States or its allies was still in motion.

"Getting hammered isn't a bad idea, I guess," Cooke said equably. "*Except* for the whole 'being arrested, interrogated, and then beheaded' deal, that is. Which I *thought* we all agreed we should avoid."

"Jeez, always with the negative waves," Hynes retorted.

The Virginian smiled back at him. "Can't help that, Cole. It's just my naturally fearful side talking." As if to make his point, two police cars with flashing lights and warbling sirens raced past them at high speed, headed back the way they'd just come.

Flynn checked his watch. Dubai's authorities were a little faster off the mark than they'd hoped. He leaned forward. "We still okay?" he asked.

"No sweat," Hynes told him with supreme confidence. He spun the wheel again, making a right turn onto a wider avenue that would take them back onto the E11 Highway heading north. But they'd only be on the highway for less than a mile before exiting again—this time into the maze of surface streets that paralleled Dubai Creek, the tidal inlet that divided the city into its two main sections. "I've got our whole escape route memorized, sir. By the time the cops figure out what kind of vehicle they should be looking for, we'll be long gone."

ON THE WATERFRONT, DUBAI
ONLY MINUTES LATER

Having ditched the Nissan in a small parking lot several blocks away, Flynn and the others ambled casually across a wide boulevard to the waterfront. He, Cooke, and McGill were carrying the big plastic shopping bags containing their discarded clothing, weapons, and gear. Hynes toted the duffel bag packed with the items they'd snatched from the Russians.

Ahead, just past a park laid out with rows of palm trees and low, trimmed hedges, they could see dozens of lateen-rigged boats tied up along three jetties. This was the Dhow Wharfage, a holdover from the long-gone days when Dubai's inhabitants had made their riches more from trade around the Persian Gulf than from oil and international high finance. While the times had moved on, the teak-hulled dhows moored here still crisscrossed the waters of the gulf, carrying small cargoes and passengers.

Flynn led the way out onto the closest jetty. There, about halfway along, one of the long, thin-hulled boats—manned by a couple of young Arab men and a gray-bearded captain shouting orders—was getting ready to cast off.

Catching sight of Flynn and the others, the captain waved them aboard with a ferocious scowl. "Took your time getting here, didn't you?" he scolded them loudly in Arabic. "You're just lucky I promised your uncles and cousins in Doha that I'd ferry you back!"

Flynn hung his head in mute apology, a gesture imitated by the rest of his men.

"Well?" the captain demanded. "Do you think I'm running some kind of charity here? My time is worth something, even if yours isn't." Grumbling, he ostentatiously took the handfuls of UAE dirhams they each meekly offered and stuffed them away in a satchel. Apparently satisfied, he swung back to his tiny crew and bawled out more orders.

Grinning, the young men obeyed, quickly hauling in the lines that had moored them to the jetty and coiling them down. Slowly, the dhow edged away from the dock and turned out

into the channel. Heading west, it motored out into the open
waters of the Persian Gulf—to all appearances bound for Doha,
more than two hundred miles away.

Seated in the stern, Flynn kept his eyes fixed back on the
coastline until it was nothing more than a low, brown blur punc-
tuated by the soaring silver towers of Dubai's forest of skyscrapers.
To his relief, there was no sign of pursuit. He breathed out.

Once even the shore had vanished in the afternoon haze,
the captain came over across the gently rolling deck. "We're out
in very deep water here," he said with a genuine smile. "In case
you've got anything you'd like to dispose of."

"As it happens, we do," Flynn told him with a nod. He got
to his feet and motioned Cooke and McGill over to join him.
One after another, the weighted shopping bags with all their
weapons and fake uniforms splashed overboard and sank swiftly
out of sight.

"I hate to throw away decent gear," McGill mused, watching the last traces of foam eddy away. He shrugged. "But I guess
it's definitely not worth the risk of being caught with it in our
hot little hands."

"Amen," Cooke said from beside him.

Privately, Flynn doubted that the UAE's police investigators
would have cared much about the niceties of ballistics, DNA,
and fiber matching. Not when presented with a case involving
the sudden violent deaths of several foreigners, one of them,
whoever he really was, seemingly very wealthy and influential.
And certainly not if they'd managed to lay their hands on several other foreigners who might have done the job. Brute-force
interrogations were frowned upon in most Western countries.
However, they were a fact of life in other jurisdictions, especially
where possible questions of national security and large sums of
money were involved.

Still, he reminded himself, every passing hour and every unrolling mile of open sea made it less and less likely that anyone would connect the four young, Arab-looking men who'd boarded a boat bound for Qatar with the three trained assassins who'd shot up an office in the Al Garhoud district while masquerading as army counterterrorist soldiers. Not in time for it to matter, at least.

Flynn leaned against the stern rail while the dhow sailed onward toward the setting sun. He sighed, watching as its long wake curled whitely away across the surface of the sea. Glad as he was that this operation hadn't gone even worse, one vital question remained unanswered. If Pavel Voronin wasn't really in Dubai as they'd believed, just where the hell was he?

MINISTRY OF THE REVOLUTIONARY ARMED FORCES, HAVANA, CUBA
THAT SAME TIME

Pavel Voronin sat listening with feigned interest to Major General Ulises Castellano, the deputy chief of Cuba's general staff, pontificate. It was difficult, since the man was only repeating the same fervent assurances Voronin had already been given by others in Havana's regime earlier in the day. These military types were much the same, he thought, whether they were Russian or some other nationality. Once such a man carried a general's stars on his shoulders, his sense of self-importance ballooned out of all proportion.

"And so, señor Voronin," the general said with a flourish, "you can be confident that the special installation you require will be ready when necessary. In fact, our construction work is already well ahead of schedule. When your team of specialists and security personnel arrive, they should have no complaints."

Voronin glanced at the short, slender man next to him. He ignored the ugly burn scars crisscrossing the right half of Fyodor Maresyev's face. Before the fiery crash that disfigured him, Maresyev had been one of Russia's most experienced and decorated Tu-22M Backfire bomber pilots. Forbidden afterward to fly from a cockpit but still determined to excel in his profession, he'd shifted over to the Air Force's newer, more technologically advanced operations. Now he worked for the Raven Syndicate.

In answer to Voronin's unspoken question, Maresyev nodded. "Major General Castellano is quite correct. Everything—including the provision of the additional backup power sources we will need—is well in hand." He indicated the tough-looking Cuban colonel seated at Castellano's right hand. "And Colonel Hidalgo and I have arrived at a good working understanding of the security measures that will be necessary once CASTLE KEEP is fully operational. We should have no trouble moving forward as planned."

That was good, Voronin thought icily. He'd certainly paid the men who ruled Havana more than enough—both through official channels and under the table into their private accounts—to count on their complete cooperation. Just then, he saw the door to this conference room open and started to frown in irritation at this unexpected interruption.

But it was Navashin, one of his own aides. The former SVR officer hurried to his side and leaned over to whisper in his ear. "Sir, there's been an incident in Dubai. A bad one. All of our people assigned there have been killed. They were shot to death during an apparent raid on our office."

Dubai? Voronin fought to avoid revealing his sudden unease. It was essential to maintain the confidence of his Cuban "allies" in this endeavor. As far as they could be allowed to know, CASTLE KEEP must appear to be proceeding without the slightest hitch. Tight lipped, he thanked the general for his time and left.

Minutes later in his car, which had been searched meticulously for listening devices, he stabbed a finger at Navashin. "Explain!" he snapped.

Nervously, the other man ran through a summary of what little was known so far. Details of the attack were still sketchy, but journalists in the region were speculating that it had been carried out by either the Iranians or the Israelis. Given the rumors circulating that Wickham Imports was considerably more than just an ordinary trading concern, there were theories the company could have been some kind of covert player in the ongoing, undeclared war between Tehran and Jerusalem—though on whose side was unclear. Officially, the UAE's government was denying any involvement in the massacre, despite eyewitness accounts that it had been carried out by men dressed as special forces commandos from the Presidential Guard.

Voronin took the news in silence. He stared out the window at Havana's rain-drenched streets. Was the death of his agent known as Jones just a coincidence? Or was it somehow connected to his own recent use of that same false identity to cover his movements in Mexico? He scowled. Given the tight security surrounding his trip, that seemed highly unlikely, but he knew the possibility could not be completely ruled out. He fought down a wave of apprehension. A leak, any leak, from the Brotherhood of Blood could be completely catastrophic.

Then he shook his head. He had far too little information to yield to such fears. Right now, the most critical task was to establish how much of their operational security might have been breached by this unexpected attack. Still frowning in thought, Voronin took out his smartphone and began to compose an urgent encrypted text to Vasily Kondakov, his deputy in Moscow.

OUT IN THE PERSIAN GULF
SEVERAL HOURS LATER

Nick Flynn stared out into the darkness off the dhow's port side. With the moon still below the horizon, only the stars speckling the night sky provided any natural illumination. A dull glow on the southern horizon marked the city lights of Abu Dhabi. But there, not far away, a small bright light started winking in quick, rhythmic flashes. Beside him, he could hear the gray-bearded captain muttering under his breath, piecing together the coded message they were being sent.

When the signal light clicked off, the older man nodded. He raised a flashlight of his own and flicked it on and off a few times, sending a fast reply. He turned to the American. "Your friends are here, as expected."

Moments later, with a throaty rumble of powerful outboard motors, a yacht glided into view and then turned to come in right alongside. The dhow's two young crewmen tossed lines from fore and aft to men waiting aboard the faster vessel. As soon as they were secured, Flynn saw a short, white-haired man wave politely to the Arab captain. "*Alsalam alaykum*, Masoud," Gideon Ayish called out. "Peace be upon you."

"And with you, Gideon," the bearded man replied with a big grin. "I have those fish you wanted."

Ayish nodded. "Then send them over, my friend. Your payment will be as agreed."

"Have you ever failed me?" the Arab retorted with a shrug. He turned to Flynn and the rest of his team, who'd all gathered near the railing. "Here we part. May God go with you."

They nodded their thanks and climbed awkwardly over the railing and onto the powerboat. The moment they were aboard, the two crews released the lines holding their vessels together.

With a dull rumble, the yacht pulled away, curving back around to the south onto a course that would lead them to Abu Dhabi.

Flynn caught the older Israeli by the arm. "Voronin wasn't there," he said flatly. "Whoever this guy Simon Jones really was, it wasn't him. He was Russian, for sure, but definitely not the one we were after."

Ayish stood still for a moment, considering the ramifications. "That is surprising," he said finally. "Based on the list of names, our intelligence seemed conclusive."

"Except for that quick, otherwise unexplained stop in Havana," Flynn pointed out tiredly. "My guess is that's where they made a switch. Jones from Mexico, a.k.a. Voronin, got off, and the Jones headed for Dubai got back on."

"A reasonable assumption," the older man said. "I'll pass the word to Fox and the other stations." He touched Flynn on the shoulder. "In the meantime, Nick, it's time for you and your men to become yourselves again."

With that, Ayish ushered Flynn and others belowdecks. The yacht had a single washroom, sufficient for them to rinse out the dyes darkening their hair and skin and to remove their fake beards and mustaches. Western-style khaki shorts and polo shirts were laid out across a couple of bunks. By the time the boat tied up outside the villa they were using as a safe house, anyone seeing them debark would assume the little group of Western businessmen was just returning from a daylong sight-seeing trip along the gulf coast. And since they were all set to leave the next day, heading back to America and Europe on different flights, no further cover stories would be necessary.

THIRTEEN

WARSAW, POLAND

TWO DAYS LATER

Nick Flynn climbed out of the taxi that had brought him from Warsaw Chopin Airport. He leaned back in through the rolled-down front seat window and handed the driver enough zlote for his fare and a generous tip. One of the rideshare services like Uber might have been cheaper, but cash was still king for someone who wanted to avoid leaving electronic credit card traces of his movements. With a cheerful wave, the cab driver pulled out from the curb and soon vanished into the steady flow of cars, trucks, and buses on the busy thoroughfare.

Watching him go, Flynn shivered a bit as a cold, damp gust of wind whistled down the pavement. He zipped his jacket up and buried his neck in his collar. Poland in the spring was a far cry from the sun-drenched warmth of the Middle East. A wry smile tugged at the edge of his mouth. His travel wardrobe wasn't exactly cut out for this unexpected side trip.

He'd been in Heathrow the day before, waiting for his

connecting flight back to the States, when he'd received a coded text from Fox instructing him to detour to the Polish capital instead. And then, after he'd landed this morning, he'd received another message directing him to this address in Warsaw's Mokotów District.

Flynn took careful stock of his surroundings. His instructors, first in Air Force intelligence and later in the Quartet Directorate, had all pounded home to him the critical importance of situational awareness for an agent in the field. He remembered the unique way one of them, a former member of MI6, had phrased it. "In the days of air-to-air dogfighting, the old mantra was 'Beware of the Hun in the sun.' On our considerably murkier and often less honorable field of battle, it's 'Watch out for the seemingly innocent passerby. She might be carrying a gun.'"

Mokotów was one of the few sections of the city left unscathed by the ravages of the Second World War, and it was densely populated. The district was also home to several foreign embassies and many multinational corporations that did business in Poland. From what he'd been able to gather, most of Mokotów's streets and neighborhoods fell into the category so beloved by real estate agents of being fashionable, bustling, and prosperous. The area was widely known as a place where Poles and foreign visitors alike could dine on trendy international cuisine, shop for designer fashions, and party late into the night in glittering nightclubs and wine bars. Less widely known was that Poland's foreign intelligence agency, the Agencja Wywiadu, or AW, had its headquarters nearby. Considering this carefully arranged rendezvous, Flynn had a hunch that little detail wasn't just a random coincidence.

This particular block, however, seemed to have been bypassed by all of the Mokotów District's vaunted prosperity.

On this side of a divided six-lane boulevard, several drab gray concrete two-story buildings daubed with swirling tags of spray-painted graffiti sat adjacent to one another. Apartments occupied the upper floors, marked by windows closed off with blinds. Large windows at the sidewalk level advertised the presence of a couple of local businesses, including a tailor's shop and a convenience store selling mostly alcohol, cigarettes, and lottery tickets.

Flynn checked his phone. The address Fox had texted for their meeting belonged to a little Vietnamese café. Beneath a red awning, a green-trimmed glass door opened into the restaurant. He went in. A handful of square tables crowded the small dining room. Along the back wall, a pair of swinging double doors opened into a tiny kitchen. The atmosphere was pleasantly warm, almost steamy, and full of the pungent aromas of fermented fish sauce, lemongrass, garlic, and peppers.

Fox waved him over to the only occupied table. The head of Four's American station was seated beside a somewhat stockier man of about the same age. Everything about the other man, especially the way his watchful gaze cataloged, measured, and dissected Flynn's appearance while he walked up to join them, practically shouted *senior spook*.

And if Flynn had any doubts about the value of his instincts, Fox's low-voiced introduction dispelled them. "Nick," the older man said, "this is Mikolaj Soliński, my central European counterpart."

With a start, Flynn recognized the other man's name from classified briefings during his days in US Air Force intelligence. Up to a year ago, before he'd retired from his government service, the Pole had headed the Agencja Wywiadu. This guy was a senior spook, indeed.

"Mr. Flynn," the Pole responded, with a minute nod.

"Since, for the moment, we can't safely approach anyone inside our own government's intelligence organizations, I've enlisted Mikolaj's help to figure out a few of the mysteries raised by your operation in Dubai," Fox explained.

Flynn nodded. Ordinarily, they could have run the data he and the others had retrieved past friendlies in the US intelligence community—using the government's vast databases to filter out vital information from meaningless chaff. Unfortunately, since they strongly suspected Voronin had his own people in place inside those agencies, such a move would now be far too dangerous. If the slightest hint of anything—names, pictures, computer files, and the like—connected to their hit on the Raven Syndicate base in Dubai reached the wrong people, it would be like sending up a flare for their enemy to zero in on.

"I relayed the identity photos of the four men you killed to a trusted former colleague in AW," Soliński said. "He ran them through my old agency's computer systems, looking for matches."

Flynn raised an eyebrow. "Any luck?"

"With three of them? No. They didn't turn up in our files."

Fox shrugged. "My assessment is that those men were probably junior officers in the Spetsnaz, SVR, or GRU before they joined the Raven Syndicate."

"Goons, not command types," Flynn realized.

"Exactly," Soliński agreed. "Absent some compelling reason, we generally don't track those without command responsibilities or unusual skill sets."

Flynn nodded and asked, "And the fourth man?"

"There we scored a hit," the Pole said. He passed a color photograph across the table.

Flynn studied it for a moment. The photo was obviously a copy of a formal portrait. It showed a middle-aged man in the dress-blue tunic of the Russian Air Force. The rank insignia displayed on his gold epaulets was that of a full colonel. There wasn't any doubt about it. That was the man Flynn had seen and shot in Dubai. The man who'd been calling himself Simon Jones. He tapped the image. "Who was this guy in real life?"

"His name was Georgy Bazhanov," Soliński said.

Flynn looked back at the picture. "He wasn't a pilot?" he asked. Unexpectedly, Bazhanov's uniform tunic didn't show a set of flying wings.

"No," the Pole replied. "According to our intelligence, Bazhanov was an aviation-engineering specialist attached to the Gromov Flight Research Institute at Zhukovsky Air Base."

Flynn frowned. Zhukovsky, about twenty miles southeast of Moscow, was the equivalent of Edwards Air Force Base, the US Air Force's premier test center for advanced aircraft.

"Bazhanov was on our 'radar' because he was believed to be one of Russia's top experts in stealth technology," Soliński continued. His mouth creased in a slight smile at his own small joke.

"So what's a guy like that, with top-notch and top-secret technical expertise, doing running a covert operation for Voronin?" Flynn wondered. Up to now, most of the Raven Syndicate agents they'd encountered had been veterans of the covert operations world, mostly officers with Spetsnaz, GRU, or SVR experience. Bazhanov's background as a heavy-duty scientific and engineering guru didn't correlate at all with the usual background for someone involved in cloak-and-dagger work.

"A very good question," the Pole admitted. "And one we desperately need answered."

From the chair beside him, Fox nodded solemnly in agreement. "The computer and smartphones your team collected are on their way to our technical experts," he told Flynn. "If we're lucky, our people might be able to break far enough into them to obtain the information we require."

"And if we're not lucky?" Flynn asked.

"I've alerted all of Four's other country and regional stations," Fox said, "asking our colleagues around the world to dig up whatever they can on Bazhanov's travel history. His access to that Bombardier jet suggests it must have been extensive. It's just possible that analyzing flight records, credit card data, and other similar information will yield some clues about what he was really doing for Voronin."

Soliński nodded. "I will set the wheels going here in central Europe," he said. "We Poles, and our friends in the Czech Republic, Hungary, and other nations, have a great many reasons to distrust Russians, especially when they lie about who they really are. If we find any evidence of this so-called Mr. Jones operating in our backyard, you can be sure that we'll relay it to you right away."

"I'm counting on that, Mikolaj," Fox said. "Somewhere, somehow, there's a trail out there for us to follow. We just have to find it."

Flynn sighed. "*And* we have to find it in time to matter," he reminded the older man. "I thought we were getting inside Voronin's decision loop by hitting his operation in Dubai. Now, though, I've got the bad feeling that we're still lagging way behind that Russian son of a bitch."

"An occupational hazard, I fear," Soliński observed. "Turning the tables on a predator like Voronin is no easy task. But you will have every assistance my people can provide." He rose from the table and extended his hand. "In the meantime, Mr. Flynn, *udanego polowania*. Good hunting."

Flynn took it gratefully. "My team and I will do our best, sir," he promised. When the café door closed behind Soliński, he turned back to Fox with an apologetic look. "I'm really sorry about the foul-up in Dubai. I figure I got so fixated on the idea of nailing Voronin that I didn't even consider the possibility he could have pulled a switch on us."

"None of us did, Nick," Fox said with a slight shrug. He peered at Flynn over his glasses. "We acted on the best information available. That it turned out to be in error is no one's fault—especially given the speed with which we were forced to move."

"Yeah, maybe so," Flynn said, hearing the almost unwilling agreement in his own voice. He rubbed at his gritty eyes. The string of too many long airline flights across too many time zones with too little sleep along the way was starting to wear on him, he realized. He wasn't exactly ready to crater, but there wasn't much doubt that the mix of coffee and adrenaline wouldn't keep him upright for a lot longer. Sometime soon he was going to need to catch some shut-eye. He dropped his hand and looked across the table at Fox. "In hindsight, I guess, it's easy enough to see how the mix-up happened."

The other man nodded. "We should have paid more attention to your earlier intuition about how easily passport checks could be evaded in Belarus. It's likely that Voronin actually boarded the executive jet during its refueling stop in Minsk, taking on the Simon Jones cover identity for his own purposes in Mexico. Whether this man Bazhanov stayed aboard for that trip or flew separately to Havana in order to rejoin the plane on its return flight is unclear. What is clear, though, is that Voronin himself must have disembarked in Havana . . . for some as-yet-unknown but significant reason."

Flynn saw what he meant. It would have been easy enough for the jet to make another refueling stop in Minsk on the way back—dropping Voronin off considerably closer to Moscow in the process. So the Raven Syndicate chief must have had some pressing reason to stay behind in Cuba. "Oh, joy," he said. "One more tangle to unravel."

"One of altogether too many for comfort," Fox agreed. Then, behind his lenses, his eyes took on a calculating look. "Nevertheless, as it happens, I think there's a strong possibility that Bazhanov might prove to be one of the keys to learning what Voronin has planned."

"Well, I sure as hell hope you're right about that, Br'er Fox," Flynn told him. "Because I'd love to stop kicking myself for plugging the wrong guy. I hate playing into the stereotype of all Americans being trigger-happy maniacs who shoot first and ask questions later."

"Even Texans?" Fox asked with the bare hint of a smile.

"Especially Texans," Flynn replied. He offered the other man a sheepish grin. "Even if, judging by my own personal inclinations under pressure, there might be a little kernel of truth in that."

FOURTEEN

MERCURY CITY TOWER, MOSCOW, RUSSIA

THE NEXT DAY

Even under the thick band of gray rain clouds stretching across Moscow, the Mercury Tower's bronze-tinted glass glowed—reflecting the lights of its neighboring skyscrapers. The soaring building drew attention to itself, whether in shadow or in sunlight. That was something prized by its wealthy and successful tenants, the owners of high-end retail stores, luxury apartments, five-star gourmet restaurants, and, naturally, the headquarters of several of Russia's most prosperous corporations. Including his own Sindikat Vorona, the Raven Syndicate, Pavel Voronin thought with pleasure. Its offices filled three whole upper floors of this reinforced-concrete, steel, and glass monument to power and prestige.

A tone chimed at the door to his office. He turned away from his breathtaking view out over the loop of the Moskva River to the Kremlin's redbrick walls and golden-dome-topped spires. Unhurriedly, he tapped an icon on his smart watch, instructing the door's security lock to disengage.

With a soft buzz, it swung open, admitting Vasily Konda-kov. The tall, balding deputy hurried in. "I've got a report on the episode in Dubai," he said.

Voronin concealed his scorn. His subordinates seemed to believe that using pale, trivial words like *incident* or *episode* would rob what had happened in Dubai of some of its grim reality. If so, they were fools. Three highly trained security officers and one of his most important operatives had been butchered—cut down in their own office without apparently even laying a finger on those who'd attacked them. With a curt nod, he sat down behind his desk and motioned Kondakov into the only chair on the other side. "Well?" he said with icy calm.

"We've managed to obtain a copy of the security camera footage," the former GRU colonel told him. "I've sent you the file."

Expressionlessly, Voronin tapped the keyboard built into his desk. A monitor glowed to life. An icon with his deputy's identifier blinked into existence in a lower corner. Clicking on that opened the video file. He watched the grainy footage in tight-jawed silence, seeing three men in military uniforms enter the building containing the Wickham Imports office and then calmly exit only a few minutes later. He closed it without comment and then looked at Kondakov. "Your assessment?"

The other man took off his glasses and polished them with a handkerchief, obviously buying himself a few seconds of time to get his thoughts in order. He put the glasses back on. "While the operation was undoubtedly noisier than they would have preferred, those involved are certainly professionals," he said carefully. "My former subordinates could not have done better."

Voronin nodded. From Kondakov, that was high praise. He had once headed the GRU's special assassination squad, Unit 29155. Under his command, its trained killers had murdered a large number of defectors, political dissidents, and even foreigners who were judged dangerous to Russia's national security. Despite his veneer of seeming bureaucratic dreariness, the man was a keen connoisseur of targeted covert killing.

"To me, they looked like Arabs. Or Iranians. Or perhaps Israelis," Voronin mused.

Kondakov shrugged. "Their appearance could simply be a disguise," he pointed out. "Facial hair and other features are easily altered, especially for a short time."

Voronin scowled, knowing the other man was right. "What else do you have?" he demanded.

"The van the attackers used was found abandoned several kilometers away, not far from where Arab sailing dhows tie up along Dubai Creek," Kondakov said. His lips thinned. "Apparently, though, the vehicle's registration papers, identification number, and license plate were all top-quality fakes."

"Which makes the vehicle a dead end?" Voronin replied grimly.

Kondakov nodded. "The make and model are quite common in the UAE," he said. "My suspicion is that it will end up having been reported as stolen. Undoubtedly from a location without witnesses or closed-circuit TV cameras."

"*Der'mo*," Voronin said through gritted teeth. "Shit."

His deputy looked apologetic. "As I said, our opponents are professionals."

"Tell me something that is not blindingly obvious," Voronin retorted. His fingers drummed hard in irritation on the surface of his desk. "You say the van was abandoned near a harbor area?"

Kondakov nodded. "The area known as the Dhow Wharfage," he clarified.

"Indicating these assassins escaped by sea?"

"That is one possibility," Kondakov said. He didn't sound very convinced. "It could also have been an act of misdirection.

It would have been easy enough for them to simply switch vehicles and just drive away."

Voronin glared at his deputy for a long, uncomfortable moment. "You don't believe these people can be caught and identified, do you?" he bit out.

"In all candor, I don't," Kondakov admitted quietly. "Not after so much time has passed without the UAE's investigators picking up any real trace of them. Even if the killers weren't merely local talent hired for the task, by now it will be virtually impossible to track them." He shrugged his shoulders again. "After all, the region's three main international airports—Dubai, Abu Dhabi, and Doha—handle a combined total of more than three hundred thousand passengers a day."

Voronin considered that. "A great ocean of fish, through which a few sharks could easily swim by unnoticed," he said at last, with a sour twist to his expression. After a moment of disgruntled silence, he turned his cold gaze on Kondakov. "Very well, then, Vasily. Do you have anything positive to report in this endless parade of disasters?"

The other man nodded vigorously, plainly eager to move onto safer footing. "We've completed our analysis of the potential risks to CASTLE KEEP's operational security," he said.

"And?"

"They should be minimal," Kondakov assured him. "Since Bazhanov had finished obtaining the special components and advanced technology we need, he was already in the process of winding down Wickham Imports."

Voronin sat forward. "So the warehouses we were using to transship sanctioned electronics and other special materials are—?"

"Completely empty," Kondakov said with certainty. "Even if the UAE authorities or others search them, they will find nothing of any use."

"What about his computer and other electronic devices?" Voronin asked. "I assume they've gone missing?"

Kondakov nodded. "They have. But they won't be helpful." He explained, "All of Bazhanov's files were encrypted to a very high standard, easily the equal of that used for our most secure military systems."

"Codes can be cracked," Voronin reminded him.

"Given enough time and computing power," his deputy acknowledged. "Which is why I made sure that none of Bazhanov's records or messages were ever preserved in plain language. Before encrypting those files, he first rewrote them in a word code of his own devising, a highly idiosyncratic system known only to himself . . . and to me. Even if our enemies break through the computer encryption, they will find only seeming gibberish."

Slowly, Voronin nodded his approval. Given the ex-Air Force aviation-engineering specialist's importance to the initial stages of CASTLE KEEP and his relative inexperience as a covert operator, Kondakov had taken on the task of acting as Bazhanov's controller in Moscow. And from the sound of it, he'd done a thorough job of training the other man in the dark arts of espionage tradecraft.

At least the news that their secrets were still safe offered a small measure of consolation. True, whoever was responsible for killing Bazhanov and his other agents had won a tactical victory. But it was a hollow achievement. Considered as a matter of strategy, their murderous effort would yield only barren fruit.

CASTLE KEEP could proceed without impediment.

FIFTEEN

AVALON HOUSE, WINTER PARK, FLORIDA

TEN DAYS LATER

Nick Flynn briefly closed his eyes. Not because he didn't like the view. Far from it. Outside the window of Fox's small office, the gardens around Avalon House were in full spring bloom, vibrant with a mass of tropical colors. Plus, Laura Van Horn was there, too, seated right beside him. Anyone who couldn't appreciate the remarkable beauty on ample display had the desiccated soul of a teetotaling corporate accountant. Or maybe, he decided, that of a government bureaucrat whose idea of fun was perusing the tens of thousands of pages of bullshit regulations in the *Federal Register*. No, he knew he'd shut his eyes out of sheer frustration. With a sigh, he forced them open again and turned toward Fox. "A total waste of time?" he asked in astonishment. "Seriously?"

The older man nodded, obviously regretting his role as the bearer of bad tidings. "I'm afraid so, Nick." His shoulders lifted and then fell again in an apologetic shrug. "Try as they might, our technical people haven't been able to break into the files on

Georgy Bazhanov's laptop. Their assessment is that the key data is hidden beneath incredibly complex levels of encryption." He sighed quietly. "In their judgment, it would take NSA's super-computers to break them—given enough time, that is."

"Yeah, except the boys and girls at Fort Meade don't do contract work," Flynn retorted with a wry half smile. "And I'm betting we can't afford to buy a supercomputer of our own, can we?"

"Sadly, I didn't win the most recent lottery." Fox shrugged. "But even if I had, we'd still be considerably short of funds."

Flynn nodded. Price tags for the incredibly advanced code-breaking computers inside the National Security Agen-cy's top-secret site in Utah ran into the hundreds of millions of dollars. And that was without including the dedicated power plants required to supply them with dozens of megawatts of electricity.

Van Horn leaned into the conversation. "Okay, that's a non-starter. So what else do we have, Br'er Fox?" she asked reasonably. "Because I know you well enough to be sure that you wouldn't call Nick and me in for a consultation just to crush our fondest hopes and dreams."

"You are correct. I don't have as much data as I would prefer. And certainly not in as much detail," Fox admitted. "But there is still enough to be intriguing . . . and for me to be very inter-ested to see what the two of you make of it." He looked down at his desk for a moment, visibly arranging his thoughts. "My requests to Four's various European stations have borne some fruit," he said at last.

"Do tell," Van Horn said with an encouraging smile. She made a show of batting her eyelashes.

Fox stifled a snort. "I'm mostly impervious to the femme fatale approach, Laura."

"Just practicing," she assured him.

He gave an imperceptible shake of his head. "Apparently, this Georgy Bazhanov traveled extensively using his Simon Jones cover identity. The various stations have confirmed a number of short visits to London, Paris, Toulouse, Munich, and Madrid over the past year or so—plus other direct flights from Dubai to Minsk."

"Those visits to Minsk were probably for meetings with Voronin or other high-ranking Raven Syndicate executives," Flynn interjected.

"Undoubtedly," Fox said with a quick nod. He continued, "Bazhanov's credit card records flesh out some of the story." Seeing their questioning looks, he explained. "We had a bit of luck there. As a member of Interpol, the UAE's government requested those records as part of their own homicide investigation. As a result, one of our allies inside the organization was able to pass discreet copies to us at the same time."

"So what was Bazhanov up to?" Van Horn asked.

"That's not readily apparent," Fox told her. "But we do know that his credit cards, all corporate accounts connected to Wickham Imports, show many quick stays in very expensive hotels in each of those cities—along with luxury car rentals and meals, often for two people, at various top-flight restaurants."

"My, what an interesting pattern," Van Horn said with a raised eyebrow. "Maybe he was showing his mistress a really good time," she suggested impishly.

"Highly doubtful," Fox said. "If Bazhanov really was playing around on Pavel Voronin's dime, the hit team that killed him would have come from the Raven Syndicate, not Four." He shrugged. "Secret organizations really *don't* approve of their agents poaching operational funds for personal romantic use," he pointed out, with a sidelong glance at Flynn and Van Horn.

"Warning duly noted, Br'er Fox," she said cheerfully.

Flynn mentally ran through the list of cities his superior had rattled off. Somewhere there, he thought, was a pattern. And it wasn't just the obvious one that they were classic European tourist spots. Despite its beauty, Toulouse certainly wasn't in quite the same tourist league as Paris or London or Madrid. He frowned. What was their special draw for a former Russian air force colonel turned spook? And then, very suddenly, like a firework exploding in a dazzling shower of sparks in a dark night sky, he saw it. Toulouse, for example, was basically the center of Europe's aerospace industry. And all the other cities on Bazhanov's list had their own links to high-tech defense industries. That was the connection. "Every city Bazhanov visited is home to one or more of the major European and British defense contractors—companies like BAE, Airbus, MBDA, Dassault, and others," he pointed out.

Van Horn nodded, seeing what he was driving at almost as fast. "All of which are deep into cutting-edge stealth-technology research and development," she said. "Which we just happen to know was good old Mr. Bazhanov's field of expertise as a serving air force officer." She shrugged. "What's the old saying? A leopard can't change its spots? Same thing usually applies to people. Which is why it never made a lot of sense to think an engineering and science careerist like him would suddenly veer off to join the wonderful world of spies on a whim."

"Unless his new job was to illegally acquire stealth tech secrets by any means necessary. Like by theft, purchase, or maybe even blackmail," Flynn said. "With his technical background, Georgy Bazhanov would be the perfect guy to evaluate whether he was getting access to useful material. Or if someone was just peddling a bunch of junk science to him—either as part of a con game or maybe as bait offered up by Western counterintelligence to ferret out hostile spies. Put that together with the rumors that Wickham Imports was in the business of acquiring stolen military technology, and it all makes sense."

Fox considered that. "Your hypothesis seems sound. Stealth-technology theft is always guaranteed to be a high-priority item for Russia's intelligence services and military," he said slowly. "But something about it doesn't jibe." His mouth tightened. "And that's Pavel Voronin's involvement in organizing and funding the venture."

Flynn saw where he was going. "Meaning that what Bazhanov was doing seems like penny-ante stuff for a guy like Voronin?"

"Exactly," Fox said. "Our experience with him is that he prefers masterminding large-scale operations. Operations that are intended to have staggering strategic consequences. Stealing Western military secrets as a middleman or contractor for the SVU or GRU seems completely out of character."

Flynn couldn't disagree with the older man's assessment. Everything they knew about the Russian oligarch indicated he was both supremely self-confident and almost insanely ambitious. Running an espionage ring whose success might, at best, earn him the insincere thanks of Moscow's Ministry of Defense and the equivalent of a few tens of millions of dollars in grudging reimbursements and monetary awards didn't add up. "Just great," he grumbled. "The more we dig at this, the longer and longer our list of things we *don't* know grows. And when you combine that with the things we *do* know that don't make any damned sense . . ." He trailed off in frustration.

"Not a particularly agreeable situation," Fox agreed.

Flynn heard the warning note in the other man's voice. "Oh, swell," he said. "There's more?"

Fox nodded. "Unfortunately, we're picking up signs that whatever Voronin put into play in Mexico has kicked into gear."

He pulled a folder out of his desk and opened it. Inside was another set of full-color surveillance photos. "These just came in from Reyes," he said. "Passed along from Colonel Herrera's informant in Durango."

Flynn and Van Horn leaned forward, studying the pictures in silence for a few moments. They showed a large twin-engine jet sitting on the tarmac of the Mexican airport. Its cargo doors were wide open, with high loaders caught in the act of unloading large black-wrapped pallets onto a number of waiting trucks.

"That's a Boeing 777F, a plane specially configured for long-haul heavy-freight operation," Van Horn realized with a slight frown. "Which is not something I would have expected to see in that part of Mexico."

The aircraft's engine mounts were colored bright orange, while dark-blue, light-blue, and vivid-orange stripes marked its tail. A name, CARGA AÉREA, was emblazoned in matching orange across the 777's light-gray fuselage. Flynn looked up at Fox. "Carga Aérea?"

The older man nodded. "An airfreight company incorporated in Venezuela. On paper, it's privately owned. But that's a facade. One of the two owners is a retired major general. The other is his brother-in-law. Both of them have extremely close ties to the upper echelons of their country's narco-dictatorship."

"Then how can we be certain this shipment, whatever it is, is somehow connected with Voronin?" Flynn asked. He tapped one of the photos, which showed cartel gunmen posted as guards around the trucks. "We know the Brotherhood of Blood has close links of its own to the thugs running Caracas. Sure, it'd be a bold move for the narcos to have some of their cocaine shipments or guns delivered directly by air, but I don't see how we can rule that out."

"Ordinarily, I'd share your caution," Fox told him. "Except

that Carga Aérea isn't the actual owner of that particular 777." He smiled dryly. "Up until a few weeks ago, the airline's entire fleet consisted of just two much-older and considerably less capable Airbus cargo planes."

Van Horn frowned. "So where did that jet come from?"

"It's been leased to them by a Moscow-based competitor."

"A company owned by Voronin," Flynn guessed.

Fox's pale eyes brightened behind his glasses. "Not officially." Then he shrugged. "But off the books? Yes, almost certainly."

Flynn's eyes narrowed. "Do we have any details about this specific flight to Mexico?"

"Only that the plane was tracked taking off from Minsk," Fox said. "And that it landed briefly in Caracas, before flying straight on to Durango."

Van Horn whistled. "At max load, a 777F like that can haul up to one hundred and four metric tons of freight. Whether it's drugs, guns, or whatever, that's one hell of a lot of cargo."

Flynn fanned through the photos. He stopped, seeing one that showed a bus with tinted windows parked close to the big jet. He looked up at Fox. "That aircraft wasn't just carrying cargo," he realized. "There were passengers aboard, too."

"Yes."

"Who and how many?"

Fox shook his head. "We don't know. Colonel Herrera's undercover man was roughly warned away by those armed cartel guards when he tried to get closer." He sighed. "Nor do we know where the cargo pallets or those passengers went after they left the airport grounds."

Flynn's jaw tightened. "Remember what I said earlier about being really fed up with not knowing what the hell we were facing?"

Fox nodded.

"Consider that repeated," Flynn told him flatly.

THE KREMLIN, MOSCOW
THAT SAME TIME

One of Zhdanov's civilian aides silently ushered Voronin into the president's private office and just as quietly and unobtrusively departed, leaving the two men alone. A gray haze of cigarette smoke hung heavily in the room, only barely stirred by an old-fashioned ceiling fan. Heavy drapes closed off any view of the Kremlin courtyard below. Irritably, Zhdanov gestured to one of the gilt chairs in front of his ornate desk. "Sit down, Pavel," he growled.

With a polite nod, Voronin obeyed. Deftly, he unbuttoned his perfectly tailored suit coat and then crossed one leg over the other. To all appearances, he was the very picture of casual, unstudied elegance. Inside, however, all of his senses were on high alert, attentive to the slightest details. "Yes, Mr. President?"

Scowling, Zhdanov crushed his cigarette in the overflowing ashtray in front of him. Then he picked up a heavy, leather-bound folder on his desk and flipped it open. His finger stabbed down at the handful of documents it contained. "It's these new authorization requests of yours, Pavel," he said tightly.

"They are all vital if we are to proceed with the next phases of CASTLE KEEP," Voronin pointed out.

The president's mouth thinned. "What you're asking me to approve is absolutely unprecedented," he said, with an edge to his voice. A tiny nerve twitched at the corner of one eye. "A delegation of my command authority which would go far beyond any ever deemed wise in the entire modern history of our Motherland."

"That is quite true," Voronin agreed.

Nettled, Zhdanov glared at him. "You seem pretty fucking calm about that," he snapped. "And about the risks you're asking me to run. The risks not only to me personally but to our nation as a whole. True, I understand that if this new plan of yours works as you promise, Russia could dominate the globe for decades, maybe even centuries. But if anything goes wrong, anything at all, the whole world could easily be plunged into chaos—and us along with it. If anything, the danger is even greater than it was in your MIDNIGHT project, which ended up as a complete disaster!"

"The risks are high," Voronin agreed, carefully ignoring the president's dig. To have come so close to success the last time only made it more important for him to triumph now. And for that, he needed Zhdanov's continued backing. "But no higher than the rewards promised by success. Besides, what alternative do we really have?"

Zhdanov's hard eyes narrowed.

"At the moment, our conventional armed forces are perceived as a laughingstock—poorly trained, poorly equipped, and corrupt," Voronin reminded him. "A decisive victory over even a fourth-rate power like Ukraine is now unachievable. And open conflict with NATO and the United States or with China would only result in our swift and sure defeat. We are caught in the tightening coils of a military, economic, and demographic trap. In such circumstances, taking the safe path is not a sensible option. It will lead only to our ruin," he argued forcefully. "CASTLE KEEP alone plays to our nation's sole remaining strength—to the special weapons we have so painstakingly and at tremendous cost developed over decades."

"Those weapons are our last guarantee of survival," Zhdanov shot back. "So long as our missiles are poised, no one dares to attack us."

Voronin shrugged. "Because no one needs to, Mr. President," he said icily. "When the day comes, as it must, and our run-down, depopulated cities are inhabited only by elderly cripples begging for scraps of bread from wealthy Chinese or American or European tourists, who will care that we still have ICBMs on alert in rusting, overgrown silos? We will be no more respected or feared than some Stone Age tribesman brandishing a flint-tipped spear."

Watching the president's face whiten in shock and anger, Voronin knew he was taking a serious risk by speaking so bluntly. As he grew older, Zhdanov had increasingly surrounded himself with bootlicking sycophants and toadies. But it was precisely that fact that justified this gamble. Somewhere inside, beyond the thin shell of Zhdanov's supremely confident public persona, was a man only too aware that his health was increasingly fragile. And with the prospect of serious illness, his hold on power was far less certain. He was a man, moreover, who knew that those same sycophantic subordinates had failed him again and again. Down one road, the president must subconsciously realize, lay only inevitable darkness—a future where he would end his days ingloriously, as yet another aging failure desperately clinging to his personal power in a dying state . . . just like so many Russian leaders before him. Voronin alone offered him the chance to alter that bleak prospect. The chance to go down in history as the Motherland's greatest, most powerful, and most daring ruler.

The fact that Voronin had a much different vision of who would ultimately reap those accolades was something he intended to keep well hidden from Zhdanov—and from everyone else for the time being. For a moment, he held his breath. The future hung in the balance. Would this old man have the guts— and the desperation, he thought cynically—to take the needed leap into the unknown and the unknowable?

Then, seeing Zhdanov's short, sharp nod, he understood that he'd won.

"Very well," the older man said with a snap to his voice. In a rapid, slashing series of motions, he systematically scrawled his name across the bottom of every special authorization document he'd been given for approval. But then he looked up with hooded, unreadable eyes. "Nevertheless, Pavel, let one thing be plainly understood between us."

"Of course, Mr. President," Voronin replied easily.

"While I've signed these authorizations, I want your personal oath that you will take no irrevocable actions without my express approval. In this matter, I, and I alone, must be the final judge of whether it is safe, or prudent, to continue. Is that clear?"

"Completely clear, sir," Voronin lied smoothly. "Nothing will be done without your permission. You will retain full control at every step."

SIXTEEN

LA CASA DE LAS SIRENAS, MEXICO CITY, MEXICO

A FEW DAYS LATER

Nick Flynn and Laura Van Horn made their way across the rooftop terrace and over to a table in the far corner. Two men, both in civilian clothes, rose politely to greet them. One, tall and spare with a gaunt, lined face, was Miguel Reyes, the head of Four's station in Mexico. And based on the file photos they'd studied before flying down from the United States, the somewhat shorter, solidly built man with him was his old friend and colleague, Colonel Antonio Maria Herrera of Mexico's military intelligence section.

"*Buenas tardes, señor y señorita,*" Reyes murmured, shaking hands with them. Herrera did the same, eyeing them with undisguised curiosity. From that, Flynn guessed he'd only been told the two Americans worked for one of their government agencies. And by the concentrated look on the colonel's face, he was currently trying very hard to decide whether that meant they belonged to the FBI, the DEA, or maybe even the CIA.

They all sat down, which gave Flynn a chance to savor the outstanding view. Their table overlooked a cobblestoned street and the historic Plaza del Templo Mayor. The ornate edifice of Mexico City's huge metropolitan cathedral rose skyward along the border of the plaza. Occupying a house originally built in the sixteenth century on foundations laid with stones torn from Aztec pyramids, La Casa de las Sirenas was now widely regarded as one of Mexico City's finest restaurants. This early in the afternoon, fortunately, they had a table off by themselves, without anyone else in earshot.

Reyes waved a hand toward two colorful platters heaped high with food set in the center of the table. "To share," he said politely, indicating the small plates and forks laid out and waiting.

Van Horn eyed the two appetizers with undisguised interest. One was a salad piled high with sliced mango, avocados, green apples, bacon, and toasted almonds. The other was a savory blend of shrimp and octopus sautéed in garlic oil and chili powders and then topped with chunks of creamy avocado. She smiled appreciatively. "Definitely a step up from the bag of peanuts and snack crackers on the plane," she allowed.

Reyes chuckled. "Ah, the joys of airline cuisine." At her pleased nod, he placed a generous helping of the mango salad on her plate. "If nothing else, the complete absence of taste greatly intensifies one's desire to get off the plane as rapidly as possible." The head of Four's Mexican station waited until their waiter brought drinks—craft beers for the three men and a mojito for her—before turning their conversation toward more important business. He looked carefully across the table at the two Americans. "So, I understand you have new information to share concerning our common . . . problem?"

"The bad boys in Durango?" Flynn said with a nod. "We sure do." He reached down into his case and took out a handful of color satellite photos. Through one of its front organizations, a nonprofit supposedly dedicated to research on deforestation and agricultural patterns in Mexico and Central America, the Quartet Directorate had bought time on one of the commercial imaging satellites orbiting the earth. Fox's analysts had put in several days of intensive study on the images retrieved during successive passes over territory controlled by the Brotherhood of Blood. Their work had pinpointed a top candidate for the destination of Voronin's secret cargo and personnel. It was a compound in an isolated valley in the Sierra Madre Occidental, about thirty miles west of Durango. Flynn slid the photographs across to the two Mexicans. "We're pretty sure the place in those pictures is where they're working with their new foreign friends," he said quietly. "The images were taken a short while back by the WorldView-3 satellite."

Herrera and Reyes took turns examining the photos. They were crystal clear, showing incredible detail. The colonel raised an eyebrow. "Quite impressive," he said. "I would have thought these photographs had been taken from a low-flying aircraft, rather than from the depths of outer space."

"Yep. That commercial bird offers resolution down to a foot from an orbital altitude of close to four hundred miles," Van Horn told him. "And since the pictures it obtains are open-source intelligence, no special security clearances are required for us to share them with you."

Flynn noticed Reyes keeping a very straight face at the element of misdirection she'd just introduced. If Herrera assumed from what Laura had said that the two Americans were in fact highly placed official agents with access to their own government's far more capable secret imaging satellites, that was perfectly fine. Friendly or not, the fewer people who knew anything about Four's existence, the better.

Herrera turned his attention back to the photos. They plainly showed a barbed wire fence surrounding a single enormous, prefabricated building with a high, sloping metal roof. Several rows of canvas tents were set up adjacent to this structure. Half a dozen home-built armored vehicles—mostly four-by-four trucks sheathed in steel plates with firing slits cut out for heavy weapons—were parked in an open field close to the tent camp. Deep ruts torn across the ground marked the passage of very heavily loaded trucks across the newly built compound. In addition, a wide strip of ground between the large building and the nearby road appeared to have been recently paved over. Finally, a number of diesel generators were lined up along the back end of the building, suggesting whatever was going on inside required a lot of extra electric power.

At last, the colonel took his gaze off the satellite images. He shook his head in amazement. "This facility, whatever it is for, is huge." Beside him, Reyes nodded.

"And that's not what you would expect?" Van Horn asked.

"No," Herrera said flatly. He sat back in his chair, took a small sip of his beer, and then set the glass back down. "No," he said again. "The Brotherhood, like most of the cartels, generally operates drug factories and storage sites that are considerably smaller. Or at least much more discreet." He prodded the photo. "In comparison, this place your satellite spotted looks practically like a full-scale manufacturing plant."

Flynn leaned forward. "Which brings us to the key question," he said seriously. "If you run this intel by the folks higher up in your government here, do y'all think your police or military would be willing to raid this Brotherhood compound?"

There was a long, awkward silence. But then Herrera and Reyes both shook their heads. Though their regret was clear, neither man showed the slightest signs of doubt.

"Such an operation would be unthinkable in the current political climate," the colonel admitted. He ran a hand over his jaw.
"Going after a target that deep in cartel territory would require
a major military operation involving hundreds of troops, plus
helicopters and armored transports. It would quickly become
a media circus."

Reyes nodded with a deep frown of his own. "And even if such
an operation could be kept secret from the Brotherhood's informers and moles, the present government would never countenance
it." He shrugged. "The ruling politicians are turning a blind eye
to most cartel activities—effectively ceding huge swathes of our
national territory to them for the pretense of 'internal peace.'"
Four's head of station didn't bother to conceal the disgust he felt
at this cowardly policy. Appeasing aggressors, whether they were
nation-states or vicious bands of criminals, might buy time and
win plaudits from a conflict-weary public and political class—but
never for very long and never with any lasting benefit.

Flynn exchanged a meaningful glance with Van Horn. The
fact that the Mexican government wouldn't intervene wasn't
much of a surprise. In fact, it was essentially what they had
both expected before making this trip. Which was why they'd
come fully prepared to propose an alternate course of action.
He cleared his throat. "All right, we understand. And that being
said, I figure we need to move on to our second-best option."

"Which is?" Herrera asked.

"Asking for your aid in infiltrating the Brotherhood's territory," Flynn told him bluntly. "Because if we're going to act
against these people somehow, we need to put our own man
on the ground first. As it is, we're seriously short of actionable
intel here."

"And just who do you have in mind for such an incredibly
dangerous task?" the other man asked.

Flynn shot him a crooked grin. "Well, Colonel, that would be me."

Van Horn nodded. "We drew straws for the honor. Nick here won."

Startled into stunned silence, Herrera just stared at the two of them for several long seconds. While he clearly believed they were working for the US government, it was equally clear that he also thought they were crazy. Finally, he hunched his shoulders and leaned forward. "Señor Flynn," he said emphatically. "What you propose is impossible. Between their guards, patrols, and paid informants in every village, the Brotherhood has the whole area around that compound locked down tight. Nobody the cartel doesn't know and trust can possibly get in or out without being spotted, intercepted, tortured, and killed." He shook his head in dismay. "Even making such an attempt would be an act of suicidal folly."

"I won't be entering by road," Flynn told him. "So getting in shouldn't be a problem. But that does leave the problem of getting out alive . . . which is where we could use your help."

Herrera frowned. "What kind of help?" he asked after a short pause to look over at Reyes in disbelief. But the other man only nodded, as if to encourage him to listen to these Americans and their *loco* proposal.

"Well," Flynn said with a disarming half smile, "first off, I do admit what we've got in mind may come across as sort of complicated, but—" Speaking directly and in detail, he and Van Horn took turns outlining the plan they'd worked up over the past couple of days—ever since Four's photo-interpretation specialists had pinpointed the cartel compound.

When they were finished, Herrera only shook his head in amazement. "This madness must be catching," he said at last. "Very well, even if I doubt my own sanity for aiding and abetting this plan of yours, I will see what I can arrange." But when they tried to express their gratitude, he only shook his head. "Please do not thank me. Right now, I feel as if I were handing a man a revolver loaded with five bullets—instead of just one—and then inviting him to play a game of Russian roulette."

Flynn only grinned back at him. "I'd say you're a pessimist, Colonel. Because by my reckoning, I've got at least a fifty-fifty shot at coming out alive. So there can't be more than three bullets spinning in this particular game."

SEVENTEEN

RURAL KANSAS

SOME DAYS LATER

Miles and miles of open, pancake-flat country stretched as far as the eye could see on either side of the ruler-straight two-lane highway. The closest town, with fewer than a thousand people, lay almost fourteen miles north up that same road. Away to the east, the tiny shapes of a lone farmhouse and a couple of adjoining outbuildings were barely visible. A few birds circled high overhead, riding the air currents as they hunted for prey. Apart from them, there were no signs of life or movement anywhere out to the horizon in all directions. The landscape seemed completely deserted.

Amid such emptiness, the presence of a quarter-mile-long warehouse fronted by acres of paved parking lot seemed doubly incongruous. The building's flat roof climbed fifty feet above the surrounding farmland, and a dozen tall bay doors closed off its cavernous interior. Patches of graffiti scattered across its aluminum siding were a clear indication that the vast structure was currently vacant and unused.

Two men stood outside the warehouse, both looking it over with their hands planted on their hips. Despite their near-identical stances, they were a study in contrasts. One of the men, a local real estate agent named Carl Phillips, was older and carried a little more weight around his gut than was healthy. The other was taller and leaner. Everything about him, from his Burberry bomber jacket down to his expensive, hand-fitted jeans and Lucchese cowboy boots, radiated wealth and big-city sophistication. According to his New York–issued driver's license, his name was Thomas Baker.

Still staring upward, the man called Baker nodded in satisfaction. His research, most of it carried out over the internet or by phone, had been accurate in every respect. He glanced over at Phillips, who'd driven all the way out from town just to show him this property. "And you can confirm that there are no serious issues with the building? No major roof leaks or hidden structural damage?"

"Not a one, Mr. Baker," the shorter man declared stoutly. "County inspectors keep a real close eye on things around here. I'd be glad to show you the reports if you'd like."

Baker nodded. That was no great surprise. This warehouse, empty though it was, was still probably the single most valuable piece of real, tangible property within forty miles or more. From what he'd learned, the taxes paid by its current owners represented a significant portion of the local government's annual revenues. And those ongoing property taxes, in turn, explained the evident eagerness of those same owners to sell out, even at a loss.

He looked back at the enormous building looming over them. It had been constructed entirely on spec by a group of middling investors—mostly retirees with decent investment portfolios and good cash flow—who'd been lured into this project by the promise that it would generate a quick, generous return on their money. They had planned to sell the huge warehouse to one of the major retail companies like Amazon, Walmart, Target, or Costco for use as a regional distribution center. But with the recent rise in fuel prices and resulting recession fears, it had been left sitting empty for the past couple of years . . . without a single interested buyer. To the investors who'd bought into the project, its vacant, echoing spaces were a constant slap-in-the-face reminder that even if you built it, *they* wouldn't always come.

Baker didn't have to be psychic to sense the other man's fervent hope that he'd finally be able to clear this expensive and, so far, useless piece of commercial real estate off his agency's books. From what Phillips understood, the New Yorker represented a much-better-capitalized private investment consortium whose business focus was picking up properties on the cheap, intending to hold on to them until the economy picked up again. If the selling price was low enough, they could afford to sit on a building for just about as long as that took. And this huge, empty warehouse was definitely priced to sell.

Made a little nervous by the continuing silence, the Realtor cleared his throat. "So, what do you think?"

Baker turned back to the other man with an agreeable smile. "I think, Mr. Phillips, that we can do business." He shrugged. "The only open question we had was whether or not this facility was in a decent state of repair. That's especially important since it's likely to sit idle for a minimum of some months more. Or perhaps even longer, given the adverse local economic conditions. But since the building is in very good shape, I should have no problem receiving approval to move forward with the purchase. By the close of business today, in fact."

"That's great," Phillips said, sounding relieved. The corners of his mouth turned down a fraction. "Though I am a little sorry to hear that your company doesn't plan to look for a corporate buyer sooner. Someone who'll put the place to use right away, I mean." He nodded at the open countryside around them. "Folks around here could use a shot in the arm and some steady jobs. Farming's a hard way of life."

Baker spread his hands apologetically. "I wish I could be more optimistic," he said. "But my employers rely heavily on their own econometric models to guide such decisions. Unfortunately, those models don't show a significant retail turnaround is likely anytime in the near future." He considered the building through narrowed eyes for a moment longer before shrugging his shoulders. "At most, it's possible that my firm could send in a work crew to do some minor refurbishment on the interior. But even that's not certain."

"If you're looking for skilled people for those jobs, I've got some contractors I know pretty well—" the Realtor started to say.

Baker shook his head. "That won't be necessary." He smiled. "As you can imagine, with so many properties in our group's portfolio, we keep several reliable contractors of our own on retainer to handle any required maintenance and renovation work."

Phillips hid his disappointment at that news reasonably well. No doubt he would have preferred being able to parcel out work to friends and relatives in the community. But he certainly wasn't going to risk jeopardizing the biggest property transaction he was ever likely to handle by pushing that angle any harder.

After the Realtor drove off in his pickup truck, heading into town to start working on the necessary paperwork, Baker walked back out to the shoulder of the rural highway. He stared carefully along it in both directions and then nodded sharply to himself. The maps hadn't lied. This road ran perfectly straight and level for miles and miles. That vital fact, combined with its easy access to the giant, empty warehouse complex behind him and the complete absence of any nearby inhabitants, meant this site more than met all of his superior's exacting requirements. Since he'd already bought up all the surrounding farmland in private, cash-only transactions, they would own everything in view once the sale of the big building went through. Still smiling, he checked his watch. It was time to report in.

Back at his rented Audi, the man who called himself Thomas Baker retrieved a satellite phone from his suitcase. Quickly, he connected with one of Russia's Raduga (Rainbow) communications satellites high overhead in a geosynchronous orbit. After confirming that he had a secure link, he transmitted a short coded text: *Prioreteny konyushni zamka. Castle stables acquired.*

VOLOGDA-20 SPECIAL-WEAPONS STORAGE DEPOT, NORTHERN RUSSIA
THAT SAME TIME

Set in a forested area close to four hundred kilometers north-northwest of Moscow, the Vologda-20 special-weapons depot was surrounded by an intricate web of defenses that included electrified wire fences, minefields, and a network of cameras and motion sensors. These defenses were ordinarily manned by the soldiers of Colonel Oleg Utkin's elite 521st Guards Motor Rifle Battalion. His soldiers, backed up by their unit's complement of wheeled BTR-82 armored infantry fighting vehicles and T-72 main battle tanks, had as their sacred duty the ultimate security of the hundreds of nuclear weapons stored in Vologda-20's massive underground bunkers. It was a duty Utkin and his troops had always executed with absolute precision during the entire time their battalion had been assigned here.

Which was why Utkin could not believe the orders he had just been given by the depot's brand-new commanding officer, the recently promoted Major General Mikhail Krylov. For a long moment, he simply stared down at the sheaf of instructions he'd finished reading. Finally, he shook himself and then slapped the wad of papers down hard against the general's desk. "What blithering idiot in Moscow came up with this prized bit of lunacy?" he demanded.

Krylov turned away from his view through the window of his office. "You have a problem, Colonel?" he asked blandly.

"Of course I have a problem!" Utkin snapped. He stabbed a finger down at the orders. "According to these astonishingly insane directives, I'm expected to take my entire battalion hundreds of kilometers away to Exercise Area Orange for what's laughably described as four days of 'intensive combat refresher training' against units of the local National Guard."

"And?"

Utkin stared at the other man. "Except for the fact that my troops will be completely wasting their time shooting blanks at a bunch of conscripts who couldn't find their asses with both hands?"

Krylov nodded dryly. "Yes, Colonel. Apart from that."

"It's a rather basic question, sir," Utkin said pointedly. "Just who the hell will be guarding this depot while my men and I are gone?"

The general shrugged. "That is not your concern, Colonel," he said. "I rather think it's mine. And mine alone." As a reminder, he tapped the shoulder flash on his uniform. It was the badge of Russia's Twelfth Main Directorate—a red shield topped by a silver mace inside a stylized atom symbol. Responsible first to the Ministry of Defense rather than the General Staff, the directorate was responsible for the maintenance and

security of all of Russia's nuclear weapons. As such, the authority wielded by its officers in their own highly specialized area of
expertise effectively superseded that of any line-infantry, armor,
or artillery commander. "All that you need to know, Utkin, is
that the president himself is satisfied with the interim security
measures I'm putting in place while you and your soldiers are
temporarily away."

Utkin scowled. "President Zhdanov is—"

"The commander in chief!" Krylov interrupted. "And the
man who has personally approved the orders you now hold. As
you should be able to tell," he went on acidly, "from his signature on the authorizing page." He glowered down at the colonel.
"Are you seriously considering disobeying a direct order from
Moscow? From the highest levels of the state? Because if so, I
might remind you that would constitute treason!"

Grudgingly, very grudgingly, Utkin yielded. "Very well, sir,"
he said. "But I want it on the record that my troops and I are
abandoning our duty post for this so-called combat exercise
under extreme protest."

"Noted, Colonel," Krylov agreed. "Now, get out of my
office. And start preparing your unit to move out—as ordered
and on time. Clear?"

Utkin stood, stiffly saluted, and stormed out.

When the door slammed shut behind him, Krylov breathed
out. One hurdle down, he thought warily. He pulled out his
smartphone and dialed a number.

Pavel Voronin answered. "Yes?"

"It's done," Krylov told him simply. "The drawbridge will
be down within twenty-four hours."

"Good work, Mikhail Sergeyevich," the head of the Raven
Syndicate said calmly. His use of the general's patronym-
ic—a middle name derived from the given name of Krylov's

father—was clearly intended to reinforce his praise, since it implied that they were now close colleagues. "You will not regret our continued association. I'll be up tomorrow morning to personally oversee the next phase." He hung up without another word.

Krylov sat down behind his desk. He fumbled to loosen his uniform collar, which suddenly felt tight enough to choke him. To carry out a previous covert operation against the United States, the one code-named MIDNIGHT, Voronin had been given approval by President Zhdanov to put a handful of Twelfth Main Directorate officers on his personal payroll. Officially, the president had never revoked that permission. And so Krylov and several others continued to receive extra payments from the Raven Syndicate that outstripped their official salaries by a factor of ten to one. Given the unlooked-for promotions he and the others had been showered with by Moscow over the past few months, Krylov tended to believe that Zhdanov still approved of this highly unorthodox arrangement. And if nothing else, the remarkable orders he had just passed on to Colonel Utkin seemed to confirm this supposition—as did the additional directives he would begin carrying out the moment the colonel and his security troops were safely out of the way.

Or so, at least, he earnestly hoped. With Zhdanov's signed order in hand, it was one thing to browbeat an underling like Utkin into submission. But the bigger risks inherent in what Voronin and the president apparently planned sent a wave of cold fear racing down his spine. If they failed, he had no illusions as to what would happen. Facing a possible military court-martial would be the least of his concerns . . . since failure in this context might well mean the complete destruction of the Motherland.

EIGHTEEN

LA PAZ, BAJA CALIFORNIA SUR, MEXICO

THE NEXT DAY

Outside the cozy seafood restaurant where Nick Flynn and Laura Van Horn were finishing their dinner, lamplit streets sloped down toward La Paz's beachside promenade. Couples strolled arm in arm along sidewalks lined with flowering trees, enjoying the cooler night air. Even this early in the evening, the nearby bars seemed busy. As the capital of the Mexican state of Baja California Sur, La Paz was the center of business for this isolated desert region. Many foreign tourists tended to flock to the coastal resorts of Cabo San Lucas and San José del Cabo, both around ninety miles farther south at the southern-most tip of this rugged peninsula. But more and more were choosing to visit La Paz, drawn by the lower prices and the opportunities for snorkeling, kayaking, and diving among the nearby coastal islands.

That explained the cover story Flynn had chosen for this visit. He was traveling as a wealthy, hard-charging Dallas executive who'd flown down to La Paz aboard his own private plane for a much-needed short break from the pressures of the oil business. Officially, Van Horn was along as his personal pilot. Whatever else any interested observers inferred about their relationship was entirely up to them. "Let 'em wonder," she'd suggested with a devilish glint in her bright-blue eyes, "about whether I'm your girlfriend or girl Friday or something in between. I'll be the international woman of mystery like I've always wanted."

Now, looking across at her in the soft, flickering candlelight, Flynn would have been very surprised if anyone still watching them had the slightest doubt about the current state of their relationship. They'd spent the morning snorkeling with whale sharks in the waters off the Baja coast. And then whiled away the afternoon lazing around on a beautiful white-sand beach north of the city. This intimate dinner was the capstone of a day seemingly devoted entirely to finding pleasure in each other's company.

And the best part, Flynn thought with some amusement, was that the pleasure was genuine. He glanced around the little restaurant. Except for their waiter, deep in conversation with the bartender, they were alone. Couple by couple and group by group, the other diners had finished their meals and departed. He turned back to Van Horn with a smile. "Gee, it looks like no one's still interested in us. I guess we're not the hot-ticket item in town anymore."

"Told you it would work," she said with satisfaction. "Eventually, even the best little worker snoops get bored and fed up watching other people having more fun than they are."

Shortly after they'd landed at La Paz's airport, they'd both spotted the discreet observers tagging along behind them. It had been a toss-up as to whether the watchers were cartel spies checking up on a rich gringo who'd unexpectedly arrived in their territory or Mexican *federales* doing the same thing. What mattered now was that Flynn and Van Horn seemed to have persuaded everyone that they were exactly what they appeared to be—rich American tourists only interested in fun, frolic, and food and drink.

With a mildly ironic flourish, Flynn raised his wineglass in a toast. "*¡Salud!*"

"Here's to your health," Van Horn echoed in English, lifting her own glass with a faint, melancholic smile of her own. "And to your getting out of this little jaunt alive, Nick. Preferably with your skin completely unpunctured by any shots fired by drug-cartel scumbags," she continued, pitching her voice so low that only he could hear. She drained her glass and set it back down. "At the moment, I sort of wish you really were an oil millionaire. As a profession, it's probably a whole lot safer."

"I suppose so," he agreed with an easy smile. It was time, he decided, to lighten her evidently darkening mood a little. Although their plan was the best one possible in the circumstances, she still hated the idea of him taking risks she couldn't share. "But I don't think Nick Flynn, oil baron, was ever in the cards." He shrugged. "See, when my grandfather came to Texas from the wilds of County Clare, he had big, big plans for becoming the Irish Rockefeller. So he worked hard, saved up a stake, and bought up a pretty good-sized chunk of land. But just when he was all set to get down to some serious exploratory drilling, he discovered his one tiny mistake."

"Which was?" Van Horn asked curiously.

"Geography," Flynn said with a shake of his head. "Turns out land in Central Texas is good for cows. Not so much for oil or natural gas."

She eyed him warily. "Is that story even a little bit true? Or is this just another one of those Flynn family legends you love so much?"

"It's all true," Flynn assured her. Raising his hand, he said, "I swear it on my sainted mother's grave."

Van Horn snorted. "Your mother," she reminded him, "is very much alive. And, from what I gather, a little too ornery for sainthood anytime soon."

"Well, there is that," he admitted. "But it's the way I heard it, nonetheless." He shrugged. "Besides, why—"

"Let a few unimportant facts get in the way of a perfectly good tall tale," she finished for him.

Meekly, Flynn lifted his hands in surrender. He looked at their empty wineglasses. "Ordinarily, I'd suggest a refill, but it's getting kind of late."

"And duty calls?" Van Horn suggested. "Whether it's welcome or not?"

"Something like that," he agreed.

She looked across at him with a serious expression. "You know, I think I've figured out what it is about you that I really like, Nick."

Flynn raised an eyebrow. "I assumed it was mostly my rugged good looks," he said lightly.

Van Horn smiled. "Well, they're not all that bad. But I learned a while back that you need more than physical attraction to make things work." She shook her head. "Nope. It's because you see what has to be done—and then you just go ahead and do it, regardless of the risks or the naysayers and second-guessers. And I'm pretty much the same way. When we make a commitment, whether it's to a task or an organization—"

"Or to a person?" he said.

She nodded. "Or to a person. Anyway, when we commit,

it's with a whole heart and mind, and body. There's nothing held back. Nothing in reserve. That seems awfully rare these days. And rare is valuable."

Under her steady gaze, Flynn felt suddenly self-conscious. His face reddened a bit.

Van Horn smiled again. "Blushing, Nick?"

"I'm just not used to hearing all my worst attributes—being stubborn and kind of reckless—praised," he admitted.

"Told you I liked you," Van Horn said with a laugh. She glanced around the empty restaurant again. "Maybe we should take pity on the staff and get out of their hair."

Nodding, Flynn got to his feet, thumbed through his wallet for the pesos to pay their bill, signaled to the waiter that they were finished, and then politely pulled out Van Horn's chair for her. She raised an eyebrow at the old-fashioned gesture. "More of that childhood etiquette training of yours?" she murmured.

"Yes, ma'am," he conceded, offering her his arm.

Smiling, Van Horn took it, and together they strolled back to their hotel in quiet contentment. Overlooking the water, their rooms were right next to each other. She opened the door to hers and then turned back to face him, the invitation plain in her manner. "Would you care to come in?" she asked huskily. "Tomorrow's going to be a long, hard day . . . and we may not have another chance like this anytime soon."

Flynn grinned crookedly. "What about Br'er Fox and all his cautionary tales about romance on the company dime?"

She shrugged. "Well, Nick, if you don't tell him, I sure as heck won't." Now her bright eyes gleamed with unalloyed amusement. "Besides, it's all part of our cover story, right? So the way I see it, this is the best of all worlds."

"Put like that, how can I resist?" Flynn asked, with a quiet laugh. Still smiling, he took her hand and led her inside.

IN A SECURE RAIL YARD,
PART OF THE VOLOGDA-20
SPECIAL-WEAPONS DEPOT, NORTHERN RUSSIA
THAT SAME TIME

It was raining, a cold, driving spring rain that lashed down across the rail yard in withering torrents. Bearing a heavy green metal crate aloft, a forklift trundled slowly across to the freight train waiting on a nearby siding. Mud splashed out from under its tires as it maneuvered over to a boxcar near the end. Men in Russian army camouflage jackets marked by the shield-mace-and-atom badge of the Twelfth Main Directorate were waiting there, already slathered in mud up to their knees. Carefully, they guided the crate through the rail car's open side door.

Once the crate disappeared inside, whistles blew shrilly. The door was slammed shut. A man wearing an officer's peaked cap stepped up to padlock and seal the door.

"That's the last of them," Major General Mikhail Krylov reported to Pavel Voronin, raising his voice to be heard over the heavy deluge splashing down around them.

"Very good," Voronin said. He raised the edge of his umbrella a little to take a better look. The uniformed men were already moving away, trudging over to a row of waiting canvas-sided Ural-5323 trucks. He smiled to himself. As far as the railway workers knew, those men were all soldiers assigned to the Vologda-20 storage depot. Only he and Krylov knew they were actually operatives of his own Raven Syndicate, disguised to avoid any unfortunate questions about how and why civilians suddenly had access to crates containing such compact and lethal weapons.

Other men, these in civilian clothing, climbed out of more waiting vehicles. They sloshed over toward the single passenger car hitched to the rear of the train. Briefly, their leader turned aside to confer with Krylov and Voronin. "My men are set," he confirmed.

Krylov nodded. "Keep your eyes peeled and your guard up, Anatoly," he ordered. "Make sure nothing happens to that cargo."

Colonel Anatoly Yakemenko stiffened to attention and then subsided, remembering that he wasn't in uniform now. He was another of the Twelfth Directorate officers in Syndicate pay. His team were former Spetsnaz soldiers, all with combat experience. They were traveling under false passports that identified them as citizens of Poland, Serbia, the Baltic states, and other eastern European countries. Their weapons were already safely stowed aboard the train. Since it was common practice for Twelfth Directorate personnel to camouflage movements outside their bases by wearing either civilian clothes or other service uniforms, the train's crew would know better than to ask any awkward questions. "You can count on it, sir," he said, already turning to go.

Krylov and Voronin watched him climb into the passenger car. The moment Yakemenko was aboard, the echoing blast of a horn sounded from farther down the line. In response to the signal, the train started moving, slowly at first, and then faster—clanking and rattling out from the siding and onto the main rail line headed south toward Moscow. Granted special clearance at every junction along the route, the special devices now sealed in those padlocked boxcars were expected to arrive in Minsk within twenty-four hours.

NINETEEN

THE NEXT DAY

With his small carry-on bag slung over one shoulder, Nick Flynn ambled unhurriedly across the airport tarmac toward his waiting plane, a Pilatus PC-12 single-engine turboprop. No one would believe the idea of anyone—not even the hard-charging Texas oil executive he was currently pretending to be—being in a rush to end a picture-perfect Mexican beach-town vacation that was already way too short. Shadows cast by the row of hangars and other buildings along the airport perimeter stretched ahead of him. This late in the afternoon, the sun was already low in the west.

Drawing closer to the Pilatus, he admired its sleek, needle-nosed lines. Pressurized for high-altitude flight, fast, and long ranged, the Swiss-manufactured air machine was the best-selling single-engine civilian business aircraft in the world. And by a not-so-strange coincidence, considering what he and Laura Van Horn had planned, the plane's U-28A Draco military variant was also a favorite of the US Air Force's Special Operations Command.

A few hundred yards away, a narrow-body Embraer 190 passenger jet belonging to Aeroméxico Connect roared down the runway and lifted off—climbing steadily as it turned over the city toward the east. Flynn ducked his head slightly against the hot, aviation-fuel-tinged gust stirred by its rumbling passage. One side of his mouth quirked upward. However quiet and scenic its beaches might be, the flight line of La Paz's relatively small international airport was just like every other in the world—hectic, smelly, and *loud*.

After a final look around, he went up the Pilatus's airstairs, ducking his head to enter the cabin. Once inside, he turned around to pull the clamshell-style door up and closed. Instantly, the background din of all the other aircraft taxiing, taking off, and landing diminished sharply.

"Hey, boss," Laura Van Horn called through the open cockpit door. From the left-hand pilot's seat, she shot him a quick over-the-shoulder grin. "Decided to get some work done today after all?" Though casually dressed in jeans and an open-collared khaki shirt, she'd already donned her radio headset. Her leather flight jacket was draped over the empty copilot's seat. The large multifunction displays set into the cockpit's instrument panels showed rows of brightly lit numbers and acronyms and diagrams. Some of them were green. Others glowed red. A clipboard resting on her knee showed that she was working through the items of her preflight checklist.

"Figured I might as well, since that lovely señorita I spent the night with up and vanished on me a while back," Flynn shot back with just a touch of a sorrowful Texas drawl. "Sure, she woke me up in the nicest possible way, but then she said something about having a job to get to. And something more about how she couldn't just lollygag around naked all day in bed, unlike some lazy-ass folks such as me."

Van Horn had the grace to blush, though only very slightly.

Holding in a laugh, Flynn moved back into the cabin. At sixteen feet long and nearly five feet wide, it was roomy by the standards of most single-engine planes. At the aft end, larger cases were stowed behind netting. They contained the equipment and clothing he would need for tonight's outdoor excursion. He dropped his bag onto one of the passenger cabin's four plush leather seats and settled back into its next-door neighbor. After buckling in, he waited patiently while Van Horn finished her preflight. When she finally put the clipboard down, he leaned forward. "Any more news from Fox?"

"Yeah, I got a coded text from him about twenty minutes ago," Van Horn said. She half turned to face him. "Our timing looks even better than we expected. Colonel Herrera's informant at the Durango airport sent in another report. That Boeing 777F flying for Voronin landed there this morning with another big load of cargo."

Flynn nodded, seeing what she meant about good timing. Their daylight satellite passes hadn't picked up anything at the cartel compound except the ruts showing where heavily loaded trucks had parked. Given that and the obvious desire by both the Brotherhood of Blood and the Raven Syndicate to avoid the risk of unwelcome satellite or aerial surveillance, it was likely the trucks headed for that isolated compound wouldn't start unloading until well after dark. If so, that would be a definite stroke of luck. He checked his watch. The sun would be down in less than an hour. "Then I guess we'd better get this bird off the ground," he commented.

"Copy that," Van Horn said. She pulled the clipboard back onto her knee and flipped to another checklist page. Rapidly, she moved through the dozen or so separate line items, verifying the positions of various switches and settings. A high-pitched whine started out low and built rapidly in volume. Quick glances out the right and left windows confirmed that there weren't any airport mechanics or other bystanders dangerously near. Then she made one last check of the lights on her CAWS—caution and warning system—display panel. No anomalies or other faults were showing.

Satisfied, she reached up to a panel above her seat and punched the starter button. Immediately, the PC-12's twelve-hundred-horsepower Pratt & Whitney turboprop began spooling up. The noise level grew rapidly. She pushed the condition lever into its ground-idle position and looked forward through the cockpit window to see the plane's five-bladed prop start turning—spinning faster and faster until it was a blur. Happy with what her gauges showed, she flipped more switches on the overhead panels, bringing both generators, her avionics, and the aircraft's environmental-control systems all online.

"Okay, everything looks good. We're ready to roll," Van Horn announced. She radioed the tower. "La Paz Tower, this is Pilatus One-Five-One; request departure from runway three-six, per approved flight plan."

"Pilatus One-Five-One, La Paz Tower, runway three-six, taxi via Alpha," the controller replied, granting permission.

Van Horn released her brakes and edged her throttle, setting up a bit. Immediately, the PC-12 started rolling. Under her control inputs, it turned smoothly onto the taxiway.

Flynn glanced out through the nearest window, watching as they passed the other passenger jets and propeller-driven planes parked outside the airport terminal. In the lengthening shadows, he could clearly make out the bright green position light glowing on their starboard wing.

Reaching the end of the runway, Van Horn swung the PC-12 around through a tight half circle until it was lined up perfectly—pointed straight north down the center line. Her eyes ran across her displays and gauges one last time. "La Paz Tower, Pilatus One-Five-One," she radioed. "Number one, runway three-six, ready for takeoff."

"*Pilatus One-Five-One, La Paz Tower,*" the controller confirmed. "*Winds light at one-seven-five, cleared for takeoff runway three-six. Have a good flight.*"

Van Horn ran her throttle forward, released her brakes again, and started her takeoff roll. The PC-12 reacted instantly, accelerating fast down the long concrete runway. At eighty-two knots, she pulled back a tiny bit on her yoke. Smoothly, the Swiss-made turboprop broke free of the earth and zoomed skyward. The ground dropped away fast below them. Still gaining speed, they crossed the coast and, minutes later, turned due east out over the Sea of Cortez—climbing ever higher while heading straight toward the quickly darkening Mexican mainland. In accordance with her approved flight plan, she leveled off at thirty thousand feet.

"Next stop, the middle of nowhere," she said, with a glance back at Flynn.

"Yep. I guess that's my cue," he agreed. He unbuckled his seat belt, got up, and moved aft to pull out the cases stowed there. Quickly, he shed his jeans and polo shirt in favor of camouflage fatigues and a Special Forces–pattern tactical assault vest. The product of a partnership between two Swiss companies, the innovative materials used in both the vest and the clothing were designed to render him very difficult to detect by either the Mark I human eyeball or more sophisticated infrared sensors. With that done, he systematically stowed pieces of equipment away in the various pockets and pouches rigged to his vest.

Then he carefully applied streaks of tan, green, and black camouflage paint to his face, neck, and ears, working outward from the lighter colors to those that were darker. Next, he carefully struggled into another complicated layer of zippered clothing.

From the cockpit, Van Horn checked him out with an undisguised smile. "Oh, look, Boris," she said with a heavy and very fake Russian accent. "Is flying squirrel."

Flynn looked down at himself with an answering grin. She had a point. The wingsuit he was now wearing shared certain elements with the tree-gliding rodents parodied in the old *Rocky and Bullwinkle* TV cartoon. Made of layers of connected nylon, wingsuits turned skydivers into human gliders. At least for a time. Fabric layers connecting a wingsuit wearer's arms and legs created an airfoil—providing lift that helped greatly extend the duration and range of any jump out of an otherwise perfectly good airplane.

Nevertheless, he knew there was a point where gravity was bound to take over in a very real and potentially lethal sense. Without some other technological intervention, the equation "initial altitude divided by angle of descent" ended inevitably in impact with the ground at a velocity that every textbook he'd ever studied described as "completely nonsurvivable." And that was where his final piece of equipment came in—a pack containing a steerable, rectangular-shaped ram parachute.

By the time Flynn had finished checking over all his gear, they'd been in the air for nearly an hour. From this high up, he could see thousands of stars gleaming brightly, speckled across a pitch-black sky. And far below, a scattered handful of tiny clusters of yellow light—little villages and isolated haciendas—dotted the rugged slopes of the Sierra Madre.

Up in the PC-12's darkened cockpit, Van Horn watched her central multifunction display closely. Set to show a GPS-integrated digital map, it tracked the aircraft's position to within a few yards. When the icon identifying the Pilatus slid through a waypoint indicator she'd set before takeoff, she nodded to herself and eased back on the throttle. In response, the plane decelerated, gradually shedding airspeed as its prop spun slower. She looked back over her shoulder. "We're roughly ten minutes out, Nick. Better get yourself set."

Obeying, Flynn shuffled awkwardly toward the tail section of the plane. Between his wingsuit and other equipment, he was now carrying more than eighty pounds of extra weight strapped to his back, chest, and thighs. He stopped next to the rear cargo hatch. "I'm in position," he called out. "Standing by."

Van Horn kept her eyes fixed on her navigation display. As always, the closer she got to a crucial decision point, the faster time seemed to run. In a fight or critical flight maneuver, everything moved in slow motion. But in the moments leading up to the event, her world always kicked into higher gear—with minutes flashing by in what felt like only seconds. "Two minutes out," she warned. "Go to oxygen." Then she shrugged into her leather flight jacket and donned her emergency oxygen mask.

At the back of the Pilatus PC-12, Flynn put on his own mask and jump helmet. He turned a small valve and heard the satisfying hiss of air flowing through the system. One less thing to worry about, he thought. They were thirty thousand feet above the ground, so the air pressure outside their plane was scarcely a third of that at sea level. Without supplemental oxygen, anyone exposed to that harsh, unforgiving environment would lose consciousness in sixty seconds or less.

He turned toward the cockpit and flashed Van Horn a thumbs-up signal.

She nodded sharply. Then she leaned forward and punched the aircraft environmental-control system's Bleed Air switch to its "Inhibit" position. In response, the engine bleed valves that ordinarily supplied pressurized air to the aircraft interior slammed shut. Next, she reached down to the CPC (cabin pressure control) switches, flipped up the safety shield over the system-mode switch, and set it to manual. *Well, here goes*, she thought. *Say goodbye to your warm and cozy ride, Laura.* Without hesitating, she opened the shield over the cabin pressure control and pushed it to "Dump." Immediately, the cabin outflow valves cycled open. In seconds, the plane depressurized.

Van Horn shivered as the cabin temperature plunged dozens of degrees to match the exterior air's below-zero readings. Suddenly this was feeling a hell of a lot more like the dead of winter above the Arctic Circle than a balmy spring night over Mexico.

Her eyes flicked to the navigation display. They were ten nautical miles beyond the valley that was Flynn's target. Her right hand eased the engine throttle back even more. Her airspeed indicator dropped again and touched ninety knots, which was very close to her stall speed in the current conditions at this altitude. Swiftly, she turned toward him and pumped her right fist in the "go" sign.

Flynn nodded forcefully in acknowledgment. This was it, he knew. There was no holding back now. Using one gloved hand to hold tight to a strap fastened next to the aft cargo door's frame, he reached out with the other and unlatched the door. Immediately, the door swung up and out into the night sky. Howling wind gusts whipped in through the opening. The Pilatus juddered violently, robbed of its streamlined shape by the door raised at an angle above the fuselage.

Van Horn gripped the steering yoke firmly and wrestled to regain full control over the aircraft—making rapid adjustments to her rudder, elevators, and ailerons to counteract the induced turbulence. The Pilatus settled out, coming back to fly straight and level. She risked another quick glance over her shoulder.

Flynn was gone. He'd hurled himself out into the open air the moment the cargo door was fully open.

She blinked away a couple of tears. *Damn cold air*, she thought irritably, knowing the freezing cabin temperature was only partly to blame. She punched the emergency door control, and an electrical winch whirred into action to pull the aft cargo door back into its sealed and locked position. The shrill, keening noise made by the wind sweeping through the cabin died away. With that done, her fingers danced back across the environmental-control panel, resetting switches to repressurize her aircraft.

Gradually, the temperature climbed, and as soon as the red "low cabin pressure" caution and warning light vanished, Van Horn took off her oxygen mask. She throttled back up and banked a couple of degrees, bringing the nose around to head northeast on a course that would take her to Torreón's international airport—now roughly a hundred nautical miles ahead. Her filed flight plan included a planned layover there, supposedly so that her "boss," Flynn, could conduct some business in the city, which was one of Mexico's most important industrial and economic centers. The beauty of it was that no one should notice that he wasn't on board. Since their flight originated domestically, from La Paz, at least there wouldn't be any awkward immigration or passport control checks for her to sweat.

TWENTY

OVER THE SIERRA MADRE

THAT SAME TIME

Caught by the blast from its spinning propeller, Flynn tumbled away from the Pilatus PC-12. In the tiniest fraction of a second, he was swept back behind the plane and out into the vast, empty night sky. Stars pinwheeled around him as he rolled over and over. Through his helmet, he could hear the rushing hiss of freezing air tugging at the folds of his wingsuit as he plunged toward the distant ground. It was time to get control of this suit, he realized. Because otherwise this would end up being one of the shortest and most futile covert airborne insertions ever attempted. Going *splat* against the side of one of the local mountains was *not* in his mission plan.

Making very gentle, very easy, very careful movements, he stretched his arms out behind and to his sides, simultaneously spreading his legs a little to form a tapered V shape. That gave his wingsuit just a bit more surface area, allowing it to bite harder into the air currents roiling past him on every side as he fell. Whenever he felt himself starting to tumble, he curled his arms back in tight to his chest to free-fall. Time and again, he repeated the movement, gradually slowing and gaining control over his descent. At last, he was able to point his face toward the ground and slant downward, with the folds of his suit fully extended in order to make a stable airfoil.

Glowing numbers counted down across the face shield of his helmet. He was descending through 26,000 feet—still high above the darkened peaks and valleys below. His navigation gear, originally designed for backcountry hikers, was equipped with electronic compasses, GPS receivers, and barometric altimeters. A tiny green dot blinked rhythmically in the center of his vision, showing the landing point he'd selected earlier. From the maps and satellite photos he'd studied, it had looked like a piece of empty country. It was also very near the eastern edge of the same valley that held the large, heavily guarded compound the Brotherhood of Blood had apparently turned over to Voronin. And according to the GPS coordinates, he was still around eight miles out.

Piece of cake, Flynn thought with a wide grin. The world distance record for a wingsuit jump was around twenty miles. Compared to that, eight miles was nothing. He was suddenly gripped by the wild, exhilarating sensation of totally unencumbered flight. Wingsuits were the closest any human being could come to realizing the ancient dreams of soaring freely through the air—independent of any machine or other mechanism.

He arrowed onward, trading altitude for distance. Gradually, the terrain ahead of him took on added shape and definition. By the time he was down to around six thousand feet above the ground, what had once been almost formless masses of shadow emerged out of the darkness to become wooded hills and open patches of pasture and fields. Dim patterns of lights dotted the rough, uneven countryside, each signaling the presence of a few tiny homes or a small village.

Passing through two thousand feet, Flynn noticed the green dot marking his planned landing point sliding a bit to the left across his face shield. A small frown crossed his face. Plunging through the stronger winds at high altitude must have thrown him off course. And there were places in the valley up ahead he definitely wanted to avoid. Dropping out of the sky right into the middle of that cartel compound, for example, had *bad idea* written all over it. He lowered his left shoulder slightly to bank a couple of degrees. His selected aiming mark moved back to the middle of his helmet display and steadied up.

Not long now, he thought, fighting against the temptation to tense up. Fifteen hundred feet. One thousand. The highest peaks of the Sierra Madre rose like black spires along the far western horizon. The valley was widening out ahead, though still surrounded by wooded high ground on all sides. Five hundred feet. He came in, gliding fast above steep slopes cut by dry streambeds that snaked away toward the valley floor.

Now! Flynn yanked the cord on his parachute pack. His rectangular chute spilled out into the air behind him and then snapped open with a sudden, sharp jolt. Tugging down on the toggle in his right hand, he spilled a little air from the right side of the billowing canopy, which sent him veering in that direction. Now he was sliding downwind toward an open stretch of what looked like empty grazing land. Covered in tall grass, the pasture lay at the foot of the nearest elevation.

The ground came up fast. Ten feet up, he yanked down hard on both toggles, flaring the parachute to drastically slow his descent. A second later, his boots thumped down in a perfect soft landing. Not bad for a ride that had started at thirty thousand feet and ten-plus nautical miles away just five minutes before, Flynn decided with an inward grin.

Moving quickly, he reeled in the fluttering canopy arm over arm—bundling it up into a compact mass of nylon fabric. It took only a few more seconds to hit the quick-release buckle on his parachute harness and shrug out of the straps. Then he pulled off his jump helmet, mask, and oxygen cylinder and set them down on top of the bundled parachute and harness. As a final step, he wriggled out of the zippered wingsuit and piled it into a heap with the rest of the items.

Freed of his encumbering and no-longer-needed jump gear, Flynn crouched down into the knee-high grass, fitted a pair of night vision goggles to his eyes, and drew his Glock 19 pistol. He spun through a slow circle, scanning his surroundings. There was nothing moving in sight. And apart from the soft chirruping sounds made by insects, everything seemed quiet.

About a mile away to the west, he could make out a few scattered yellowish lights. They marked the location of a small town near the middle of the valley. A patch of much brighter and whiter light somewhat farther north pinpointed the cartel compound that was his immediate target. Listening carefully, he thought he could make out the faint rumble of heavy engines coming from that direction.

Flynn nodded to himself. It was high time he got moving. He slid his pistol back into his chest holster. Then he shook out a tightly rolled tan plastic garbage bag from one of his vest pouches and stuffed every piece of his discarded jump gear inside.

He headed across the pasture toward the high ground in the east to look for somewhere safe to hide the bag and its damning contents. Within a couple of hundred yards, he was inside the fringes of the woods that covered the slopes. A clump of tangled undergrowth seemed like the perfect spot. Carefully, trying to avoid getting snagged, he shoved the bulging plastic bag deeper and deeper into the mass of brambles and thorns until it was mostly out of sight. With a bit of luck, by the time any of the locals stumbled across it, he would be long gone.

Moving faster now, Flynn pushed north along the forward slopes of the hill—staying inside the tree line to reduce the chances of encountering people or grazing animals. While it was still dark, he needed to find a concealed vantage point that would offer him a good view of the cartel compound. If he couldn't accomplish that task, scope out the place, and then make it back into the deeper cover of the nearby hills before the sun came up, this whole complicated operation would end in pointless failure.

TWENTY-ONE

IN THE SIERRA MADRE FOOTHILLS, MEXICO

A FEW HOURS LATER

Crouched low, Flynn darted forward from out of a small thicket of low-hanging trees and then dropped prone behind a clump of scrub brush. He was moving through a patch of waste ground adjacent to what appeared to be currently unused grazing land. A barbed wire fence marked the border between the two pieces of ground. It was in bad repair, with several weathered posts down and sagging sections of rusting wire in places.

He wriggled a little to one side to get a better view past the closest tangle of thorn bushes and tall grass. There, about fifty yards ahead, another barbed wire fence, this one brand new, cut straight across his intended path. That barrier marked the outer perimeter of the Brotherhood of Blood compound he'd come all this way to check out.

Flynn frowned. Someone had taken a chain saw to all the stands of trees and tall brush close to the fence line, hacking them away to establish clear fields of fire along the perimeter. If he wanted to get closer, working his way across that stretch of open ground without being spotted would be a grade-A bitch.

Alerted by the low, rumbling growl of a heavy diesel engine moving off to his right and growing rapidly louder, he flattened himself against the ground and froze in place. There, beyond the fence, he saw a four-by-four truck sheathed in steel plates lumbering slowly across the cleared ground. It was obviously on patrol, looking for signs of trouble. He could make out gunmen standing upright through hatches cut into the improvised armored car's roof. They were scanning their surroundings using night vision gear of their own.

Flynn buried his face in the ground, holding absolutely still while the cartel's armored car drove past. It kept going without slowing or stopping. He breathed out. The high-tech, anti-IR materials woven into his camouflage gear seemed to have worked as advertised. Maybe he'd have to write the companies involved a glowing testimonial—using a pseudonym, of course.

As the heavy vehicle's engine noise faded in the distance, he raised his head again. He had a view through the barbed wire across the Brotherhood compound. The central building, which looked from here like a prefabricated warehouse, was roughly two hundred yards away. Several big trucks were backed up to it, with large side-loader forklifts pulling long, heavily wrapped cargo pallets off them. Light spilled out across the otherwise darkened yard from the large building's wide, partially open sliding doors.

Flynn focused his night vision goggles. But it was no good. From his current position, he just didn't have the angle to get a clear look in through those half-open doors. Which meant he needed to leave this patch of waste ground, with its bushes and shrubs and small trees providing decent cover, and risk moving out into the far more open piece of grazing land on his right.

Slowly, he belly-crawled over to the dilapidated wire fence that marked the pasture's boundary. The bottommost strand between two intact posts was about eighteen inches off the ground. Maybe that was low enough to discourage wandering cows, he decided with a mild flash of humor, but it sure wasn't good enough to stop Nick Flynn, Gentleman Rustler. Gingerly, he edged his way under the barbs and on into the pasture.

Flynn froze and went facedown again as another home-brew armored car rumbled past along the compound's perimeter. When the noise receded, he lifted his head and kept going, slithering silently across the dirt and through patches of tall grass. Since cattle weren't being grazed here now, that grass offered partial concealment. And at least he didn't have to worry about spooking a herd into a stampede. But there were definitely still obstacles to be avoided, he realized as an all-too-familiar smell reached his nostrils. *What did you do in the great drug-cartel wars, Daddy?* he thought with a sudden twisted grin, mangling a famous inspirational speech by General Patton. *Well, son, I belly-crawled through dried cow shit . . .*

By the time he reached a vantage point that allowed him to see in through the doors, his face and hair were sodden with sweat. Trying to control his breathing, he willed himself to look like a rock while another vehicle patrol drove by along the perimeter. Then he pushed his night vision goggles up off his eyes and reached into one of his equipment pouches to take out a digital camera. After fitting it with a high-powered Zeiss optics zoom lens, he peered through the viewfinder.

Suddenly he could clearly see part of the warehouse-like structure's brightly lit interior. A number of Slavic-featured men wearing gray and light-blue coveralls were hard at work inside. They were clustered around large tarped shapes that were surrounded or supported by some type of metal scaffolding. Near them were carts that were piled high with power tools, what looked like color-coded coils of wiring, an assortment of mechanical parts, and stacked groups of small plastic boxes in several different colors.

Busily snapping pictures of all the activity, Flynn allowed himself a moment of surprise. Scratch that part about this building being some kind of drug warehouse or weapons armory, he thought. Whatever was going on inside made it look a lot more like a sort of factory. After a few minutes, satisfied that he'd captured images of every part of the interior in his view, he slowly lowered the camera.

For a moment, he was tempted to try moving even closer, hoping to get a different angle that would allow him to see inside more of the building. But hearing the approaching rumble of another cartel armored car, the temptation passed. The open ground up to that barbed wire perimeter fence was way too well patrolled. And even if he could make it that far without being spotted, worming his way under, over, or through that fence without raising an alarm would be almost impossible. No, he decided, his job now was to back out of here quietly, without spooking the bad guys. In the circumstances, caution was absolutely the better part of valor. He stashed his camera and, once the armored vehicle passed by, started the long, painful crawl back into better cover.

More than an hour later, Flynn reached the edge of the nearest woods. Confident that he was now safely out of sight of the Brotherhood compound, he climbed back to his feet, wincing as various muscle groups he'd worked too hard during the prolonged low crawl kinked and knotted up. Gritting his teeth, he bent and stretched and twisted in an effort to loosen them. For a moment, he felt like he was much closer to being seventy years old than somewhere just shy of thirty. *Yeah, well, it's not the years, Nick*, he told himself. *It's the miles.* And he'd sure as hell put on the equivalent of a lot of miles during tonight's furtive scouting expedition.

Straightening up, he headed out, moving up the wooded slope. Ahead, through the trees, he could already tell that the sky was starting to lighten in the east. For the coming day, his plan was to hole up somewhere out of sight. Then, after the sun went down again and it was safer to travel, he'd push on east through the jumble of ridges and valleys to reach the extraction point he and Laura Van Horn had picked out earlier.

Thirty minutes later, he stopped in the middle of a small cluster of stunted pines and oaks. The crest of this ridge was only a couple of dozen yards ahead. And already the rising sun was sending golden rays slanting down through the tree canopy. It was time to bed down, and this spot seemed as good as any. Ideally, he'd have put more miles between himself and the Brotherhood compound, but safely getting in and getting out with his pictures had taken much longer than he'd hoped. Pushing on now in broad daylight would be asking for trouble.

Setting his back against a tree trunk, Flynn slid down until he was sitting more comfortably. He had one last job to do before getting some rest. Reaching into another pocket, he pulled out his palm-sized compact satellite phone. Once he was connected to the satellite constellation, he texted a short, carefully composed, and coded status report.

Within moments, a reply came back, scrolling across the phone's inch-wide screen: *Roger, Rogue One. Act casual. Standing by.*

Flynn grinned. He should have known he could trust Laura Van Horn to be just as short and to the point herself. He leaned back against the rough bark of the scrub oak tree and closed his eyes.

MILITARY AIR STATION NUMBER 3, TORREÓN INTERNATIONAL AIRPORT, COAHUILA, MEXICO
A SHORT TIME LATER

With her mouth a thin, hard, compressed line that implied both concentration and irritation, Laura Van Horn prowled around the camouflaged Bell 206A Jet Ranger II helicopter parked on a wide square apron not far from the airport's main runway. She wore the olive-drab flight suit of the Mexican Air Force and a dark-blue flight cap bearing the three gold bars of a senior captain. She'd also darkened her hair another shade, and right now her vivid-blue eyes were concealed behind a pair of mirrored aviator sunglasses. Shannon Cooke, carrying a clipboard and disguised as a first sergeant in the same service, followed her around the grounded helicopter, jotting down notes in response to her terse comments.

Off to one side, a ground crew made up of junior enlisted men waited nervously for the newly arrived *capitana de culo duro*, this hard-ass female captain, to finish her visual inspection. A tanker truck loaded with aviation fuel was parked close by.

"You really think we're going to get away with this crazy stunt?" Cooke murmured quietly out the corner of his mouth, when they had rounded the helicopter fuselage and were temporarily out of sight of the little group of genuine Mexican Air Force personnel.

Van Horn grinned back at him over her shoulder. "Of course we are." She raised an eyebrow. "Tell me, what do all the armies, navies, and air forces around the world run on?"

"Bullshit and bravado," Cooke shot back.

Her smile widened. "Okay, fair point. But what else?"

Cooke sighed. He shrugged his shoulders, acknowledging

her point. "Paperwork, ma'am. Mounds and mounds of mind-numbing, standard-issue, fill-in-the-blank, quadruplicate paperwork."

Van Horn nodded. "Exactly. By the time anyone here figures out that something weird is going on, we'll be long gone, my worried little coconspirator."

Mentally, she crossed her fingers that her confidence was justified. After undergoing routine mechanical work by the Mexican Air Force's Fourth Air Group Maintenance Center at Culiacán on the west coast, this helicopter was being transferred back across the country to its home squadron—the 102nd—in Nuevo León, not far from the Rio Grande. Working through his old boys' network in the defense ministry, Colonel Herrera had pulled strings to have the bird stop over here in Torreón, the halfway point. And when it arrived, its two regular crewmen had been handed new orders—requiring them to report in person to Air Force headquarters in Mexico City for further instructions.

At her side, Cooke winced, clearly imagining the administrative and paperwork nightmare those two poor saps were about to encounter. Herrera had set it up so that they'd be shunted from office to office while various bureaucrats in uniform tried vainly to figure out why they were in Mexico City instead of their home base and what was supposed to happen next. Unsnarling the mess should take at least a full day or two, not counting the time needed for them to fly or drive back to Torreón. Cooke was sympathetic to their plight. In his days with the Army's top-secret Task Force Orange, any contact with the Pentagon's paper pushers had always been migraine inducing.

Van Horn finished her inspection and ducked her head to walk back under the Jet Ranger's tail boom. She marched directly over to the waiting ground crew, who stiffened to attention under her cool gaze. "I want this bird refueled and prepped for flight," she snapped in crisp, flawless Spanish. "Immediately!"

They scattered in all directions, practically running to obey her orders.

Cooke watched them go with a slightly puzzled expression on his face. "Hey, I thought we weren't supposed to pick up our wandering boy until after dark?" According to their plan, they were going to make the extraction under the guise of a nighttime training-and-maintenance-check flight. "So why the sudden hurry? From his last status report, everything's on track."

Van Horn snorted quietly. "Yeah, that's what worries me. This is Nick we're talking about, remember? Sometimes, even going in with the best of intentions, he has a special gift for stirring up trouble." She jerked a thumb at the helicopter sitting on the pad. "Which is why I want that whirlybird gassed up and ready. Just in case the wheels *do* come flying off this little sneak-and-peek exercise sooner than we expect."

TWENTY-TWO

IN THE SIERRA MADRE FOOTHILLS

SOME HOURS LATER

Nick Flynn suddenly came fully awake, and his eyes flew open. His right hand had already dropped to the butt of his 9mm Glock 19 pistol while his brain was still sorting out where he was. Moments before, he'd been dozing comfortably in the shade of the gnarled scrub oak tree. Now he was on the alert, poised, and dangerous.

What had startled him? he wondered.

And then he heard it.

From somewhere downhill to the west, Flynn picked up the sound of movement among the trees—noises accompanied by a low baaing and the sharp yips of at least two dogs. That had to be a flock of sheep, which would certainly be overseen by at least one shepherd, he realized. And from the way the sounds were growing louder, the flock was heading uphill, coming straight his way.

Reacting swiftly, he rolled to his feet and crouched low

beside the base of the tree. His mind raced, trying to figure out how best to avoid this unwanted encounter. Overhead, he noticed the oak leaves rustling in a gentle breeze . . . and he frowned. The wind was blowing toward the oncoming animals, which meant he was already too late.

Two sharp-pitched, much louder barks confirmed Flynn's assessment. They had caught his scent. Panting eagerly, two big, black-furred animals—almost more wolf than dog by appearance—bounded uphill through the woods to scout out his strange new smell and see if it represented some kind of threat to their woolly charges. Flynn stayed perfectly still, avoiding any sudden moves that might alarm them. Tongues hanging out, they circled him warily, sniffing and huffing.

"¡Oye, Paco! ¡Oye, Duro! ¿Qué pasa?" a man's voice called from somewhere not far below. "Hey, Paco! Hey, Duro! What's up?"

Responding to their master's voice, the two dogs broke off their circling movement and raced away back down the slope. Carefully, Flynn rose to his full height. He slid the Glock back into its chest holder. Otherwise, though, he stayed rock still. He earnestly hoped he'd be able to bluff his way through this sudden confrontation.

His only other realistic option, he knew, would be to kill the shepherd and both dogs. But he dismissed that thought completely out of hand. There was no damn way he was going to start shooting innocents just to save his own hide or his mission—not even for the sake of his country and its equally innocent people. That was the ends-justifying-the-means road to hell already taken by Voronin and every other evil son of a bitch.

Moments later, the shepherd came into view, striding as easily up the ridge as though it were a flat, paved street. Considerably shorter than Flynn, the Mexican was lean and wiry, with strands of long, graying hair poking out from under a battered felt hat. His pants, shirt, and leather vest were frayed and stained. Not much of whatever drug money flooded into this valley was making it into this guy's pockets, Flynn judged dispassionately.

The Mexican's eyes widened suddenly at the unexpected sight of a stranger with a camouflage-striped face wearing what clearly looked like a military uniform. He licked his lips nervously. "*Perdóneme, señor*. Pardon me, sir." He nodded apologetically at his dogs. "*No quisimos entrometernos*. We didn't mean to intrude."

I just bet you didn't, Flynn thought. Around here, an armed man was probably never good news. He waved a hand graciously, trying to signify that it didn't matter. "*De nada*. No problem."

The other man looked relieved. He backed away a few feet. "*Lo dejaremos en paz, señor*. We'll leave you in peace, sir."

"*Vaya con Dios*," Flynn replied courteously.

Within minutes, the shepherd, his flock, and his dogs were out of sight and, from the sound, moving south and back downhill away from him.

Flynn frowned thoughtfully. That was too damned easy. He felt a prickling sensation at the back of his neck as trained instincts kicked in. The old military proverb, "the easy way is always mined," seemed appropriate in this case. And what that meant now was that he needed to start moving fast . . . and to call this news in.

Tugging out his handheld satellite phone on the go, he turned sharply and trotted away to the north along the forward slope of this ridge—being very careful to stay in the cover of the trees that dotted the edge of its summit.

A couple of hundred yards back down the slope, the shepherd's eyes narrowed with concern. Like the other inhabitants of this isolated hill valley, he and his family lived under the iron fist of the Brotherhood of Blood. Fairness had nothing to do with their rule. Nor, alas, did God. Here in this place, the cartel was a force of nature—much like the summer rains that could send floodwaters cascading down the arroyos. On the one hand, the regular handouts of cash, food, and medicines supplemented his meager income from raising sheep. And on the other, the Brotherhood's punishments for perceived betrayal were always swift and particularly brutal.

He grimaced. Failing to report the presence of this outsider, who was very likely a spy for the *federales* or some rival drug gang, could all too easily cost his family their lives. A single word from one of the cartel's soldiers could result in every one of them— him, his wife, their children, and even his grandchildren—ending up as rotting corpses in shallow *narcofosas,* the local slang for the crude graves drug traffickers made their victims dig for themselves. Even the thought of such a possibility made him sick.

After darting a fearful glance over his shoulder toward where he'd met the stranger, the shepherd dug out the cheap cell phone he'd been given for just such an occasion. He punched in the only number he knew and waited while it rang. When a harsh, guttural-sounding voice answered, he nervously stammered out his message. "*Jefe*, this is Ramon! I have very important news!"

ALONG THE RIDGE,
IN THE SIERRA MADRE FOOTHILLS
SOMETIME LATER

Flynn stopped to listen. "Well, shit," he muttered. He could now hear the shrill, angry-sounding hornet whine of several engines somewhere behind him. And those noises were steadily growing louder.

He crouched down at the base of a withered-looking pine tree and looked back the way he'd just come. Plumes of dust swirled above the treetops along the wooded western slope. More dust drifted over the more open ground along the ridge crest. There were vehicles out there, on the move and heading his way, he realized with a cold chill down his spine. And given all that dust they were kicking up, they were in a real hurry. He'd bet good money that wasn't just an unfortunate coincidence. That Mexican shepherd must have blown the whistle on him.

Flynn ran uphill a few yards and dropped prone close to another tree. From here, he had a good view out across the clearer ground at the ridge's level summit.

Two vehicles tore into sight from the south, driving fast along the crest line. They were small, four-wheeled all-terrain vehicles driven by cartel gunmen with assault rifles slung over their shoulders. Those were US-made 5.56mm M4 carbines, probably pilfered or bought illegally from the Mexican army's stockpiles. *Fantastic*, Flynn thought. Well, at least if he got killed here, it would be with a weapon he'd been trained on during his own military service. Somehow, though, that wasn't exactly comforting.

With their motors howling, the two ATVs circled wide around the fringe of trees he was using for cover and concealment. They pulled up some distance to the north, off to his left. Both of the cartel "soldiers" dismounted. One raised a pair of binoculars and started scanning the tree line. Flynn held still, trusting his camouflage fatigues and face paint to keep him hidden from view. The other man unslung his rifle and went prone, sighting down its muzzle toward the wooded ground.

Flynn's jaw tightened. These guys might be thugs, but they were also playing it smart. That first man was acting as a spotter. It was his job to hunt for targets for the second gunman, who was undoubtedly the best shot.

More ATVs followed the first pair, taking up similar positions at wide intervals across the open ground. And now, from down in the valley behind him, Flynn could hear the growl of heavier engines on the move. He frowned. Those were probably some of the cartel's homemade armored cars rumbling into position to block any escape attempt to the west.

Pretty good tactics, Flynn reluctantly admitted to himself. Once those narcos finished establishing their perimeter, they could close in and flush him out of hiding. Someone out there definitely had military-style training to go with all those military-grade weapons. All of which, he decided, made the idea of waiting here like a deer caught in the headlights a quick but likely very painful way to commit suicide.

Careful to keep the tree trunk between him and the force of Brotherhood gunmen now deployed in pairs from the north to the south, he drifted back down the slope a few yards. Then, below their line of sight, he turned and loped back the way he'd come, making sure he stuck to the lengthening morning shadows cast by the scattered pine and oak trees wherever he could. He hadn't gone more than a hundred yards when wasp-like engine noises from somewhere not far ahead alerted him to the presence of more ATVs heading his way.

Flynn dropped to one knee behind a chest-high clump of brush. He risked one quick look toward the sounds. Two of the four-wheeled buggies were in sight—slowly driving north along the slope between the trees. Each was flanked by two more rifle-toting narcos on foot. These men were also wearing what appeared to be bulky Kevlar body armor. From end to end, the skirmish line of cartel gunmen and ATVs stretched about fifty yards. Like beaters driving game toward a predetermined killing ground, he realized coldly. With his precious hide as the designated prey.

He pulled back into cover. His mind felt like it was racing, raising different tactical options and just as rapidly discarding them as only likely to get him killed even faster. He frowned. This whole "Flynn's Last Stand" bullshit was going to make him look bad. No one ever praised George Armstrong Custer for blindly riding his whole cavalry regiment into a bazillion really pissed-off Sioux warriors. Well, now it looked as though he'd managed pretty much the same thing, if on a lot smaller and far more personal scale.

Flynn felt a sharp vibration from one of his assault-vest pockets. He yanked out his satellite phone and read the message scrolling across its tiny screen: *Two minutes out. Status?* He grinned more broadly. Man, Laura was *not* going to be happy about this. And if he somehow lived through the next few minutes, she would never let him forget it. But now that he knew a ride was on the way, the elements of a plan—though still one that was pretty desperate—fell into place in his mind.

Quickly, he scrolled through the message presets he'd loaded in before this mission started. The most appropriate one was close to the top, indicating his subconscious must have had an inkling of how this outing was likely to end up. He sent the highlighted text: *SNAFU*. The military slang term meaning *Situation Normal All Fucked Up* was also the code word used by Four to indicate that an agent was surrounded, with enemies closing in. Then, carefully, he typed in *PUNCHOUT*, signaling that he intended to break out of this trap before its jaws snapped shut. With his decision made, he didn't have the time or need to send any further messages, so he tucked the phone safely away again.

Flynn eased his pistol back out. His pulse sped up. This was going to get hairy fast. Another cautious glance around the large bush he was using for concealment showed that the skirmish line of Brotherhood ATVs and gunmen was headed right toward him. His mouth thinned. These guys were about to learn the hard way what happened when the hunted decided to become the hunter instead.

He counted down silently. *Three. Two. One.* Now.

Flynn stepped out from behind the clump of brush with his weapon already up and moving through a short arc. The closest ATV was only a few yards away. The driver's mouth fell open in surprise at his sudden appearance out of the shadows. The Glock's front sights settled on target, and Flynn squeezed the trigger twice. Two 9mm rounds moving at 1,200 feet per second slammed into the other man's face. Without a sound, the narco folded over the handlebars of his buggy in a spray of bright-red blood and shattered white bone. Its driver dead, the ATV veered slowly toward Flynn and rolled to a stop only feet away, with its motor still ticking over.

One down, he thought calmly.

Flynn swiveled and fired two more times. The nearest gunman on foot dropped in a boneless heap, shot through the head before he could even begin to react to this unexpected ambush. But given a second's more grace, his partner yelled out in horrified alarm—frantically fumbling to bring his own short-barreled M4 carbine to bear.

Too late, Flynn thought. He squeezed off several more rapid shots. Hit multiple times in the torso, the cartel gunman spun around through a half circle and went down. The rifle he dropped whirled through the air before thudding to the ground. *That guy might not be dead,* Flynn realized, since the Kevlar he was wearing could be good enough to stop 9mm rounds, even ones fired at point-blank range. But at a minimum, that narco would be out of the fight for a time—battered by mule-kick-like impacts, scared shitless, and probably not very inclined to make a target of himself again by scrambling after his lost weapon.

Down the wooded slope, the driver of the second Brotherhood ATV dived out of the seat and down behind his four-wheeled buggy. And in the same moment, the last two cartel gunmen in the group threw themselves prone and opened fire from where they were—wildly shooting in his general direction without spending a lot of time aiming.

5.56mm rounds whipcracked low over Flynn's head, ripping pieces of splintered bark and shredded leaves off the nearby trees and sending clumps of dirt flying high in all directions. *Well, this neighborhood's gone to hell*, he thought tightly. Which made it time to bail out of here, before one of those panicked Brotherhood thugs got lucky and punched a bullet into him.

Moving like lightning, he lunged forward and grabbed the M4 carbine dropped by one of the men he'd shot. Hurriedly, he slung it over his right shoulder, muzzle down. Then Flynn hauled the dead ATV driver out of the saddle and dropped him over the side. In that same motion, he swung aboard the low-slung vehicle. Leaning forward over the handlebars, he put the buggy back in gear and slewed it around through a hard, tight turn that sprayed loose dirt and rocks out from under the tires. More rifle rounds slashed by on all sides.

Pointed almost straight up the slope now, Flynn gunned the ATV and accelerated with the throttle open wide. Swerving wildly to avoid crashing headlong into trees, he roared uphill and burst out into the open terrain at the top of the ridge.

There, some miles off to the east, but rapidly drawing closer, he saw the small shape of a green-and-tan-camouflaged helicopter low in the sky. Sunlight glinted off its clear canopy. Flynn held on tight as the four-wheeler bounced up and down over the rough, rocky ground. He risked a glance back over his shoulder. Alerted by the sudden burst of gunfire, the Brotherhood gunmen who'd been deployed to watch the tree line had obviously spotted him. In ones and twos, they were mounting their own ATVs and turning after him in hot pursuit.

Tight lipped, Flynn swung back around. There was no way he was going to outrun that many cartel gunmen, he realized. Not and get far enough away for an easy helicopter extraction. This was their home turf, so they knew all the ins and outs of the local terrain. That left him only one serious option: stand and fight until retrieved. Spotting a small thicket of scrub oaks and brush a few hundred yards away, he steered toward it and sped up.

TWENTY-THREE

ON THE RIDGE

MOMENTS LATER

Just a few yards from the little patch of stunted oaks, Flynn braked hard, skidding to a stop in a whirling haze of dust and sand. Immediately, he rolled off the motionless ATV and sprinted across and into the shadowed edge of the thicket. Swiftly, he yanked a smoke grenade off his tactical vest, pulled the pin, and lobbed it back toward the center of the tiny clump of scrub trees.

With a muffled bang and then a snakelike hiss, the grenade ignited. In seconds, a thick cloud of bright-green smoke billowed skyward—marking his position for the incoming helicopter. Then, unslinging the M4 carbine he'd grabbed, Flynn dropped to his stomach and wriggled forward until he could see out of the edge of the thicket. Now he needed to buy some time.

Calmly, he sighted down the barrel of the weapon, tracking on the closest Brotherhood ATV as it sped across the ridgetop toward his position. He opened up, squeezing off one aimed shot at a time. The M4's stock slapped rhythmically back against his shoulder as he sent rounds keening downrange. Dust fountained up around the oncoming four-wheeler. Hit at least once, its driver screamed shrilly, threw his arms out wide, and tumbled off to lie sprawled and limp. Riderless now, the vehicle slowed and then swung away, curving through an arc until it came to a complete stop some yards away from the dead man.

Out across the ridge, the other cartel gunmen reacted fast. They braked to a stop and dived off their own ATVs, going to ground. Within moments, repeated flashes from near the motionless vehicles marked their return fire. Flynn pressed his face hard into the dirt as 5.56mm rounds slashed through the thicket at supersonic speed—shredding tree limbs and vegetation.

And then, with a pounding, deafening roar from its turboshaft engine, the Bell 206A Jet Ranger flew right over his head. It was already flaring out to land only a few scant yards from the grove. Dust and torn pieces of tall grass swirled crazily in a man-made tornado, whipped up by the wash from its spinning rotors.

Through eyes narrowed to slits against the stinging cloud of rotor-blown debris, Flynn could make out Laura Van Horn seated in the helicopter's right-hand pilot's position. She wore an expression of absolute concentration while her hands danced over the Jet Ranger's cyclic and collective controls—determinedly holding the helicopter down on its skids while the machine's combination of thrust and lift tried to bounce it back into the air. On the other side of the helicopter, Shannon Cooke was leaning out the open cabin door, shooting back at the Brotherhood gunmen with his HK417 carbine.

Ignoring the rounds still ripping through the thicket, Flynn bounced to his feet and bolted for the grounded helicopter. In less than a second, he plunged into the dust cloud kicked up

by its whirling rotors and kept going. Half expecting to feel the
shattering impact of a bullet at any second, he lowered his head
and ran even faster—sprinting across the short interval with
ever-lengthening strides. Straight ahead, the Bell 206 loomed
up through the haze, taking on solid form. Without slowing,
Flynn dived headfirst through the open door past Cooke—and
abruptly saw red when he smacked painfully into one of the
cabin's metal fittings.

The moment he was aboard, Van Horn lifted off, swinging the helicopter around through a fast 180-degree arc that
generated an even thicker cloud of rotor-blown sand and dust.
WHANG. WHANG. WHANG. The Bell 206 rattled and shook
as rifle rounds punched through its fuselage and tail boom and
exploded out the other side. Still only a few feet off the ground,
she lowered the helicopter's nose slightly and transitioned to
level flight—slashing low across the top of the ridge to the east
at more than one hundred knots.

"Oh, fuck!" Cooke yelled suddenly from the left-side door.
He'd turned to fire back behind them, hoping to suppress the
Brotherhood gunmen still shooting at them. "SAM! SAM at
our six!" he warned.

Ignoring the blood spattering from his gashed forehead,
Flynn whipped around to stare back through the open right
door. A small dark shape had streaked skyward out of a billowing cloud of pale-gray smoke. Trailing a plume of fire, the
missile was already turning to home in on their heat signature. Jesus Christ, he thought in dismay. Who had sold these
drug-running bastards shoulder-launched antiair missiles? Some
crooked supply officer in the Mexican Armed Forces? Their
Venezuelan narco allies? Voronin?

"Hang on tight!" Van Horn snapped, barely audible over
the high-pitched roar from their turbine engine. She took them

out over the crest of the ridge at high speed and then pushed her collective control forward—sending the Bell 206 plunging down into an arroyo on the other side. The dry canyon twisted back and forth like a snake as it wound eastward through the Sierra Madre foothills. With her right hand busy on the cyclic stick and her feet on the rudder pedals, she rolled the helicopter back and forth through a series of incredibly tight turns to follow the arroyo without smashing into its steep sides.

In the aft cabin, straining to keep from being thrown out through the open side door, Flynn suddenly noticed tree branches flashing past outside . . . branches that were now *above* the speeding helicopter. Holy crap, he realized in sheer amazement. Van Horn had taken them right down in among the sparse woods that lined the slopes of this narrow canyon, and now she was weaving in and out among the very tallest trees. Without warning, with a bone-shaking jolt, the Bell 206's rotor blades sheared right through a couple of treetops. Tiny scraps of sliced and diced pine and oak bark sleeted through the door in a burst of aromatic splinters.

WHAAMMM.

A huge flash of blinding orange and red lit the sky close behind them. The missile on their tail had just slammed into another tall tree and detonated. Hit by the shock wave and a rattling hail of razor-edged fragments, the helicopter shimmied and shook from end to end, like a wet dog coming out of the water. Somehow, despite everything, Van Horn retained control. She leveled out just above the floor of the little canyon and flew on eastward, still throwing the bird from side to side in wild evasive maneuvers.

"Anybody hit?" she called out.

On the other side of the cabin from Flynn, Cooke stared down. He looked flabbergasted to find himself in one piece. "I'm okay," he reported over the intercom. Then he checked Flynn over. "So's Nick. Except for a shallow-looking gash on his fore-head that I think he must have got diving aboard."

Flynn grabbed the headset offered to him by the other man and plugged it into the intercom. He swiped at the blood trick-ling down his face. "I'm fine," he reassured Van Horn.

"Figured you would be, amigo," she retorted. "That head of yours has never been your most vulnerable spot."

Peering forward toward the cockpit, Flynn could see that it was a mess. The helicopter's clear canopy was starred and cracked by shards of metal hurled outward from the blast. Smoke curled out of the damaged instrument panel. And the sleeve of Van Horn's arm was turning red. "You're wounded, Laura!" he blurted out in sudden worry.

She glanced down at her torn flight suit. "No sweat," she assured him coolly, opening and closing the fingers of her left hand to show him there was no major damage. "Just a clean through-and-through. Get me some bandages and a stiff Scotch once we touch down, and I should be good to go."

They flew on to the east, heading for Torreón at very low alti-tude. Behind them, a pillar of dark-gray smoke curled higher, fed by the missile-set fire now spreading through the little canyon.

WEST OF TORREÓN INTERNATIONAL AIRPORT
AN HOUR LATER

Five miles west of the city, Van Horn cautiously pulled the damaged helicopter into a shallow climb. They needed to clear a chain of low, rugged hills just ahead—hills that marked the border between the states of Durango and Coahuila. Torreón was just across the line. At around a thousand feet above the ground, she leveled out again. Suddenly, the Bell 206 shuddered violently, and the howling roar of its turboshaft engine grew even shriller.

Holding on to a safety strap, Flynn leaned out through the open side door and looked aft toward the helicopter's tail. He frowned. "Uh, Laura," he said over the intercom. "I hate to say this, but we're starting to trail smoke."

"Well, crap," Van Horn replied. "Is that smoke black . . . or gray?" Her tone was almost conversational, as though she were discussing the weather.

"Black."

Flynn could almost hear her nod. "Yeah, I was afraid of that. I figure one of those pieces of shrapnel must have nicked an oil line. And now, I bet the line's busted open . . . which means we've got hot oil spraying across the engine mounting."

Flynn exchanged a glance with Cooke. "Let me guess. That's bad."

"Oh yeah." Van Horn tapped her damaged instrument console. "Our fire-suppression system's kaput. And so are most of these gauges. So I can't even tell how much oil we're losing."

"Which means—?" Flynn asked.

"If we're really unlucky, a full-on fire starts, spreads to the fuel tanks, and we blow up," she said, still sounding remarkably unfazed. "And if we're only a little bit unlucky, then the engine seizes up when all the oil's gone."

Flynn saw Cooke mouth, "Oh, just fricking great." He nodded and keyed the intercom mike again. "So what happens then?"

"Well," she said meditatively, "best case is that we autorotate down for a hard landing. The worst case is that we fall out of the sky and slam nose first into a building or some rocks or some other piece of extremely unforgiving terrain." A couple of hundred feet below, the last of the hills they'd just flown across fell away behind. Seemingly perfectly serene, she tweaked the helicopter controls some more. Still spewing smoke, the Bell 206 descended again, until it was skimming low over the rows and rows of flat-roofed houses and other buildings on the out-skirts of Torreón. The buffeting grew worse.

Flynn sighed. "Sorry I asked."

Van Horn's mouth tightened into a thin grin as she saw the square helipad at the Torreón military air station coming into sight. "Relax, guys," she said. "I've got this."

As the helicopter clattered low over a four-lane highway bordering the airport, she started working the pedals, cyclic stick, and collective control to slow their airspeed. The helipad grew bigger through the canopy. Barely moving forward, they settled down toward the pad . . . and with a muffled bang, the engine suddenly died. With its rotor still spinning automati-cally, the Bell 206 dropped the last few feet and slammed down hard on its skids.

"Everybody out," Van Horn ordered. Her hands danced across the instrument panel in front of her, quickly flicking as many switches as were in working order to their off positions. "This thing could still blow."

They all piled out and walked away fast from the smoking, shrapnel-riddled helicopter. A car sent by Colonel Herrera was waiting for them across the tarmac. Members of the air station's ground crew rushed past them, heading for the smoldering Bell 206 with handheld fire extinguishers.

The senior man, a sergeant, stopped dead in his tracks before them. His mouth was open as he stared at the battered wreck they'd just left. "Mother of God, Captain," he stammered. "What happened?"

Van Horn swung round on him. Her mouth curled into a

deep frown as she put her hands on her hips. "Isn't it obvious?" she snapped.

"Señora?" the sergeant said in total confusion.

"It failed its maintenance check." Without waiting for a response, she spun back around and rejoined Flynn and Cooke.

Before the stunned Mexican Air Force sergeant could recover his wits, the three agents were on the move again. They slid into the waiting car, and it immediately drove away—heading straight for the Pilatus PC-12 turboprop parked at the other end of the airport.

TWENTY-FOUR

THE BROTHERHOOD COMPOUND, IN THE SIERRA MADRE

TWO DAYS LATER

Pavel Voronin stepped down out of the bus that had ferried him here from Durango's airport. He'd come in aboard the Boeing 777F on its most recent cargo flight from Minsk. The freight-hauling jet's limited crew and passenger accommodations were a large step down in comfort and luxury from those of the Bombardier Global 7500 he'd used the last time he visited this godforsaken part of Mexico. Recent events, however—Bazhanov's murder and now this report of an intruder spying on the compound—had persuaded him to travel even more discreetly than before.

Two men were there waiting for him. One of them, burly and bald headed, was a former Russian Air Force colonel named Arkady Anokhin—the leader of the Raven Syndicate engineering and technical unit assigned to this compound. Before resigning from the military to join the Syndicate, Anokhin had overseen a special maintenance depot dedicated to unmanned aerial vehicles. The other was Joaquin Lopez, the Brotherhood of Blood's second-in-command.

Voronin noted that the cartel leader was not wearing an expensive suit this time. Instead, he was dressed in a plain green T-shirt and faded blue jeans—clothing that deliberately showed off the array of gang and prison tattoos covering his arms and neck and part of his face. Thick gold neck chains completed Lopez's transformation into the archetype of the flamboyant drug lord called a *buchón* in narco slang. His facade of sophistication and education was gone. Plainly, for this meeting at least, Lopez wanted to be seen for what he truly was—a cold-blooded killer and criminal boss.

The Russian hid his distaste at this loutish, *nekul'turny* display of machismo. For all their wealth and power, the Brotherhood's leaders were simple thugs, a bare step above the sort of imbeciles one could find in any provincial Russian prison. But for the moment, he needed these men and the secure secret staging area they had promised to provide for CASTLE KEEP.

A promise the Mexican cartel had singularly failed to fulfill, Voronin reminded himself. Given the number of Brotherhood gunmen and armored vehicles patrolling the compound itself, he could be reasonably sure this mysterious intruder hadn't escaped with any significant information on his operation. But even the faint possibility of a leak was disconcerting. It was essential that the Americans learn nothing of what was in store for them. He fixed his pale-gray eyes on Lopez. "So, Joaquin, have your men identified this spy yet?" he demanded without preamble. If the other man wanted to butt heads to see who was the stronger here, Voronin was more than ready to oblige him.

Clearly angry at being forced on the defensive right at the start, Lopez frowned. "Not yet," he admitted with obvious reluctance. He folded his arms. "But since this *cabrón*, this bastard motherfucker, escaped aboard a helicopter in Air Force camouflage and colors, he was almost certainly a *federal* or some other sort of government agent."

Voronin raised an eyebrow. "Oh?" he said. "And yet, despite your vaunted network of informers supposedly planted in every nook and corner of your country's police and law enforcement apparatus, you *still* had no warning that this spy was operating so freely in your own territory?"

Lopez scowled. "Only God knows all," he snarled back. "In any case, this man was not *operating freely*, as you claim," he said through gritted teeth. "He only got away from my *soldados*, my soldiers, by the skin of his teeth."

"But not before killing three of them, I understand," Voronin pointed out, with a thin, dry smile. Seeing Lopez turn pale with renewed anger, he moved on. "What matters is that this spy did, in fact, escape." His smile vanished. "Which raises the question of the overall security of this facility—security that is entirely your Brotherhood's responsibility according to our agreement." He nodded at the bustling compound around them. "Should I worry that your government's next move will be a large-scale police or commando raid aimed at my operation here?"

"You can rest easy on that score," Lopez told him, apparently feeling on somewhat firmer footing now. "A lone-wolf agent is one thing. A major assault? That's another. We would certainly be informed of any such operation being planned days or even weeks ahead of time. And frankly, I doubt the politicians in Mexico City would have the balls to order such a thing. The last time they tried to fuck with us, they walked into a meat grinder."

Voronin nodded. That much of what Lopez said, however boastfully, was accurate. A major effort by the Mexican National

Guard to capture a drug lord in the neighboring state of Sinaloa had ended in disaster when it turned into an all-out pitched urban battle between the outnumbered soldiers and hundreds of cartel gunmen, all of whom were heavily armed. In the end, the National Guard had been forced to release their prisoner in exchange for the return of captured soldiers and their families. The central government's prestige in this region had never fully recovered from that humiliating defeat.

"Besides, we've taken steps to lock this valley down even tighter," Lopez assured him. "Right now, not even a bat could get anywhere near here without being spotted and shot out of the sky."

"Let us hope your confidence is justified," Voronin said coolly. "At least this time." He turned to Anokhin. "And your part of this project, Arkady? Are you still on schedule? As you've promised?"

Standing there, listening to the two other men argue, the former Russian Air Force colonel had studiously maintained a neutral expression on his broad-featured face. Voronin was his employer. But Lopez was in charge of the notoriously hot-tempered and trigger-happy narco gunmen who ruled the surrounding countryside. A serious falling-out with the Brotherhood could easily have lethal consequences for Anokhin and his team of technicians and aeronautical engineers. Given that, it was decidedly *not* in his interest to insert himself into their quarrel.

But now that the discussion had turned to his own area of responsibility, Anokhin's rigidly disinterested expression altered, transforming into one that was noticeably more confident and in command. In answer to Voronin's blunt, hard-edged question, he gestured at the large prefabricated building ahead of them. "Come inside and see."

Voronin and Lopez followed him in through the open doors. Under the powerful overhead lights illuminating the interior, the reason for Anokhin's look of confidence was clear. Twelve batwing-shaped gray aircraft were lined almost wingtip to wingtip in two rows of six each. No windows or cockpit canopies broke their smooth lines. A number of scaffolds, heavy loaders, and other pieces of complex machinery lined the building's back wall, but almost all of the existing space was taken up by the force of unmanned aerial vehicles.

After a long, admiring look at the Mora drones, Voronin turned to his subordinate. "Are these machines fully assembled?"

"They're all flight ready," Anokhin confirmed. He shrugged his powerful shoulders. "Of course, as long as they're parked here in this facility away from prying eyes, we don't have enough room to construct more."

Voronin nodded his understanding. Right now, the inside of this building, large as it was, appeared far more crowded than the hangar deck of any navy aircraft carrier. "Don't worry about that, Arkady," he assured the other man. "Your assembly teams will be able to get back to work soon enough."

Anokhin stared at him.

"The designated payloads for this first wave of Moras are being trucked in from Durango now," Voronin explained. "They came in with me aboard the most recent 777 cargo flight." He carefully avoided saying exactly what those "payloads" were. So far, Lopez and his boss, Diego Barros, hadn't shown any great curiosity about what their ally planned to fly into the United States. And this was definitely not the time to whet their interest.

But from the tiny beads of sweat that suddenly appeared on Anokhin's wide forehead, Voronin guessed that—up to this moment—the former Russian Air Force officer had not fully considered the real-world implications of the missions planned for the UCAVs he and his team were assembling. Up to now, Voronin strongly suspected, the other man had seen his part of CASTLE KEEP as primarily a complicated and difficult technical task; one, moreover, that had to be completed under somewhat primitive conditions. All of that had just changed. Once the devices aboard those trucks arrived here and were safely stowed aboard the Moras, it would no longer be possible for Anokhin to treat this as a purely aeronautical engineering challenge. The hard truth could no longer be avoided. They were involved in an extremely daring and dangerous bid to forever alter the world's current strategic balance, with all the risks that entailed.

"And what about *my* cargoes?" Lopez demanded. The Brotherhood leader ran his eyes over the twin rows of strange-looking flying machines with a look that reflected a hint of both awe and pure mercenary calculation. It was equally clear that he, at least, hadn't fully understood the scale of the aircraft assembly work the Raven Syndicate had been carrying out in this isolated valley.

Voronin glanced over at him. "Are they ready for shipment?" he asked blandly.

"Naturally," Lopez said.

"Then you have nothing to worry about," Voronin said. "We will honor our agreement to the letter. Each of our Moras will fly out with one hundred kilograms of your *products* aboard, exactly as promised." Immediately, he saw the unsuppressed gleam of greed in the drug lord's gaze. The street value of even a single unmanned aircraft load of fentanyl would come to almost fifty million US dollars—almost as much as it had cost to build each of the sophisticated stealth drones in the first place.

TWENTY-FIVE

THE MORA COMPOUND

THE NEXT NIGHT

From a vantage point out near the barbed wire perimeter fence, Voronin closely observed the large aircraft assembly building a couple of hundred meters away. At his right shoulder, Lopez was doing the same. On his left, Arkady Anokhin was watching a digital timer count down on the screen of his smartphone. "And . . . now," he heard Anokhin murmur to himself. The burly man raised his smartphone to his lips and ordered, "Move the aircraft into position, Dmitri."

In answer, the main compound lights blinked out, leaving a few hooded lamps along the outer fence as the only illumination. The area immediately around the assembly building was plunged into darkness.

Voronin and his two companions lifted night vision binoculars to follow the next steps. They watched intently as several of Anokhin's technicians rolled the building's large central doors all the way open. Slowly and carefully, an aircraft tug—a small, one-man tractor—towed one of the bat-shaped Mora UCAVs out onto the paved apron in front. Once the aircraft was in position, the tug unhooked from it and then went back inside to haul out a second. When there were two of the UCAVs lined up outside, the Syndicate technicians hauled the doors closed again.

Standing behind Voronin, one of his aides was on a secure satellite phone. "Flight control reports solid, encrypted communications links established with both Mora One and Mora Two," the aide stated.

"Very well," Voronin acknowledged. He swung toward Lopez. "Are your people along the border ready?"

The cartel leader's teeth gleamed in the darkness. "They are indeed," he said. "The gringos are going to be very busy. Don't worry, señor Voronin, we will open the holes you need."

Voronin nodded. Over the next several nights, Brotherhood of Blood coyotes, human smugglers loyal to the cartel, had been instructed to orchestrate a series of mass crossings of illegal aliens at key points along the US-Mexico border. Their plans had been deliberately leaked to the Americans in order to lure the Border Patrol into concentrating its heavily outnumbered personnel into those same carefully selected sectors. That would leave vast stretches of the frontier unwatched and unguarded by anything except automated sensors.

A tight, humorless smile slid across his face. Conventional military thinkers and strategists were remarkably unimaginative, he thought coldly. They viewed conflict almost solely in terms of so many soldiers deployed in one place, so much firepower delivered in another, and the like. But what they completely failed to comprehend was that desperate people—men, women, and, especially, children—could be employed as equally effective weapons. He, on the other hand, had a much wider and more creative understanding of warfare. His stealthy unmanned aircraft were already invisible to the balloon-mounted radars the Americans used to detect ordinary drug-smuggling planes attempting to sneak across the border. But by stretching the Border Patrol to its breaking point, his weaponized deliveries of thousands and thousands of migrants should help ensure that the low-flying Moras weren't picked up by sight or sound when they breached US airspace.

Voronin glanced back at his aide. "Signal control to commence flight operations," he ordered.

The other man relayed his order, listened to the reply, and then looked up. "Havana is go for engine start," he said.

Seconds later, the wing-buried turbofan engines in both UCAVs spooled up with low whines that steadily increased in both pitch and volume. Control surfaces along the trailing edges of their wings flexed slightly. Voronin nodded to himself, understanding what he was seeing. Pilots based more than two thousand kilometers away from this darkened valley were busy running through their preflight checklists.

"Moras One and Two are both ready for takeoff," the aide reported, relaying what he was being told by the remote control center.

Voronin focused his night vision binoculars. The first unmanned aircraft started rolling slowly across the apron, followed closely by its twin. In succession, they turned out onto the narrow paved road that ran past the Brotherhood compound. Braking to a stop again, they were lined up one behind the other, now pointed straight north. For a few moments more, they held in place. With a shrill howl, their engines keened louder and louder as they ran all the way up to full power. And then, quite suddenly, the first UCAV was in motion up the road—which now served as an improvised runway. It picked up speed fast, accelerating smoothly. The second aircraft followed in its trail. Moments later, having reached the necessary velocity, the first Mora broke away from the ground and climbed higher, its landing gear already retracting out of sight into its gray belly. The second drone took off only seconds later.

Staying low, scarcely five hundred feet above the ground, both UCAVs headed north along the eastern edge of the Sierra Madre. Their pale-gray shapes soon vanished entirely, swallowed up by the dark, moonless night.

Voronin lowered his binoculars with a feeling of intense satisfaction. After so many months of careful planning, enormous expense, and intensive preparation, his chosen weapons were on their way—beginning the intricately plotted 1,800-kilometer flight that would take them deep into the heartland of the unsuspecting United States.

RURAL KANSAS
SEVERAL HOURS LATER

Former Russian Air Force major Ivan Strelkov lifted his night vision binoculars and carefully scanned the southern horizon. From up here on the flat roof of the quarter-mile-long abandoned distribution center now owned by the Raven Syndicate he could see out across the surrounding countryside for nearly fifteen kilometers. There was nothing in sight yet.

Lowering his binoculars, he glanced down at the glowing dial of his watch. Soon, he thought. Based on his rough estimates of flight distances and average airspeed, the events he and his men had been waiting for should occur within the next few minutes, at most.

And high time, too, in Strelkov's judgment. He and the others in his covert operations unit had arrived a week ago and had been secretly occupying the unused warehouse complex ever since. On the plus side, its cavernous interior offered plenty of room to conceal their trucks and other special equipment, which included a tanker leased from Pemex, Mexico's state-owned oil company—a tanker truck full of aviation fuel. But ample space or not, no one could say it was a particularly comfortable existence. Ordered to avoid any contact with the locals, they had been subsisting on surplus American military rations, the so-called MREs, or meals ready to eat, and camping out in sleeping bags on the cold, hard concrete floor of the empty, echoing distribution center.

Strelkov smiled sardonically. After their first experience of eating the individually packaged ration packs, two things had become clear. One, they were admittedly a little more palatable than the Russian army's own equivalent emergency ration, the IRP. At the same time, however, his experience of the glutinous mess laughably labeled *Chicken Chunks* strongly suggested that only the middle part of the MRE acronym, the *R* for *ready*, was really accurate. The MREs they'd been given were not really meals in any genuine sense of the word. Or very edible, for that matter.

Then again, he reminded himself, their mild discomfort would be well worth it. At least assuming they managed to avoid being arrested by the Americans as spies. And if all of CASTLE KEEP went according to plan. The huge bonuses promised by Pavel Voronin for the successful completion of this mission would guarantee Strelkov and the others in his command very comfortable lives of leisure and luxury once they returned to Russia.

Strelkov's phone beeped suddenly. He checked the screen

and read a message relayed circuitously from Havana: *Delivery truck in your neighborhood. Confirm driveway is clear.* Rapidly, he typed in a confirmation. He had two of his men watching the highway to both the north and the south. At this late hour, the rural two-lane road was usually completely empty of any traffic. And tonight was no exception. Besides, across this flat, featureless farmland, the headlights of any oncoming vehicles would be visible all the way out to the horizon.

He raised his night vision binoculars again. And there, to the south, he caught sight of a tiny pulse of infrared light low in the sky. He focused and caught a glimpse of a pale shape growing larger as it flew his way. It was descending gradually, shedding altitude and airspeed. The lead Mora UCAV was on its final approach—aimed directly at the stretch of rail-straight highway beside the big warehouse. The pilot seated behind a console in distant Cuba was guiding on the pairs of IR beacons Strelkov's aircraft-handling team had set up at fifty-meter intervals along the road.

The Russian watched, holding his breath, as the plane's landing gear unfolded from inside its fuselage and locked in position. Moments later, the Mora touched down, braked gently, and then taxied off the highway into the huge parking lot outside the distribution center. A tug driven by one of his men was already there, waiting to tow the UCAV into concealment within the empty building.

Strelkov lifted his binoculars again and saw the second drone making its own landing approach. He watched closely as it slid down out of the sky, kissed the improvised runway, and slowed to a complete stop beside its identical companion. He let out his breath in relief. The men in Moscow would be pleased. Phase II of CASTLE KEEP was now successfully underway.

TWENTY-SIX

AVALON HOUSE, WINTER PARK, FLORIDA

THE NEXT MORNING

Nick Flynn carried his cup of coffee in through the ballroom's double doors. He walked over to the semicircle of folding chairs facing a projector screen in the middle of the large room. Decades ago, the wealthy New York banking family who had owned the mansion held black-tie dinner dances here. This morning's gathering was considerably more casual—just a mix of men and women in everyday clothes. It was a lesson, however, in just how deceiving appearances could be.

In those long-ago days when a band or orchestra filled the ballroom with tunes and perfectly dressed couples swirled or swayed in time with the music, the worst consequences of a mistake in judgment might be hurt feelings, or maybe even a broken engagement. The stakes for today's assembly were much higher. Fox had called this all-hands meeting of the Quartet Directorate agents currently based at Avalon House specifically to go over the new intelligence acquired by Flynn during his reconnaissance foray into drug-cartel territory. A significant error in analysis now could easily cost lives—either of Four personnel or of innocent civilians.

Besides Fox, himself, and Laura Van Horn, those already present included the members of Flynn's action team—Cole Hynes, Tadeusz Kossak, Wade Vucovich, and Shannon Cooke—plus Gwen Park and a few others. Despite the relatively early hour, they all looked attentive and wide awake.

Flynn took the seat on Van Horn's right and carefully set his coffee down next to his chair on the worn hardwood floor. Casually, her hand slid into his and squeezed gently. He glanced over at her. "I missed you this morning," he said in a low voice.

She nodded. "Br'er Fox ordered me to go in for a med eval." She raised her left arm slightly. "He wanted me to have that splinter wound I took down in Mexico a couple of days ago checked out. So since the doctor could slot me in at the crack of dawn, I trotted in like the good little doobie that I really am."

Flynn resisted the urge to grin openly. Van Horn had a well-earned reputation for obeying orders she approved of—and ignoring those she didn't. The term often used by Fox in conjunction with her was *force of nature*. Flynn turned in his chair to face her more fully. "And? What was the diagnosis?"

She shrugged. "It's like I thought. No big deal. There's no significant tissue or muscle damage. To quote Doc Halloran, 'The wound should heal by first intention.' He put in a few stitches and then gave me the usual warnings to avoid overtaxing my arm for a few more days."

Flynn nodded. The Quartet Directorate retained the well-paid services of some discreet surgeons and other medical professionals, often with their own private clinics and practices—skilled men and women who could be relied on to avoid reporting any treatment of gunshot wounds and other injuries to the overly inquisitive authorities. "What, no prolonged bed rest?" he teased.

Van Horn's generous mouth curved in a playful smile of her own. "Bed, I wouldn't mind," she told him with a throaty murmur that couldn't be heard by anyone else over the quiet buzz of other conversations. "The rest part I can probably do without."

From where he stood near the projector screen, Fox cleared his throat gently. "Ladies and gentlemen, if I may?"

The room fell silent immediately. Anyone meeting him for the first time might assume Fox was just the boring money manager or midlevel government bureaucrat he so often pretended to be. But when it counted, Flynn knew, the older man had a forceful command presence—one easily capable of bringing to heel even the sort of square-peg-in-a-round-hole mavericks who were naturally attracted to Four's brand of high-risk covert operations.

Fox used a small wireless remote to bring up the first set of images Flynn had shot through the half-opened doors of the cartel compound's big central building. The pictures had been enhanced and cropped to make them as clear as possible. He scrolled through them until he stopped on one in particular. Of all the dozens of photos Nick had taken, this one offered the best combination of details of both the mysterious work being done . . . and the men who were doing it. "Our task now is to make some broader sense of the new information we now possess, thanks to Nick and those who brought him out safely."

Heads nodded around the room.

Hesitantly, Wade Vucovich raised a hand. Flynn hid his surprise. The lanky man was ordinarily the quietest in any room. "That looks kinda like a factory," he said. He pointed toward the lower portion of the current photo shown on the projection screen. In it, a large tire was partially visible, poking out from under one of the concealing tarps. "Maybe they're building better versions of those mechanized beasts the narcos like so much?" Vucovich suggested. "The ones they've got are pretty fricking crude looking . . . just a bunch of steel plates bolted onto truck chassis. Could be Voronin's promised these Brotherhood guys their own heavy-duty armored fighting force—one that can whack the other cartels and even give the Mexican government some serious heartburn."

Flynn considered that. It wasn't a bad hypothesis, but something about it didn't feel right. It came back, he realized, to their assessment of Voronin's character. The Russian simply did not strike him as someone who would ever be happy playing a supporting role of any kind—especially one as an arms supplier to a gang of comparatively uneducated criminals. Whatever he did, Flynn suspected, the head of the Raven Syndicate would always need to be the ringmaster, the man in a top hat and tails at the center of the circus tent's spotlight.

From beside him, Van Horn spoke up. "I think you're right about this place being some kind of factory, Wade," she said slowly. "But not for making armored cars." She got up from her seat and moved closer to the screen to eye the photo frozen there. Her hands moved through the air, as though she were trying to trace out the shapes hidden beneath those heavy-duty tarps. Then she nodded to herself and turned back to Fox. "My bet is that what we're looking at here is a small-scale aircraft plant."

"Seriously, ma'am?" Cole Hynes blurted out. "You really think that rat fucker Voronin is building his own air force down there in the Mexican boonies?"

"From scratch? No, I don't," Van Horn corrected him. She studied the pictures more carefully. "But what I do think is that his guys are *reassembling* aircraft that have already been built, tested, and flown in Russia before they were taken apart for shipment."

Flynn saw immediately what she was driving at as she explained her idea to them. It was a practical solution to an old strategic logistics problem. During the Second World War, there were only two real ways to move large numbers of combat aircraft from America's incredibly productive home-front factories to the Pacific and European theaters. One was by flying them along ferry routes—with all the attendant risks of losing planes and crews to mechanical failures, navigation errors, and bad weather. The other was by loading them aboard cargo ships in separate pieces—fuselages, wings, engines, and other components—and then putting them back together once they arrived in the war zone. Applying that same method, only this time using a big airfreight jet like that Boeing 777F, would make a lot of sense for Voronin. So far, they'd tracked three separate flights from Minsk through Caracas and then on to Durango. Taken in total, that could easily mean the Russians had already shipped more than three hundred tons of aircraft parts, machinery, and other equipment to the heavily guarded Brotherhood compound Flynn had scouted out.

One after another, the others in the room nodded. Her hypothesis seemed sound.

"Very well. Let's take that as the strongest possibility of what our enemies are doing," Fox agreed with a terse nod of his own. He stared at the screen. "The question then arises," he went on, "what sort of aircraft are Voronin's people assembling here? And for what purpose?"

In answer, Van Horn frowned. Clearly deep in thought, she leaned closer to the screen. Fortunately, some of the workers on the attached scaffolding gave her a sense of scale. She swung back toward the older man. "At a first guess, Br'er Fox, these things can't be that big. Not compared to most aircraft types anyway." She pointed at the screen. "For sure, they're a lot smaller than most modern combat fighters. Or most business jets, for that matter." She shook her head. "Based on what we see here, I don't think their wingspans can be more than six to eight meters. Maybe with a total loaded weight of around ten thousand pounds. And possibly less than that."

Fox tapped his chin reflectively, considering her analysis. An aircraft on that order was only a fraction of the size of even a comparatively small and lightweight US jet fighter like the F-16 Fighting Falcon. "So," he said slowly, "they may not be intended for a serious warlike purpose?"

Van Horn shook her head. "I didn't say that." Her mouth tightened. "Given sufficiently advanced technology, you can fit one hell of a lot of lethality into a very small package these days." She looked thoughtful. "In fact, I suspect anything that small is probably unmanned. Take out the need for a cockpit and the other systems required for a living, human pilot—oxygen, heating and cooling, and an ejection seat, for example—and you shave off a lot of weight and overall size."

From the murmurs around the room, it was plain that she'd made her point.

Flynn saw something else that was likely to be true. "Manned or unmanned," he interjected, "the aircraft Voronin's guys are assembling are almost certainly designed for maximum stealth."

Slowly, Fox nodded. "Thanks to Bazhanov," he said quietly.

"Bingo," Flynn said. "That's got to be the connection between this project and what Georgy Bazhanov, a.k.a. the late and unlamented Simon Jones, was doing. We were pretty sure his job was to siphon up as much advanced stealth technology as he could. Well, now we know why that was so important to Voronin. Because I'm pretty damn sure that same stolen tech is being used in these mystery aircraft the Raven Syndicate is deploying down in Mexico."

"Nick's on target," Van Horn agreed. "The Russians have developed stealth aircraft designs and materials of their own, but they've had a crapload of trouble making the transition from prototypes to full-scale production."

She had that right, Flynn knew. The Russians had a version of their first real stealth fighter, the Su-57, in the air way back in 2009. But in all the years since, they'd only managed to build a relative handful of combat-ready aircraft. Stealing proven specs, radar-absorbent materials, and top-of-the-line avionics and software from the various Western defense companies working on stealth allowed Voronin to bypass the production obstacles imposed by Russia's inefficient and less developed aviation- and computer-manufacturing capabilities.

"Here are some examples of what we may be looking at," Van Horn told them. She pulled up a number of images on her own smartphone and transferred them to the bigger display using Avalon House's secure wireless network.

Fox and the others watched in silence as pictures of the different stealthy unmanned combat aircraft under development by all the major powers appeared: BAE's Taranis, Dassault Aviation's Neuron, India's Aura, China's Lijian (Sharp Sword), Russia's own Mikoyan Skat and Sukhoi S-70 Okhotnik, Boeing's X-45C, Northrop Grumman's X-47B, and others. While their wing and fuselage dimensions and weights varied significantly, all of them shared the same rough features—including a highly blended flying-wing design. Their proposed combat uses ran the gamut from covert reconnaissance to air-to-air combat to strike missions against heavily defended ground targets.

"Unfortunately, without hard data on whatever engines and sensors are installed in the UCAVs Voronin is assembling, any assumptions we make about their range, speed, and payload capacity aren't going to be worth much," Van Horn admitted. "Everything in combat aircraft design is a trade-off between weight, thrust, maneuverability, range, and bomb or missile load. And we just don't know enough right now to even guess at what kind of trade-offs the aeronautical engineers who designed these planes actually made."

Fox frowned, deep in thought. At last he sighed. "Given that, we need to try working out this problem in reverse order: from the back to the front. Ordinarily, of course, that's a remarkably bad analytical technique. But in the absence of facts, I'm afraid that the application of educated guesswork is our only real remaining option."

"You mean, if we can figure out how Voronin intends to use this force of stealth aircraft, we might be able to draw some reasonable inferences about their capabilities?" Gwen Park asked.

Fox nodded.

Flynn shook his head. "I see where you're going, Br'er Fox. Trouble is, I can easily think of half a dozen things he could be planning—all of them extremely bad news for us or for our allies."

"Indulge me, Nick," the older man said patiently.

"Okay," Flynn replied. After a moment to organize his thoughts, he quickly ran through some of the nightmare scenarios his vivid imagination had just kicked up.

One was the possibility that Voronin planned to employ his aircraft in an assassination campaign that targeted important American and allied political and military leaders. Using stealthy drones to nail the president, influential state governors, powerful senators, and high-ranking generals and admirals could easily throw the entire country into political chaos. Better yet, the use of unmanned aircraft of a new design could make the assassination deniable—without any easy way to tie them back to Moscow. In fact, that could be another reason why Voronin would choose to build his UCAVs with stolen Western technology and components, instead of relying on identifiably Russian hardware and software.

Or Voronin might be planning to carry out equally deniable precision-guided weapon strikes against high-value American government facilities—national science and R&D centers like Lawrence Livermore, Argonne, and Los Alamos, or the NSA's computer server farms, space launch sites, and similar targets. Equally possible would be a terrorist-style campaign to sow panic inside the United States by using the drones to drop chemical or nerve agents over cities and towns or sports stadiums or outdoor concerts and other mass gatherings.

Flynn shrugged. "The sad truth is our air defenses are pretty much crap, except where NORAD is on alert against Russian bombers or cruise missiles coming in across the Arctic. We've got a few SAM units stationed around the Washington, DC, area to protect the White House, but it's not clear how effective they'd be against small, stealth targets."

When he finished, there was silence for several long moments. Then Cooke whistled softly. He looked down the row of seats at Flynn. "Man, Nick. Those are some genuinely vicious ideas. Has anybody ever told you that you've got a seriously evil streak?"

"All the time," Flynn said with a rueful smile.

"And that's just his mother," Van Horn cut in with a straight face.

That broke the tension. But once the laughter died down, Hynes raised his hand. "What about nukes?" he asked. "We know the Russians already smuggled one to the Iranians for that EMP attack we stopped last year. Could these drone aircraft carry nuclear bombs?"

His blunt question triggered another uncomfortable silence. Fox turned to Van Horn with a questioning look in his eyes.

She nodded soberly. "Sure they could. Modern nuclear warheads aren't actually significantly bigger or heavier than conventional weapons."

"The issue would be what Voronin could possibly hope to gain by arming his unmanned planes with nuclear weapons," Fox pointed out. "His earlier attempt to set off an EMP weapon in orbit was explicitly planned to hide Moscow's involvement in the attack. There would be no way to do anything of the kind in a case where several nuclear weapons were detonated inside the continental US. One such bomb going off might be judged a terrorist attack. But there are considerably fewer suspects with significant nuclear arsenals, all of them nation-states."

Fox shook his head. "The most likely result of any such attack would be an almost immediate American retaliatory strike against comparable Russian targets. And that would almost certainly lead to a full-scale nuclear exchange."

"You're basically talking World War Three," Hynes realized.

"Yes, I am. And such a conflict would only end with both our nations in radioactive ruins," the older man confirmed. "Now, while Pavel Voronin is quite clearly a psychopath more than willing to kill millions to further his own ends, he is not a fool. Nor is he completely insane. The risks involved in carrying out a nuclear attack against us are simply too great. No perceived reward could conceivably justify running them."

Hynes looked stubborn. "Yeah, I get your point, sir," he said at last. Then he shrugged his shoulders. "I sure hope we're reading this guy right, is all."

Silently, Flynn found himself echoing the sentiment.

Cooke leaned forward in his chair. His expression was somber. "Why wait to find out what he's planning?" he asked.

"We know right where the son of a bitch has his people putting these drones together. So let's send a strike team down there and blow the shit out of them. End of story."

That drew a quiet murmur of agreement.

Fox shook his head in regret. "I wish we could. But unfortunately, carrying out a successful attack on that cartel compound is no longer possible." He toggled the remote control again. New pictures appeared. These were satellite images of the compound itself and the surrounding hills and valleys. Time stamps showed that they had been taken within the past twenty-four hours.

Flynn shook his head at what he saw. The whole area was now an armed camp. The Brotherhood of Blood must have called in muscle from all over the territory it controlled, bringing in hundreds of reinforcements. Dozens of new vehicles were parked around the compound itself and in other places up and down the valley. The neighboring villages appeared to be full of armed men. Even more remarkable, he saw indications that the cartel had its men digging bunkers or other weapons emplacements with clear fields of fire across the neighboring hills and ridges.

Fox was right, he realized. It would require either a full-scale Special Forces assault or an all-out air strike to penetrate those defenses—neither of which was within Four's power. Flynn's jaw tightened. The only organizations with that kind of firepower were the Pentagon and the CIA. And there was no way in hell anyone from the Quartet Directorate would be able to persuade the officials who ran either place to take decisive action, even if by some miracle they could gain a hearing.

He knew in his gut that their guesses about what Voronin was planning were on the right track. But to outsiders, especially those who were slaves to bureaucratic inertia and political considerations, their intelligence would appear fragmentary and almost entirely speculative. Certainly, no one in the current administration would approve a bombing raid, commando assault, or cruise missile strike that deep in sovereign foreign territory, even if it was effectively controlled by a criminal drug cartel. Not on the basis of a few photographs showing unidentified men working on what were completely unidentifiable machines. The resulting political and diplomatic blowback from even a successful attack launched that far into Mexico would be colossal.

All of which meant, Flynn understood with a sudden sinking feeling, that the Quartet Directorate was again completely on its own. No one was coming to the rescue. Hell, no one else was likely to even accept the reality of this developing threat, let alone be willing to meet the challenge head on. Which left the task up to him and the others here with him. A reluctant smile tugged at the corner of his mouth. *Those are some mighty bold words*, he thought. Because one other thing was damned sure: as of this moment, he didn't have the slightest clue of what to do next.

TWENTY-SEVEN

HEADQUARTERS OF THE BROTHERHOOD OF BLOOD, WEST OF DURANGO, MEXICO

THAT SAME TIME

Pavel Voronin followed Joaquin Lopez into the so-called study of Diego Barros. The drug cartel's bald, barrel-chested leader was seated behind an empty desk, waiting for him. The room did not contain a single book or genuine work of art. Instead, its plain, whitewashed walls displayed a morbid collection of both ancient and modern instruments of torture, along with color pictures of murder victims photographed in their own blood—all of them probably former rivals of Barros.

Inwardly, Voronin sneered. He supposed this crude display of torment and death was supposed to intimidate him. Instead, it only confirmed his evaluation of the Brotherhood chief as a savage. Someone who could be useful under certain circumstances, but who could just as easily be discarded if it proved necessary.

This time, Barros did not offer him a chair. There were none besides his own. He did offer the Russian a thin-lipped smile, though it was one that never reached his dark eyes. "El Frío tells me your invisible robot airplanes work," the cartel leader said flatly. *El Frío*, the Cold One, was the nickname first acquired by Lopez back in the days when he was a Brotherhood enforcer renowned for killing efficiently, emotionlessly, and utterly without remorse.

Voronin nodded. "As I promised," he said. He met the other man's cold eyes straight on. "Your first shipments of drugs have already arrived and will be delivered to your people inside the United States at the agreed-upon drop."

Barros ignored that. "In fact, your aircraft work so well," he continued, "that we must renegotiate our agreement, I think."

Ah, Voronin thought with unconstrained cynicism. He could practically see the gears turning in the other man's mind— the mind of a treacherous peasant who believed himself to be clever. It was just as the Russian had expected. "If you want more space for your drugs aboard our flights, I regret to say that is impossible," he said calmly. "Every kilo of payload and fuel is precisely calculated. There is no extra margin for additional cargo. None whatsoever."

Barros smiled. It was an unpleasant expression completely devoid of any humor or goodwill. "You misunderstand me, señor. I do not want to cram more of our product aboard your drones. What I want is one of these fancy aircraft for my own. You see, it has occurred to me and to my people that such a powerful capability would be very useful to us. In any number of different enterprises."

Voronin felt as though he could almost read the other man's thoughts. Barros, like most uneducated criminals who had attained power through brute force and innate viciousness, had a mostly one-track mind. There wasn't an ounce of subtlety or genuine intelligence in his head, only a sort of native shrewdness. The cartel leader was convinced that, armed with a remotely piloted stealth plane of its own, the Brotherhood could assassinate rival gang leaders, blow up their drug factories, and terrorize the authorities with impunity. At a minimum, it would certainly allow the cartel to enormously expand its current territory. Perhaps such a capability could even enable the Brotherhood to become the undisputed criminal power behind the facade of a legal Mexican government.

Voronin feigned surprise. "You do understand that these aircraft, our Moras, are not fully automated," he said carefully. "They require a trained pilot to fly them remotely. And mechanics to maintain them in working condition."

Barros snorted. "Pilots and grease monkeys are no problem. We can buy them ourselves." He waved the issue aside. "What I need from you is one of those control stations, those fake cockpits . . . and training for one of my men in how it is used."

Voronin carefully kept his face immobile. "And if I refuse your request?" He sensed Lopez stiffening beside him.

But Barros only chuckled coarsely. "Oh, I really would not advise such a thing, señor Voronin," he said. "Terrible accidents could so easily happen to your men and to your other precious machines." He shrugged. "That would be tragic, of course, but such events are very, very difficult to avoid when business partners become . . . unsympathetic." The cartel leader nodded meaningfully at the photographs of murdered men crowding his study's walls.

"A cogent argument," Voronin said coolly.

Barros smiled again. "Do not get the wrong idea, my friend. I have no wish to rob you. Only to buy one of your planes. Just one."

Voronin arched an eyebrow. "And how much are you

offering to pay me in return?" he asked, not bothering to hide his skepticism.

"A single aircraft load of product, our best fentanyl. One hundred kilos of a substance ten times more precious than gold," the cartel leader said with mock graciousness. "And it will be yours to keep and use as you wish. Fifty million American dollars' worth. I think that's a fair price."

Voronin said nothing for a few moments. In truth, however, he was delighted. The arrangement Barros proposed was perfect for his own purposes. Finally, he nodded in agreement. "Very well," he said at last, forcing a note of reluctance into his voice. "I agree to this."

He saw the triumphant look Barros shot his subordinate and guessed that Lopez had originally been unsure whether this was a good idea. If so, he thought, *El Frío* had more common sense than his master. But not enough to matter. "However, it will take some time to fly in the computers and other equipment you will need to set up a piloting station here," he warned. "And more time to train someone, even someone with flying experience, to safely operate one of our Mora drones at a distance."

Both Barros and Lopez shrugged, apparently unfazed by the prospect of the necessary delay. And no wonder, Voronin thought coldly, when it was abundantly clear that his operation here would be effectively held hostage until he made good on his promise.

TAVERNA OPA, ORLANDO, FLORIDA
THE NEXT DAY

Besides its theme parks, hotels, nightclubs, and other attractions, Orlando's International Drive was also home to hundreds of restaurants, ranging from popular chain options to locally owned hot spots. One of them, Taverna Opa, happened to be one of Laura Van Horn's favorites—sometimes for the sheer wild energy of its crowded, noisy, exuberant dinner hour, complete with belly dancing—but at other times as a place for a quieter lunch outside on its shaded patio. Times like today's afternoon outing with Nick Flynn.

"Enough moping, Mr. Flynn," she had ordered earlier, after finding him in the Avalon House study hunched over a computer screen filled with digital maps of the terrain around Voronin's aircraft-assembly building. He'd been plotting the Brotherhood defenses shown on their satellite photos and trying, futilely so far, to figure out some way a small force could penetrate them without getting shot to pieces in the process.

"I'm not moping," he'd protested. "I'm planning."

Van Horn had only shaken her head dismissively. "Planning is when you're contemplating action with some chance of success, however small. Moping is when you bang your head over and over against a tactical problem that can't be solved. *This*"— she'd pointed at the screen—"is moping."

With a rueful shrug, Flynn had yielded. "Okay, so I'm not getting anywhere here. What's your idea?"

She'd smiled down at him. "We go elsewhere. Specifically, out to lunch. The world may look brighter with some food and a couple of drinks in you. And if not, well, hell, it still won't hurt you any. Or me, for that matter."

Slowly, Flynn had allowed a smile of his own to appear. "All right, I surrender. I'm willing to be distracted for a bit." He looked her up and down. "After all, it's not every day that a beautiful woman offers to buy me lunch."

Van Horn had raised a haughty eyebrow. "Me? Buy *you* lunch? Oh, no, Mr. Flynn, this is your treat."

"Hey!" he'd blurted. "You practically order me to take you out for a meal, and then I wind up paying for it? How does that work?"

In answer, she'd smiled pityingly. "Beautiful woman, remember?"

Flynn hadn't seen any way to argue against that.

Now they were seated at a table outside the main restaurant. It was a sunny, warm spring day, with only a few towering white masses of cloud on the horizon to warn that the usual late-afternoon thunderstorms were possible. They were sharing a couple of small plates—a traditional Greek salad of cucumber, tomato, red onion, and olive, as well as crispy slices of zucchini with kasseri cheese and tzatziki, a yogurt sauce with hints of garlic, cucumber, dill, and other herbs. A pitcher of sangria sat between them.

Distractedly, Flynn poked at the food in front of him. Try as he might, he couldn't stop niggling at the problem of how to get at the unmanned aircraft Voronin was building—at least long enough to destroy them. Well, that, and also how to do the job without being killed. The Quartet Directorate recruited men and women who were willing to risk their lives for a larger cause. It did not enlist would-be kamikazes.

Van Horn waved a hand in front of his face. "Hey, nonfly-boy, up here. Remember me? Your charming and, if I do say so myself, reasonably attractive lunch companion?"

He looked across the table, feeling his face redden slightly. "Sorry, Laura," he apologized. "I feel a little like a mouse stuck in a complicated maze. I know there's a piece of cheese out there somewhere, if only I could find it."

With a dry look, she wagged a finger at him. "I respect the work ethic, boyo. But all work and no play risks making Nick a very dull boy." Then she nodded over toward the plaza beyond the patio. Taverna Opa was on the second level of a collection of stores and restaurants and theaters. From where they were seated, they had a view out across a row of palm trees and a sparkling fountain. "Besides, you need to smile. We're on candid camera here."

Flynn saw what she meant. A small quadcopter drone was flying out over the plaza, zooming around only a couple of dozen feet above the surface. It jigged and slid through the air, pausing now and again to hover motionless. He glanced around and saw its controller, a teenage boy, seated a few tables over from them. While the other members of his family were busy with their food and animated conversation, the kid was totally fixated on the small handheld controller he was using to fly his little rotor-driven craft.

Neat toy, Flynn thought. He wouldn't have minded having one like it when he was that same age. Of course, he probably would have ended up in detention or juvenile hall for trying something crazy like rigging the drone to drop lighted firecrackers over a rival school's marching band or football team. So all in all, it was probably just as well that he'd missed his chance.

With an amused snort, he started to turn back to Van Horn . . . and then froze, still eyeing the controller in the kid's hand. *Jesus*, he thought, in amazement, *that's it.* That was the answer he'd been looking for all along.

"Um, Nick, are you okay?" he heard Van Horn ask. "Because you're just sitting there with your mouth practically hanging open and a wild look in those eyes of yours. Kind of like the maniacal expression a movie mad scientist gets right before he starts shouting, 'It's alive! It's alive!'"

With an effort, Flynn dragged his gaze away from the teenage kid flying his drone. He shook his head. "I'm fine. I think." He looked across the table at her. "It's just that I suddenly realized we've been coming at this problem of wrecking Voronin's operation from totally the wrong angle."

Van Horn cocked her head slightly to one side. "Okay, shoot."

"Since we can't preemptively destroy those unmanned aircraft on the ground, we have to find another chink in the Raven Syndicate's armor, right?"

She nodded. "Sure. One nice opening between a couple of steel plates and some sharp, pointy daggers in our hot little hands equals a very bad day for our Russian friends." She frowned in thought. "So what do you have in mind?"

"Their command and control node," Flynn said.

Van Horn stared at him for a moment. Then she glanced over at the teenager flying the drone. One side of her mouth quirked upward in an approving smile. "You mean, if we can't take out the machines themselves, we nail the men behind those machines, instead?"

"Yep." His calculus was simple. The Raven Syndicate's drones could probably fly autonomously in some circumstances, but they almost certainly needed humans to pilot them remotely for any complicated maneuvers—or to carry out missile launches or bombing runs against important targets. There was intensive research going on to develop the hardware and software solutions needed for unmanned air vehicles to fly and fight entirely on their own, but no one yet seemed to have fully cracked that code. All of which meant that Voronin would need a control center somewhere, one equipped with secure satellite communications, data links, and remote-piloting stations.

Van Horn's grin widened. "I like your idea. We cut the Gordian knot by zapping a bunch of Russian drone jockeys instead of beating our brains out trying to smash the aircraft themselves. In that case, if he winds up without any working command

and control over his pet air force, Voronin is screwed." Then she sighed. "Unfortunately, that still leaves us facing some big damned challenges, Nick."

He nodded. "Yeah, like, can we even find this hypothetical control center, for one thing. Let alone organize a successful attack against it."

"If the remote-piloting center is sited somewhere in Russian territory, we're probably out of luck," she warned. "Even setting aside the logistical nightmares involved in sneaking a strike force of any size across the frontier, the politics of it likely make that a total no-go. I sure can't see Four's various heads of station approving the idea. An act of sabotage maybe. But they definitely won't green-light a significant use of armed force on Russian home soil."

Flynn knew she was right. From its start in the earliest days of the developing Cold War, the Quartet Directorate had relied on a collegial approach to leadership. Its founders, all veterans of the war against Nazi Germany and violently opposed to Stalin's Soviet tyranny, were only too aware that power corrupted and absolute power corrupted absolutely. They wanted no part in creating an organization that tried to run its secret war against the enemies of the free world from the top down. So as a safeguard, and if there was time for consultation, all of Four's large-scale or unusually dangerous operations required explicit approval from the separate national stations around the world. Short of being able to prove that it was either that or seeing the United States destroyed, the odds of winning permission to carry out a major assault inside Russia itself were probably somewhere between slim and none—with the emphasis on *none*.

But would Voronin really want his remote-piloting center sited on Russian soil? Flynn wondered. At every other stage of this operation—whatever its real intent—he seemed to have been exercising extreme caution to minimize the evidence of Russian involvement. Whether it was orchestrating his stealth-technology thefts through a phony import-export company based in Dubai or shipping aircraft parts into Mexico aboard a plane nominally owned by some Venezuelan airfreight company. Maybe he was trying to insulate Moscow from culpability if the operation was blown too soon. Or maybe he wanted to run his own show, without the chance of interference by Zhdanov or others in the Russian president's inner circle.

When Flynn said as much out loud, Van Horn nodded. "Yeah, I can see that. Voronin is pretty much the poster boy of the 'does not play well with others' side of the human race." She considered the possible options. "Could he be stashing his pilots and their equipment somewhere else in the Brotherhood's territory?"

Flynn shook his head. "The same reasoning applies. Voronin's too smart and too controlling to want to give a bunch of drug-running thugs complete veto power over his plans. As it is, I bet he's not really that happy he has to depend on the narcos to guard his aircraft-assembly plant."

"So where then?" she asked reasonably.

"Some country that's friendly to Russia," he said, working it out. "But not one like Belarus that's practically controlled by Moscow. If he tried to run his operation out of a place like Minsk, for example, he might as well just hand over the keys to Zhdanov or the regular Russian military."

"You're thinking about Venezuela," Van Horn realized.

"Or Cuba," Flynn agreed. "We know Voronin's spent time recently in both countries. And up to now, we didn't know why. Well, maybe now we do." He started to get up from his chair.

Van Horn laid a hand over his wrist. "Whoa there, cowboy. Just where do you think you're going?"

He stared at her. "We need to ask Fox to lease some more satellite time," he said.

"We sure do," she replied. "But *not* until after we finish lunch." She smiled up at him. "Relax, Nick. Wherever that SOB Voronin has his remote-flight ops center, it's sure as hell not going to up and disappear anytime in the next half hour or so. Is it?"

Slowly, Flynn sat back down. "I guess not," he conceded.

"Besides," she went on, with a hint of amusement now plain in her voice, "you haven't paid the check yet. And *nobody* stiffs Laura Van Horn on a lunch date." She laughed. "Well, not anyone who's ever lived to tell about it, anyway."

TWENTY-EIGHT

UPPER-FLOOR STUDY, AVALON HOUSE

SOME DAYS LATER

Irritably, Flynn scrolled through to another pair of satellite photos on his laptop screen. These showed an area near El Libertador Air Base in the central region of Venezuela. A key click split the screen in half, with the newest picture of this area on the left and an older one obtained from public databases on the right. He zoomed in across both images, slowly panning across the array of barracks, hangars, aircraft shelters, and other structures. It was careful, painstaking work—requiring intense concentration over a period of several minutes to be even reasonably sure he wasn't missing anything.

In fact, Flynn was staring so hard that the screen suddenly seemed to blur. He pinched his nose tight and blinked rapidly a few times to clear his vision. The pictures swam back into focus. Not that it made any difference, he realized bleakly. There were no significant differences between the two images. They were virtually identical. His mouth tightened. *Scratch one more possibility*, he thought. A quick mouse swipe sent both satellite photos to the shared computer folder he and Laura Van Horn were using to hold sites they'd evaluated and ruled out.

It was just as well the hard drive storage folder was digital, he decided dryly. If they'd been stacking printed photos onto the desk between them, the pile would be at least a foot high by now. Or more likely, he knew, one of them would have hurled the whole damned stack halfway across the room in frustration—strewing photos across the floor every which way.

Over the past few days, Flynn and Van Horn had spent dozens of hours combing through hundreds and hundreds of satellite photos taken from orbit over Cuba and Venezuela. Although plenty of others—Cooke, Hynes, and the rest—had volunteered to help, they were the only two people at Avalon House with anything like the specialized training required to do the work. Photo interpretation was almost as much an art as it was a science.

On the theory that military form almost always followed function, they were using orbital photos of existing US Air Force installations dedicated to UAV operations as their models. These ROCCs (remote operations control centers) could generally be identified by clusters of large satellite dishes parked close to highly air-conditioned buildings and trailers. Remote-piloting stations relied on serious computing power, and computers needed to stay cool and dry to run efficiently.

Flynn frowned. So far, all he and Laura had managed to do was establish the yawning chasm between theory and practice. They'd eyeballed images of military bases, airfields, government installations, and other compounds across the length and breadth of both Venezuela and Cuba—looking for signs, any signs at all, of the new structures and equipment that might signal the construction of a UAV remote-piloting center. To no avail. Good as his hunch at Taverna Opa had seemed at the time, they'd come up empty handed.

Exasperated, he pushed his chair back and stood up to stretch his sore back and shoulders. "Christ," he muttered. He could hear the deep, deep tiredness in his own voice. Caffeine and catnaps could keep him going for a long time, but there were limits. And right now, sheer exhaustion, coupled with the sense that they were getting nowhere fast, had him right on the edge of a crash. "What if we're wrong about this?" he wondered.

Van Horn looked up from her own screen and rubbed at her bloodshot eyes. "Then we're out of luck, Nick," she told him with a quick twist of her shoulders. "And we move on to plan B."

Flynn stared at her. "What *is* our plan B?"

Van Horn grinned back at him. "Oh, hell if I know. I leave all the intricate operational details to ground-pounding weenies like you." More seriously, she went on. "But see, I figure we're *not* wrong. Your basic reasoning is solid. Voronin's got himself a remote ops center, all right. And ten to one it *is* sited somewhere in Cuba or Venezuela."

"Then why haven't we been able to spot it yet?" he demanded.

"Because I'm beginning to think that while we are looking in the right places, we might not be looking for the right visual cues," Van Horn said quietly. "I mean, if nothing else, the CIA and our other government intel outfits pour huge resources into satellite reconnaissance. And they've got thousands of specialists employed full time analyzing all those pictures, right?"

"Sure," Flynn said.

"Well, since we know Voronin isn't an idiot, he's got to figure that even the goofballs at Langley might start wondering why something that looks like a brand-spanking-new UAV control station has just popped up outside Havana or

Caracas or wherever," she reasoned. "Especially since neither
Venezuela nor Cuba has a real fleet of unmanned aircraft, outside of a couple of dinky, relatively short-ranged types." She
shrugged. "And the last thing he wants is for anyone in DC
to start taking a closer look at his operations. Not if whatever
he's planning depends as much on surprise and misdirection
as we believe."

Flynn nodded. Then he sighed. "But there are still real limits
to how much anyone can disguise the kinds of high-powered
dishes you need for secure, high-speed data links to military
communications satellites," he argued. "So even if Voronin's
swaddled his Satcom dishes in camouflage netting from top
to bottom, we should still be able to pick up some differences,
however small, when we compare our new satellite photos with
the older images of the same area."

"Why assume that Voronin is planning on using military communications satellites to link with his remote-piloted
planes?" Van Horn asked gently. "After all, sometimes a satellite
is just a satellite, isn't it?"

For a long, frozen moment, Flynn stared at her in silence.
Memories of the hundreds of images he'd studied so closely
rushed through his mind in a dizzying torrent. *Son of a bitch*,
he thought, stunned that he'd missed something so obvious
on the first pass. He *had* seen something in one of those sets
of photos. An anomaly he'd briefly wondered about and then
foolishly discarded as irrelevant because it didn't fit his precon-
ceptions. And that, he realized with a feeling of embarrassed
dismay, was just as much a mistake in intelligence work as it
was in science. The moment you ignored an observed fact because it didn't match your theories was the moment you strayed
into fundamental error.

"I'm an idiot," he growled, dropping back into his chair

and pulling his laptop back closer. His hands flew across the keyboard, rapidly inputting search terms to cull through their shared discards folder for two particular satellite photographs.

"Don't be too hard on yourself, Nick," Van Horn said consolingly. She shot him a dry look. "There are probably plenty of people dumber than you out there in the world. Maybe even hundreds of them."

Flynn refrained from any retort to her affectionate teasing. He had it coming. Just then, the two images he'd been searching for popped onto his screen. He stared hard at them for several seconds. Damn, he thought. There was the answer. He looked up at her with a gleam in his eyes. "Dumb I may be," he said. He entered a new command on his keyboard. "But I think you just might be a certified genius."

Van Horn shrugged. "Well, yeah," she said. "So much for all those *muy macho* clowns in flight school who thought I was nothing but a pretty face—" She broke off as the two satellite images he'd just sent to her computer appeared.

"Take a look at those," Flynn said simply.

The first picture, taken just a couple of days ago, showed a large, squat, apparently windowless concrete building surrounded by at least half a square mile of farmland and light forest. The isolated building's flat roof was dotted with a dozen white domes. Judging by the scale, each dome was somewhere around the height of an average man and shaped something like a golf ball. They were arranged in three rows of four separate domes. Cables connected them and ran into some sort of metal junction box at one end of the roof.

In the second satellite picture, taken during a pass several months before, that same stretch of flat roof was empty.

Van Horn's eyes narrowed. She tapped the side of her screen. "What do you think those white dome things are?"

In answer, Flynn entered another search query, pulled up a third photo, and sent it to her. "Weatherproof protective radomes covering Starlink satellite internet antennas," he said.

She studied the image, drawn from the internet. Taken at a Starlink ground station, it showed an array of very similar-looking white domes. She frowned. "You think Voronin plans to connect to his unmanned aircraft through the Starlink constellation?" Starlink was a massive new commercial enterprise designed to provide high-speed internet to every part of the globe. Several thousand of its tiny satellites were already in low earth orbit, with hundreds more being launched at a rapid tempo.

"Why not?" Flynn asked. "The guys in our own military already want to piggyback onto the Starlink system, since it's usually faster, with significantly less lag, than connecting through our bigger, dedicated com satellites higher up in geosynchronous orbit. Voronin would see the same advantages." He smiled crookedly. "Plus, it's not a Russian-owned platform."

"One more piece of plausible deniability," Van Horn acknowledged. "And of course, there's the juicy, ironic evilness of using the well-intentioned efforts of an American-owned company to assist the Raven Syndicate's dirty work." She darted a finger at the satellite photos. "Okay, so where is this place?"

"Just outside Havana," Flynn said. He leaned over to point at a larger complex east of the building now covered in Starlink satellite antennas. It was a campus of other, taller buildings connected by broad avenues and tree-lined walkways. Interspersed throughout this area were what looked like sports fields, parking lots, and some kind of residential housing. "That used to be the Lourdes Signals Intelligence Station, the largest Soviet spy base in the entire Western Hemisphere."

She raised an eyebrow. "I thought Lourdes was shut down when the Cold War ended?"

"It was," he said with a quick nod. "But the Cuban government took over the whole facility and expanded it into what they're calling their University of Information Sciences."

"Which means what?"

Flynn grimaced. "From what I can see, cybersecurity work and a lot of other high-tech buzzwords that I really don't have time to dig into. The kind of stuff they call 'bioinformatic engineering.'"

Van Horn winced in sympathy. "Ugh. I see what you mean."

"Anyway," he continued more enthusiastically, "what better place to hide a control center for unmanned aircraft than right next to a high-tech campus already bristling with computers?"

She nodded cautiously. "Or maybe those Starlink stations are just a coincidence," she warned. "They could just represent an investment to bring faster internet connections to Geek Squad U there."

"Could be," Flynn allowed. "Which is why we'll need to do some digging into the source of those Starlink antennas. To see who paid for them, for example." He shrugged. "Personally, though, I'm willing to take odds that their sudden appearance has a lot to do with Voronin's otherwise unexplained stopover in Havana a while back."

"Ah," Van Horn said in understanding. "The whole: once is happenstance, twice is coincidence, and three times is—"

"Enemy action," Flynn said quietly, finishing the classic Ian Fleming quote from *Goldfinger*.

He waited patiently while she brought up new satellite photos from the wider area around the old Lourdes intelligence base. Her lips pursed as she noted its proximity to Havana and the sizable Cuban army garrison there, a major fighter base, and multiple surface-to-air missile sites. When she was done, Van Horn turned back to him. She had a slight worried frown on her face. "You know, Nick," she said, "I kind of hope that you're wrong about this. Because if you are right, that damned place is the very definition of a hornet's nest. And hitting it is going to be one grade-A, Do-Not-Pass-Go bitch of an operation."

TWENTY-NINE

MORA REMOTE OPERATIONS CENTER,
SOUTHWEST OF HAVANA

THAT SAME TIME

Pavel Voronin paced briskly down the corridor separating the two rows of flight control bays. At the entrance to each cubicle, a flight-suited pilot, all veterans of Russia's Air Force now working for him, stiffened to attention as he passed by. Behind each man there was a workstation crammed full of computer hardware, a large display screen, a keyboard, and a pair of flight controllers.

Voronin nodded to himself in satisfaction. All of that sophisticated equipment enabled each of these pilots to fly one of the Mora drones remotely from takeoff to landing or weapons delivery—using the information supplied by its cameras and other sensors. Through their secure satellite data links, the men safely inside this reinforced concrete-and-steel bunker would send the soulless machines under their command into battle.

He glanced down at the shorter man striding beside him. "You've done well, Maresyev."

In response, the left side of Fyodor Maresyev's face twitched. The right side, crisscrossed by burn scars, remained immobile. "So far, we're on track," the former Tu-22M bomber regiment commander agreed.

"And you've had no problems on your flights north?" Voronin asked. He'd read the other man's written reports, but he'd learned long ago to put a higher value on information delivered in person. It was harder to successfully gloss over unpleasant facts or events when someone was staring you right in the face.

"Major challenges? No," Maresyev said. He shrugged. "Minor glitches? Of course. Several of my pilots have experienced small periods of greater-than-expected data lag on the transfer flights from Mexico. But only over isolated mountain regions . . . places that are not yet fully served by the existing Starlink constellation."

Voronin nodded. "So you do not expect to encounter similar problems on your attack flights?"

"None at all," Maresyev told him with confidence. "True, each small individual American satellite isn't nearly as capable or powerful as the military communications satellites we have deployed in geosynchronous orbit. But there are thousands of these smaller satellites in orbit now. What each may lack in size, they more than make up when operating as a coordinated whole. When the day comes, my pilots won't have any trouble flying their Moras into striking range of every target you've assigned them."

Voronin's smile in response was almost wolfish. "Quantity has a quality all of its own," he said with approval, using a phrase often attributed to Stalin.

They reached the solid, inches-thick steel door that separated the flight operations center from the compound outside. Two ex-Spetsnaz commandos were on guard there, bulky in combat helmets and body armor. Each carried a compact 9mm SR-2M Veresk submachine gun at the ready.

"I take it you prefer to provide your own security inside this building?" Voronin asked in an undertone. "Rather than rely on our Cuban . . . auxiliaries?"

Maresyev nodded in reply. "Colonel Hidalgo's troops are extremely competent," he said. "But I thought it unwise to post any of his men in here." He indicated the row of computer flight consoles. "Especially since we often run full-scale attack simulations which include detailed maps and digitized aerial views of our planned targets. Along with computerized assessments of the damage inflicted by our weapons."

"Sensible," Voronin approved. "There are indeed key elements of CASTLE KEEP that our allies should not comprehend. Not, at least, until it is far too late for them to get cold feet." He turned to face the shorter man. "Good work, Fyodor. Keep the Cubans in the dark as much as possible. After all, they're being amply paid to provide the soldiers and heavy weapons we need to guard your outer perimeter. Beyond that task, they don't need to know anything."

NEAR THE MARINE TERMINAL, SAINT PETERSBURG, RUSSIA
A COUPLE OF DAYS LATER

In all its gray drabness, the ferry building hovered over the waterfront. Veneers of curving concrete around the windows lining each floor were supposed to suggest canvas sails caught by the wind. Instead, stained by decades of exposure to the elements and pollution, they reminded observers more of the heavy drapes preferred in lower-end hotels where housecleaning was not a priority and the darker the rooms were kept, the fewer complaints the management would receive.

Standing outside the terminal, Major Leonid Kazmin checked his watch for what seemed to be the thousandth time. And also for the thousandth time, he saw that the ferry to Helsinki was not scheduled to board its passengers anytime soon. It would be at least forty-five minutes, which was just one minute sooner than the last time he'd looked. The youngest and lowest ranking of the Twelfth Main Directorate officers in Voronin's pay was painfully aware that his nerves were rubbed raw. He'd contemplated getting a couple of drinks to settle them, but the noise level inside the ferry building bar had been even more shattering—as had been the prospect of having to crowd in elbow to elbow with the other travelers headed to Finland.

He felt inside his jacket to make sure the forged passport and other false identity papers he'd been given were still there. His throat felt dry. Voronin had assured him over and over that the documents were good enough to stand up to close scrutiny. Now, faced with the prospect of having to rely on them to avoid arrest, interrogation, and likely imprisonment as a spy, those promises seemed hollow. The Finns were no longer even pretending to be neutral in the new cold war between Russia and the West. If they caught a Russian military officer traveling incognito, especially one with access to highly classified nuclear secrets, the consequences would be unthinkable. Although, Kazmin considered worriedly, *unthinkable* was probably the wrong word, since he found himself able to think all too clearly about his probable fate if this trip went wrong.

The major started to check his watch again. This time, though, he was able to stop himself from glancing down at his wrist. It would be better, he decided, to at least mentally run through the plan to covertly infiltrate him into the United States.

Step one was getting to Helsinki. Once there, he would assume another identity, this time a Ukrainian businessman, and travel by rail to Stockholm. From Sweden, he had tickets for a commercial air flight to Canada. Shortly after arriving in Toronto, he was supposed to cross the US border using his third set of false papers, ones that identified him as a naturalized Canadian citizen of eastern European origin.

Kazmin sighed, thinking about the ordeal ahead. His language skills were good, which was one reason he'd been selected for this assignment. There was no use, however, in pretending he was a trained intelligence operative. But when he'd tried making that point, Voronin's reply had been pointed. "I don't need another spy in the US, Major," he'd said icily. "But I do need a weapons specialist. And the odds of slipping you safely across the American border are considerably higher than the odds of somehow training a GRU operative to become a nuclear expert in the next few days, are they not?" Remembering the implied threat in Voronin's pale-gray eyes, Kazmin shivered. As cold as the brisk wind coming off the nearby Baltic Sea now felt, those eyes had been colder still.

Kazmin looked up suddenly as a long black Aurus Senat L700 limousine pulled up to the curb right beside him. With its Porsche-developed, twin-turbocharged 4.4-liter V8 engine, the Senat was the Russian equivalent of a top-of-the-line Cadillac or a Rolls-Royce Ghost. They were only available to the very rich and the very powerful. Men like Pavel Voronin.

Doors popped open on the limousine, and two tough-looking men in dark jackets climbed out. One stepped up to him. "Get in the car . . . Major Kazmin," the man said in a low, harsh voice.

The major swallowed hard. Obeying, he slid into the back seat. The door slammed shut behind him.

But instead of Voronin, Kazmin found himself face to face

with President Piotr Zhdanov himself. On instinct, he tried to stiffen to attention, a futile gesture while seated, even in the limousine's spacious passenger compartment.

"Relax, Major," Zhdanov said. His gaze hardened. "But listen carefully. Very, very carefully."

Kazmin bobbed his head. "Sir."

"I'm here to make one addition to your orders for this mission to the United States," the president said. He then shrugged. "Nothing extraordinary, of course. Just a small piece of extra insurance I consider essential for the security of the state." His mouth thinned. "And I have been assured that what I ask is well within your competence, Major."

"Yes, Mr. President," Kazmin hurried to reply. There was no other possible response.

Zhdanov nodded, evidently satisfied. "Excellent." He lifted a briefcase up onto the seat between them. "Now, to business." He popped the catches on the case and spun it around to face Kazmin. "This is the equipment you will need to fulfill my instructions."

The major stared into the open briefcase. He saw what looked like a smartphone case. Next to it was a very small gray metal cylinder and an even tinier twelve-volt power supply. Together those two items were no bigger than a ballpoint pen.

"Camouflaged inside that phone case is a special circuit card," Zhdanov told him. "Once you have the opportunity to study this card more closely, you should not have any difficulty recognizing its type and intended purpose."

Kazmin licked lips that suddenly felt as dry as the arid Kazakh Steppes, where the old Soviet Union had tested its nuclear weapons for decades. "Yes, sir."

Zhdanov touched the gray cylinder. "And this is a VLF, very low frequency, radio antenna. Together with its power supply, this is the second component I need you to install—as I direct." Then, carefully and very precisely, he told the major exactly what he wanted him to do.

When the president finished, Kazmin was pale.

Zhdanov eyed him sternly. "You realize, I hope, Major, that it is not necessary, nor would it be wise, for you to repeat this conversation to anyone else—most especially not to our mutual friend Pavel Voronin. Is that quite clear?"

"I understand completely, Mr. President," Kazmin stammered, aware of his pulse pounding in his ears. He felt queasy. This was a game far above his pay grade. "And I will do exactly as you order."

Zhdanov nodded curtly. "A sensible decision." He pushed a button on the armrest at his side. Immediately, the car door next to Kazmin was pulled open by one of the bodyguards. Quite evidently, this clandestine audience was at an end.

As the younger man slid out with the briefcase in his hand, sweating now despite the cold sea breeze, Zhdanov leaned toward him. "Good luck on your mission, Major," he said. There was absolutely no trace of warmth in the president's eyes, only a steely resolve. "But remember, do not fail me. Do not fail Russia. Because if you screw this up, I promise that your life will be short and extremely unpleasant."

THIRTY

AVALON HOUSE, WINTER PARK

THAT SAME TIME

For several minutes, Fox examined the satellite photos in absolute silence. At last, he looked over toward where Nick Flynn and Laura Van Horn sat on the other side of his desk. "You're sure about this?" he asked.

Flynn nodded. "Yeah, we are. The Lourdes site is definitely our target." He leaned forward. "We've spent the past couple of days tracing the purchase of those Starlink antennas. It turns out they were 'donated' to Cuba's University of Information Sciences by a privately owned company."

"Let me guess," Fox said. "By Wickham Imports and Exports of Dubai."

Flynn grinned. "Got it in one." He sat back. "Georgy Bazhanov, alias Simon Jones, seems to have been a very busy boy. And generous as hell for a guy without any discernible above-the-table source of income."

"The total cost for all that Starlink gear runs to around a

million bucks," Van Horn cut in. "And rich as he is, we don't see Voronin approving one of his operatives doling out that kind of money just to boost internet speeds for a bunch of budding Cuban computer engineers."

Fox smiled thinly in agreement. "It would be out of character."

"We enhanced the most recent photos of the area around that concrete, bunker-like building," Flynn went on. "And we're confident that there are vehicles and other military hardware camouflaged and dug in all around it to form a defensive perimeter. Most are probably concealed inside those patches of woods just north and south of the building. But there's a weird shadow clearly visible in one early-morning pass—stretching out of the tree line across some open ground. We enlarged that section, and the shadow's definitely being thrown by a good-sized vehicle with some type of weapons turret."

Van Horn nodded. "And nobody deploys tanks to guard civilian tech-nerd internet hubs. Not even in the Silicon Valley."

Fox frowned. "I don't see any sort of perimeter fence in those photos," he said carefully. "Or any other kind of fixed defenses."

"Nope," Flynn said. "Then again, what's the first thing you'd think if you saw a barbed wire fence surrounding a building? Or pillboxes guarding the approaches?"

"That there was something worth guarding inside it," the older man realized.

Flynn nodded. "Voronin's got to be walking a fine line here. That building's important enough for him to deploy a serious amount of firepower to protect it. But at the same time, he sure as hell doesn't want to call any unwanted attention to what he's doing there."

"How much firepower?" Fox asked. "Give me your best guess, Nick."

Flynn shrugged. "That's tough to say." He narrowed his eyes. "But based on the amount of ground they need to defend, I'd estimate at least a company-sized force—probably a mix of infantry and light armored vehicles and heavy weapons. That'd let them keep a platoon, say thirty or forty troops, on alert at any given moment."

"A company of soldiers," Fox repeated. "As a local garrison?"

Flynn nodded.

"And Havana itself is—?"

"Roughly six miles away," Flynn admitted.

"With how many Cuban army troops and other security forces based in and around the city?"

Flynn gave him a rueful grin. "A bunch. As in several thousand at least, with attached armor and artillery."

Fox took a short breath and then let it out. "Plus, if I remember correctly, there's also a major military airfield nearby?"

This time it was Van Horn's turn to answer. "Yep, about eight miles off," she said. "But the best intelligence I've seen is that the Cubans can't have more than a handful of MiG-23 fighter-bombers and MiG-29 interceptors stationed at that base."

"MiG-23s and MiG-29s," Fox said with emphasis. "Against which any civilian aircraft or helicopter would be—?"

"Dead meat," Van Horn acknowledged. "That is, assuming those Cuban planes ever got off the ground, of course." She smiled. "But we might have a say in that question. If we do things intelligently, that is."

Fox shook his head. "All right. You've sold me that this Lourdes site is where the pilots for Voronin's unmanned aircraft are based. But I cannot see any practical point in attempting an attack on the operations center there, especially considering the strength of its defenses." His mouth thinned. "Besides, even if, by some unforeseen miracle, we could knock it out, we wouldn't achieve any lasting effect. Voronin would simply recruit new pilots and set up new flight control stations—this time in some location that's entirely out of our reach. Once that's done, he'd be ready to pull the trigger again at a moment of his own choosing."

"That remote flight control center doesn't represent a single point source of failure for his operation," Van Horn agreed easily. "Not like knocking those drones out of the sky or, better yet, blowing them up on the ground."

"Which we are manifestly *not* in a position to do," Fox said with a gloomy expression on his narrow face. "Not while they're so closely guarded by the cartel."

She shook her head. "Oh, it's worse than that, Br'er Fox," she said. "Because I'm pretty sure we don't actually know where those unmanned aircraft are right now. Or at least not most of them."

He stared at her. "What am I missing?"

"I've been running the numbers," Van Horn explained. "We tracked at least five of those freight-jet deliveries to Durango, right? That's more than five hundred tons of cargo. And there's no way—no way on God's little green earth—that much stuff fits inside the compound Nick scouted. Not if it's being turned into completed airframes, anyway."

"Wonderful," Fox murmured. He looked across the desk at the two of them. "Do you have any thoughts on where these stealth planes might be going?"

"Somewhere north," Flynn said.

"Somewhere inside the US or Canada," Van Horn amplified.

Fox looked as though he'd bitten into something sour. "Is there any evidence of that?"

"Beyond a weird uptick in ranchers near the border claiming to have heard UFOs flying overhead at night? No," Van Horn said. Then she shrugged. "But where else makes sense? Those drones sure aren't headed for Cuba or Venezuela. If nothing else, our intel agencies in DC still keep their beady little eyes open watching for funny business in both of those two places. But like Nick said earlier, the deserts and mountains between us and Mexico are wide open to penetration by stealth aircraft."

"Which leaves about seven million square miles of possible hiding places," Flynn clarified. "This is a big, big country with a lot of elbow room. And Canada's even bigger. Even if we rule out areas that are too close to densely populated urban centers or active-duty Air Force and other military bases, there's a hell of a lot of rural countryside and uninhabited wilderness to choose from. And it's not like Voronin even requires a bunch of infrastructure. All he needs is some place to park those aircraft out of sight until he wants to use them."

"You don't think they'd need a landing strip or runway?" Fox asked.

Van Horn shook her head. "Nope. We already know that you can operate heavy modern fighters off stretches of highway in wartime. As small and light as these Russian UCAVs probably are, my bet is they can land and take off on any good-sized piece of road . . . so long as it's relatively straight and reasonably level."

A long, heavy silence followed while Fox contemplated the bad news he'd just heard. The probability that Voronin now had unmanned combat aircraft hidden somewhere in the vastness of the North American continent was ugly enough. What made it even worse was the Quartet Directorate's complete inability to conduct any kind of realistic search. Even calling in every part-timer who worked for Four on a contract basis, the odds of them zeroing in on wherever the Russian was concealing his planes were about the same as using a soup spoon to strain the Atlantic for an earring lost overboard.

At last, Flynn broke in on the older man's dour thoughts. "We don't really have a choice here," he said. "Either we sit back and do nothing, or we hit the one solid target we've been able to identify—Voronin's remote flight control center. At a minimum, destroying it buys us time. Maybe months. Certainly a few weeks."

Almost unwillingly, Fox nodded. "And perhaps the horse can learn to sing," he mused, remembering the old story of the thief under sentence of death who'd promised a king he could teach his horse to sing within a year. When challenged by a fellow prisoner for the sheer lunacy of his pledge, the thief had said, "Much can happen in a year. The king may die. I may die. And maybe the horse will learn to sing."

Flynn grinned, catching the reference. "Besides that, a successful smash-and-grab raid also gives us a shot at picking up intel about where those drones are based," he continued. "Intel that might be solid enough to prod the national security powers that be into doing their damn job for once."

"It sure would be nice to see our tax dollars at work for a change," Van Horn agreed with a sardonic smile.

Fox nodded slowly. "I see your point." Then he shook his head. "However, the problem with your analysis of this situation is the word 'successful.' Because judging from what you've told me about its defenses, I cannot see how a raid against that control center would be anything but an exercise in futility." He sighed. "The need to risk agents' lives to accomplish vital missions is something I live with every day. It's a responsibility that comes with my job as the head of this station. What I do not accept is the idea of wasting those same lives for no possible gain."

"Well, as one of those lowly agents, I certainly appreciate that sentiment, Br'er Fox," Flynn told him gravely. "But here's where appearances may be deceiving. Despite our hard-earned reputations, neither Laura nor I are completely crazy."

Fox studied him for a moment. "Meaning the two of you have come up with a plan?"

"One that might even work," Flynn told him with a quick smile. He unfolded a large-scale topographical map of the area around Havana across the older man's desk. He and Van Horn had spent a couple of hours before this meeting marking the location of every Cuban army and security-force garrison and every known fixed surface-to-air missile battery in the region. The military airfield at San Antonio de los Baños, eight miles south of Voronin's control center, was ringed in red.

Fox stared down at the map briefly, absorbing the information it contained. He looked up. "All right, Nick. Brief me."

"Task one is eliminating the local security forces guarding Voronin's flight operations center," Flynn said. He tapped the map at that spot. "That's doable, if we hit them hard and fast. And if we can catch the defenders with their pants down." His grin tightened. "Speed and surprise are the key force multipliers for every part of this plan. With them, we have a chance. If we lose the element of surprise or bog down, we're fucked."

Fox nodded in understanding. Given sufficient surprise, even a small group of attackers could wreak tremendous damage on an opposing force.

"Task two, naturally, is destroying Voronin's remote control center once we eliminate the outside security force. And, of course, retrieving as much intelligence as possible about his plans, especially the location of those unmanned aircraft." Flynn's finger moved south to the airfield at San Antonio de los Baños. "Task Three involves suppressing or eliminating the MiG-29 and MiG-23s based here so that our raiding force can extract safely."

Fox took in the totality of the ground and air defenses highlighted on the map. "Sadly, Four is fresh out of tactical nuclear weapons of its own," he said sarcastically, looking back up at Flynn and Van Horn.

"A nuke would be nice," she agreed with a slight smile. "Fortunately, all we really need is an air assault force, an aircraft carrier, and some other special equipment that Nick has his eye on."

"Is that all?" Fox said. Ostentatiously, he pulled his wallet out and riffled through it. He shook his head. "Alas, I fear that we're short several billion dollars. Not to mention the difficulty involved in persuading the US Navy to part with one of its most prized combat vessels . . . and the services of several thousand highly trained sailors and aviators along with it."

Flynn grinned at him. "Like I said, Br'er Fox, we're not completely crazy. What we need is a ship big enough to carry some gear I've got in mind for the assault force. Not anything close to a Nimitz class. I've checked, and there are a number of the right type of commercial ships available for lease just now. It turns out that what's bad for the offshore oil business is good for us."

"Exactly what kind of gear do you have in mind?" Fox asked slowly.

"Somewhere around ten of these new machines," Flynn told him, sliding a couple of glossy marketing-brochure-style photos across the desk. Mentally, he held his breath. After all his promises to the older man that they were still sane, revealing this part of what they had planned was going to push the envelope on that some. "Probably five of each design."

Fox stared down at the pictures. His eyes widened just a bit. He lifted his head. "Are those things real? I would have thought concepts like that were pure science fiction."

"They're real enough," Flynn assured him. "Just past the prototype stage, admittedly. So these are the first working models."

He nodded at Van Horn. "Laura's run her critical eye over the aeronautical-engineering specs."

"Once you cut past all the PR hype, the performance numbers for both designs are solid," she confirmed. "Payloads, range, and speed, they all add up to what we need."

Fox's eyes narrowed. "And you've already contacted the manufacturers?" he guessed with a hard look at Flynn. "To put in a rush order for this equipment?"

Flynn did his best to look innocent. He failed. "Well . . . yes," he admitted finally. "On a tentative basis, anyway. Subject to your approval."

"And just how did you explain your urgent need for such . . . unusual . . . flying machines?" Fox wondered. The hint of a smile appeared on his face. "I trust there was no mention of your intention to use the devices in a military-style commando raid on targets in Cuba?"

Flynn laughed. "I figured that might be a bad idea." He dug out a business card from his pocket. "I had a few of these left over from last year when my team and I were doing all that wingsuit training. This gave me a cover story that seemed plausible, so I ran with it."

Fox took the offered card. His thin smile widened a fraction. The fake business card read: FLYNN'S FLYING CIRCUS—TEAM AEROBATICS AND STUNTS. AIR SHOWS AND MOVIE SPECTACULARS OUR SPECIALTY.

"And they believed you?"

"Cold hard cash buys a lot of belief," Flynn said simply. Out of the corner of his eye, he noted Van Horn miming the *kapow* of a grenade going off. Oh boy, he thought, this was where the camel, a.k.a. Nick Flynn's brilliant plan, had to thread the eye of the needle—the hard reality that the Quartet Directorate's resources, though significant, were not unlimited.

Fox cleared his throat. "How much cash?"

"Six hundred thousand dollars for each machine," Flynn said. "Six million in total."

The older man stared at him for a long, long moment. "You're serious about this?" he said at last.

"Dead serious," Flynn assured him. He shrugged. "Look, Br'er Fox, I know this is painfully expensive. Then again, this whole plan is risky as hell. And try as I might, I just can't see any other workable options to get our assault force in . . . or to extract any survivors once the job's done. Helicopters are out. Cuba's air defenses may not be top of the line, but they're good enough to swat slow movers out of the sky. And making a drop by wingsuit this time is a nonstarter since there'd be no way to evacuate our guys." He reached out and prodded the pictures in front of Fox. "This experimental hardware, pricey as it is, is our best bet."

Slowly, Fox nodded. "You make a good case." Behind his glasses, his eyes were intently focused. "But that still leaves you with another problem, doesn't it? An even bigger one?" He indicated the map. "Three mission tasks. At two separate sites. Sites that are several miles apart. Carried out by who, exactly? Your action team, for one, I suppose. But that's only five men, counting you."

"Five men and one woman," Van Horn corrected him. "Counting me."

"Numbers are my biggest worry," Flynn said. "But I've already contacted Tony McGill. He's agreed to commit the team he's assembling for Four's European stations."

Fox considered that. "Eleven in total, then." He shook his head dismissively. "That's not enough. Not nearly enough for the magnitude of the operation you're contemplating here."

"I can't argue that," Flynn said quietly. "But the Quartet

Directorate happens to be very short of trained commandos at the moment. So while I admit that I'd be more comfortable going in with a larger number of reliable shooters, the job's still got to be done. We don't have much of a choice here. Not unless we're just going to give up and pray that somebody else, somewhere else, somehow else figures out the threat Voronin poses and steps in." His jaw tightened. "Which I really don't see happening."

"No, I concur," Fox said in reply. His dry smile was back. "Prayer has its purposes, I'm told. But they also say God helps those who help themselves." His gaze took on a more distant view. "As it happens," he said carefully, "I may have a solution to your manpower problem—especially since the attack you're planning is aimed, at least in part, at Cuba's communist regime."

Seeing the puzzled expressions on both Flynn's and Van Horn's faces, he only shrugged. "All I can tell you now is that Four has always been a very farsighted organization, one that takes a much longer view of history than is possible for any ordinary government. During the very dark days after the Bay of Pigs landings failed and Castro's tyranny consolidated its grip on power, our founders took certain measures. And as a result, we have a number of allies available—allies who might be very willing to risk their necks for the benefit of this harebrained scheme of yours."

THIRTY-ONE

PERICARD AND SONS MARITIME BROKERS,
HOUSTON, TEXAS

THE NEXT DAY

The offices of Pericard and Sons occupied an entire floor of one of Houston's tallest steel-and-glass structures. Two miles west of the elegant and expensive River Oaks neighborhood, the forty-six-story skyscraper towered over the neighboring commercial buildings and local restaurants. On a clear day, Giles Pericard III, the privately held company's chairman and CEO, could see all the way east to the soaring star-topped San Jacinto battlefield monument—and beyond to the glistening waters of the Houston Ship Channel, the ultimate source of his family's prosperity.

Today, however, Pericard's attention was wholly focused on his visitor, a thin, middle-aged man with graying hair and thick wire-rimmed glasses. According to his credentials, Carleton Frederick Fox was the managing director of a firm named Sykes-Fairbairn Strategic Investments. Quick digging by Pericard's staff before this meeting had turned up relatively little hard data on Sykes-Fairbairn, only enough to confirm that it was both a long-established enterprise and one that handled its worldwide business affairs with remarkable discretion.

Pericard frowned slightly. Although he was quite sure that he personally had never had any business dealings with Fox or his firm, something about the Sykes-Fairbairn name rang a faint bell in his memory. Perhaps it was something mentioned by his father, the previous CEO, before he retired? Or no, he thought, more likely something shared by his grandfather before his death. The old man, a refugee from war-torn France who'd built this thriving maritime brokerage business from the waterfront up, had been a prodigious teller of tales. And many of them, his grandson had come to realize with the passing years, had even been true—most astonishingly those concerning his exploits in the Resistance during the Second World War.

He shook his head impatiently. Either the long-buried memory would come back to him, or it would not. One could not force such things. What mattered now was dealing with the remarkable request this Mr. Fox had just made. Pericard raised an eyebrow. "This is a genuine proposition?"

Fox nodded. "I rarely joke about business matters." He indicated the set of documents he'd brought with him. "As I said, my firm would like your company to arrange a short-term lease of MarCor's *Dynamic Voyager* for us. I understand the vessel is currently available?"

Pericard nodded. The *Dynamic Voyager* was a specialized supply ship, one of dozens built around the world to ferry cargo to and from offshore oil platforms. Ordinarily at this time of year, the 260-foot-long, 4,200-ton vessel would have been at sea, crisscrossing the waters of the Gulf Coast region between various ports and offshore rigs—carrying everything from food and water stores for the drilling crews to machinery and spare parts. Unfortunately, thanks to recent federal restrictions on US energy exploration and production, the ship was currently swinging at anchor out in the Houston Ship Channel, eating away at its parent company's profits in harbor fees and other costs. Given the current economic and regulatory outlook, there was little prospect of any change in that situation soon, which would result in MarCor leaping at any reasonable offer he made on behalf of this client.

But that was precisely the problem, Pericard thought. Try as he might, he could not figure out why this Mr. Fox and his investment firm would want to hire such a vessel in the first place. Since its founding, Pericard and Sons had brokered ship leases and purchases for a wide range of clients, but never before for a financial-management company. Besides, beyond the pure strangeness of Fox and his associates using their anonymous investors' money this way, rather than in purchasing traditional stocks or futures contracts, there were plenty of other ships available that would be far better suited for almost any other imaginable freight-hauling job. With its long, open aft cargo deck and high bridge structure directly behind its large inverted bow, the *Dynamic Voyager* was anything but an ordinary merchant vessel.

When in doubt, be blunt, he decided. Pericard and Sons had a hard-earned reputation for both shrewd business dealing and integrity. It would be foolish to risk either asset merely for the short-term gain involved in brokering this transaction. He leaned forward. "May I ask how you intend to use the ship?"

Fox shook his head. "I'm afraid that is proprietary information."

Pericard's frown grew deeper. "I will need more than that, Mr. Fox. I'm sure you understand that my company cannot be party to anything illegal or immoral," he said stiffly.

"And I can assure you that neither the *Dynamic Voyager* nor the crew we'll provide will be involved in anything immoral," Fox said solemnly.

The maritime broker noted the complete absence of any such promise about illegality. He shook his head. "Not good enough," he said. "I don't believe we can do business together." He started to get up from his chair, intending to usher this peculiar fellow out of his office as quickly as possible.

The other man only smiled. "Before you make your final decision, Mr. Pericard, I recommend that you examine some of your company's original documents. Specifically, there will be a folder among your grandfather's oldest papers labeled 'Quatre.'"

Pericard stared at Fox. He vaguely recalled seeing a folder like that, with a faded and yellowing tag, in among all the other papers relating to the company's founding. They were kept in a filing cabinet in his outer office, more as a matter of tradition than of business necessity. How the devil did this Mr. Fox know anything about them?

He sat back down and punched a button on his phone to connect with his personal assistant. "Ms. Climpson," he said. "I need a folder from the corporate history files. It should be marked 'Quatre.'"

When his assistant bustled in moments later, Pericard took the folder from her and set it down carefully on his desk without opening it. The moment the door closed behind her, he looked down. There it was, he realized, the yellowing, faded label he'd dimly remembered, a label in his grandfather's strong, distinctive handwriting. Feeling strangely as though he were opening a door into the distant and far more dangerous past, he flipped the folder open.

It contained only a single sheet of paper with the torn half of a playing card—the four of diamonds—paper clipped to it. On the paper was a short message in ink, also in his grandfather's unmistakable writing: *These are good and honorable men, men to whom our whole family owes its very existence. Their cause is just. Therefore, when you are shown the other half of this card, you will do whatever is necessary to aid their endeavors. This I instruct. Giles Pericard, known during the war as Sculpteur.*

Pericard shivered. *Sculpteur, sculptor* in English, had been his grandfather's code name in the Resistance. The old man's reference to that name must mean that whatever this debt was, it had its origins in the terrible years when France lay broken and bleeding at the feet of its Nazi occupiers. Slowly, he looked up from the opened folder. "Do you have something to show me, Mr. Fox?" he asked carefully.

In answer, the other man reached into his suit pocket and pulled out the equally torn half of a four of diamonds.

Numbly, Pericard took the ragged piece of playing card and compared it to the portion his grandfather had left in that folder so many decades before. They matched perfectly. He sighed. Dead though he might be, the old man's word was still law for his descendants. Breaking it was unthinkable. "Very well, Mr. Fox," he said softly. "I will do as you ask."

THE MORA COMPOUND,
IN THE SIERRA MADRE, MEXICO
LATER THAT NIGHT

Hiding his disgust, Arkady Anokhin watched the Brotherhood of Blood's number two man, Joaquin Lopez, strut down the row of aircraft parked wingtip to wingtip inside the assembly building. These were the second group of drones his engineers and mechanics had finished putting back together from their separate parts flown in aboard Voronin's Boeing 777F cargo jet.

The cartel leader had a possessive look in his eyes that Anokhin did not like and did not trust. More than ever, he regretted the Raven Syndicate's need to rely on these criminals for the safety and security of this aspect of CASTLE KEEP. The fact that there were no alternatives was no real comfort. *We are playing a dangerous game with these men*, he thought, a game where the consequences for losing would be horrific.

Apparently satisfied, Lopez turned on his heel and stalked back to where the Russian waited. "Impressive as usual, señor," he said. He nodded back over the row of Mora drones. "But which of them has been allocated to us?"

"The aircraft on the far right," Anokhin said shortly. "My crews finished checking its systems this morning. Everything— its avionics, engine, and other systems—is in perfect condition."

Lopez smiled. "And our pilot, Bernardo?" he asked. "How is he progressing?"

The Russian nodded toward the far end of the building, where his men had installed a remote-piloting station. Right now, the primary seat was occupied by a slender young man with jet-black hair. Before deserting from Mexico's Air Force shortly ahead of his arrest for selling drugs to the ground crews at his base, former lieutenant Bernardo Suárez had flown Pilatus PC-9M attack aircraft. While his moral character might be that of a coldhearted snake, his flying skills were not in doubt. "Reasonably well," Anokhin said. "His instructor tells me your man should be able to complete all the necessary simulation coursework within ten days at the most. Perhaps a week."

"Even better," Lopez said with a terse nod. "My *patrón* is not a particularly patient or understanding man. He is eager to finish this transaction of ours." He showed his teeth. "As I'm sure is your own employer, since there has been this regrettable but necessary delay in his plans."

Anokhin only shrugged. Voronin knew the Brotherhood intended to keep half of the aircraft he'd just finished assembling here on the ground hostage until they were fully satisfied that their pilot could handle one of the Moras. To his surprise, when he'd apologized for the operational pause needed to accomplish this unexpected task, the Raven Syndicate's leader had seemed unworried. "Don't be too concerned, Arkady," he had said coolly. "A few days more here or there means nothing in the end. Not when it will enable us to finish all our business with the Brotherhood so satisfactorily and so thoroughly."

Now that he'd received his final coded instructions, along with the materials required to carry them out, Anokhin understood far more clearly exactly what Voronin had meant. He studiously controlled his expression. Lopez might be a thug, but he was not a complete fool. So for the time being, it was crucial that the cartel leader remain satisfied that the Brotherhood retained the upper hand in this uneasy alliance of convenience.

THIRTY-TWO

RURAL WEST CENTRAL FLORIDA

A COUPLE OF DAYS LATER

With a quiet sigh, Nick Flynn shrugged out of the sensor-studded harness he'd been wearing for the past several hours. By itself, the MILES gear—multiple integrated laser engagement system—wasn't really very heavy, only a little under four pounds total. No, the sense of relief he was feeling was because being able to dump the array meant the end of the most recent in a series of intensive combat drills he'd organized. Running around shooting blanks and using low-powered lasers to judge simulated hits and kills wasn't as stressful as real battle, but it was the next-best thing. Make that the next-worst thing, actually, he thought with a crooked grin, remembering how many times he'd heard both the double-beep tone that indicated simulated rounds slashing nearby and the shrill, flat-line tone that confirmed that he'd been taken out by somebody on the opposing side—all too often by someone he'd never even known was there until it was far too late to react effectively.

For most of the day before and all of today so far, his action team and Tony McGill's guys, newly flown in from Europe, had been prowling across the local countryside, taking turns to attack and defend or to patrol and ambush. This part of central Florida was thinly populated, mostly agricultural or set aside as state parks and nature preserves. The blend of light and heavy woods, dried-up circular lake beds that were now stretches of tall prairie grass, farm fields, and wide-open cow pastures offered a good mix of tactical challenges, besides being reasonably similar in nature to the ground around Voronin's remote operations center.

Now with his MILES harness in one hand and his HK417 carbine slung over the other shoulder, Flynn walked toward the large wood barn he and the other Four agents were using as their living quarters and base. This particular farm was owned by a long-retired Quartet Directorate operative who was more than happy to rent out his land to his old organization for training purposes.

Flynn pulled open one of the barn's big central doors and went inside. To clear room for them, the farmer had stacked most of his equipment along one wall. A loft at the very back held piled bales of hay. Otherwise, the large building had been turned into a combination of living quarters, an armory, and a chow hall. Rows of cots filled about half the space. Several long, picnic-style tables, some folding chairs, a couple of portable refrigerators, and cooking gear took up most of the rest. One whole wall was now lined with weapons cabinets and pegs for sets of body armor, helmets, and other tactical gear. They had a portable shower rigged up in one of the neighboring outbuildings, along with a few portable latrines.

The rest of his team—Shannon Cooke, Cole Hynes, Tad Kossak, Wade Vucovich, and Laura Van Horn—were already seated at one of the long tables with their own equipment off and hanging up. They all had cold beers in front of them.

Flynn stopped dead in his tracks. "Hell, you folks sure don't waste any time," he said in mock outrage. "While your glorious leader was still out there sweating his ass off and getting shot to shit by the new guys, you decided to call it a day?"

Hynes offered him a devious grin. "Hey, sir, when the whistle blew, we figured it was time to display some of that famous individual initiative you're always preaching on."

Cooke nodded. "It was either that or wait around to see if you'd decided there was maybe, just possibly, enough time to squeeze in one more itty-bitty field problem—which would inevitably lead to us crawling through more dust and dirt and bugs and cow crap for another couple of hours."

"I would never do anything like that," Flynn said, donning as pure and harmless a look as he possibly could. He had the immediate recollection of trying to pull off the same "who me?" act at home as a teenager—over the small matter of a curfew violation, a speeding ticket, and a couple of outraged cows that had, by some unfathomable mystery, ended up in the locked cafeteria of their crosstown rivals. Unfortunately, he remembered that he'd failed to be very convincing then, too.

Van Horn grinned at him. "Sure you would, Nick," she said. "If you thought it was important for quote 'unit readiness and tactical cohesion' unquote." She shook her head. "It's why we love you so."

Flynn snorted, eyeing their relaxed poses. "I'm not exactly feeling the love here."

She patted the empty chair beside her. "Hey, we saved you a seat." Then she reached down and pulled out another beer from the cooler next to her. "And a drink."

With a sheepish laugh, Flynn hung up his equipment and

then took both the offered chair and the beer. He savored a deep swig to wash the dust out of his throat and sighed. "Okay, now I feel better," he admitted.

Tadeusz Kossak nodded in approval. "This proves you are not crazy." His teeth gleamed. "Or not any more so than the rest of us, I suppose." He raised an eyebrow meaningfully. "Which includes these *new guys*, of course. The ones Tony McGill has brought to join our little party."

Cooke looked around. "Speaking of whom," he said carefully, "where is Tony's merry little band of European cutthroats?"

Flynn had the grace to look slightly abashed. "He took them off on a reconnoiter of the surrounding area. Just to get in a little more practice in moving tactically through this kind of country."

"See?" Hynes told the others with a satisfied look. "Told you so. The captain here hasn't changed any since me and Wade served under him in Alaska. If we hadn't bugged out when we did, we'd be rucking it now, too."

Opting for discretion over valor, Flynn said nothing. Instead, he simply shrugged. "Well, seeing as how we do have a little privacy at the moment, what's your honest-to-God assessment of Tony's people?"

Van Horn and the others nodded, understanding the purpose of his question. If this mission into Cuba got off the ground, they would be relying on McGill and his team—still relative strangers despite the intensity of the past two days of shared combat drills—to help get them home safely. The fact that it worked both ways went without saying. If they screwed up their own part of the mission, nothing the European action team did would really matter.

Kossak went first. "The Czech, Tallich, is very good," he said matter-of-factly. "He has an excellent eye for ground. And his marksmanship is top notch."

Flynn nodded. Mikolas Tallich was a veteran of his own country's elite 601st Special Forces Group, and like Kossak, the middling-tall Czech with a deceptively young face under his stubble beard was a crack sniper. From painful experience, Flynn had also learned that Tallich, though animated enough in conversation, had the uncanny ability to blend in with even the smallest piece of cover—lurking silent and motionless until his intended target wandered into his sights. "Are his shooting skills as good as yours?"

"Let us say that it would be a very interesting match," the Pole admitted with a small shrug.

"Well, one thing's for sure: that guy Piero Lucente has to be a seriously shit-hot helicopter pilot," Van Horn offered.

Flynn smiled. "You guys swapped flying stories?"

She shook her head with a smile of her own. "Nope. For a tall, dark, and handsome flyboy, and an Italian one at that, Lucente is remarkably tight lipped. Not a boaster at all." She cocked her head to the side, considering. "But I know his old outfit. Nobody who served with them was anything but the best." She took a sip of her beer. "Because if they weren't, they probably died. Flying through the Alps or the Apennines with your skids only a couple of feet off some very rocky, very unforgiving ground separates those with the right stuff from those without it pretty fast."

Flynn agreed. He didn't have Van Horn's firsthand flying experience to judge from, but Italy's Third Special Operations Helicopter Regiment, the Aldebaran, had a remarkable record of courage and daring and skill—both in its known combat deployments and in far less widely known antiterrorist and other covert operations.

He turned slightly toward Hynes and Vucovich. "How about Haugen, the Norwegian?"

"Einar's a good guy," Vucovich said simply. For the normally quiet soldier, that was almost an oration. Clearly, Haugen, who had experience as a member of Norway's Forsvarets Spesialkommandos, its Special Operations Commandos, had impressed the big man.

"He's got a quirky-as-shit sense of humor, though," Hynes chimed in. "I saw some big, nasty-looking snake slither right across his boots out in the field. Well, I was 'dead' at the time, so I couldn't move, even though I sure as hell wanted to. Anyway, when I asked him why he didn't stomp that scary-looking motherfucker into paste when he had the chance, he only shrugged and said it was a matter of professional courtesy— one cold-blooded killer to another."

Flynn felt a laugh welling up. Clearly, Haugen, outwardly the spitting image of a stereotypical Viking, with his short-cropped yellow hair and square jaw, had hidden depths.

That left one remaining member of McGill's European action team to consider. Before joining Four, the Lithuanian, whose name was Rytis Daukša, had been a long-serving member of the small Baltic nation's highly secret Aitvaras antiterrorist unit. While the Lithuanian special forces unit was named after a mythological nature spirit, *aitvaras* also meant *kite*, like the bird of prey, and Flynn had the passing thought that Daukša's narrow, sharp-nosed face, bright-blue eyes, and graying brown hair gave him more than a little resemblance to a fierce avian predator.

Flynn glanced at Cooke, whom he'd observed spending some time with the older man during their infrequent breaks between combat exercises. "Any thoughts about Daukša, Shannon?"

The Virginian pondered the question for a moment. "You know how my old specialty in the US Army was covert infiltration into hostile countries?"

Flynn nodded. Cooke had demonstrated his ability to blend unnoticed into different populations and situations over and over—first for Task Force Orange and later for the Quartet Directorate.

"Well, this guy Rytis is cut from the same cloth," Cooke told him. "If I had to pick one word to describe him, it would be 'sneaky.'"

"I object," they all heard a somewhat muffled voice with a distinctly eastern European accent say from somewhere above them.

Their heads swiveled toward the hayloft. There, digging his way out of one of the stacked hay bales, was Rytis Daukša. The Lithuanian wore his radio headset and throat mike, showing that he'd been in constant contact with McGill and the rest of his own team while eavesdropping on their meeting. "'Subtle' I would accept as a description," he said, brushing away stray pieces of hay with a pained expression. "'Sneaky,' however, seems overly harsh."

Cooke rolled his eyes at Flynn. "See what I mean," he muttered. "The guy's sneaky. Definitely sneaky. A good sneaky, sure. But totally fucking spooky sneaky."

Flynn nodded and felt a wide answering grin cross his face. Whatever lingering doubts he might have had were erased. Unquestionably, McGill's action team had the skills and toughness to more than pull its own weight during the coming test of fire.

Which left, he realized, the remaining unknown factor: these mysterious "allies" Fox had promised to seek out.

THIRTY-THREE

THE FARM

THE NEXT DAY

The reinforcements Fox had pledged to find arrived very early the next morning, aboard a rented minibus and accompanied by the head of the American station in person. When the vehicle pulled up in front of the barn, Fox was the first one out. Nine other people— seven men and two women—clambered down behind him. They were all relatively young, in their late twenties or early thirties at most, tough looking, and plainly physically fit. Although they wore ordinary civilian clothes, everything else about them screamed ex-military to Flynn. They also all appeared to be Hispanic.

Or more accurately, he corrected himself, thinking back on what Fox had said about Four cementing an alliance after the failed landings at the Bay of Pigs, Cuban Americans.

"Nick, these are members of the Regimiento de Navarro, the Navarro Regiment," Fox said as an introduction. The men and women grouped behind him were already forming up in a disciplined group.

Flynn listened closely while Fox gave him a quick rundown on just who these people were. The Navarro Regiment was a secret paramilitary unit sponsored by the Quartet Directorate. Its origins went back to the early 1960s, when it had started becoming painfully clear that Fidel Castro's spies had deeply penetrated both the CIA itself and several of the larger Cuban exile groups run under Langley's aegis. Too many resistance groups on the island were being blown and too many covert operations betrayed to the communist regime's secret police to draw any other reasonable conclusions. In desperation, a handful of farsighted exiles had resolved to build a whole new force—one entirely untainted by any connections to the CIA. The Quartet Directorate had stepped in to aid them with funding and clandestine-operations training. Ever since, the Navarro Regiment and Four had periodically collaborated in operations aimed at the Cuban regime and the terrorist groups and guerrilla movements it sponsored.

Named to honor Tomas Navarro, a courageous young Cuban freedom fighter who'd fought bravely at the Bay of Pigs and then later risen to high rank in the US Army while serving his adopted country, the Navarro Regiment drew its recruits first from the sons and daughters, and now from the grandsons and granddaughters, of those who'd resisted Havana's brutal dictatorship from the outset. They had all served honorably in the US armed forces, both out of a deep sense of patriotism and from a desire to gain the combat and other special skills that might one day help them free Cuba from its oppressive government.

So when Fox approached the group with the news of a chance to strike another blow against the regime and its mercenary Russian allies, the Navarro Regiment's council had quickly approved his request for a small handful of trained and highly skilled volunteers.

Even without being given any details other than that the operation would be extremely dangerous, more than fifty of the unit's members had stepped forward—a far greater number than Flynn's force could possibly use to fill out its thin ranks. Thus, the nine Navarros finally selected were among the best of the best.

If that small group's leader, Alejandro "Alex" Zayas, was typical, Flynn thought after being introduced to him, the regiment's standards were high indeed. Built like a middleweight boxer, Zayas was a former captain in the US Army's Special Forces with decorated combat service in Afghanistan, Syria, and other hellholes.

"Why you'd leave the service?" Flynn asked bluntly.

Zayas shrugged. "Because they were going to bump me to major. Which meant I was looking at spending even more of my time at a damned desk and not enough with my soldiers. And I hate paperwork with an undying passion."

Flynn nodded his understanding. Every grade after captain meant less time in the field and more time in an office, handling administrative matters. Like most military bureaucracies, the Pentagon seemed to specialize in drowning enthusiasm, leadership, and initiative in a morass of meaningless forms and other red tape.

"Plus, I signed up to kill communists. Not to become one," Zayas said with only the flicker of a sardonic smile.

Again, Flynn nodded. The current American military hierarchy's obsession with trendy politics at the expense of real soldier skills had passed the point of being truly funny. Recruiting and retention numbers were well below where they needed to be, with qualified officers, noncoms, and enlisted men leaving the services in droves when their tours were up. Which ironically, he realized, had probably worked to Four's benefit in this particular case.

Studying the row of unfamiliar faces while Zayas ran through the names and backgrounds of his comrades, Flynn resolved to do his very best to get to know these men and women as quickly as possible. Because time was tight. The next several days, if they were allowed even that much, were going to be extraordinarily grueling. Rigorous, almost nonstop training and rehearsals would be essential if he was going to succeed in melding his own team, McGill's European unit, and now these Cuban American volunteers into a cohesive operational force.

Flynn got things rolling by issuing the newcomers personal weapons and equipment. He could tell they were impressed by the array of small arms and explosives laid out inside the barn. One of them, a powerfully built Ranger veteran named Andy Cavada, started in surprise when he spotted a couple of shoulder-fired antitank missile launchers. The weapons were about three feet long, with wide, bulbous front muzzle brakes and smaller apertures at the back. He turned to Flynn and the Four agents with an astonished and equally admiring look on his face. "You guys have NLAWs? Where the hell did you get them?"

Produced by Saab Bofors Dynamics, the NLAW—next-generation light antitank weapon—was a single-use, man-portable missile designed to allow infantry to destroy enemy armored vehicles at ranges anywhere from twenty to eight hundred yards. Thousands were in service with armies around the world, including Sweden and the United Kingdom, but the antitank missile was very definitely *not* a weapons system anyone ordinarily expected to find in private hands.

"They fell off the back of a truck," Flynn said blandly.

McGill grinned broadly. "Point of order, Nick," he said with a wink at Cavada. "That truck was in England, so it was technically a lorry."

In truth, this arms cache was the fruit of many years of

carefully orchestrated "equipment losses" by American and allied military units, along with discreet purchases from various friendly arms manufacturers. All for a good cause, of course. Weight considerations would inevitably make it impossible for them to bring all the weapons, ammunition, and other gear Flynn wanted, but at least he had the consolation of knowing that he and his people would be going in as well equipped as a regular commando force undertaking a similar deep-penetration raid.

Alex Zayas chuckled along with the others. But then he turned to Flynn with a quizzical look. "This is a sweet collection of hardware, all right," he said. "But what's your plan to get it—and us, for that matter—into the target area in Cuba? Are we going in by boat? Or by air?"

Tony McGill nodded. "I have the same question, Nick," he said. Looking around the intent and interested circle of faces, which now included those of his own men as well as those of Flynn's team and the Cuban Americans, he continued, "If nothing else, we need to know so we can get a sense of just how much kit we can really bring on this op."

Flynn paused for a moment, considering how best to break the news of the plan he and Laura Van Horn had concocted. Pretty much straight to the point was probably best, he decided. "Well, the short answer is that we're not going in by boat, at least not all the way," he told them. "Nor are we going in by air. Not in any conventional sense, anyway."

They all stared back at him. "Last time I checked," McGill said carefully, "there weren't any bridges connecting Florida to Cuba. And there's certainly not a tunnel under the Straits of Florida either, unless the technical lads in your CIA are a lot cleverer than I'd ever supposed."

"See, Nick, I think you're gonna need to give them the *long* answer," Van Horn told Flynn. Her amused expression left absolutely no doubt that she'd been looking forward to this moment ever since they'd arrived at the farm.

He nodded. "Yeah, I reckon so." He surveyed the assembled men and women. "How many of you are fixed-wing or helicopter pilots?"

Five hands, including Van Horn's, went up.

"And how many of you can ride a motorcycle?"

More hands, most of them, in fact, were raised.

Flynn met that with a slight smile. "Good," he told them cheerfully. "Because that's going to make our training on the new machines a lot easier. A couple of examples are here now. The rest of them are supposed to arrive sometime in the next twenty-four hours."

"What kind of new machines?" asked one of the women, a former navy helicopter pilot named Daina Perez.

"I'll show you," Flynn said in answer. Offering the little crowd a "follow me" nod, he went back outside and across the yard to one of the adjoining outbuildings. It was an equipment shed the retired Four agent turned farmer ordinarily used to keep his small John Deere 3 series utility tractor out of the weather. Flynn took a key out of his pocket, unlocked the padlock holding the shed doors shut, and slid them all the way open with a clang.

Inside were two distinctive, tarped shapes. Neither was more than eight feet long nor more than three feet wide, and both were under three feet high.

At Flynn's nod, Van Horn grabbed hold of one tarp and yanked it off, much like a stage assistant unveiling a magician's latest stupendous and astonishing trick for the audience. Then, still grinning, she turned and did the same to the second cloaked machine. "Welcome to the future of personal combat aviation, boys and girls," she announced.

"Holy shit," someone muttered from the back. Everyone else was too busy staring to say anything.

Sitting in front of them were two futuristic-looking vehicles. One resembled a flying speeder bike straight out of a *Star Wars* movie. Eight small, swiveling turbojet engines mounted in pairs surrounded what otherwise looked very much like a two-seat motorcycle chassis. The other design somewhat more closely resembled a conventional quadricycle, until anyone noticed the jet engines mounted in the middle of each rotatable wheel and two more angled backward out from the undercarriage.

Flynn pointed to the first machine. "What you're looking at here is a fully functioning flying speeder," he said flatly. "The company that built this hopes to sell others like it to the military for use as personal battlefield transports, for medevac, and as light-cargo lifters."

"How fast can this so-called speeder fly?" Piero Lucente asked. The Italian looked intensely interested.

"Like a bat out of hell," Van Horn assured him. "Max speed is around one hundred and fifty knots up to an altitude of fifteen thousand feet. Those four turbojets you see produce around twelve hundred pounds of total thrust."

That drew admiring whistles. "Sounds like a hot ride," one of the other pilots commented. "But a really easy way to get killed."

"Yep," Van Horn agreed. "Fortunately, it's fully stabilized, with a lot of computerized flight controls to assist. You can fly it manually, but the software does a great job of keeping it in a safe flight envelope."

Daina Perez looked the speeder bike over with a critical eye. "Something that small can't be carrying a lot of fuel," she said. "What's the range like?"

"It's got a combat radius of around thirty-five nautical miles," Van Horn answered. "Or close to seventy miles out and back." Her mouth quirked. "Which I agree isn't far in the greater scheme of things, but it's just enough for our purposes."

McGill moved over to get a closer look at the second machine, the one with four wheels. "And this thing?" he asked. "What's the story here?"

Flynn smiled. "That's a bird of two very different feathers, Tony. The French company that designed it wanted something that could function both as a conventional ground transport and as a turbine-powered flier. For road use, it's got an electric motor with a range of around sixty miles. Transitioning into flight mode only takes about a minute—and it's got enough kerosene fuel for twenty minutes or so of flying time."

"So then, it's somewhat slower and shorter ranged compared to the speeder bike?" Lucente observed.

Flynn nodded. "Plus, it's limited to very low altitudes, more like a hoverbike than a full-on flier."

"Why use two different designs, with such different capabilities?" Zayas asked.

Van Horn shrugged her shoulders. "Because both of these machines are straight out of the prototype phase and barely in production," she explained. "The only way we could assemble the force we're going to need—ten fliers able to carry twenty personnel—was to buy everything currently available and tailor elements of our mission accordingly."

"The assault unit tasked with neutralizing the San Antonio de los Baños military airfield has the farthest to fly and the least need for stealth once the balloon goes up," Flynn told them. "So they get the speeder bikes."

"Makes sense," McGill acknowledged. He shot a quick grin at Lucente. "It's your lucky day, Piero."

The Italian pilot smiled back slightly. "*La fortuna favorisce i veloci*," he agreed. "Fortune favors the fast."

"And the rest of us, those hitting the control center itself, will use the hybrids," Flynn went on. "In electric mode on the ground, they're pretty stealthy . . . so that's how we'll make the final approach to our jump-off point." He eyed the assembled group. Their faces now bore a range of expressions. Some appeared eager and excited. Others, probably those with the most experience under fire, looked more somber and thoughtful. But for all of them it was obvious that seeing physical examples of the brand-new flying machines that would carry them into Cuba had brought home the reality of what they were planning. This operation was no longer purely theoretical.

"One more thing," he told them. "The code name for this mission will be GRYPHON. Which makes us Gryphon Force."

As he'd expected, that drew approving nods. His choice of a mythological beast with an eagle's head, wings, and talons and a lion's body, tail, and back legs was perfect.

THIRTY-FOUR

THE MORA COMPOUND,
IN THE SIERRA MADRE, MEXICO

SEVERAL NIGHTS LATER

Arkady Anokhin raised his night vision binoculars and watched closely as one of the six remaining Mora unmanned aircraft brought its turbofan engine to full power. The keening howl increased steadily in volume and shrillness, until it seemed to echo back from the neighboring hills. He took his eyes away long enough to catch sight of the equally rapt expression on Joaquin Lopez's tattooed face. The Brotherhood of Blood's second-in-command was completely absorbed, studying the drone preparing for takeoff as though his very life depended on a successful flight.

Which it very well might, the Russian suddenly realized. If the Mora crashed, Lopez's superior, Diego Barros, would not be at all pleased. Inevitably, the bloodthirsty cartel boss would come looking for a scapegoat, someone to blame for such a disaster. And it would be a coin toss as to whether his choice of victim fell on a complete outsider like Anokhin or on his own closest subordinate, the man who would most likely someday challenge Barros's control over the Brotherhood.

As its engine reached maximum thrust, the unmanned drone abruptly started moving—rumbling up the road that served as their runway as it picked up speed. Moments later, it lifted off, wobbling slightly as it rose into the air and banked into a gradual, spiraling climb. Higher and higher it ascended, until finally the pale-gray aircraft, almost invisible against the night sky, leveled out and began orbiting several thousand feet above the valley.

Lopez watched it for several minutes. His taut face relaxed and he nodded in pleasure. He turned to one of the cartel soldiers who'd accompanied him on this visit to the compound. "Tell Bernardo that it's time to bring his steed back to the barn."

"At once, *jefe*," the man barked. He trotted off to the aircraft-assembly building to relay the order to Suárez, the Brotherhood's newly trained remote pilot.

Moments later, the UCAV broke out of its circling flight and began descending. Both Anokhin and Lopez watched it line up with the road and make its final approach. The landing gear whined down and locked in place. The Russian darted a quick look at Lopez. The cartel leader appeared considerably more at ease now.

Anokhin hid his surprise. Lopez *was* an amateur when it came to aviation, he suddenly realized. He did not realize that landings were at least as difficult and dangerous as takeoffs, perhaps even more so. After all, when in the air, a well-designed plane was in its natural element. But many things could go wrong when it returned to earth—everything from mechanical failures, losing an engine or having the landing gear collapse, to simple pilot error. Mistakes that might include a poorly chosen angle of approach, coming in too fast, or, perhaps even worse, shedding speed too rapidly, stalling out, and crashing short of the runway. And on this particular test flight, the Russian knew, the odds of pilot error were at least double that of any ordinary landing.

He held his own breath as the Mora dropped lower still. At last, its wheels touched the road surface, bounced slightly, and then settled back into firm contact. Slowing, the drone rolled down the road toward the Brotherhood compound. Engine spooling over softly at very low power, it taxied across the apron and finally came to a full stop next to the large assembly building. Once the rest of Voronin's aircraft departed for their own flights north into the United States, the empty building would serve as a permanent hangar for the Brotherhood's newly acquired stealth plane.

Lopez turned to Anokhin. "Well?" he asked. "What do you think?"

"I congratulate you," the Russian replied, choosing his words with infinite care. "Your pilot has learned his lessons well."

Lopez nodded. "In that case, our business here together is finished."

Anokhin tensed. This was the critical moment. Would the Brotherhood make new demands now? Before it gave away its remaining leverage over the Raven Syndicate? Voronin, he knew, had plans in place for almost any contingency. What was less certain was whether those alternate plans gave the Syndicate personnel based here a reasonable chance of survival. "Then the rest of my aircraft and my men are free to go?" he asked tightly.

Lopez smiled graciously. "Of course. My *patrón* and I are men of our word. Your planes and your technicians will be allowed to depart safely." His eyes glittered. "With one caveat. No one goes until the practice bomb for tomorrow night's demonstration is loaded aboard our drone plane. Or until I am sure that my own mechanics know how to repeat this evolution with real weapons when the time comes." His smile returned in full force as he contemplated the Mora UCAV now parked beside the assembly building. "Never fear, the little gray bird you have sold us will earn its wings very, very soon."

Anokhin followed his gaze. "Of that, señor, I have absolutely no doubt," he said evenly.

For the next few hours Anokhin kept a close guard on both his expression and his mouth while his remaining planes were slowly towed out of the hangar one by one, ran their engines up to full power, and then soared away into the star-speckled sky on their long flights north. When all of them were gone and the cartel's UCAV was loaded as promised, he joined the rest of his engineers and technicians and climbed onto a bus for the ride to Durango's airport—where Voronin's Boeing 777F waited to ferry them back to Minsk on the first leg of a journey that would eventually bring them home to Russia.

Only once they were safely on board the big jet did Anokhin allow himself to relax. Smiling far more genuinely now, he punched in a preset number on his smartphone. It was the number for the Mora remote operations center outside Havana.

Fyodor Maresyev answered immediately. "Yes, Arkady?" he said tersely. "Were there any problems?

"None," Anokhin assured him. "Tell your man he did an excellent job of duplicating the Mexican pilot's control inputs. No one could tell the difference. Not even me."

RURAL KANSAS
THE NEXT DAY

More than twenty gray-winged Mora unmanned combat aircraft were now parked throughout the cavernous interior of what was once intended to be a giant American retail distribution center. A tangle of hoses snaked across the bare concrete floor—connecting the Pemex tanker truck full of jet fuel to the newest arrivals from Mexico. Men from Ivan Strelkov's covert aircraft-handling team were busy topping up their tanks.

Crouched inside the opened weapons bay of one of the first Moras to arrive, Major Leonid Kazmin paused in his task. Tugging a rag out of one of his pockets, he wiped the sweat off his forehead and then stuffed the cloth back into his coveralls. It wasn't at all warm inside the vast warehouse. In fact, it was so chilly that he could see his breath condensing on the highly polished green metal casing of the cylinder slung inside the bay. But this was painstaking work—the sort that required intense concentration and attention to the smallest details. The consequences of even the slightest mistake could be enormous.

Ever since he'd arrived in this godforsaken corner of the American heartland, he had been inspecting the drone payloads from nose cone to tail fins—obsessively checking, double-checking, and even triple-checking every single system and circuit. Except for breaks to sleep and eat, he spent all his time gently poking around the innards of each device. He was the only special-weapons officer at this covert base, so there was no one else qualified to handle the job.

Essentially, it was Kazmin's responsibility to make sure every Mora payload was ready for operational use. At first, he'd been so overjoyed to make it safely through all the potential counterespionage snares awaiting a Russian military officer entering the United States illegally that the work itself had seemed easy. It was, he knew, more than anything else simply a question of training and education coupled with a passion for meticulous precision and close observation.

But in the long, exhausting days since, Kazmin had become more and more conscious that he was running out of time. With every weapon he confirmed ready for use, Voronin's audacious CASTLE KEEP operation moved that much closer to fruition. And the arrival late last night of the last five unmanned aircraft from Mexico left him without any more excuses for delay. Putting off installing the final safeguard President Zhdanov had insisted on was no longer an option.

He leaned closer to the inspection port he'd opened on this particular weapon. What to any untrained person would have appeared a tangled mess of cabling and circuitry was as easy for him to read as a schoolboy's first book of ABCs. This was the heart of the device's permissive action link—the electronic lock that made all the difference between this complicated device being nothing more than a collection of disparate, inert components . . . and it being one that would function, for a millisecond, as a unified mechanism aimed only toward one very final result.

Gently, Kazmin teased aside a handful of color-coded wires and then, using a thin-bladed tool, very, very carefully unfastened several tiny screws. With that done, he carefully wiggled one of the credit-card-sized circuit boards back and forth until it came loose. Easing the board outside the port, he slid it away out of sight into a pocket. Then, from another, he pulled out what appeared to be an identical assembly of integrated circuits, diodes, resistors, and other components. This was the special piece of electronics Zhdanov had provided, the one originally camouflaged inside a smartphone case.

Taking infinite pains, Kazmin installed the new card in place of the original and reconnected it. Small status lights glowed green, indicating that it was live and that the other mechanisms accepted it as genuine.

Kazmin breathed out in relief. Despite that, he made sure not to rush the rest of this job. If anything, he realized with a sudden icy feeling, it was more important than ever that this particular

device be ready to operate exactly as commanded—should the
eventuality arise. His movements, if it was possible, became even
more precise as he systematically reinstalled the remaining elements of the system and closed the weapon back up. Finished at
last, he wriggled back out from under the Mora drone. He wiped
his fingers carefully, delicately removing any lingering traces of oils
or dust. Much like Pontius Pilate washing his hands of Christ's
guilt or innocence, he thought bleakly. But orders were orders.
And if all went as planned, nothing of what he had just done
would matter, he reminded himself. Not in the slightest.

Seeing the Twelfth Main Directorate officer emerge from
under the aircraft's wing, Strelkov came over to join him. The
senior Raven Syndicate operative had been supervising his fuel
handlers while they finished tanking the newly arrived aircraft.
"Is that it, Major?" the older man asked, not hiding his own
concern. He and his team of trained aircraft mechanics could
make sure these machines took to the air. What they could not
do was guarantee that the UCAVs would complete their assigned
missions. "Did you run into any problems?"

Kazmin forced himself to appear calm. "Nothing significant," he said. He shrugged his shoulders. "Only a few small
adjustments here and there." Seeing the sudden worried look
on Strelkov's face, he explained more fully. "Sir, many of these
weapons have been sitting in cold storage for twenty years or
more. After all that time, it's not at all surprising that I've had
to replace a few minor electronic components or a bolt or screw
here or there."

"Then they'll all detonate?" Strelkov asked. "There won't
be any duds?"

"None," Kazmin guaranteed. "All the major elements of
each device are in perfect working order. Trust me, they will go
off . . . exactly as ordered."

Evidently reassured, Strelkov visibly calmed down. "So you're finished here?"

"Not quite," Kazmin told him. He opened his satchel and pulled out the tiny VLF radio antenna array and power supply Zhdanov had given him back in Saint Petersburg. "All I need to do is install this little item somewhere high up; near the roof would be my first choice."

Strelkov stared at the small antenna, obviously curious. "And what is that?" he asked.

Kazmin had anticipated the question. "This?" he said, trying hard to sound casual. "It's a radiation sensor and data relay," he lied.

The older man looked nervous. "A radiation sensor?" He glanced around to make sure none of his men were in earshot and lowered his voice. "Tell me, Major, is there a risk we'll get a hard dose here?"

"Don't worry," Kazmin said with confidence. "You're not in any real danger from radiation leaks." That much was the truth. "This is just a routine precaution, part of the standard operating procedure for handling these types of weapons. Trust me; I've inspected all their casings quite thoroughly, and I can promise you that there won't be any accidents. None whatsoever."

Strelkov's face lightened. "I'm very glad to hear that, Major," he admitted. He glanced down at his watch. "And you've certainly completed the rest of your work in excellent time. Once you're ready to go, just say the word, and I'll have one of my men drive you to the airport."

"You can count on that," Kazmin said gratefully. He turned away to find a ladder. Now that he'd obeyed President Zhdanov's secret orders, the sooner he was out of the United States and safely on his way home to Russia, the happier he would be.

THIRTY-FIVE

BROTHERHOOD OF BLOOD HEADQUARTERS,
WEST OF DURANGO, MEXICO

LATER THAT NIGHT

Surrounded by a crowd of their lieutenants—their top subordinates within the cartel—Diego Barros and Joaquin Lopez stood on the low, flat roof of the hacienda's central building. Under the nearly full moon, the rooftop was bathed in a pale, silvery glow, adding to the gathering's festive mood. The smells of tequila, cigarettes, and other, more illicit substances hung lazily in the relatively cool night air.

From here, the assembled cartel bosses could look out over the neighboring fields and orchards. About a kilometer away, a large circle had been chalked into what had once been prime grazing land. This was the aiming point selected for tonight's demonstration of their new Mora remotely piloted aircraft. While seeing dirt thrown up by a practice munition would not be as exciting as watching a live bomb go off, it would still make the necessary point. Under the leadership of Barros and Lopez, the Brotherhood was now more powerful and more dangerous than ever before—with capabilities beyond any possessed by rival cartels.

Lopez held his smartphone to his ear, listening to the running commentary provided by Bernardo Suárez. The Brotherhood pilot was twenty kilometers away, flying the Mora UCAV from his computer station inside what had been Voronin's aircraft-assembly building.

"*One minute out,*" Suárez reported calmly. "*I'm coming left to zero two zero. I'm throttling back. My airspeed is now three hundred knots. Altitude is fifteen hundred feet.*"

Lopez turned to Barros. "The plane is close, coming in from the south. We should see it soon." They swung around to stare off in that direction, gazing out over a moonlit patchwork of rugged hills and softer, more settled country. Other Brotherhood bosses, overhearing Lopez, did the same.

Moments later, a small gray shape came into view low on the horizon. Growls of anticipation greeted its appearance. Some of the men on the rooftop, those who'd been guarding the Raven Syndicate's compound, had seen aircraft like this one before. For others, this was their first look at the drone's menacing, high-tech batwing configuration. But for all of them, the knowledge that the organization they'd pledged their lives to now owned a weapon of such sophistication and lethal striking power was deeply satisfying.

Accompanied by the shrill whine of its turbofan, the UCAV slid fast across the night sky. It was flying a course aimed directly at the chalk circle. "*Target acquired. Payload bay opening,*" Lopez heard the pilot say over their phone connection. The younger man sounded more excited now. "*Holding my course straight and level. I am ready to make my attack!*"

Lopez frowned suddenly. From his vantage point, it looked as though the Mora was turning again—and certainly *not* flying straight and level as Suárez claimed. Instead, the unmanned aircraft seemed to be banking very sharply left, coming around fast onto a heading toward the hacienda itself. It was also descending to a very low altitude. "What the hell are you doing, Bernardo!" he snapped. "You're heading straight for us! Not the goddamned target!"

In his ear, Suárez's voice was suddenly shrill with panic. "Jefe! *The aircraft isn't responding to my controls! I can't steer it—*"

And then a long, finned shape dropped from under the oncoming drone—slanting down out of the sky straight toward the Brotherhood of Blood's leaders and their top lieutenants gathered on the hacienda's flat roof. Lopez's eyes barely had time to widen in horrified understanding. "*Carajo,*" he whispered. "Oh, fuck."

In the sky directly above them, the KAB-1500 thermobaric bomb went off. First, a single small explosive charge detonated, splitting the fuel container that made up most of the weapon's mass. Instantly, a thick fog of atomized fuel expanded outward, still plummeting toward the hacienda below. A split second later, the weapon's second charge triggered—igniting that spreading cloud of fuel in a massive, searing explosion. A huge orange-and-red fireball lit the night sky, consuming everything and everyone caught within 150 meters of the blast point. The fireball was accompanied by an enormous, lung-rupturing shock wave that raced outward at many times the speed of sound—killing anyone within 500 meters of the explosion.

When that brief, blinding light faded into blackness, leaving only the pale glow of the moon behind, the Brotherhood of Blood's hacienda was a broken, burning mound of rubble.

There were no survivors.

OUTSIDE MOSCOW
THAT SAME TIME

Pavel Voronin sat at his desk in the private office on the second floor of his villa. The monitor of his computer carried a live, zoomed-in video feed transmitted from one of Russia's Persona electro-optical reconnaissance satellites as it swept south to north along the inclined path of its orbit. As the satellite crossed high above the darkened Mexican hinterland, the brief, blinding orange-red flash outside Durango was plainly visible.

A text message appeared in the lower left of his screen. It was from Fyodor Maresyev at the Mora remote operations center outside Havana: *Detonation confirmed. Target obliterated. As planned, the UCAV itself was inside the blast radius. Only unidentifiable fragments will remain.*

An arctic-cold smile appeared on Voronin's face. So much for Barros, Lopez, and the rest of their ignorant followers. He picked up a secure phone, one that offered him a direct, encrypted line to Zhdanov's own office in the Kremlin. When the older man answered, he said simply, "I've handled our small Mexican problem, Mr. President. Accordingly, we are ready to move into the next phase of CASTLE KEEP. I'll be on my way to join you shortly."

With his hand, he signaled Kondakov. The former GRU officer nodded and hurried out to issue the necessary orders to his staff. By the time Voronin finished his call, the rotor blades of the Kazan Ansat utility helicopter parked outside were already starting to turn.

GRYPHON FORCE TRAINING AREA,
WEST CENTRAL FLORIDA
A SHORT TIME LATER

Turbojets howling, the hybrid hoverbike streaked low across the neighboring farmland, trailing a curling plume of dust that showed white in the moonlight. Seeing the outline of the barn looming up in his night vision goggles, Nick Flynn throttled back and felt his speed dropping. Automatically, the bike's computer instructed its wheel-mounted engines to swivel slightly toward the ground, adding lift to keep him in the air as he slowed down.

Flynn noted Fox already waiting for him just outside the barn. His jaw tightened. The radio call had come in just as he was about to run his section of Gryphon Force through another low-level, cross-country training flight. But the verbal code word the older man had used, *PARAMOUNT,* signaled that his message was both urgent . . . and best given orally and in person. Their tactical radio net was as secure as they could make it, but the Quartet Directorate avoided taking risks whenever possible, especially with high-level intelligence information. Over the long history of human espionage, poor communications security had doomed more agents and operations than anyone could count.

He tapped an icon on the small glowing instrument panel set between the motorbike's handlebars. The howl from the two turbojets mounted on its undercarriage faded away, replaced by a somewhat shriller whine as its wheel jets powered up briefly to compensate for the lost thrust. They swung down and locked in place. Now pointed straight down, all four engines reduced thrust simultaneously, bringing the bike in for a vertical landing on the hard-packed yard next to the barn.

Flynn switched everything off and dismounted. Pulling his helmet off, he cradled it under one arm and turned to Fox. "What's up, Br'er Fox?" he asked.

"We just received word from Colonel Herrera in Mexico City," Fox said. "His informant at the airport in Durango says someone just wiped out every significant leader in the Brotherhood of Blood, including Diego Barros and Joaquin Lopez."

Flynn stared at him. "Wiped out?" he repeated in surprise. "How?"

Four's head of station looked suitably grim. "Apparently with some sort of exceptionally powerful bomb. Beyond that, the details are sketchy. Herrera's man says there's nothing left of the cartel's headquarters outside the city except for smoldering wreckage."

Flynn whistled quietly. "When our pal Voronin decides to clean up some loose ends, he doesn't screw around, does he?"

"Apparently not," Fox said.

Flynn's eyes narrowed in thought. "Which likely means he's getting ready to kick off whatever even bigger nastiness he's got planned for the US as a whole. And if that's true, we're also running out of time to stop him before it's too late."

Fox nodded. "A reasonable supposition, Nick." The lines on his face were deeper. "Much as I hate the idea of pushing you and your people into action without more training and rehearsal, I don't see that we have much choice here."

"No, we don't," Flynn agreed. The only way the raid they planned made sense at all was if they could smash Voronin's operations center *before* his drone aircraft took off from wherever they were currently based. Going in too late would simply result in men and women who were now under Flynn's command dying without achieving anything meaningful for their sacrifice. He frowned. "But I will say that I'm sure getting awfully tired of dancing to the bad guys' tune."

Fox nodded again, this time without speaking.

"Is our ship in position?" Flynn asked, his eyes distant as he ran through various options.

"I spoke to Captain McLennan a few minutes ago," Fox confirmed. "The *Dynamic Voyager* is currently holding station about six miles off the coast, due west of Turtle Beach."

Flynn pulled up his mental map of the local Florida area. That put the oil platform supply ship roughly twenty-eight miles from this spot as the crow—or, in this particular case, their speeders and hoverbikes—flew. He shook his head. "You know we're going to raise all kinds of hell just getting our gear on board."

Originally, they had planned to move their tarped flying motorcycles and speeder bikes to the ship aboard trucks, discreetly keeping them well away from prying eyes and ears. But now, given this sudden need for speed, subtlety and stealth were no longer possible. Instead, Flynn and the others would have to fly directly out to the ship and make a landing at sea. Spending the extra fuel was okay. They had additional supplies waiting on the ship, so they could refuel while at sea. But since much of Florida's coast was densely populated, their flights would inevitably trigger a flood of irritated 911 calls from beachside residents complaining about late-night, low-altitude passes by crazy pilots.

Fox shrugged. "What can't be changed can't be helped." A thin smile appeared on his own face. "We'll just have to risk the noise citations."

"True that," Flynn said. "Besides, the cops would have to

catch us first . . . and my guess is no town constable's going to have a speedboat on standby to chase after us." He sighed and straightened his shoulders. Then he keyed his radio mike. "Gryphon Lead to all Gryphons, rally on home plate, pronto. We're going up to bat in the majors. Spring training is over."

He listened carefully while startled acknowledgments flooded through his headset. Up to that moment, the widely dispersed sections of his force had been busily engaged in carrying out a range of different live-fire and flight training. But now, with a single quick order, he'd told them that their time of preparation was over. Whatever they had learned—about tactics, about their brand-new equipment, and about working as a cohesive whole—would have to be enough. Because now they were headed into battle.

Satisfied that everyone had gotten his message, Flynn turned back to Fox. "You know," he said with a thoughtful look, "at least this is going to make Laura happy." Noting the quizzical expression on the older man's face, he explained. "Because she's finally going to get a chance to fight instead of just flying the getaway plane."

THIRTY-SIX

KOSVINSKY KAMEN NUCLEAR COMMAND
BUNKER, DEEP IN THE NORTHERN
URAL MOUNTAINS, RUSSIA

THE NEXT DAY

Thirteen hundred kilometers west-northwest of Moscow, the snowcapped granite dome of Mount Kosvinsky Kamen rose more than fifteen hundred meters above the neighboring valleys. The mountain's summit lay buried under meters of hard-packed snow and ice, while the lower two-thirds of its slopes were cloaked in stands of Siberian pine, fir, larch, and birch trees. Scattered throughout those forests were camouflaged S-500 antiballistic missile launchers. Battle-management radars sited high up on neighboring peaks were online, ready to feed tracking and engagement data to their tied-in missile units. Barbed wire fences backed by roving security patrols sealed off the entire area.

The reason for those layers of defenses was buried far under the mountain, below more than three hundred meters of solid granite. The Kosvinsky Kamen nuclear command bunker was the ultimate nerve center of Russia's strategic air, rocket, and ballistic missile submarine forces. From its deep subterranean vaults, protected against anything but direct hits by the most powerful and accurate nuclear earth-penetrator warheads, Moscow's political and military elites could both unleash Armageddon and then hope to ride out the terrible consequences in relative safety.

Now those leaders were meeting inside a secure conference room located at the heart of the mammoth multilevel bunker. Vault-like armored doors guarded by squads of heavily armed soldiers closed off this chamber from the rest of the complex. No one without the very highest security clearance was ever admitted to this innermost sanctum with its computer-driven situation maps and shielded communications links to Russia's ICBM launch control centers, strategic bomber bases, and fleet headquarters.

From his place at the Russian president's right hand, Pavel Voronin studied Zhdanov's other close advisers. Difficult though it was, he forced himself to conceal his contempt for them. They were like the dinosaurs, he thought idly, staring up at an incoming asteroid without the slightest comprehension of what was about to happen—except possibly for some small nagging sense of instinctive fear. None of them had any idea of why they had so urgently been summoned to the sheltered underground confines of Kosvinsky Kamen. Certainly, none had any understanding of what else was now in motion. Of all the men seated around the U-shaped conference table, only he and Zhdanov were privy to the secrets involved in CASTLE KEEP.

The silent, intimidating presence of four of the president's personal bodyguards along the back wall of the conference room only added to their small but growing sense of unease. By now, it must be clear to even the dimmest member of Zhdanov's inner circle that whatever was happening here was not simply a routine exercise to test the readiness of Russia's strategic command and control systems.

Voronin waited patiently while Zhdanov lit another cigarette and took a long, pensive drag. Nicotine was the older man's primary vice these days. With a meditative glance around the room, as though he were evaluating the true worth of everyone seated at the table, the president blew out a lungful of smoke. Then, with a shrug, Zhdanov turned to him. "Why don't you go ahead and update our friends here, Pavel. It's time they learned the current situation."

Voronin noted the sudden looks of mingled alarm and irritation on several faces. The realization that, once again, they had been kept out of the loop by Zhdanov in favor of an outsider whom they considered rash and dangerous and far too ambitious must be especially galling. Some of them were probably even shrewd enough to sense just how far his real ambitions extended. The president would not live forever. And in the ordinary course of events, one of the other men at this table might have expected to become his successor. Well, Voronin thought, they were about to learn that nothing about the world's immediate future would be ordinary—not in any sense of the word.

He leaned forward slightly. "Gentlemen, the top-secret operation I'm briefing you on is code-named CASTLE KEEP. The reasons for this should be immediately obvious." He touched a key on the control pad in front of him. The large wall screen they were all facing lit up in response. Its main panel showed a detailed map of the United States. A single blue dot blinked rapidly near the very center of the other country, deep in its heartland.

Astonished murmurs ran around the room.

"And what the devil is that?" Gennady Kokorin, the minister of defense, rasped.

"The key to Russia's future as *the* global superpower . . . and to the destruction of America as a functioning nation-state," Voronin answered evenly.

Zhdanov's other advisers stared at him in utter disbelief. Kokorin recovered his voice first. A cynical frown appeared on his deeply wrinkled face. "The key to the future? A flyspeck in the middle of nowhere?" The old man had to peer hard even to read the map. "In this Kansas place?" He snorted. "How can you seriously make such an absurd claim?"

Voronin smiled, allowing himself to savor the moment. With luck, the shock of what he was about to say might kill a couple of these old fossils—clearing away a little more of the deadwood obstructing his path to power. "Because this 'flyspeck,' as you call it, happens to be the site where more than twenty highly advanced unmanned stealth aircraft are currently based." His voice hardened. "Based, I might add, right under the noses of the completely unsuspecting Americans."

Lieutenant General Yvgeny Rogozin, the head of Russia's Air Force, gaped at the map in open-mouthed consternation. "That's impossible! We have no such stealth drone aircraft. Not in service, at least."

Voronin shrugged. "*You* do not, General." He allowed a hint of irony to enter his own voice. "But *I* do . . . or more accurately, *the president* does—thanks to the efforts, extraordinary investments, and expertise of my organization, the Raven Syndicate." He tapped a key, and another panel of the wall screen came to life. This one showed an image of one of the Mora UCAVs—complete with the details of its range, speed, stealth characteristics, and payload capacity.

Rogozin reddened with anger. Even a cursory glance at those numbers showed that these new aircraft were far more capable than anything in the Russian Air Force's current operational inventory, or even in its near-term research and development pipeline. Seeing the evidence that his official research facilities and contractors had been leapfrogged by the Syndicate—a group Rogozin must view as a mercenary band of hired killers and bandits—was undeniably infuriating. The general stabbed a finger at the image of the Mora on screen. "And how have you armed these unmanned planes of yours?" he demanded.

Zhdanov abruptly ground out his cigarette.

With mild interest, Voronin noted the small, almost invisible tremor in the president's hands. The older man's show of nerves was understandable, though unnecessary. The balance of power in this subterranean room had long since shifted.

Voronin smiled at Rogozin, though it was a thin, mocking smile that never reached his cool, calculating eyes. "I am happy to inform you that each Mora carries a one-hundred-and-fifty-kiloton nuclear warhead," he said. His tone was that of a man stating certain cold, hard facts.

For a long, increasingly uncomfortable moment, the assembled generals, admirals, and cabinet ministers stared back at him, seemingly unable to comprehend what they had just heard. At last, one of them, Aleksandr Ivashin, head of the General Staff's military intelligence agency, the GRU, blurted out, "You've deployed atomic weapons onto American soil? You must be completely mad!"

"On the contrary," Voronin contradicted him quite calmly. "President Zhdanov and I are both wholly sane. And since we are capable of grasping key facts, we are also able to see clearly what will befall our beloved Motherland unless we act . . . and act quickly." He adopted a tougher tone, taking on some of the mannerisms of a professor lecturing a classroom of dullards on facts they should already know. "It's high time you learn to face reality, harsh though it may be. Our population is aging rapidly.

Our industries are obsolete and riddled with corruption. In total, our gross domestic production lags behind that even of Italy!"

He shook his head in disgust. "The time to stay cozily wrapped in the comfortable illusions we've clung to for decades has passed. The sad truth is that Russia is already a third-rate economic and conventional military power." Voronin's eyes roved around the table, daring anyone to deny what he was saying. No one took up the challenge. "One thing only gives us even the semblance of geopolitical strength—our strategic rocket and ballistic missile submarine forces."

That drew approving nods, particularly from Colonel General Anatoly Gruzdev, the commander of Russia's Strategic Rocket Forces, and Admiral Golitsyn, the head of the navy.

But then Voronin merely shrugged his shoulders, visibly dismissing the importance of such weapons. "But of what real use have those missiles ever been to us, even after we've spent trillions upon trillions of rubles designing, building, and storing them away? None! They sit idle in silos, on mobile launchers, and locked inside steel cans circling aimlessly under the sea."

"They deter the Americans from destroying us utterly!" Gruzdev snapped back, plainly nettled.

"Your theories are outdated," Voronin countered effortlessly. "Even a child can see that the Americans have *no* intention of attacking us militarily. Why should they? The correlation of political and economic forces is entirely in their favor. Time is *their* ally, not ours. All Washington needs to do is wait patiently while we shrink, shrivel, and finally implode entirely."

From the thoughtful, considering looks appearing on some of the faces around the table, he could tell that he'd scored a point. Political, economic, and military intelligence analysis confirming what he had said was not popular reading in Moscow's highest circles, but it existed nonetheless. And some of these men, however willfully ignorant they might otherwise be, had obviously seen those same reports.

Breaking the silence, Zhdanov rapped the table sharply. Russia's president might have risen to the top of the heap through intrigue and sheer ruthlessness, but his political skills were undeniable. If nothing else, he knew how to read the mood of an audience. "Pavel is right," he declared forcefully. "CASTLE KEEP offers us a chance we badly need—a chance to break out of the box we're in. The opportunity to reverse decades of decline, to destroy our single most formidable and dangerous rival, and to restore Russia to its rightful place as the world's foremost power."

Kokorin cleared his throat. "All things devoutly to be wished, Piotr," the minister of defense said, speaking slowly and with careful deliberation. "But the risks of taking such action—"

"Exist, Gennady," Zhdanov said sharply, cutting off the older man. "Nevertheless, given the choice between taking some risks now and facing an inexorable collapse in the not-so-distant future, I choose to act." He glared around the table. "There is no room for debate on this question. The decision has been made. The weapons are in place. There is no going back now." He shrugged. "Even if it were desirable, exfiltrating the Mora drones secretly at this stage would be impossible." The president glanced aside at Voronin. "Continue your briefing on the attack plan, Pavel."

Voronin nodded. His fingers entered more commands on the control pad at his place. They triggered a sophisticated computer program cued to his voice so that as he spoke, icons appeared and moved on the conference room's map displays— visually hammering home the elements of the CASTLE KEEP strike plan as he laid them out. "Once our team inside the United States is given the final 'go' code by the president, the

Mora UCAVs based there will take off at precisely timed intervals. As soon as they are airborne, our stealth aircraft will proceed to their preselected targets along flight paths selected to minimize any risk of detection."

Rogozin frowned. "And just what are those targets?" he asked heavily.

"A range of critical strategic sites," Voronin said. "Among them: Washington, DC, and the Pentagon; the Raven Rock and Mount Weather command bunkers; NORAD headquarters near Cheyenne Mountain; the US Strategic Command headquarters in Nebraska; the two American ballistic missile submarine bases; and all three of their B-2 and B-52 bomber bases." As he listed them, red targeting symbols blinked into existence on the digital map, scattered across the length and breadth of the United States.

"A decapitation strike," Rogozin said in dawning realization.

Voronin nodded. "Exactly so, General. Every weapon will be timed to go off over its chosen target at precisely the same instant. Quite literally in the blink of an eye, our Moras will completely annihilate America's political and military leadership, smash its strategic bomber force, cripple much of its ballistic submarine fleet, and wreck any chance the survivors have of communicating effectively with their remaining forces."

Colonel General Gruzdev scowled. "And yet," he pointed out with a gloom-ridden face, "the American ICBM force will remain intact in its own hardened silos, ready to take its vengeance on us—and on our people."

Zhdanov banged his fist down on the table, startling the Strategic Rocket Forces commander into silence. "Not if you do your own fucking job right, Anatoly!" he barked.

"Mr. President?" Gruzdev said hesitantly, clearly at a loss.

Zhdanov's jaw tightened. "Think it through," he said with

cold emphasis. "The moment our early-warning satellites detect our bombs going off over the CASTLE KEEP targets, you will launch a massive follow-on strike on the American Minuteman III missile fields using our own ICBMs."

They all stared at him. The implications were clear enough. With America's political and military leaders vaporized in the radioactive ruins of Washington, DC, and elsewhere, the US military wouldn't be able to react—not in the brief thirty minutes between the moment Russia's ballistic missiles blasted aloft out of their own silos and that deadly instant when hundreds and hundreds of nuclear warheads rained down across the Minuteman III complexes in Wyoming, North Dakota, and Montana. When the resulting deluge of fire, shock wave, and radiation came to an end, the United States would be left with only a handful of submarines at sea. And America would find itself without any ability to retaliate effectively—not without accepting the massacre of its civilian population by Moscow's own remaining weapons. The "war" would be over in less than an hour . . . and with it any future for the United States except as a starveling beggar nation—one entirely dependent on whatever scraps Russia deigned to hand out.

Gennady Kokorin stared at Zhdanov in absolute horror. "This is Petrov's plan," he muttered. "A plan created by a dying madman with nothing to lose."

Both Voronin and the president shrugged. That much was true, in a sense. Of necessity, CASTLE KEEP incorporated many of the same elements of the strike intended two years before by Colonel Alexei Petrov, using the cruise missiles aboard a stealth bomber prototype he had stolen. At the time, left without any alternatives, Zhdanov had been prepared to go along with Petrov's scheme, though under duress.

The events of the past years, however, had only proved that

the colonel's analysis of Russia's strategic situation was accurate. And further study of Petrov's proposed attack plan had also revealed that the aims he intended could have been achieved, if only the PAK-DA bomber prototype hadn't mysteriously crashed before the renegade colonel could launch his cruise missiles.

In retrospect, Zhdanov had increasingly come to regret Petrov's ultimate failure, however relieved he had been at the time. Left unstated, Voronin knew, was the president's own increasing awareness that his time in power was growing short. Either he acted decisively now, or he risked sliding into feeble irrelevance as his health inevitably declined.

For Voronin's part, he understood the dangers involved, at least to those tens of millions who might be caught outside the sanctuary offered by this massive bunker and its hundreds of meters of granite shielding. But they were far outweighed, in his judgment, by the useful chaos that would be unleashed by CASTLE KEEP. For now, he had made himself Zhdanov's most trusted counselor. But the men of the old guard were only waiting to pull him down the instant the president lost his own grip on power. If, however, the unmanned Mora aircraft he had created actually succeeded in opening the door to the destruction of the United States, Voronin would have made himself untouchable. No one would be able to stop his rise to power, not even, he thought coolly, Zhdanov himself.

Silently, he watched while the men of the Kremlin's inner circle exchanged frightened, ineffectual glances. He fought down the urge to laugh out loud. They would yield to the president's will—and to his. What real choice did they have?

But then, to Voronin's surprise, Gennady Kokorin forced himself up out of his chair. The defense minister's face was ashen, almost bloodless, but clearly determined. "This madness must stop, Piotr!" he said forcefully. "Before it drags us all into the abyss!" He stabbed an accusing finger at Voronin. "This young fool you've allowed to delude you plays with the lives of tens of millions, perhaps hundreds of millions, as though they were nothing more than pieces on a giant chessboard. But this is no game! You cannot put the Motherland at risk like this!"

Zhdanov stared back at the older man. "Are you refusing to obey my orders, Minister Kokorin?" he asked.

"Of course!" Kokorin snapped back. He turned his gaze to the others in the room. "As should everyone else in the chain of command. Before it's too late and this insane operation ignites the apocalypse."

Voronin leaned closer to Zhdanov. "This is treason," he pointed out quietly.

Zhdanov nodded sternly. He gestured to his bodyguards. Two of them came forward from the back of the conference room and grabbed Kokorin's arms. The defense minister's eyes widened in surprise. "Enough, Gennady!" Zhdanov growled. He turned to a third bodyguard. "Deal with this traitor. Immediately."

The two security personnel pinning Kokorin's arms hustled him toward the armored door leading into the hallway beyond. The third guard followed behind, already unbuttoning the flap of his holster to pull out his 9mm MP-443 Grach pistol. The fourth bodyguard activated the door controls. It swung open.

Kokorin and his captors passed through the door. It closed behind them, but not before those still seated in shock around the conference table heard the muffled sound of a shot. Moments later, the armored door swung back open. One of Zhdanov's bodyguards came back in. He nodded formally to the president. "The problem has been dealt with, sir."

"Good," Zhdanov said heavily. "Make sure the mess is cleaned up." He turned back to the rest of his advisers with a feral gleam in his eyes. "Do any of you have further objections? If so, you are free to resign. Effective immediately."

That shut them up, Voronin noted with satisfaction. Kokorin's sudden execution had settled the matter. Rogozin and the others could no longer doubt the fate in store for anyone who opposed the president or his plans. Anyone who wasn't immediately liquidated on Zhdanov's order would certainly be tossed outside the bunker's sheltering embrace—at a time when the threat of all-out nuclear war loomed very large indeed.

When none of the remaining generals and cabinet officials responded, Zhdanov turned back to Voronin. "Send the appropriate codes to your men in Kansas and in Cuba, Pavel," he ordered. "You have my approval for CASTLE KEEP's final phase."

Voronin checked his watch. According to his plan, the first Mora drones, those with the farthest to fly, were scheduled to take off at midnight, US Central Standard Time—roughly sixteen hours from this moment.

"I will do so at once," he agreed. How fortunate, he thought, that he would never have to reveal to Zhdanov that no such coded orders were necessary. No matter how this "discussion" had gone, it had always been Voronin's intent to present the president and those around him with a fait accompli. He smiled. "And may I suggest that the appropriate term for the precise instant our drone-carried nuclear weapons will detonate is *Vremya Unichtozheniya*?"

Zhdanov nodded with a grim smile of his own. "A fitting choice, Pavel. *Vremya Unichtozheniya*, Obliteration Time, it is. Which makes this—?"

"U minus nineteen hours and counting," Voronin replied.

THIRTY-SEVEN

CIA HEADQUARTERS, LANGLEY, VIRGINIA

THAT SAME TIME

Miranda Reynolds, head of the CIA's Directorate of Operations, waited with decreasing patience for the briefer to finish his presentation of all the supposedly significant intelligence and geopolitical developments that had occurred around the world in the past twenty-four hours. In her jaundiced view, these daily meetings for Langley's high-ranking executives were a complete waste of time. That went double for this seemingly endless Key Events briefing. Given the agency's internal politics, every section head in every CIA directorate felt it was imperative to shoehorn at least one item related to his or her fiefdom into the morning presentation for Charles Horne, the director of Central Intelligence. The result, Reynolds thought sourly, was a mind-numbing laundry list of minor events, gossip, rumors, and pure speculation compiled in no particular order of true importance. In fact, if she had to guess, she'd have estimated that roughly four-fifths of the items discussed so far today had about as much real significance as hearing about the president's current favorite flavor of ice cream.

From the satisfied expression on his jowly face, however, it was evident that Horne did not share her feelings. The DCI had a deep, almost reverential devotion to the whole concept of staff meetings. No issue seemed real to him until it had first been broken down into bullet points, read out verbatim with excruciating dullness, and then thoroughly beaten to death in the course of an around-the-table discussion where every CIA executive present felt compelled to make some comment, no matter how trivial.

Reynolds grimaced. Winston Churchill had once pithily said that "jaw-jaw is better than war-war." The current CIA director's version of that quote might well be "jaw-jaw is better than work-work." Certainly no one stuck around this top-floor conference table was getting any serious part of their real job done right now.

"Meanwhile, we've received confirmation of that earlier report of a massive explosion outside Durango," Henry Markham, the briefer, recited gravely, reading off the PowerPoint slide they could all quite plainly see for themselves. Markham was a middle-ranked member of the DCI's personal staff with delusions of importance. "Apparently, it was centered on a large compound believed to be the headquarters of a major drug cartel, La Hermandad de la Sangre, the Brotherhood of Blood. Estimates of the numbers of dead run close to a hundred, all of them apparently senior cartel leaders and enforcers."

"Gee, what a terrible shame," the head of the Science and Technology directorate said dryly.

"I think we can safely resist the temptation to send condolences," Horne agreed with an equally sardonic smile. He turned to Christine Heseltine, who had recently been appointed to manage the Directorate of Analysis. "Any guesses as to who did it? And how?"

Heseltine, petite, with dark-blond hair and horn-rimmed glasses, leaned forward. "I've spoken to my people in the Latin American section," she said. "They're inclined to point the finger at some of the other cartels. There's certainly no love lost between the Sinaloa organization and the Brotherhood, for instance. This probably came to a head as part of some undeclared gang war for control over drug and human trafficking in that region of Mexico. As to the method?" She shrugged. "Probably a truck bomb. A big one. At a guess, something involving ammonium nitrate."

Heads nodded in agreement. Bombs created out of commercial fertilizers had tremendous potential explosive power if they were carefully designed. They had long been a weapon of choice for terrorists and criminals.

"What about the rumor that a couple of the local farmers are saying it was actually a bomb dropped from an airplane?" someone else asked.

Heseltine shook her head dismissively. "I think we can definitively rule that out." She ticked off her reasons with precision. "First, realistically speaking, an air attack of that magnitude could only be carried out by a government. It's not the sort of operation that even a powerful cartel like the Sinaloas could hope to pull off. And second, I cannot see any circumstances that would motivate the current Mexican government to wipe out the Brotherhood's leadership like this. Mexico City's whole policy up to now has largely been to turn a blind eye to cartel operations, in the hopes of securing some illusion of domestic peace."

"Maybe the people in power in Mexico City don't have the motive or the means to bomb the crap out of a bunch of narcos," the head of Science and Technology said. He raised an eyebrow. "But we certainly do."

Reynolds noticed faces turning in her direction. In the past, CIA black-ops paramilitary units, the Navy's SEAL teams, and the Army's Delta Force were known to have carried out secret operations deep inside Mexico aimed at the drug cartels. She shook her head with a tight, small smile. "This was not our baby," she said flatly.

"Folks up on Capitol Hill and in the White House will be wondering about that," Horne commented.

Reynolds nodded. "I'd recommend taking the usual line," she suggested. "The bit about not being able to comment on anything that might involve sensitive intelligence and national security matters."

That drew the sort of cynical grins she'd expected. The wording was a term of art expressly intended to create useful uncertainty—rather than unhelpful clarity. Some would understand it as a denial of CIA involvement. Others would take it as a dark hint that Langley had, in fact, played some role in wiping out the Brotherhood's senior leadership. If nothing else, just leaving open the possibility would boost the agency's reputation as a player in the region, even if it was complete nonsense.

Horne jotted down a note to himself. "Very good, Miranda," he said approvingly. He turned back to the briefer. "Do you have anything else this morning, Henry?"

"Only one more item," Markham said. He scrolled down to the next bullet point. "Apparently there are some indications that the senior Russian leadership may be conducting another strategic-command readiness exercise. We've tracked a couple of flights from Moscow out to Yekaterinburg, including one that might be President Zhdanov's personal plane."

Horne looked momentarily blank.

"That's the closest airfield to their Kosvinsky Kamen nuclear command bunker," Heseltine reminded him.

The DCI's face cleared. "Ah."

"On top of that, SIGINT and other technical intelligence we've collected over the past twenty-four hours may indicate that the antiballistic missile units and radars around the mountain have been brought to a higher state of readiness," the briefer continued.

Horne turned to Heseltine. "Is this anything we need to worry about?"

The head of Analysis shook her head. "I strongly doubt it, Director. Moscow runs these kinds of exercises more for domestic political consumption than any serious military purpose." Her tone was laced with irony. "It's all the stuff of propaganda, the usual 'our heroic Strategic Rocket Forces stand ready to guard the Motherland against a treacherous sneak attack by the evil West' nonsense."

"Which we have absolutely no intention of ever doing," Horne said, sounding amused.

Heseltine nodded. "Exactly, sir. This has to be just a show, another excuse for Zhdanov to strut around in front of his generals and look tough. After the last few years, everybody knows that Russia's conventional forces are largely a joke—at least in a strategic sense. For the boys in the Kremlin, their nuclear weapons are the only thing left propping their country up as a player on the world scene. Every so often, they have to remind everybody of that."

"And your recommendations?" Horne asked.

Heseltine considered her response for no more than a few seconds. "Just that we continue to observe. It's possible we could pick up some useful technical intelligence about their real command and control methods by watching this exercise unfold."

Reynolds leaned in with a suggestion of her own. "You might also want to alert the White House and State Department to expect some more meaningless saber-rattling by Moscow, Director."

"Oh?"

She nodded. "We've seen the pattern before. Zhdanov comes back full of beans after hearing all about his oh-so-powerful nuclear missiles. And then he feels compelled to go out in front of a bunch of TV cameras and blow off steam by uttering the standard-issue dour threats against the sinister machinations of Big Bad NATO and its greedy American paymasters."

Horne snorted. "None of which he actually means, I suppose."

"Oh, I've no doubt whatsoever that Zhdanov means every single word," Reynolds told him. She shrugged. "But he's also not stupid or crazy enough to believe Russia could ever win a major war against us. And ultimately, of course, that's all that really matters."

ABOARD THE DYNAMIC VOYAGER, IN THE GULF OF MEXICO, WEST OF FLORIDA
A SHORT TIME LATER

The crew dining area took up most of the forward superstructure's second level, with a serving hatch that opened into the galley. The tables and chairs now filled with the men and women of Gryphon Force were bolted to the deck as a precaution against bad weather. For the moment, however, that was a completely unnecessary safety measure. The ship rode easily, steaming south at twelve knots under a bright, almost cloudless sky. White foam curled away from its broad bow as it shouldered through a succession of low, rolling waves.

Nick Flynn read through the long email message he'd just received on his smartphone. Ostensibly from an old high school friend, it was full of family news—all about vacations taken or planned, kids in school, mutual acquaintances, and memories of the teenage pranks they'd pulled together. It all sounded completely plausible. And not one word of it was true.

In reality, this email was from Fox—one sent using the plain-language word code created by the Quartet Directorate to pass messages that wouldn't attract attention from hostile or even friendly government intelligence agencies. Groups like the UK's Government Communications Headquarters (GCHQ), the US's National Security Agency, Russia's Foreign Intelligence Service (SVR), and China's Ministry of State Security routinely siphoned up all emails, text messages, and phone calls—relying on supercomputers to sift them for anomalies, indications of unusually strong encryption, and various key words and phrases.

Part of Four's training for its agents required the rote memorization of hundreds of seemingly ordinary phrases and words in a wide range of different languages. Each of these phrases or words had very specific secret meanings, which changed depending on how they were used in any given sentence. Apparently a simple idea, it was also fiendishly complex in practice. But thanks to a near-perfect memory and an excellent ear, Flynn had mastered the system over several weeks of painful and painstaking practice shortly after he'd joined the Quartet Directorate.

Now, his eyes narrowed as he read the final lines of Fox's message: *Give my best to your folks and the rest of the family, even that crazy distant cousin of yours. What was his name again? Something like Paul, wasn't it?*

"Oh shit," Flynn murmured as different coded phrases shook out in his mind. He felt cold.

"Trouble, Nick?" Laura Van Horn asked from across the table they were sharing.

With a sigh, he looked up from the phone. "Hell, yeah. More than you can imagine, I'm afraid."

"I don't know," she said coolly. "I can imagine quite a lot. Try me."

Sooner and not later, he was going to have to share some of what he'd been told with the rest of the team, so he might as well start with her. "Fox just received some new intel from one of his remaining sources at Langley," he said.

"Let me guess. This wasn't the good kind of intelligence," Van Horn said, watching his eyes. "The kind where we all join hands and sing glad hosannas because the bad guys have seen the light of reason and given up their evil ways?"

"Not hardly," Flynn agreed. "Because from what we can tell, Zhdanov and his top advisers have just started what's being described as a strategic nuclear command readiness exercise. Apparently, they've all flown out of Moscow and gone deep underground in one of those big bunkers in the Urals."

Van Horn stared at him for a long second. "Well, crap, Nick," she said at last. "You weren't kidding."

He smiled ruefully. "I sure wish I was."

"So the Russian stealth drones Voronin's got hidden somewhere in the States *aren't* going to be carrying conventional bombs or missiles. And he sure as hell isn't planning to launch some sort of deniable terror campaign," Van Horn said softly.

"Nope."

Her mouth tightened. "Which boils down to the probability that those UCAVs will be carrying nukes, after all."

Flynn nodded with equal grimness. "I figure that's the case. So does Br'er Fox. It's the only way any of the pieces fit now. Otherwise there's no reason for Zhdanov and his goons to hightail it to the Urals." He frowned. "I bet Voronin sold his bosses on the idea of using nuclear-armed stealth drones to kick the shit out of our command and control. All of our warning systems and defenses are oriented against threats coming in over the polar ice cap or out from across the Pacific or Atlantic. So nobody on our side will even see an all-out attack coming from inside our own territory, let alone be able to do anything that might stop it."

"Which sounds an awful lot like the plan that son of a bitch Petrov blabbed to you aboard that stolen Russian stealth bomber, just before you crashed his crazy ass into a ridge in northern Alaska," Van Horn said.

Flynn nodded grimly. "Yeah, it does."

"Well, then I guess that leaves just us," Van Horn realized. Slowly, almost imperceptibly, a tiny hint of amusement flickered into life in her eyes.

Flynn stared at her. "What's so funny?"

She shrugged. "It's only this, bucko. Nothing's really changed, has it? Nukes or no nukes, it's not like we were going to sit back and let that rat bastard Voronin hit our country unchallenged anyway."

"The stakes just got a lot higher," he pointed out. "If we fail this mission—"

Van Horn just smiled at him.

"Right," Flynn said slowly. "Failure is not an option."

"It never was," she reminded him. "With your shield or on it, as the Spartan mothers used to tell their sons before battle. We win this fight. Or we don't come home. Because there won't be a home left to come back to anyway."

THIRTY-EIGHT

CASTLE KEEP MORA UCAV HANGAR, RURAL KANSAS

SOME HOURS LATER

Ivan Strelkov bent his head to clear the underside of Mora Zero-One's wing and moved forward to where one of his aircraft handlers was fitting the clamp of a tractor tug to the drone's nose wheel. He glanced down at his watch. The local time was just past 2300 hours. His pulse quickened. In a little less than an hour, this unmanned machine would lift off under the control of a pilot based in Cuba and fly westward toward its designated target—the American ballistic missile submarine base at Bangor, Washington.

As soon as it arrived overhead at a precisely calculated moment, the UCAV would dive straight into Delta Pier, a colossal structure where up to four of the enemy's eighteen-thousand-ton Ohio-class submarines, each carrying twenty-four Trident II D5 missiles, were usually berthed. Strelkov smiled, imagining the result. At point-blank range, the detonation of the Mora's

150-kiloton nuclear warhead would leave nothing but twisted and half-melted radioactive hulks littering the bottom of the Hood Canal.

The handler finished attaching his tow tug, climbed aboard, and started up. Strelkov stepped back out of the way as the pale-gray flying wing began rolling toward the nearest tall bay door. He watched it go with satisfaction and then turned to where another of his men was busy with a second aircraft tug, readying Mora Zero-Two for its own short journey outside the cavernous warehouse facility that they'd turned into a hangar building. Like its companion, Zero-Two needed to fly more than two thousand kilometers to reach its own target, the Pentagon. One after another, the twenty-one remaining drones would follow at precisely selected intervals, each set to obliterate a vital American military or political target.

Faced with the need to launch all the Moras in so short a time, Strelkov had opted to move as many of them as possible to their taxi positions outside the huge distribution building. Since it was late at night and the closest town was far away, he was willing to gamble that no one would notice the futuristic-looking aircraft scattered across the vast unlighted parking lot.

Or at least no one who would live long to ask any inconvenient questions, he thought. His observers were already in place along the two-lane highway outside. They were disguised in the same blue-gray uniforms and felt campaign hats worn by the Kansas Highway Patrol. Any cars or trucks that approached while the UCAVs were deploying and taking off would be stopped—and those inside quickly and efficiently dispatched.

By the time any bodies were found, it would be far too late. Strelkov and his team already had their personal gear stowed aboard the convoy of SUVs and semitrailer trucks that had brought them to this isolated complex several weeks ago. Their escape route had been carefully mapped to stay well away from any American strategic targets that would be nuked by Russia's follow-on ICBMs.

The time for caution and concealment was nearly over.

ABOARD THE DYNAMIC VOYAGER, OFF THE COAST OF CUBA, IN THE STRAITS OF FLORIDA
THAT SAME TIME

From his position on the ship's bridge wing, Nick Flynn swept a pair of binoculars through a slow arc. A dull orange glow in the southeast, far off the starboard bow, marked the location of Havana's urban core. Farther west, the dark night sky was broken here and there by isolated patches of brightness. This far out to sea, the coast itself was well below the horizon. What he was seeing was the light haze from the handful of small towns and villages along a sixteen-mile stretch between the outskirts of the Cuban capital and the port of Mariel.

"We're in position, Nick," a gravelly voice said from over his shoulder. "Twelve nautical miles north of the beach at Punta Barlovento."

Flynn lowered the binoculars and turned to face Captain Ewan McLennan. Short and wiry and white haired, the merchant marine officer was one of Four's part-timers—agents who could be activated when their special skill sets were needed. The older man looked a little ragged around the edges. A ship the size of the *Dynamic Voyager* ordinarily operated with a considerably larger crew than Fox had been able to put together, so McLennan and his fellow sailors had been pulling double shifts on the voyage south from Florida, never getting more than four hours off duty at any time. Flynn nodded gratefully. "Thanks, Captain. Y'all have done wonders to get us here this fast."

"Not a problem," McLennan assured him. "And we'll do our damnedest to be right here waiting for you and your people when the job's done." He looked back through the open hatch at Jeff Sandoval, one of two other merchant marine officers on the bridge. "How's it looking, Jeff?"

"We're all clear on radar, Skipper," Sandoval reported, after a glance at his screen. "There are no air or sea contacts anywhere in visual range at present. Got a commercial airliner or two heading for Havana's José Martí International, but we've been listening in on the circuit, and conveniently enough air traffic control's routing them well away from our position."

Flynn handed the binoculars back to McLennan. "Then I guess we'd better git while the going's good."

The captain nodded. He stabbed a finger at Sandoval. "Okay, Jeff. Let's darken the ship. There's no sense in making it any easier for anyone to see that we're here—or what we're up to."

The other man moved to a panel and began flipping switches. One by one, *Dynamic Voyager*'s red and green marine-navigation and white masthead lights vanished. The ship's interior lighting was already doused, so now they were in almost total darkness, except for faint glows from bridge repeaters and control panels, and from far out to sea behind them, where the moon was just beginning to rise in the east.

Running dark like this was a total violation of all maritime safety regulations and laws. Then again, Flynn thought with a sudden, wild stab of humor, was it really a big deal that they were breaking more of the sea's traditional "rules of the road"? Not compared to the much louder hue and cry that could be triggered by Gryphon Force's band of heavily armed private commandos blowing up military installations inside a sovereign nation. Hell, piracy was probably the least of the crimes they'd be charged with if this operation went sour and any of them were taken alive.

McLennan's eyes gleamed in the sudden blackness. "Reminds me of old times in the Mekong Delta," the captain commented. "Just gliding along real quiet and waiting for Mr. Charles to put in an appearance. And usually hoping like hell he wouldn't." As a much younger man, McLennan had put in two tours with the US Navy's riverine patrols in South Vietnam—trying to interdict the flow of supplies and manpower to the Vietcong guerrillas.

He stuck out his hand. "Good hunting, Nick."

Flynn took it in a strong grip. Then he pulled down his night vision gear and switched it on. The murky, unlit world around him blinked back into clarity—a razor-sharp vista of black and white. He swung onto a ladder that descended all the way to *Dynamic Voyager*'s long, open aft cargo deck and went down it fast.

The men and women of his two strike units were gathered at the foot of the ladder, waiting for him. Between their body armor, helmets, weapons, and equipment pouches loaded with extra ammunition and other gear, they were all carrying a lot of extra weight. Flynn's eyes sought out those of Tony McGill, who would lead the assault group tasked with hitting the Cuban military airfield at San Antonio de los Baños.

The ex–SAS sergeant grinned back at him. His teeth were startlingly white against the rest of his dark, camouflage-painted face. "All set, Nick?" he asked cheerily.

"We've reached our planned launch point off the coast," Flynn told him, raising his voice a little so that everyone could hear over the soft lap of waves against the hull and the deep, throaty rumble of the ship's big diesel-electric engines turning over at low RPMs. "And there's no sign yet that we've been spotted."

"And since there's no point in waiting around for the enemy to wake up and notice that we're out here off their coast, we're going now?" McGill guessed.

"We're going," Flynn agreed.

McGill glanced at his watch. "It's just past midnight. Do you still reckon your team needs a head start before my guys kick things off?"

"Yeah, I do," Flynn said firmly. "We'll push on as fast as we can once we're feet dry, but I figure we need to build in some extra time in case we get hung up somewhere."

"Friction's a nasty, bloody bitch," McGill said with an approving nod of his own. "Because she always gets her say." In war, even the simple things were hard. And moving a unit at night in unfamiliar territory was among the most difficult of all military tasks. Flynn's team was almost guaranteed to run into delays along their route.

Early on in their mission planning, it had become clear that the two Gryphon Force teams should lift off from their improvised aircraft carrier in two waves, setting out at two staggered times. The hoverbikes Flynn's unit would be using were both slower and shorter ranged than the speeders equipping McGill's team. On the other hand, they were also considerably quieter. So his section of Gryphon Force would depart first—flying straight to a stretch of little-used country road just inland from the beach. Once there, they'd land, switch the hoverbikes back to ground mode, and drive the rest of the way to a concealed jump-off position near Voronin's remote operations center. Relying on the machines' silent electric motors should keep the noise level to a bare minimum. But the same need for stealth meant following a circuitous route that avoided towns and major roads. Navigating a maze of narrow dirt farm lanes and even heading cross country through fields and over irrigation ditches in the dark was bound to be slow going.

Flynn turned toward Van Horn and the rest of his team, which now included the former Ranger, Andy Cavada; Daina Perez, the ex-Navy helicopter pilot; and two other members of the Navarro Regiment, Roberto Cuellar and Bill Martinez—the first a former Marine with Force Recon experience and the second a veteran of the Army's 160th Special Operations Aviation Regiment. "Okay, guys," he said quietly. "We're on the clock. Saddle up!"

Responding instantly, they scattered across the deck—trotting over to the tarped hoverbikes lined up along the ship's open stern. It took only moments for them to haul off plastic sheeting that had sheltered the fliers against weather and observation, and not much longer to loosen the cables tying them down. In pairs, they mounted up. Practice had confirmed that their best pilots were Flynn, Van Horn, Perez, Martinez, and Cooke. The other members of the team hopped on behind those five, with Tadeusz Kossak riding behind Flynn.

"Gryphon Leader to Gryphon Red Team, com check," Flynn said into his throat mike. Acknowledgments rippled through his headset. With a nod, he switched frequencies, first confirming that McGill and his people were tied in on their tactical radio net, then checking in with Captain McLennan on the ship's bridge, four stories above them. "Gryphon Leader to Voyager, do you read me? Over."

"*Voyager to Gryphon Leader, we read you five by five,*" McLennan replied, confirming that his transmission was both strong and coming in with perfect clarity. "Winds are very light from the south. We're not picking up any new air or sea radar contacts. You are cleared for takeoff at your discretion."

Flynn's finger poised over the hoverbike's starter button. "Gryphon Leader to Red Team. Go for engine start." He punched the button. Immediately, the machine's six turbojets spun up with a low, tooth-grating whine. His eyes darted over the tiny screen set between his handlebars. All six icons representing the engines lit up bright green, signaling that they were operating perfectly. He throttled up, feeding more kerosene into the turbojets. Steadily, the engine whine increased, becoming ever shriller. Slowly, the hoverbike lifted off the deck, wobbling just a bit as it climbed several feet straight up in the air.

Flynn glanced over his shoulder. The other four bikes were all airborne behind him, bobbing gently on thrust reflected off the ship's deck plates. "Gryphon Leader to Red Team," he radioed. "Follow me!"

Smoothly, he transitioned from hover to horizontal flight. Picking up speed rapidly, the hoverbike zoomed low across the deck and plunged off the stern—dropping to within a few feet of the sea surface before coming back level to slash low above the wave tops.

Flynn felt a wild devil-may-care grin flash across his face. Come what may, this kind of high-speed, low-altitude flying was exciting as hell. As a passenger, it had always made him nervous. Being the one at the controls made all the difference. He swung the handlebars sharply left, leaning into a tight turn as the hoverbike curved out over the sea, and then sped south— trailing a rooster tail of spray and foam blasted skyward by its jets. One more quick glance over his shoulder showed that Van Horn and the others were right on his tail. They flew on toward the Cuban coast, hugging the waves to stay off enemy radar.

The Gryphon Force's Red Team was headed into battle.

THIRTY-NINE

NEAR PUNTA BARLOVENTO, CUBA

A SHORT TIME LATER

With Flynn in the lead, the five Gryphon Force hoverbikes streaked low over an empty, moonlit beach and immediately started decelerating. A hundred yards inland, the shoreline's expanse of sand, rocks, and low-lying scrub gave way to a mix of trees, thicker brush, and tall grass. A narrow dirt trail, bordered by trees on both sides, ran south deeper into the Cuban countryside.

Flynn brought his hoverbike in for a vertical landing on this trail. The others came in right behind him. The instant they touched down, Tadeusz Kossak and the other passengers slid off and fanned out around the little knot of landed vehicles—with their rifles up and ready to meet any unexpected surprises. Flynn and the other pilots switched off their turbojets. The shrill howl faded away, leaving only silence. Quick button pushes started the process of transitioning the bikes to electric-powered ground mode. Smoothly, each hoverbike's four tires rotated back upright and slid into position in two linked pairs, turning them into quadricycles again.

The procedure took less than a minute to complete.

At a hand signal from Flynn, Kossak and the others on guard remounted. Together, the five bikes headed south—ghosting deeper into Cuba. Only the faint hum of electric motors and a soft crunch of gravel and dirt under their tires marked their otherwise silent trek.

RAIL CROSSING, EAST OF BAUTA, CUBA
A SHORT TIME LATER

Flynn drove slowly across the tracks. The hoverbike's four big tires bumped over the railroad's gravel bed and blocky concrete ties and came back down onto the narrow dirt path on the other side. This was a crossing point for field hands on foot or bicycle who were working the neighboring fields of sugarcane and pineapple. Just across the rail line, the path veered sharply to the right to avoid a tangle of overgrown trees and brush, probably the remains of a long-abandoned orange grove. Over the whir and rustle of insects stirring among the trees, he could hear the soft whining noises made by the four other quadricycles a little ways behind him.

Flynn checked his mental map of their route. They were still about four miles west of their target, and his best guess was that they were now several minutes behind their ideal timetable, just as he'd expected. But he resisted the urge to speed up straight away. Doing so before Van Horn and the others had joined him on this side of the double-tracked rail line would only increase the chances that someone might fall back and take a wrong turn, or run into some other kind of trouble without anyone else noticing.

Suddenly, a bright spotlight speared out of the darkness ahead. Hit full on by the beam, his night vision gear automatically switched off its light intensifiers to avoid overloading his sight.

"*¡Alto!* Halt!" a voice snarled in distinctively Cuban-accented Spanish. "Stop that machine and get your fucking hands in the air! Now!"

From behind him, Flynn heard Kossak mutter, "*Cholera.* Shit." Narrowing his eyes against the glare, he could now make out two men pointing pistols at them. Both wore pale-blue shirts, dark slacks, and gray berets, the uniform of Cuba's National Revolutionary Police. The spotlight practically blinding him was fixed to the driver's side window of their compact patrol car, a Peugeot 106 mini hatchback. The car had been evidently backed in among the overgrown orange trees for concealment.

Bringing the hoverbike to a stop, Flynn slowly raised his hands, palms outward, an action imitated by Kossak. The last thing he wanted to do was spook these guys into shooting first and asking questions later. "Easy there, comrades," he said, using the same Cuban version of Spanish—deeper toned and faster, with a lot more sounds simply dropped or elided, than the Spanish spoken by Tejano relatives on his mother's side of the family. "What's the problem here?"

One of the policemen, a corporal by the single chevron on his shoulder boards, glanced nervously at his superior. His 9mm Makarov pistol wavered slightly. "Uh, Sergeant?" he said hesitantly. "I don't think these are the smugglers we're hunting. They look like soldiers."

"No shit, Felipe," the older man growled back. "What gave it away? The guns? The helmets?" His pistol didn't budge an inch from Flynn and Kossak. "The question is: Whose soldiers, exactly? I served my time in the army. And I never saw *any* gear or uniforms like that."

Flynn saw a possible opening—one that might at least buy them some time. "You're quite right, Sergeant," he said briskly. "We're part of a brand-new unit, the Revolutionary Guards Special Battalion. We're out on a night training exercise, practicing silent infiltration tactics." He smiled disarmingly. "And evidently we have a lot more to learn, since you and the corporal here ambushed us so easily." He nodded with his chin toward one of the pouches on his tactical vest. "I can show you my identity card, if that would help?"

The police sergeant jerked his pistol slightly. "You do that, *comrade*," he said, practically spitting out the last word. "But you lower one hand only. And you do it very, very slowly. Because if I see anything but an ID card coming out of that pouch, I'll blow a fucking hole in your fucking face. Clear?"

Flynn nodded carefully. "Definitely clear."

Without turning his head, the Cuban sergeant snapped an order to his subordinate. "Meanwhile, Felipe, you call this into headquarters. See if they know anything about a bunch of soldiers operating in our patrol area tonight."

"Yes, Sergeant," the corporal responded. He started to back up toward the car.

Damn, Flynn thought. A bead of sweat slid down from under his helmet lining. So much for buying time. The moment that radio call went through, this mission was completely blown. Given the stakes—what looked like an all-out nuclear attack on the United States in the works—they'd have to press on regardless. But there'd be no chance of achieving surprise, either at Voronin's control center or at the San Antonio de los Baños airfield. And without surprise, they were basically all dead.

Van Horn's calm, cool voice ghosted through his headset. "Nick. Tadeusz. Lean right . . . *now.*"

He obeyed, as did Kossak—inclining sideways in their hoverbike seats. The police sergeant scowled. His pistol swiveled to stay centered on them. "I *said*, don't m—"

Pop-pop-pop-pop. Four rapid-fire shots erupted from close behind them, only partially muffled by a suppressor.

Hit twice, once in the chest and once in the forehead, the sergeant's mouth opened wide in horrified amazement. No sounds emerged. His Makarov pistol wavered and then fell out of his suddenly nerveless hand. He slumped forward, dropped first to his knees, and finally collapsed facedown on the ground. Rivulets of blood, black in the glaring white spotlight beam, trickled across the dirt.

The younger man, also shot twice, spun around and went down hard. A hand scrabbled frantically for the weapon he'd dropped. "Damn it," Van Horn said quietly. She fired a fifth shot. This one hit him high up in the back. He shuddered once and lay still.

Flynn breathed out. That had been much too close. He swung round in the seat. Except for Van Horn, the other members of his force were staring, either at him or at the bodies sprawled just ahead of them. She was busy unscrewing a suppressor from the muzzle of her SIG Sauer P226 pistol.

Immediately, his mind shifted back into gear. His job was to lead. Not to stand around with his mouth hanging open because he was still surprised to find himself alive and unwounded. "Cooke! Vucovich!" he snapped. "Shut off that fricking spotlight and shove that car back deeper into those trees. Martinez and Cavada, drag those bodies off a ways, somewhere out of sight." He checked the time. "We're burning up our margin for error fast, people. Step on it!"

OUTSIDE THE REMOTE OPERATIONS CENTER, SOUTHWEST OF HAVANA
A SHORT TIME LATER

Cradling his HK417 rifle, Flynn low-crawled up to the edge of the tree line. The rest of his team slithered into position on either side of him. They'd left their hoverbikes parked out of sight farther back in this dense stand of sumac, mariposas, and dwarf palms. He flipped his regular night vision goggles higher up on his helmet and pulled a pair of powerful light-amplifier binoculars out of one of his vest pouches. The others did the same.

Following his lead, they scanned the ground stretching ahead of them. Switching to binoculars made sense because, from this far away, higher levels of digital magnification were necessary to pick out useful details. A squat, windowless, thick-walled concrete building with rows of white domes across its flat roof sat about three hundred yards to the east. Since there were no lights set outside the structure, the entire area was cloaked in darkness.

Flynn frowned in concentration. At first glance, their primary target looked abandoned, as though it were only an old storage facility left over from the long-ago Cold War days when this whole area was still a major Soviet intelligence base. But the brand-new satellite internet dishes under those white protective domes told a very different story. Behind those solid walls, Voronin's pilots were almost certainly readying their US-based squadrons of remotely controlled stealth drone aircraft for flight.

From here, Flynn and his team also had a good view of the local access road that connected the operations center to a wider boulevard about a half mile away—one running due east to the larger campus of Cuba's University of Information Sciences. The single-lane access road came up from the south and then made a right turn into a small parking area directly in front of the building. Except for the road and parking lot, there was just a wide-open stretch of grassland between their current position and the building. Occasional small rises and hollows across that cleared ground offered a couple of possible concealed avenues of approach for anyone who stayed low, but none that would be easy.

Easy or not, Flynn knew, taking advantage of every piece of potential cover and concealment was the only way his team was going to get closer to Voronin's operations center without being cut to pieces. Now that they had a clearer view into the patches of light woods flanking that building on either side, the true extent of its ground defenses came into very sharp and painful focus.

Trenches had been dug around the outer edges of each clump of trees. Heaped sandbags marked firing positions for machine guns and light mortars. And range stakes planted out in the open ground showed that the defenders already had their small arms and other automatic weapons zeroed in.

Flynn grimaced. At a guess, those trenches, machine gun nests, and mortar pits could shelter up to two platoons of troops, a total of more than forty Cuban infantrymen and gunners. Probably no more than a couple of squads, say roughly twelve to sixteen men, would be standing to on the alert at any given time, but the rest wouldn't take more than a minute or so to man those defenses once an alarm was raised.

As if that weren't bad enough, he could also see that whole stands of trees had been cut down to create clearings that were now occupied by several armored vehicles—sitting silent and motionless at the moment, but full of latent fighting power and menace. To hide those vehicles from aerial and satellite surveillance, the Cubans had strung thick swathes of camouflage netting overhead to mimic the treetops and leaf-covered branches that made up a real forest canopy.

In the woods to the north of Voronin's operations center, the most dangerous of the vehicles Flynn could identify was a forty-one-ton T-62 main battle tank. Even modernized as it was, with thicker armor and an upgraded fire control system, the Soviet-era tank would be no match for a US M1A2 Abrams. Which made it too darned bad they didn't have an Abrams with them, he thought wryly. Because that T-62 could grind his small band of commandos into the dust under its huge treads once it got moving—or, more likely, simply shred them with its 115mm smoothbore main gun, 7.62mm coaxial machine gun, and 12.7mm DShK turret-mounted heavy machine gun. Beyond the T-62, he could make out the shapes of two smaller vehicles. One was a four-wheeled BRDM-2 scout car. The other looked like an eight-wheeled BTR-60 armored personnel carrier.

Three more armored vehicles were positioned in the other patch of woods, the one to the south. One of them appeared to be a PT-76 light tank. The other two were about the same size, but they were tracked BTR-50s—old Soviet-era troop transports. Flynn sighed inside. Antiquated though this oddball assortment of armor might be on a modern battlefield, the collection of vehicles still mounted more than enough firepower to pulverize a squad-sized light infantry assault in seconds.

He swallowed hard against the taste of bile rising in his throat. Whoever had said there were no unwinnable battles was a moron. Gritting his teeth, he forced himself to resume his careful survey of the Cuban defensive positions. Somewhere, somehow, there might be a weakness he could exploit. Realistically speaking, failure—despite his earlier brave words—might actually be an option in these circumstances. But giving up and turning tail sure as hell wasn't.

From farther down the line of prone Four agents, Hynes rattled off a litany of soft-voiced but deeply heartfelt profanities.

He lowered his own binoculars and glanced toward Flynn with a worried look. "You know, sir, this is beginning to seem like a really fucking bad idea."

Flynn forced himself to offer the other man a lazy smile. "You just noticed that, Cole? Remind me to sign you up for another refresher course on tactics when we get back to the States."

His retort drew fast answering grins from the others, including Hynes. Maybe what he'd said wasn't very funny, but the fact that he could still make the effort to joke around mattered to those under his command. No matter how much he might agree with Hynes, one of his chief tasks was to keep up their morale—even in circumstances that made optimism seem like complete and total bullcrap.

Flynn raised his binoculars again. They swept across a pair of sentries standing behind the raw earthen scar that marked the edge of one of the Cuban trenches. Both had AKM assault rifles slung over their shoulders. Neither wore body armor. *Score one at least for the good guys*, he thought. The ballistic plates he and the rest of the Gryphon Force wore might not stop high-velocity rifle rounds all the time, but the extra protection against fragments and pistol-caliber bullets they offered still provided a real edge in combat.

He started to scan away from them, going farther down the trench line . . . and then stopped. *Hold on*, he thought, aware of something important, something he'd just seen, niggling at the corner of his mind. He refocused his binoculars on the two sentries. Only one man wore night vision gear, with what looked like early-model Russian-made goggles clipped to his helmet. The other Cuban soldier simply had a flashlight mounted on the barrel of his assault rifle.

Which had to mean the defenders were desperately short of the high-tech equipment they needed to fight effectively at night,

Flynn suddenly realized. No other explanation made sense. With only a fraction of his force on alert at any given moment, the Cuban commander would otherwise have made sure all of his sentries were as well equipped as possible. No doubt the Cubans had spotlights rigged in places, along with mortar-fired parachute flares, to illuminate a nighttime battlefield . . . but those would only matter in a set-piece engagement—one where the defending troops engaged an attacking force charging straight across the kill zone created by all that open ground.

With lightning speed, the bare-bones sketch of a plan began taking shape in Flynn's mind. And best of all, he hoped, it was a plan that might even work—at least given a lot of luck and skill working in tandem. Quickly, he stuffed his binoculars back into their vest pouch and turned to his team. "Listen up," he said quietly. "Here's how we're going to play this—"

A couple of minutes later, with Flynn in the lead, eight of the ten members of Gryphon Force's Red Team darted out of the tree line in ones and twos, crouching low to stay out of sight of the Cuban sentries posted in the woods a few hundred yards ahead of them. They dropped flat almost right away and started crawling toward the enemy positions, using the minimal cover offered by the open grassland's low hummocks and shallow dips to hide their movements wherever possible.

Tadeusz Kossak and Andy Cavada, each tasked with a separate mission, stayed behind at the very edge of the trees. Kossak lay prone, sighting through the night scope of his Finnish-made TRG-42 sniper rifle. Cavada, the Cuban American Ranger veteran, knelt down next to a tree trunk several yards away, carefully balancing the twenty-eight-pound weight of their unit's single NLAW on his shoulder. His eyes were glued to the missile launcher's telescopic night optic.

Both men waited patiently, ready to act the instant Flynn

gave them the necessary orders . . . or if the situation went very badly wrong before that moment came.

MORA REMOTE OPERATIONS CENTER, NORTHERN DEFENSE OUTPOST
A SHORT TIME LATER

Cuban Revolutionary Army Colonel Agustin Hidalgo sat at his field desk. Under the canvas tarp roofing this earthen dugout, a single small battery-powered lamp provided barely adequate illumination for the paperwork in front of him—a handful of the requisition forms needed to request the transfer of more pieces of night vision gear from Cuba's special forces, colloquially known as the Black Wasps, to his own garrison unit. Frowning, he took off his reading glasses and massaged his aching eyes. This request, his fifth so far, would probably be denied like all the others, but if nothing else, the effort soothed his conscience. As far as his superiors in the Ministry of the Revolutionary Armed Forces were concerned, the equipment he wanted was expensive and scarce, which meant only a handful of pieces could be doled out to any one unit—especially to one that owed its existence more to Cuba's ever-pressing need for hard currency than to any of the island nation's legitimate national security concerns.

It would be helpful to his cause, Hidalgo thought bitterly, if their Russian paymasters ever decided to fill him in on the precise timetable for their operation—whatever it really was. That, however, was quite clearly *not* going to happen. His counterpart, Fyodor Maresyev, had made it abundantly clear that their two groups—his veteran pilots and Hidalgo's conscript soldiers—existed in two very different worlds. In the Russian commander's view, the Cuban colonel's real "need to know" began and ended

with the terse admonition, "You and your troops will guard our
outer perimeter until further notice. That is your only duty,
Comrade Colonel Hidalgo. Nothing else should concern you."

Hidalgo looked up in irritation as one of his subordinates,
a first lieutenant, brushed aside the curtain that screened off his
portion of the small dugout from the outside. "Sir!" the younger
man said quickly. "I think something's going on."

Hidalgo grabbed his pistol belt and rose from his desk.
"Show me, Fuentes," he ordered.

He followed the lieutenant up a few short steps cut out of
hard-packed dirt and emerged into darkness. Off to the east, the
rising moon was still so low that it spilled only a tiny amount of
silvery light under all these trees and camouflage netting—just
enough to allow him to make out the huge silhouette of their
attached T-62M tank parked some meters away.

Blinking rapidly while he waited for his eyes to adjust, Hidalgo snapped, "Now, what is it?"

"Listen, Colonel," the young officer said urgently. He waved
a hand at the night sky off to the west.

And then Hidalgo heard what he meant—the shrill, keening
wail of high-pitched jet engines streaking past some kilometers
away. From the sounds, those aircraft were flying at very low altitude as they came racing from somewhere to the north before
beginning to curve back east at high speed. Toward the airfield
at San Antonio de los Baños, in fact.

He suppressed an exasperated snort. It would do no good to
lose his temper with Fuentes, especially since it was proving so
difficult to teach his junior officers the importance of taking initiative—instead of always waiting for direct orders. He clapped
a kindly hand on the lieutenant's shoulder. "It's nothing for you
to worry about, Ignacio," he said patiently. "My guess is that's
only some of the MiG pilots in our glorious air force showing

off their low-level night-flying skills—and incidentally scaring the devil out of every civilian between here and the coast." His lip curled. "I suspect their base commander will very soon be receiving a large number of extremely angry telephone calls from Havana."

Fuentes nodded, obviously relieved. "Yes, sir."

Straightening up, Hidalgo turned back to his dugout. He wouldn't be able to get to sleep until he finished filling out those tiresome requisition forms. Behind him, the shrill noise of jet engines faded. The MiG fighters they'd heard must be landing, he thought tiredly, already beginning to dismiss the entire episode from his mind.

FORTY

SAN ANTONIO DE LOS BAÑOS MILITARY AIRFIELD

THAT SAME TIME

Five carbon-black jet speeders blazed low across the darkened countryside in a loose diamond formation. Fields of tobacco and sugarcane, orange groves, and stretches of brush-choked waste ground dotted with palms and other trees flashed beneath them, looming up out of the darkness with startling swiftness and then vanishing astern just as rapidly. To avoid being picked up by Cuba's air defense radars, they were practically right down in the dirt—flying barely fifty feet above the ground on a carefully preplotted course that dodged around towns and villages.

Aboard the lead speeder bike as it swept through a turn that brought the formation around to fly east-northeast, Tony McGill craned his head slightly to the side. Buffeting from the slipstream pummeled his visored helmet, but he wanted to be able to see past his pilot, Piero Lucente. There, directly ahead and only a few miles away, he spotted two parallel gray lines stretching across a patchwork quilt of fields and buildings. On this heading, they were aimed straight along the axis of the air base's main runway and its adjoining primary taxiway—and closing in at nearly 120 knots, covering two nautical miles every minute.

Bright lights twinkled across the sprawling complex, outlining rows of barracks, machine shops, warehouses, maintenance hangars, and offices, as well as additional paved strips that led off the runway to separate clusters of camouflaged aircraft shelters. A somewhat dimmer gleam higher up marked where a glassed-in control tower rose to the right of the runway and taxi strip. This was the fighter-interceptor base closest to Havana, Cuba's political and military center of power. Even without MiG-29s or MiG-23s currently in the air, the Cuban Air Force controllers on duty needed to be ready to handle possible flight operations at any time, day or night.

Struck suddenly by the sheer size of the base they were streaking toward, McGill frowned. Studying maps and satellite photos had been one thing. Seeing this large complex spreading out ahead of them in real life was quite another. If there was any consolation, he thought, it was that the collapse of the old Soviet Union had forced Cuba's authoritarian regime to drastically downsize its military establishment. Without hundreds of billions of rubles a year in subsidies from Moscow, the island nation had been forced to rely on its own limited resources—and modern combat aircraft were enormously expensive. So instead of thirty or forty MiG fighters and fighter-bombers, there ought to be a mere handful stationed here now. On the darker side of that equation, even if the Cubans had only five or six operational aircraft hidden in their camouflaged shelters, those planes would still be backed by dozens of ground staff and security personnel—which meant his ten-man Quartet Directorate team could easily be outnumbered by twenty to one, or more.

And if even a single Cuban MiG got off the ground, the

ex–SAS sergeant realized somberly, the whole Gryphon strike force—Flynn's section included—would be in grave danger, hammered by bombs and high-velocity cannon fire from the air, and completely unable to extract safely to the ship waiting for them off the coast.

Which was simply not an acceptable price, McGill decided. He keyed his mike. "Gryphon Two Leader to Gryphon Blue Team," he radioed. "Attack as briefed. Go in hard and fast," he reminded them. "We have the edge in mobility. Use it wherever possible. Don't get bogged down in prolonged firefights. If you run into a strongpoint, engage the bastards only long enough to rattle them. But then shift double quick to another target before they even figure out you've buggered off."

"*One-Three to Lead. Basically, you're just saying we should use our Muhammad Ali ninja-fu,*" Javier Torres, one of the Cuban Americans attached from the Navarro Regiment, replied, sounding amused. The powerfully built former Marine had been his unit's light heavyweight champion. He was riding behind Cristina Ros, who'd flown MV-22 Ospreys for the US Air Force's Special Operations Command. Their assigned call signs were Gryphon One-Three and One-Two respectively. "*Float like a butterfly and sting like a bee.*"

"Bloody well put, One-Three," McGill admitted. Obviously, he'd allowed his own case of nerves to lead him astray. Everyone on his team was a combat veteran. They knew what to do. He glanced past Lucente. The base runway was coming up with breathtaking speed. It was high time he readied his own weapons. Thankful for the quick-release harness that held him securely in the speeder's rear seat as they moved low above the ground, he lifted his slung HK417, pulled a 40mm HE grenade out of the bandolier across his chest, and slid it into the launcher fitted under the rifle's barrel.

Lucente veered slightly to fly straight down the taxiway paralleling the wider main runway. Two of the four other jet speeder bikes in their loose diamond formation stayed on his tail about two hundred yards back but slid into echelon off to his left side. The remaining pair veered away, aiming for their own initial targets.

The onetime Italian Army helicopter pilot eased back on his throttles as they screamed past rows of low, flat-roofed outbuildings. The speeder shed velocity as it reduced thrust. To compensate, all eight paired jet engines swiveled slightly toward the ground, adding lift to keep their vehicle aloft. The airfield's four-story-high control tower loomed out of the darkness ahead of them, growing larger and ever more distinct with astonishing rapidity. Thanks to glowing radar screens, computer monitors, and other active electronic equipment inside, the large windows enclosing its darkened uppermost level were plainly visible against the night sky.

McGill raised the HK417 rifle to his shoulder. He took the grip of the attached under-barrel grenade launcher in his left hand. *One. Two.* The speeder slashed through the air, no more than twenty yards from the top of the control tower, and he had a fleeting impression of shocked faces inside looking up from their equipment—caught completely off guard by the sudden earsplitting noise made by jet engines howling past right outside.

He squeezed the launcher's trigger. *FOOMMP.* There was almost no recoil. A window shattered, punched inward by the 40mm grenade he'd just fired.

McGill craned his neck around as they sped onward. *WHUUMP.* A blinding white flash silhouetted the control tower's upper level from within as the grenade detonated. Instantly, all the windows blew out in a glittering cascade of shattered glass and burning debris. A cloud of dirty gray smoke billowed outward, veiling the scene.

Lucente banked the speeder into a hard, tight turn, coming around over the runway itself to fly back west. Just ahead to their left, McGill saw two dazzling orange flashes light the night. The pair of jet speeders following them—one flown by Ros with Torres as her gunner, and the other by Rytis Daukša with Einar Haugen in the second seat—had swept low over a row of five Cuban Mi-8 helicopters parked on a paved apron. With superb aim, Torres and Haugen had just hit two of those helicopters with 40mm thermobaric grenades.

Both Mi-8s shuddered violently, torn apart inside by powerful fuel-air explosions. Their own fuel tanks ruptured, spraying hundreds of gallons of blazing aviation kerosene across the apron. In seconds, all five parked helicopters were on fire from nose to tail rotor. Clouds of thick, oily black smoke boiled higher into the sky.

Alert sirens keened across the air base, rising and falling in eerie, discordant howls. Lights were going on in buildings across the compound as Cuban air and ground crews and security troops who'd been asleep or otherwise off duty began scrambling for their clothes and gear and weapons.

McGill saw two half-dressed soldiers burst out of a barracks farther down the flight line. One crammed a Soviet-style steel helmet onto his head as he ran. The other was bareheaded and still shrugging into his tunic. Frantically, they sprinted toward a nearby antiaircraft gun position. The weapon inside the protective ring of stacked sandbags was a Russian-made ZU-23. With a trained crew, that twin-barreled autocannon was capable of firing hundreds of 23mm rounds per minute. "Eleven o'clock low, Piero!" he warned.

Lucente nodded. "I see them." He swung into another tight turn and chopped his throttles to slow the speeder bike drastically. They dropped lower, descending at an angle to just a few feet off the ground. Dust and gravel and bits of torn grass whirled away in their wake, ripped loose by the blast of sharply angled jet engines.

McGill sighted down the barrel of his HK417, leading the two running men as the speeder slid past them about sixty yards away. He squeezed off several shots in rapid succession. Spent 7.62mm shell cases spun away from the right side of his weapon. One of the Cubans folded over and instantly went down. The other staggered and reeled away across the gravel, clutching at his stomach. McGill let him go, knowing he was out of the fight and probably dying.

Quickly, McGill shifted his grip back to the under-barrel grenade launcher and slotted in another HE grenade. Then he half turned against the tug of his harness, aiming back toward the two-story building those gunners had just darted out from. It was obviously still used by the base garrison. Light spilled out from its open main doors. Men were grouping there, either still readying their weapons or trying to nerve themselves up to charge outside. "Too late, chums," the ex–SAS sergeant murmured. He fired the grenade straight through the doorway. It went off in a quick burst of bright-white flame and a puff of grayish smoke. Agonized screams echoed sharply from inside the barracks, audible even over the crackling roar of the fuel-fed flames consuming the Mi-8 helicopters.

And then a roiling wake of heated jet engine exhaust slammed down across him as the speeder flown by Cristina Ros flashed by low overhead, streaking down the center of the runway toward another ZU-23. Torres was leaning past her, shooting toward the sandbagged gun. Shredded bits of burlap sacking and pulverized sand sprayed in all directions.

Suddenly, a glowing curtain of tracers rippled outward from the gun position—ripping through the darkness like gouts of molten rock hurled by a volcano. Flashes erupted all around Ros and Torres as multiple proximity-fused HE rounds exploded within yards of them. Caught by a deadly hail of jagged splinters, the jet speeder rolled over and slammed into the runway at more than sixty knots. Mangled wreckage slid onward across the concrete in a blinding shower of sparks, already blazing as its fuel ignited on impact.

Too late, McGill realized the 23mm antiaircraft gun was already manned. Swearing frantically, he thumbed in another grenade from his bandolier. The Cuban gun was more than three hundred yards away, well outside his grenade launcher's effective range against point targets. But maybe he'd get lucky.

Lucente saw the threat in the same moment and accelerated. Staying right on the deck, he brought the jet speeder through another hard, tight turn. A glittering torrent of 23mm tracer rounds slashed low across the runway, sliding ever closer. The Four pilot jinked hard left and then back right, trying to shake off the Cuban gun crew's aim as they desperately tried to bring their autocannon to bear on the small, agile flying machine zooming closer at high speed.

McGill felt his stomach muscles tighten with fear. Now it was a race, he understood. With life or death as the prize.

"Hold on!" Lucente yelled. He pulled back sharply, sending the jet bike arrowing almost straight upward—trading speed for altitude. Tracers rippled past well below them. The Cubans had failed to react quickly enough to their zoom climb. Three hundred feet off the deck, the Italian leveled out. His hands danced across the controls. Responding, the speeder's eight paired turbojet engines pivoted to point straight down. Balanced on their thrust, the bike hovered almost motionless in midair.

Reacting immediately, McGill leaned out over the side of the bike, sighting down the barrel of his HK417. He could see the ZU-23. Its twin barrels were elevating rapidly toward them, coming back on target. Operating on instinct, he squeezed the trigger of the attached launcher.

His 40mm HE grenade burst right on target inside the gun position in a searing flash of white light. Fragments scythed across the two Cuban gunners, tossing them up against the sandbagged walls in a welter of blood.

McGill breathed out in relief and risked a quick look around the ground below them. From this high up, he could see fires burning out of control in various places around the air base. Smoke coiled across the complex and the runway and taxiways, a dense, impenetrable cloud in some areas but only a thin gray haze in others.

The steady crackle of small-arms fire echoed from several directions. Bodies were strewn across the pavement outside some of the buildings, showing where other members of his Gryphon Force had successfully ambushed Cuban pilots, ground crews, gunners, and others as they rushed to their action stations.

With sudden amazement, McGill realized that no more than a couple of minutes could have elapsed from the moment they'd started their attack. He felt a sudden wave of sorrow at the loss of Ros and Torres and fought to hold it back. If he lived through this night, there would be time later to grieve their deaths. Right now, the ability to compartmentalize emotion was key. He needed to regain some measure of control over this increasingly chaotic battle. He spoke into his mike. "Gryphon Two Leader to Blue Team," he said. "Report status."

"*Gryphon One-Seven to Lead,*" Alex Zayas radioed back. "*Cruz, Rodriguez, Tallich, and I are working our way on foot through the northeast quadrant. We parked our bikes behind some woods in sector one. The control tower's totally out of action, and we've wrecked what looks like their local HQ.*"

McGill nodded to himself. Their mission rehearsals had shown that the speeder bikes were best suited to the very early stages of any attack, during the moments when they still retained almost total surprise. That was when the mobility and sheer striking power conferred by the two-man flying machines offered enormous advantages. Losing Ros and Torres so quickly didn't mean their tactical appreciation had been wrong. Sadly, their deaths had been one of the rotten fortunes of war, he thought, where Murphy's law ruled supreme—whatever could go wrong would. But those same planning exercises and drills had shown that as any action went on, it was safer and more effective for Four's raiders to move and fight dismounted, where they could take full advantage of any cover and also shoot more effectively. Hitting targets at anything beyond close range from the back of a speeding jet bike was never an easy task. "Any casualties in your group?" he asked.

"*Rodriguez took some grenade fragments clearing the HQ,*" Zayas reported back. "*But he's still good to move and fight. Right now, we're pushing toward what looks an awful lot like an armory of some kind. I figure if we can blow that, we'll take a lot of the fight out of these communist sons of bitches.*"

"Copy that, One-Seven," McGill acknowledged. Zayas's plan was a good one. In most circumstances, only security personnel on duty would be carrying anything heavier than personal sidearms. The rest of the base's infantry-type weapons—assault rifles, submachine guns, grenades, machine guns, and the like—should be under lock and key in armories. While it was possible, perhaps even likely, that a base this size had more than one secured storage area for weapons, seeing a significant fraction of their arsenal destroyed before they could arm themselves ought to seriously dent the morale of the Cuban defenders. And given the odds against McGill and his team, every enemy soldier who became more interested in saving his own skin than in fending off this bolt-from-the-blue surprise attack was good news.

Einar Haugen's voice came through over their radio net next. *"Gryphon One-Five to Lead,"* the Norwegian commando veteran said. McGill could hear the high-pitched rattle and crackle of rapid rifle fire in the near background. Haugen and his Lithuanian teammate were evidently in the middle of a firefight. *"Rytis and I are deployed in the fruit orchard at the edge of the southwest quadrant."*

"Situation?" McGill asked.

"The Cubans are making a real push here," Haugen replied. *"They've made three rushes in our direction already. I'd say we've killed or wounded about fifteen so far."*

McGill frowned. "Then fade back and break contact, Einar. We're here on a raid, not to fight pitched battles."

"Negative on that, Lead," the Norwegian said simply. *"Some of those we've shot are wearing flight suits. And they all seem very determined to get to that cluster of hardened aircraft shelters a couple of hundred meters behind us. Or to die trying. So far, we have been able to oblige them on that score."*

And then McGill understood. All along, the question they had not been able to answer was which of the Cuban air base's forty or so camouflaged aircraft shelters held real MiG-29 interceptors or MiG-23 fighter-bombers. Most were certainly empty, maintained in working order solely to absorb bombs or cruise missiles in the unlikely event that the United States ever decided to attack the hostile island nation not far off its shores. So the desperate attempts the Cuban pilots and ground crews were making to break past Daukša and Haugen were a clear indication—the military equivalent of a poker tell—that those particular shelters actually contained flyable combat aircraft.

McGill took a deep breath. Everything they'd done so far to

destroy this air base's command and control and to sow chaos and confusion was all to the good. But knocking out those MiGs was the team's primary mission objective. If they could destroy those planes, they would strip the Cubans of any ability to intervene against Flynn's force from the air—or to hunt down the Gryphon Force as it withdrew back out to sea.

In their original plan, Cristina Ros and Javier Torres had been tasked with destroying any aircraft found on the ground. Now that they'd been killed, the job fell on his shoulders and on those of Piero Lucente.

"Understood, One-Five," McGill told Haugen. "You keep the bastards pinned. We'll take care of those shelters." He leaned forward in his seat and clapped the pilot on the shoulder. The Italian's head turned. "Let's go, Piero," he said, pointing toward the group of camouflaged shelters Haugen had identified. From the air, a paved stretch of what looked like a street seemed to split four ways—into short roadways that simply seemed to vanish into clumps of trees and brush. In reality, he knew, those were taxiways right up to the doors of enormous reinforced concrete hangars. Each hangar was built into an artificial mound of dirt and rock to prevent thermal and radar scans from revealing whether it was in use. "I think it's high time we blew the living shit out of some bloody Cuban MiGs."

Lucente nodded. "*Sí*, Tony." He switched their turbojets out of hover mode and dived again, picking up speed on the way. He leveled out a few feet off the ground, and they flew south across rows of crops planted adjacent to the runway.

McGill shook his head. The base garrison must have to grow some of its own food, a clear sign of Cuba's economic distress. No wonder Voronin had been able to secure the cooperation of Havana's authoritarian regime. Offer the communist kleptocrats in charge enough cold hard cash, and they'd do anything the Raven Syndicate asked. Well, he thought grimly, noting the rapidly spreading fires and smoke shrouding the air base, if nothing else, Cuba's rulers were in the process of learning the hard way that helping Voronin incurred its own punishment.

Lucente set them down in one corner of a field, close to a small group of trees, near to where the taxi strip split apart into four paths. Dust, leaves, and grass swirled around the speeder bike in a miniature cyclone as they came in for a vertical landing. The roiling currents slowly subsided when he shut their engines down.

As soon as the turbojets spooled to a stop, McGill hit the quick-release buckle on his harness and scrambled out of his seat. He went down to one knee with his HK417 up and ready to fire while he scanned their immediate surroundings. Lucente had chosen well, he decided. Their landing site was mostly out of view of both the runway and the orchard ahead, where Haugen and Daukša still seemed to have the Cubans pinned down and unable to advance.

The Italian dismounted and readied his own rifle. Then he unfastened the straps securing a heavy rucksack to the back of their jet speeder. The large camouflaged bag contained an assortment of demolition charges and detonators they would need to complete this part of the mission. With a grunt he hoisted it onto his back and slid his arms through the straps. He nodded to McGill. "You lead the way, Tony. Okay?" A smile flashed across his face. "Aircraft, bombs, and missiles, I understand. But explosives themselves?" He shrugged. "Those I will leave to the expert."

McGill grinned back at him. The truth was he felt a lot safer on solid earth. The jet speeders were wonderful weapons in their own way, but you couldn't exactly dive for cover while you were in midair. Not unless you wanted to wind up with a broken neck. "Well then, you've come to the right shop," he said. "Because blowing things up just happens to be one of my specialties, courtesy of years of training provided by Her former Majesty's government."

With McGill out ahead, they sprinted toward the nearest aircraft shelter. Here on the ground, the reinforced steel door sealing it shut was plainly visible. The top of the door was more than thirty feet off the ground.

They were only yards away when everything went to hell. A machine gun opened fire on them out of a stand of trees and brush several hundred yards away to the west, not far from the main runway. 7.62mm rounds whipcracked past on all sides. Lucente cried out once and fell sprawling. McGill felt his rifle torn out of his hands, ripped away by a machine gun bullet moving at more than three thousand feet per second. He threw himself prone. *Shit, shit, shit*, he thought dazedly. Some of the Cuban security troops must have been posted on sentry duty near the western edge of the runway when the attack started. And as a result, they'd been in a perfect position to ambush anyone heading for the hardened MiG shelters.

Tony McGill started to raise his head and then buried his face in the dirt again as another machine gun burst ripped low through the field—shredding leaves and sending clumps of damp red clay fountaining into the air. "Bloody fucking hell," he snarled, suddenly aware that his part of the Gryphon Force operation was, in the slang of his misspent youth in pubs, right on the verge of going "totally arse over elbows" and ending in complete disaster. The Cubans were reacting far faster than he'd anticipated, and his own casualties were skyrocketing.

FORTY-ONE

MORA REMOTE OPERATIONS CENTER

THAT SAME TIME

Fyodor Maresyev paced slowly up and down the corridor between the center's two rows of aircraft control bays. From here,
he could keep a close watch on the activity of the pilots under
his command. And what he saw around him was pleasing,
indeed. His men were busy in their cramped, computer-filled
cubicles, preparing for their flights with long-practiced efficiency. Each was a veteran aviator, with years of experience flying
either Russia's heavy Tu-160 and Tu-22M strategic bombers
or its smaller Su-24 and Su-34 strike aircraft. Right now, they
were working through their individual flight plans—checking
and cross-checking both the most recent weather forecasts and
real-time US air traffic data, so thoughtfully provided by the
American Federal Aviation Administration to websites across
the internet.

Maresyev was well aware of the underlying tension in the
crowded remote operations center. He felt it himself. They

were on the brink of launching the most critical strike mission ever carried out by Russian-flown aircraft, the culmination of months of intensive training and practice, first at home in Russia and now here in Cuba. Their first two bomb-carrying Mora unmanned aircraft—those with the farthest to fly—were scheduled to take off in less than thirty minutes. Others would follow at precisely timed intervals, taking to the skies over an unsuspecting United States. When the countdown clock for *Vremya Unichtozheniya*, Obliteration Time, reached zero, all twenty-three stealth planes, each carrying a 150-kiloton nuclear warhead, should be directly over their critical strategic targets.

And in that single destructive instant, Maresyev estimated, hundreds of thousands of Americans—military personnel and civilian men, women, and children alike—would die. Many would be stripped to atoms by nuclear fireballs six times hotter than the temperature at the center of the sun. Others would be crushed inside buildings smashed by shock waves. Others still would be trapped by the gigantic firestorms sweeping across towns and cities and forests in the wake of each weapon's detonation. Unconsciously, he rubbed at the scars covering the right half of his face. He knew only too well what happened to those trapped amid flames. In such circumstances, a quick death by suffocation or smoke inhalation would probably be a comparatively merciful one. More deaths would follow in the days and weeks and months to come, the result of radiation sickness and other plagues unleashed by the inevitable collapse of civil order following Russia's merciless onslaught.

Maresyev supposed that he ought to feel something other than profound satisfaction at the thought of the death and destruction his Moras were about to wreak on the United States—some sense of regret or remorse, perhaps. But in truth, he could not do so. World power was a zero-sum game. For one nation to dominate the globe, others must fall. Russia had long suffered the consequences of its defeat in the Cold War. Now, he knew, it would be America's turn to experience humiliation and anarchy.

Maresyev shrugged his shoulders. Wars were either won or lost. There were no consolation prizes for those who played fair and failed. It was his duty, and that of his pilots, to make sure CASTLE KEEP succeeded—no matter how many so-called innocents died as a result.

He finished his circuit and strode back to his own station, a ring of desks not far from the building's thick armored door. His deputy, Ilya Perskyi, like him a former bomber pilot, looked up at his approach. "What's the latest news from Strelkov?" Maresyev asked.

"Everything is proceeding on schedule," Perskyi said. He indicated the computer at his desk. A diagram showed the current position of each unmanned aircraft, including those parked outside the Syndicate's improvised hangar. Six of the Moras had already been towed into their taxi positions. He highlighted those planes with a flick of a mouse button. "Should we have our pilots establish their satellite links to these drones?" he asked. "Now that they're outside the warehouse facility with all its structural steel and siding, there won't be any interference with our signals."

Maresyev shook his head decisively. "No, Ilya. Tempting as it is to accelerate the process, let's stick to the timetable." Bringing the sophisticated electronic systems and computers aboard those unmanned aircraft to full readiness would require significant electrical power—power that could only be provided by their backup batteries or generated by starting their turbofan engines ahead of schedule. Saving a few minutes now wasn't worth the resulting drain on those batteries. There were margins built into each Mora's flight plan to cover unexpected contingencies, but they were very tight. That was especially true for these first planes Strelkov had moved into position, those with the greatest need for as much fuel aboard as possible. Since everything was going as planned so far, there was no reason to run any added risks.

A phone at the corner of his own desk buzzed sharply. He stared at it in surprise. That was the direct line to Colonel Hidalgo's field command post. What the devil did the Cuban want at this late hour, well past midnight? He picked it up. "Remote operations center. Maresyev here," he answered tersely.

"This is Hidalgo!" the Cuban officer shouted. "The airfield at San Antonio de los Baños is under attack! We're only getting fragmentary radio reports, but it's clear someone's blasting the hell out of them—both from the air and by a commando assault on the ground! For God's sake, the whole damned sky to the south is lit up by fires and antiaircraft tracers!"

Maresyev scowled, holding the phone away from his ear to avoid being deafened by the overexcited Cuban. The fighter base was only fourteen kilometers south of them, but since it wasn't part of his Raven Syndicate command, he hadn't seen a need to set up secure communications to the air units stationed there. Given the requirement to keep their remote-piloting operation secret, the fewer people who were aware of a Russian force on the ground in Cuba, the better. For many of the same reasons, plus a desire to avoid tipping off American reconnaissance satellites that something unusual was going on here, Voronin had decided against asking the Cubans to station surface-to-air missile units or antiaircraft guns in the near vicinity. Perhaps, he thought now, that had been a mistake.

"Did you hear me?" Hidalgo demanded.

"I heard you," Maresyev replied, biting down on the

temptation to respond far more harshly. "Are there any signs of a hostile air or commando attack force headed our way?"

"None," the Cuban said. "Everything's still quiet out here." It was obvious that he was fighting for control over his own voice. "And since that is so," he went on a fraction more calmly, "I plan to lead my armored vehicles and infantry south to reinforce our people at San Antonio and take the enemy commandos from the rear. The other Havana-based army units aren't on high alert like we are. They won't be ready to move until it's far too late, not for an hour or more. The Yanquis or whoever is carrying out this raid will be long gone by then. But my troops can be on the road in five minutes!"

Maresyev grimaced. Was Hidalgo insane? Or just stupid? "Absolutely not! Your request is denied!" he rasped. Foolish or not, it was now clear that there wasn't any way he could avoid an argument with the Cuban colonel. So be it, he thought, and be damned to the diplomatic niceties usually involved in dealing with allies. "Maybe it seems quiet outside right now, but whatever's going on down at that airfield might be just a diversion—one that's deliberately intended to strip this operations center of the protection provided by your troops and tanks!"

Hidalgo said nothing for several seconds. When he spoke again, his voice was icy. "Do I understand you correctly? You're forbidding me to go to the aid of my comrades now under attack by imperialist forces?"

"Correct," Maresyev said bluntly. "Remember, Colonel, by the direction of your own General Staff, you're under my direct orders for the duration of our contract. Until its terms expire, you obey me. No one else. Is that clear?"

Over the line, he thought he could actually hear the other man's teeth grinding together in suppressed fury. It was a remarkably unpleasant sound.

"Very well," Hidalgo said finally. Every word emerged with cold deliberation and obvious contempt. "Then what are your orders?"

"Have your troops stand to and man their trenches and fighting positions. And have your tank and other vehicle crews get their engines turning over," Maresyev told him, with considerably more patience than he felt. He'd successfully cracked the whip, reminding the Cuban of just who was the master in their relationship. There was nothing to gain by humiliating the other man further. In fact, he decided, it was time to throw Hidalgo a bone to soothe his injured pride. Maresyev would give the other man just enough of the truth for him to appreciate how vital it was for his soldiers to repel any attack on this remote operations center.

"Maybe whatever's happening at San Antonio isn't actually aimed at us, Agustin," he said. "But we can't afford to take any chances just now. You see, the operation we've been planning is moving forward to completion tonight. In just a matter of hours, in fact. So it's critical that we proceed as planned—without any interruptions or delays. You and your troops will do more for Cuba by remaining at your posts here, guaranteeing this outcome, than you could by rushing blindly into battle at the airfield." He tried to make his next words sound sincere, an effort made easier by the fact that they were, quite literally, true. "Because by the time our job here is finished, I swear to you that your countrymen who've been killed tonight will have been avenged ten thousand times over."

Hidalgo snorted. "I'm certain that will be of great comfort to their widows and orphans," he said tightly, clearly not inclined to take the Russian at his word. "In the meantime, since I have no choice but to obey the explicit orders you've just given me, I'll get to it. Garrison commander out!"

Maresyev heard the connection break abruptly. He frowned. His eyes sought out the two submachine-gun-armed ex-Spetsnaz troopers guarding the center's solid armored door. For a brief moment he was tempted to order them outside . . . just to make sure the Cuban officer and his men really did follow his instructions. But then he shook his head. Short of executing Hidalgo for disobedience, what could he really expect his Syndicate security guards to do? Better to hope that the colonel was enough of a professional to eventually see the sense involved in securing this facility against an attack—rather than rushing off on a wild-goose chase in pursuit of some unknown raiding force that would unquestionably be long gone by the time his column reached the air base.

His eyes moved to the timer counting down across the top of his own computer screen. Their first nuclear-armed Moras would take off in a little over twenty-five minutes. Once those UCAVs were airborne and most especially once they reached their designated targets, it would no longer matter why the Americans had decided to attack San Antonio de los Baños airfield tonight—whether it was simply a random act of superpower malice or whether somehow they'd gotten an inkling that something going on in Cuba was a serious threat to their national security. No, Maresyev thought with a touch of renewed satisfaction, the moment those flame-laced mushroom clouds rippled into the atmosphere over Washington, DC, and all the other sites marked for destruction, whatever the Americans imagined they knew would become completely irrelevant. The destruction of the United States would be both inevitable and irreversible.

FORTY-TWO

MORA REMOTE OPERATIONS CENTER,
NORTHERN DEFENSE OUTPOST

THAT SAME TIME

Colonel Agustin Hidalgo slammed the field phone down into its cradle. "Fucking Russian pricks," he growled.

"Sir?" the corporal manning his command post's small portable switchboard asked.

Wearily, Hidalgo smiled. "I suggest you forget what you just heard, Marquez."

"I didn't hear a thing, Colonel," the corporal assured him stolidly. "As it happens, I've always been a bit deaf when it comes to anything said about our beloved Russian benefactors."

"A wise disability," Hidalgo agreed absently, thinking about his next moves. Maresyev's orders might not leave him any discretion as far as the troops deployed outside the Russian operations center were concerned, but he still had one card left to play to aid the defenders at San Antonio de los Baños. "Connect me to Captain Agüero," he said.

The corporal obeyed, disconnecting the field telephone's jack from one connection on his switchboard and inserting it into another. "It's ringing, sir."

Hidalgo picked up his receiver. "Agüero here," a voice said crisply. "Yes, Colonel?"

"You've heard all the noise?" Hidalgo asked. "From the air base?"

"Yes, sir," Agüerro, the commander of his special unit's Third Platoon, acknowledged. Even for a military that had downsized as drastically as had Cuba's in recent years, having captains filling slots that were ordinarily the province of first lieutenants was almost as odd as having a full colonel like Hidalgo overseeing a force that was barely the equivalent of a badly understrength battalion. But Voronin had insisted on officers of demonstrated ability and experience command the elements of his paid garrison force—no matter what their nominal ranks decreed. "And I've seen the fires burning. From the look of things, those poor bastards must have stored ordnance cooking off. A lot of it."

"It's not an accident, Raul. A hostile force is attacking San Antonio," Hidalgo explained. "From both the air and on the ground."

"Mother of God!" the captain muttered in shock.

"That's why I want you to bring your platoon to full alert," Hidalgo said. "And prepare for a rapid road march south to assist."

"At once!" Agüerro said. But then he continued in a more cautious tone, "Though it will take some time. My men are a bit . . . dispersed . . . this evening."

Hidalgo nodded. "I understand, Raul. Do your best." Indeed, he thought, he did understand. Faced with the need to provide security for the Russian operations center on a twenty-four-hour basis for an indeterminate period, he'd opted for the least bad option. Two of his three infantry platoons, along with their attached armored vehicles, were on duty around the bunker at any given time. That allowed him to periodically rotate a third of his force to requisitioned billets a short distance away, at the University of Information Sciences. This gave the lucky troops on rotation an opportunity to sleep in real beds for a couple of days, eat better food, and even take a few hours off duty. That was good for both morale and, ultimately, combat effectiveness, since fatigued and unhappy soldiers never fought well. Unfortunately, the fact that Agüerro's platoon was out of the line right now would make it difficult for the captain to round his men up quickly. Most of them were probably out eating or drinking in local bars or cafés and trying to pick up female students from the university. "Anything you can get on the road quickly, even just a squad or a single vehicle, could make the difference between victory or defeat."

"Yes, Colonel!" the captain responded. "I'm on it."

Hidalgo put the phone down, stood up, and trotted back up the dugout steps. Lieutenant Fuentes and the two captains commanding his First and Second Platoons were just outside, waiting for him. The soldiers manning this northern outpost were stirring, awakened as the news of the apparent attack on the air base spread from tent shelter to tent shelter. A few of them, anticipating his likely orders, were already struggling into combat webbing and checking their AKM rifles. Most of the younger conscripts especially were clumped together in small groups, chatting in low, nervous-sounding voices as they tried to figure out what was going on.

Hidalgo scowled even more deeply now. It was time to bring some order out of this confusion. He spun back toward his worried-looking junior officers. "All right, gentlemen. We're going on full alert! Get your men—"

And a .338 Lapua Magnum rifle round hit him right in the back of the head. Still moving at more than three thousand feet per second, it punched out through the front of the colonel's skull—spattering his shocked subordinates with blood, shattered bone, and brain matter. Just starting to tumble, the same bullet smashed into the face of a second man, the captain commanding the southern defense outpost. Both Cuban officers folded over and went down. They were dead before they hit the ground.

GRYPHON ASSAULT FORCE
THAT SAME TIME

Lying prone in the cover provided by a clump of brush and dwarf palms more than three hundred yards away, Tadeusz Kossak gently squeezed the trigger of his TRG-42 sniper rifle again. A third Cuban officer crumpled. "Two to Gryphon Lead," he radioed. "Peacock leaders are down." Through his night optic, he could see the closest soldiers staring down at their dead commanders for a fraction of a second—before exploding into action, diving for cover in the nearest trench or scrambling up into their armored vehicles. "But now they *definitely* know we're here."

"*Copy that,*" Nick Flynn acknowledged in barely a whisper.

From this spot, Kossak couldn't see any of his teammates, except for Andy Cavada, who was concealed in the same stand of trees and bushes just a few yards to his right. But he knew they were only a few yards from the Cuban trench lines, carefully concealed in patches of dead ground—places where minor undulations in the landscape hid them from view. Flynn, Laura Van Horn, Hynes, and Vucovich were in position just outside the northern outpost, the one they'd labeled Outpost Alpha, while Cooke and three of their Cuban American allies, Daina Perez, Bill Martinez, and Roberto Cuellar, had wormed their way right up to the very edge of the southernmost redoubt, Outpost Bravo. It had taken them what seemed an eternity to snake their way across the open ground without being spotted—something that had probably only been possible because most of the sentries were distracted, paying far more attention to the sudden explosion of noise and light miles away to the south than to the sectors they were supposed to be watching. The other Gryphon Force team's assault on the airfield had gone in at exactly the right time.

"*Gryphon Lead to Gryphon Seven*," Flynn continued. "*Take out that T-62, Andy.*"

"Roger that, boss," Cavada said. The former Army Ranger already had the Cuban tank zeroed in on the optical sight of his NLAW antitank missile launcher. He squeezed the front-firing grip, which was set right behind the weapon's bulbous muzzle brake. *KA-WHUMMP.*

Cavada was briefly silhouetted by a spurt of flame and gray smoke out the back end of the launcher. Torn leaves and pieces of plant matter whirled behind him. The NLAW had a greatly reduced backblast compared to many antitank missile systems, but it was obvious that "reduced" wasn't the same thing as "none."

Propelled by a gas-pressure soft-launch system, the missile popped out of the tube and flew downrange. At a safe distance a split second later, its rocket motor ignited with a crackling hiss. Trailing fire, the missile accelerated rapidly across the open ground, covering the remaining couple of hundred yards to its still-stationary target in just over a second. Zooming in under the tree canopy, it darted low right over the T-62's turret and detonated in an orange-white ball of flame—punching a superheated jet of molten metal downward through the tank's relatively thin top armor.

Within moments, the T-62 was burning. A pillar of fire licked upward through the open commander's hatch, setting the camouflage netting strung above the vehicle ablaze. No one in its four-man crew made it out alive.

Flynn felt the ground under him shudder when the NLAW missile fired by Cavada went off. He scrambled to his feet with a yell. "Gryphons! Let's go! Light 'em up now!" He raised his HK417 carbine and tucked it firmly against his shoulder, already sprinting forward. Ahead, the flames wreathing the burning T-62 sent eerie shadows dancing across the Cuban outpost. Pale faces, eyes wide with shock, turned toward him from the nearest stretch of trench.

Flynn started firing, squeezing off shots on the move. Cuban soldiers spun away and fell, hit repeatedly. He dropped down into the trench and advanced along the hard-packed dirt surface, sidestepping the sprawled corpses of those he'd already killed.

Laura Van Horn dropped into the same trench right behind him. But she turned in the other direction, pushing ahead to clear that sector of the enemy's defensive works. A few yards on, she came around a corner and practically ran into a pair of Cubans manning a light machine gun. They had the gun perched up on the edge of the parapet, and they were firing frantically out across the open field to the west, shooting blind in the hopes of pinning down whoever had just killed most of their officers and blown up their single T-62 main battle tank. Van Horn's mouth tightened. As far as she knew, there wasn't a single member of the Gryphon Force anywhere near where those guys were shooting. Then again, she thought coldly, she might be wrong. She fired several times, feeling the rifle kick back against her shoulder. Hit from behind at point-blank range, both gunners slid down the side of the trench, dead or dying.

With the HK417 still up and ready, she moved on, looking for more Cubans to engage.

Back the other way along the trench, Flynn crouched. He checked the clear polymer magazine of his carbine. It was almost empty. He dropped it out and tucked it away in a pouch on his assault vest. Given the number of enemy soldiers they were probably still facing, the time might easily come when even a single round or two could mean the difference between living and dying. Then he slapped in a fresh magazine and moved on. He spoke quietly into his mike. "Gryphon Leader to all Gryphons. The northwest sector of Outpost Alpha is clear."

Shots crackled from all over this outpost and from its twin in the woods to the south. Voices came through his headset as the other members of his Gryphon assault force reported their own progress. Half the northern outpost's perimeter trench had already been emptied of enemy troops. The same was true of the southern bastion being assaulted by Cooke, Perez, and the other Cuban Americans.

Flynn nodded. Incredible as it might seem, so far he and his people were winning this battle—despite being so heavily outnumbered.

Then again, he knew inside, this wasn't a fair fight at all.

Their high-tech night vision gear turned everything around them into a bright, monochrome version of daylight. Most of the Cuban soldiers were not so fortunate. Forced to fight without thermal or light-intensifier goggles of their own, they found themselves locked in a close-quarters battle with half-seen foes who seemed to flicker in and out of pitch-black shadows and pale patches of moonlight with incredible speed—spotted for an eyeblink here and then gone in the next. And meanwhile, all around them, their friends and comrades were dying.

Flynn grimaced. Okay, yeah, this wasn't a fair fight. But so what? Back when he'd been in the service, one of his Air Force Special Operations tactics instructors had put it in perspective. "Fighting fair is for suckers. Or for guys who don't mind ending up dead because some hajji with a first-grade education put a bullet in them. You want to be chivalrous, Flynn? Buy some fucking medieval plate armor and sign up for a Renaissance festival somewhere. In the real world, your damn job is to kill the enemy—and do it at the lowest possible cost in friendly casualties."

Suddenly, Flynn noted movement off to his right. A handful of Cuban troops had jumped into a shallow mortar pit about twenty yards in from the trench. They were lining the edge, shooting wildly across the compound. Not far away, both the BRDM-2 scout car and BTR-60 were clanking into motion. Inside the scout car's turret, a gunner had gotten its 14.5mm KPVT heavy machine gun into action. Dazzling flashes strobed out of the end of its thick barrel. Wherever those powerful rounds struck, sandbags exploded and tree trunks shattered into flying splinters.

Christ, Flynn thought, suddenly feeling a whole lot less confident. Shooting blind or not, those armored behemoths could still inflict horrendous losses on his team and break the back of their assault. After all, if you threw enough lead into an area, you were bound to hit something. And right now, that KPVT gunner was punching out dozens of rounds a minute. Worse, the BTR-60 next to the scout car had a heavy machine gun turret of its own. Just as soon as one of the Cuban troops scrambling aboard the slow-moving APC remembered that, things were going to get a hell of a lot worse.

"Lead to Gryphons Five and Six!" he snapped. "We've got armor on the move!"

"*Yes, sir,*" Flynn heard Hynes say calmly. "*Me and Wade are on it.*" And then a couple of seconds later: "*Uh, sir. You're awful*

*close to those armored cars. You might want to eat some dirt . . .
right about . . . now!"*

Oh shit. Flynn dived for the bottom of the trench and curled
up tight to tuck as much of his body as he could under the protection offered by his helmet and ceramic back armor plates.

BOOOMM. BOOOMM. Two echoing blasts rolled across
the ground, loud enough to be heard despite the chattering
roar of the Cuban heavy machine gun and the rising crackle of
small-arms fire. They were followed almost instantly by deafening *WHAANG* sounds as shaped-charge warheads struck
thin armor and exploded inward. Torn bits of smoldering steel
rained down across the ground.

A moment later, Flynn uncoiled and cautiously peered
out over the edge of the trench. Hit squarely by the two M72
LAWs—disposable, man-portable light antitank rockets—fired
by Hynes and Vucovich, both Cuban armored vehicles sat slewed
sideways. Flames and oily black smoke curled away from the
wreckage. He swallowed hard. That had been close.

But that still left the soldiers lining the rim of that nearby
mortar pit. They were acting as a knot of resistance around
which a more cohesive and organized defense could form. And
that was something Flynn could not allow. The longer this battle
went on, the more likely the Cubans would realize they both
outnumbered and outgunned the attacking force by a consid-
erable margin. Which meant he had to finish this part of the
fight. And quickly.

And there was the problem. He could probably nail one or
two or even three of those enemy soldiers using his rifle. But then
they'd figure out where all the fire was coming from and start
shooting in his very specific direction . . . which would suddenly
make this a very bad day for Mama Flynn's dark-haired boy.

Well, when in doubt, Flynn thought, *go with high explosives.*

He tugged a ball-shaped fragmentation grenade out of one of his equipment pouches. Flicking the safety clip away using his left thumb, he twisted the pull ring and yanked it out. That released the pin. In the same fluid motion, he lobbed the grenade across the intervening space. "Frag out!"

As it sailed through the air, the grenade's safety lever popped open and came loose. The grenade itself dropped into the middle of the mortar pit, unnoticed by any of the flash-blinded Cuban troops blazing away into the surrounding darkness.

Flynn ducked below the lip of the trench.

The grenade detonated with a sharp-edged *craaack*. Metal fragments whined outward through a fifty-foot radius—killing or badly wounding every single enemy caught inside the mortar pit. When their agonized screams faded away, an eerie, almost shocked silence seemed to fall across the battlefield for a brief instant. But then the noise of gunfire broke out again. Now, though, all the shots sounded like they were coming from the HK417s carried by his team.

Cautiously, Flynn lifted his head. What was left of the Cuban garrison in this northernmost outpost was running, scattering away from the scene of so much carnage like a flock of birds spooked by a hunting dog. Most had discarded their weapons and were in full flight. A few, those who were still armed, stumbled and fell sprawling across the grass—shot down by Kossak, Andy Cavada, Van Horn, and the others as they ran.

"Cease fire! Cease fire!" he radioed as soon as the last of the defenders vanished from sight. Even assuming any of their officers or sergeants survived to try to rally them, it would be a very long time before those panicked survivors were good for anything but cowering somewhere deep in cover, hoping desperately to be left alone.

The sound of firing died away.

"Lead to Gryphon Four," he called to Shannon Cooke. "What's your status?"

The ex–US Special Forces operator sounded exultant, but equally weary. "*We've cleared the southern outpost, Nick,*" he reported. "*Whatever's left of the enemy is skedaddling, and I'm letting them go. I don't see any sense in interfering with folks who've decided to leave us alone.*"

"Good move," Flynn agreed. Suddenly feeling exhausted himself as the extra adrenaline pumped into his bloodstream dissipated, he fought the temptation to just sit down in the trench and wait for his nerves to settle. It was time he started acting more like the overall commander he was supposed to be. "How're your casualties?" he asked quietly.

"*Cuellar got shot in the leg,*" Cooke told him. "*He can't move very fast, but he can still shoot. For the rest of us, it's just scrapes and cuts.*"

Flynn felt a wave of relief. He glanced around, his expression darkening as he saw the crumpled bodies tumbled along the trench he'd cleared and out across the surrounding woods. Waves of heat rippled off the burning Cuban T-62 and the two smaller armored vehicles not far from his current position. If anyone ever doubted the importance of tactical surprise, superior fighting skills, and a technological edge in combat, he thought somberly, here was the brutal, bloody proof of their value.

Painfully, he levered himself up out of the trench and slowly walked back to the edge of the trees. Van Horn joined him, as did Hynes and Vucovich, the latter now sporting a bloodstained field dressing around his upper left arm.

"Took an AK round there at the end, just after I nailed that lousy BTR," Vucovich growled, looking embarrassed. Getting shot seemed to make him a little more talkative. "Guess I waited a little too long before ducking back into the trench."

"It's not too bad," Hynes assured him. "More a graze, really." He shook his head. "But man, Wade's gotta be a damn bullet magnet. I mean, first he gets hit aboard that Iranian tanker. And now by some Cuban goon?"

Vucovich lowered his head. "Sorry, sir," he muttered to Flynn.

Flynn grinned at him. "Consider yourself reprimanded for carelessness, Wade." He looked out across the intervening ground toward the woods concealing the southern Cuban outpost. Flickers of dull orange and spiraling columns of smoke marked the funeral pyres of two of the three armored vehicles that had been parked there. The third, one of the BTR-50 personnel carriers, sat motionless with its nose poking out of the woods. Bodies draped limply over its sides showed where Cooke or one of his people had knocked it out by lobbing a grenade into the BTR's troop compartment through its open roof hatches.

Next to him, Van Horn lowered her night vision binoculars. She'd been studying the solid-looking concrete bunker housing Voronin's operations center. Its windowless walls were broken only by a single massive steel door. She shook her head. "That place is built like a fortress. We aren't exactly going to be able to shoot our way inside."

"Nope," Flynn agreed. "Which is why we brought along a ruck full of wall-breaching charges, remember?" He keyed his mike. "Lead to Seven."

"*Seven here,*" Cavada replied.

"We're going to need your bag of tricks, Andy," Flynn said.

"*On my way,*" the other man promised.

Flynn focused his own binoculars on the clump of trees to their west. He was in time to see Cavada grab a heavy rucksack beside him, throw it across his shoulders, and lope out into the open ground between them and the Russian-occupied bunker. Flynn started to swing back to Van Horn and the others. "Okay, once we set the charges to blow that armored door, we'll—"

The sudden, sharp thump of a rifled cannon drowned him out.

Stunned, Flynn saw Cavada disappear just as suddenly inside an orange-lit cloud of dirty-gray smoke. Dirt erupted high in the air, pattering back to the earth as it drifted slowly downwind. Flynn's eyes widened in horrified understanding. "Oh, hell." A high-explosive shell had just exploded right at the former Ranger's feet.

Reacting on instinct and training, they all dived for cover.

Now they could hear the rumble and clank of another Cuban tank grinding its way toward them up the narrow access road from the south. Much smaller than the T-62 Cavada had destroyed earlier, it had a sharply angled forward bow, a low flat-decked chassis, and a rounded turret mounting its main armament. From the bottom of its treads to the top of its turret, the whole vehicle couldn't be more than eight feet, Flynn realized. It was another PT-76—an amphibious light tank with a 76.2mm gun. A searchlight flicked on, sending a dazzling beam of light sweeping back and forth across the ground ahead of the oncoming tank as the turret spun from side to side, its gunner seeking out new targets or possible threats.

The PT-76 reached the point where the road turned east toward the bunker. Treads squealing loudly, it swung to face them and rocked to a stop, over three hundred yards from the two defense outposts now held by Flynn and his team. Its turret whined through a slow, deliberate arc, sweeping the searchlight beam from north to south and then back again—obviously probing for any signs of movement.

"Jesus," Hynes muttered, facedown in the dirt as the dazzling cone of light flashed past low overhead. "Where the hell did that thing come from?"

"The Cubans must have another unit stationed nearby," Flynn said. A unit that he hadn't spotted on the satellite photos he'd studied. And unfortunately, whoever commanded it had reacted quickly and intelligently to the sudden burst of firing and explosions from their outposts around the Russian control center.

Right now, that PT-76 sitting out there had them pinned down. It could blow away anyone leaving the cover of the woods and trenches using either its main gun or its coaxial 7.62mm machine gun. And whether that tank crew realized it or not, Flynn thought, in this case a stalemate was as good as a win for the Cubans and their Russian allies. Which left it up to him to change the tactical situation and soon, before the enemy troops they'd broken rallied or more Cuban reinforcements arrived on the scene. "Gryphon Lead to all Gryphons," he called. "Anybody have a LAW left?"

"*I've got one, Lead,*" Bill Martinez radioed back from the southern woods.

"Can you get a shot on that tank?" Flynn asked.

Martinez hesitated briefly. "From my current position, maybe. But it's a heckuva long way," he warned. "I make it a little over three hundred and fifty yards."

Flynn chewed on that. Effective range for the M72 LAW was only a bit over two hundred yards. The 66mm rocket inside the launcher's disposable tube was unguided, which meant its only aiming system was the unassisted Mark I human eyeball. Hitting even a stationary target at three hundred and fifty yards would be very difficult.

"*Maybe I can work my way a little closer,*" Martinez offered.

"Negative on that," Flynn replied, watching the searchlight beam as it swept past overhead again—casting the trees around them into stark outline. "You wouldn't get more than a few yards before that tank gunner spotted you. It's not worth the risk."

"*You're the boss*," Martinez agreed, sounding relieved. Flynn knew the former Army helicopter pilot would have gone out into the open ground if ordered, but he obviously hadn't been under any illusions about his chances of making it alive. "*Wait one. I'll take the shot from here.*"

There was a sudden bright flash near the edge of the trench lining the southernmost group of trees. Unlike the NLAW, when the M72 was fired, its rocket ignited in the tube, producing a powerful backblast of hot gases that could reach 1,400 degrees Fahrenheit.

Avidly, Flynn followed the tiny, almost invisible dot of the twenty-inch-long rocket as it arced high toward the Cuban tank. At the same time, he was aware of the PT-76's turret slewing fast toward the burst of light that had just pinpointed Martinez's firing position.

The ex-Army helicopter pilot had made a spectacular shot, one that few others could have equaled. But it wasn't quite good enough. The LAW warhead fell short by a couple of yards. It exploded in a puff of orange-white flame and gray smoke. Fragments of its casing and shattered paving rattled harmlessly off the Cuban tank's chassis and turret.

THUUMP. The 76.2mm main gun fired.

More dirt fountained high along the tree line as the HE shell it had lobbed detonated. A tree caught in the blast leaned over drunkenly, then toppled with a crash. The PT-76's coaxial machine gun cut loose, hosing down the southern patch of woods with tracer fire. Dirt, rock fragments, scraps of sandbags, and shredded tree branches and bark pinwheeled away from wherever those rounds slammed home. A second high-explosive shell blew more trees apart.

And then, just as suddenly as it had begun, the fusillade ended.

To his amazement, Flynn saw that the Cuban tank was reversing away at high speed. It backed up a hundred yards or so, slewed around again in an earsplitting squeal, and clanked off to the south—heading back the way it had first come at more than twenty miles per hour. He felt some of the weight lift from his shoulders. "Is everybody okay?" he radioed.

Replies cascaded through his headset, confirming that no one had been hit. "*Trenches are very, very good places to be under fire*," Bill Martinez said devoutly. "*Hell, from now on, I'm seriously thinking about taking an entrenching shovel with me everywhere I go.*"

"Even Walmart?" Van Horn asked with an air of innocence.

"*Especially Walmart*," Martinez retorted. "*You ever been caught in a Black Friday sale in one of those places? It gets seriously hairy.*"

From his position, Hynes raised his head, watching the tank vanish over a low rise about a couple of thousand yards away. He shook his head slowly and then glanced over at Flynn. "Uh, sir? What the hell just happened? Did that tank commander seriously bug out? Because we fired one lousy antitank rocket at him? A shot that missed, I might point out."

Flynn shook his head. "Not exactly, Cole." Carefully, he explained what he guessed of the Cuban tanker's reasoning. True, the PT-76 had only been fired at once. But even at very long range, the LAW had nearly hit home, and the crew had to have heard the fragments from that near miss banging off their vehicle's relatively thin armor. Worse still, they didn't have any way to tell how many more antitank weapons they were facing. What the tankers did know for sure was that the hostile force that had overrun their comrades in those two fortified

outposts had already destroyed six Cuban tanks and personnel
carriers. Those mangled, burning wrecks were plainly visible
through the trees. And no tank commander in his right mind
ever wanted to tangle with well-hidden and protected infantry
armed with antitank weapons—not in tight terrain like these
woods . . . and especially not without foot soldiers of his own
to probe ahead for ambushes.

"So you think that son of a bitch is going to come back,"
Hynes realized.

Flynn nodded. "Just as soon as he rounds up some infantry
support. And once that happens, that PT-76 is going to head
this way again—loaded for bear. Or Gryphons, in this case,"
he amended.

Van Horn got back to her feet and slung her rifle. "In that
case, Nick, we'd better get a move on and finish this job before
that happens."

Flynn joined her. He lowered his voice. "Small problem
there." He jerked a thumb back to where Andy Cavada had been
killed. It was painfully obvious, even at this distance, that the
HE shell fired by the PT-76 had blown the veteran Ranger to
pieces, along with all of his equipment. "Without those demolition charges, we don't have any way to break into that operations
center."

Van Horn smiled narrowly at him. "Ah, that's where *my*
plan B comes in."

"Do you really have a plan B this time?" he asked.

She nodded. "Oh yeah. See, while we were all being hosed
down by that Cuban tank, I had some spare time to think. Unlike
the rest of you mere mortals cowering in terror, I might add."

Flynn let that one go. Van Horn could even be telling the
truth, he thought. He'd certainly never met anyone else who
was as cool under pressure as her.

She took his shoulder and turned him around to look at the large bunker. She pointed up at its flat roof, to where the twin rows of white domes sat. "There's plan B," she said simply.

He raised an eyebrow. "The Starlink satellite dishes?"

Van Horn nodded. With a grin, she held up a ball-shaped fragmentation grenade. "How solid are those radomes around the dishes?"

"Not very," Flynn said, smiling back as he realized what she meant. "They're probably just fiberglass."

"Exactly," Van Horn said. "So what happens to all the electronic hardware inside them when a half dozen of these babies"—she jiggled the grenade in her hand—"explode all across the top of that roof?"

"Sizzle-crack-pop," Flynn acknowledged, imagining the effects of hundreds of jagged steel wire fragments sleeting through all those satellite internet dishes and their connecting cables. "As in, fried and gone to hardware hell." Without thinking about it, he gave her a quick, hard kiss and whirled away, already radioing the necessary orders to the rest of Gryphon's Force Red Team.

FORTY-THREE

SAN ANTONIO DE LOS BAÑOS MILITARY AIRFIELD

THAT SAME TIME

Another angry-wasp-sounding burst of machine gun fire burned past just over the top of Tony McGill's helmet. He lay flat, pressed hard against the field's damp clay soil. *See the furrow, be the furrow*, one corner of his mind repeated—the one isolated corner not raging in fury at Piero Lucente's death or metaphorically pissing itself in fear at his own predicament. He knew the only reason he was still alive was because the Cuban gunner shooting up this piece of cultivated land couldn't quite depress the muzzle of his automatic weapon low enough to hit the inches-deep depression he was using for cover. But by the same token, he couldn't so much as twitch a muscle in one direction or another—not without being instantly hit and killed.

"*One-Six to Lead, hold tight where you are,*" Rytis Daukša radioed. "*On the way now.*"

From where he lay prone, McGill heard the shrill whine of turbojets powering up somewhere in the distance. The noise grew louder very fast. Careful not to rise up even a fraction of an inch, he turned his head slightly to one side, trying to get a look at what was happening.

And he saw the carbon-black shape of a jet speeder flash low across the sky from east to west—accelerating past a hundred knots with astonishing quickness. The bike flew just a few feet higher than the clump of trees separating this field from the base runway. Immediately, the machine gun fire slashing over his head lifted, curling away higher across the rows of crops as the unseen Cuban gunner tried vainly to knock the Lithuanian's speeder down before it got too close.

More tracers, much larger and brighter ones, ripped through the air not far behind Daukša. McGill swore. Those were 23mm rounds coming from the direction of the runway. The Cubans must have managed to get another of their ZU-23 antiaircraft guns in action. Treetops that were impacted by its mix of HE and armor-piercing rounds simply disintegrated in blinding flashes.

The Lithuanian angled his machine downward again, crossing into the shadow of the small band of trees and then darting onward across the wide stretch of open ground separating him from the thicker woods where the enemy machine gun was deployed. He jinked right and left to throw off the aim of the gunners trying to zero in on him.

McGill saw the two streams of tracers—those from the ZU-23 and those from the light machine—cross. But they were still falling behind the speeder bike as its eight jet engines kicked out more thrust, pushing the machine even faster through the air. Hitting a small, agile target like Daukša's jet speeder was a remarkably difficult task without radar fire control.

Seizing his chance, he rolled over to where Lucente lay dead. The Italian's rifle was next to his outstretched hand. McGill grabbed the weapon. Quickly, he sighted through its night optic—scanning the woods where the Cuban light machine gun team was positioned.

Daukša streaked low past that same clump of trees and bushes, still weaving back and forth in sharp, tight evasive maneuvers. Unable to bring their machine gun around fast enough to track such a close, fast-flying target, the two Cuban soldiers stopped firing. And then dived frantically for cover themselves as the ZU-23's gun crew, obviously unaware that there were friendlies in the area, pummeled the woods with HE and armor-piercing shells—still doggedly attempting to bring the speeder down.

"Oh, Rytis, you clever, sneaky lad," McGill murmured in admiration, watching explosions ripple through the trees. "You bloody well did that on purpose."

The speeder bike veered south and howled around, now flying so low that the antiaircraft gun couldn't see where it had gone. Trailing dust and pieces of plants ripped loose by its exhaust, the jet-black machine tore right past McGill at high speed—heading back the way it had come. His job done, Daukša was obviously returning to help his comrade, Einar Haugen, fend off the Cuban pilots and ground crews desperately trying to fight their way to the hardened aircraft shelters where their MiG fighters and fighter-bombers were hidden.

The ZU-23 stopped firing.

Through his rifle sight, the ex–SAS sergeant saw a helmeted head lift cautiously out of a pile of torn vegetation and broken tree branches. McGill's finger stroked the trigger twice. *Crack-crack.* Hit in the temple, the enemy soldier shuddered once and fell facedown, clearly dead. He swung the rifle muzzle a little to the right. There, magnified by the optic, McGill caught sight of a second Cuban desperately clearing away debris from the machine gun to get it back into action. He fired two more times and saw blood splash away from the other man's chest as the gunner slumped over his weapon.

McGill got to his feet and slung the HK417 over his neck and shoulder. Then he knelt down next to Lucente's body and pulled the heavy rucksack containing their explosives off the other man's back. "Sorry, Piero," he said quietly, aware of a deep feeling of sadness. Too many good people had died tonight. Opening the ruck's flap, he took a quick look inside. Its contents appeared undamaged.

Aware that precious time was slipping away, he scrambled back up, grabbed the heavy bag in both hands, and lugged it over to the camouflaged aircraft shelter he'd identified earlier as the best target. It was one of the pair closest to the main taxiway. Its huge steel door climbed high above his head, looking as solid as a bank vault.

No problem, McGill thought. Or so he hoped, at any rate. Swiftly, with the ease and economy of motion granted by intensive training and practice, he began assembling a wall-breaching charge. First, he unfolded a three-foot-wide corrugated plastic circle, what was known in the demolitions trade as a silhouette. Next, he carefully slotted a thick, encased five-foot-long coil of explosives into place around the silhouette and secured it with Velcro tabs. With that done, he picked up the circle, ripped away covers over the adhesive patches on its other side, and firmly pressed that side against the hangar door—setting it about chest high. A two-legged plastic stand wedged the circular silhouette into position. It took him another twenty seconds or so to wire short lengths of detonator cord to each end of the coil of explosives. In turn, he tied those pieces of det cord into a coil of twin shock tubes. These were thin, flexible plastic tubes that contained small particles of HMX/aluminum explosive powder that could be triggered by

an igniter, sending a shock wave racing toward attached detonators at more than 6,500 feet per second.

Satisfied that everything was set, McGill slung the rucksack
over one shoulder and slowly backed away around the corner
of the hangar, carefully unreeling the shock tubes as he went.
When he'd gone about thirty yards, he crouched next to the solid
mass of earth and rock and yanked on the twin igniter rings.

A brief, blinding orange-red flash ripped the darkness surrounding him as the explosive charges went off. The ground
trembled under his feet.

Wha-WHUMMP.

McGill dropped the length of the smoldering shock tube
and darted back around the side of the aircraft shelter. Through
a swirling haze of acrid gray smoke, he could see that his breaching charge had blown a three-foot-wide hole right through the
solid steel door. Its ragged edges glowed cherry red in spots.

He bent down slightly to peer inside. There, parked well
back near the far end of the vast hangar, he could make out
the deadly, twin-tailed shape of a MiG-29. A mix of air-to-air
missiles, air-to-ground rockets, and bombs hung from the hard
points beneath its wings and fuselage. This must be one of the
base's alert aircraft, McGill realized, which meant it was also
fully fueled and ready for immediate takeoff. Sadly, the large jet
fighter seemed completely undamaged by any of the steel door
fragments blown inward by the breaching charge.

Well, he thought, there was a remedy for that. Rummag-
ing around inside the rucksack produced another demolition
charge. This one was much smaller and simpler. Basically, it was
just a half-pound block of Mylar-wrapped C-4 plastic explosives. Moving deftly, he worked a nonelectric blasting cap deep
into the pliable block and then crimped a two-foot length of
black-power timer fuse to the blasting cap. It took only moments

more to screw a pull-ring mechanical igniter to the other end of the fuse. One side of McGill's mouth quirked upward. Compared to the rapid breaching kit he'd just used, this was all very old school. In fact, the only way it could have been any more old fashioned would have been if he'd thought to light the fuse with a cigar.

Holding the charge in one hand, he peered through the hole again—judging distances. A half pound of C-4 would go off with a tremendous amount of explosive power, but it was always better to have that happen as close to the preferred target as possible.

Right, McGill decided. Now to see if this would work out the way he hoped and planned. He tugged the igniter ring sharply. With a muffled bang and a hiss, the fuse ignited. Tendrils of smoke curled away from the end. *One. Two. Three.* He waited a couple more seconds to be sure the fuse was burning properly. Then, with a smooth, powerful sidearm throw, he pitched the demolition charge through the door breach. It sailed into the hangar, thudded to the concrete floor, and slid another few yards—ending up very close to the MiG-29's left wing. Thin wisps of smoke trailed away from the burning fuse.

Without waiting any longer, McGill spun around and ran— heading off to the side as far and as fast as he could. When he figured he was a couple of hundred yards from the aircraft shelter, he dropped flat. His mental clock was still ticking down. *Let's see*, he thought, *two feet of fuse burning for x many seconds should equal a big kaboom just about—*

WHAAAAMMMM.

A huge explosion rocked the hangar behind him. Flames jetted out through the jagged hole in its massive door. Only seconds later, a whole new series of explosions—even bigger than the first—tore through the structure as the MiG-29's missiles

and bombs cooked off and detonated. Channeled by the shelter's thick reinforced concrete walls, these blasts tore away whole
sections of its roof, lighting up the sky for miles around. Huge
chunks of shattered concrete, twisted sections of rebar, and even
whole trees were hurled skyward . . . and then came crashing
back down with tremendous force. Smoke billowed high into
the air.

Dazed and with his ears still ringing from the enormous
noise, McGill pushed himself back up. He stared back toward
the ruins of the collapsed hangar, now only a huge mound of
rubble laced with rivulets of burning jet fuel. Masses of debris
were strewn across the paved taxi strip leading to the three remaining hardened shelters, completely blocking them.

Job well done, Tony, my lad, he thought with satisfaction.
None of the combat aircraft parked in the other hangars would
be able to get past those obstacles to reach the runway. Not in
time for it to matter, anyway.

McGill turned away toward where Lucente had landed their
speeder. It was time to sound the recall and get the survivors
from his team back to the ship waiting for them off the Cuban
coast. He keyed his radio mike. "Gryphon Two Leader," he
started to say and then stopped dead.

There, barely a quarter mile away, a large camouflage-painted
MiG-23 fighter-bomber was lumbering along another of the sev-
eral taxi strips connecting to the airfield's main runway. Its big
R-35-300 turbojet engine was already winding up to full power.
"Oh, hell," McGill muttered.

In all the confusion, a Cuban pilot and his ground crew
had somehow managed to reach one of the remaining aircraft
shelters on another part of the base. And once the MiG-23 was
safely airborne, all of Gryphon Force—his Blue Team and Flynn's Red Team alike—was doomed. Between its bombs and

rockets and 23mm nose-mounted cannon, that fighter-bomber could swat their slower-moving hoverbikes and jet speeders out of the sky like flies.

McGill recovered fast. He was the only one with any hope of doing anything. He grabbed his slung HK417 and charged ahead, running all out across the field and straight into a narrow strip of woods bordering the runway. He crashed through a tangle of bushes at full speed, ignoring thorns and leaves and twigs that ripped and tore at his clothing and equipment vest. The smoldering trunk of a tree lay across his path. It must have been blown down when the ZU-23 opened fire on Daukša's jet speeder. He hurtled over it without slowing and sped on.

When he burst back out into the open, he spotted a sand-bagged antiaircraft position about fifty yards ahead. It was sited very close to the edge of the runway. Its two-man crew had their weapon aimed toward where the control tower and its neighboring barracks buildings were now fully engulfed in flames. He could see the gun's loader standing on top of the waist-high wall of sandbags and staring off into the distance—probably trying to pick out a valid ground target for their 23mm autocannon. A distinct *pop-pop-pop* of gunfire indicated that Alex Zayas and the three men of his Blue Team section were locked in battle with Cuban troops somewhere deeper in the air base complex. More small arms rattled behind him, from where Haugen and Daukša had the other Cuban flight crews still pinned down.

Off on his left, McGill caught sight of the MiG-23 again. It was turning slowly onto the runway. He grimaced in dismay. That big fighter-bomber would be in position to start its take-off roll in a matter of moments.

Still sprinting at full speed toward the antiaircraft gun, he threw his HK417 to his shoulder and pulled the trigger. Nothing happened. The rifle had jammed. Some part of its firing mechanism must have been knocked out of whack by one of the several powerful explosions he'd set off and then ridden out. "Bugger," he growled.

Knowing he didn't have time to clear the malfunction, McGill simply dropped the jammed rifle. At the same time, he drew his 9mm pistol, a Glock 17, and ran even faster, digging in to close the remaining distance.

Ahead, the loader glanced his way and saw him coming. The Cuban screamed a shrill, frantic warning and jumped back down into the gun position. He scrabbled desperately for the AKM assault rifle leaned up against the sandbag parapet. But he was too slow. Far too slow.

McGill vaulted over the low wall and shot the loader dead at point-blank range. The soldier spun away and collapsed heavily across the base of the ZU-23. The gunner seated behind the twin-barreled autocannon was even slower to react to this completely unexpected attack. Eyes wide in terror, he tried to scramble out of his seat while at the same time fumbling ineffectually for the pistol holstered at his own waist.

McGill fired two more times. Hit in the stomach and chest, the Cuban gunner slumped back. His mouth went slack.

Straining with effort, McGill yanked the dying man out from behind the ZU-23, pushed the body aside, and then dropped into the seat he'd just emptied. He cranked the traversing wheel fast, activating the mount's electromagnetic motor to spin the big gun back around to face the runway.

The Cuban MiG-23 came roaring down the runway, accelerating with amazing swiftness. A long jet of orange-blue flame streamed out behind its tail. The pilot had gone to full afterburner, trading huge amounts of fuel for added thrust in a bid to get his heavily loaded fighter-bomber into the air that much sooner.

"No, you don't, by God," McGill snarled. He swung the twin-barreled gun on target and yanked the trigger. The ZU-23 cut loose with a deafening roar—unleashing a withering hail of high-explosive and armor-piercing shells. Caught just as it was lifting off, the MiG-23 staggered visibly in midair. Bits of metal flew away from under its fuselage and wings.

And then, wreathed in fire, the heavily laden aircraft rolled over. At wing height now, the burning fighter-bomber veered away, slammed into the ground just off the runway, and blew up with shattering force. Twisted pieces of burning debris hurled away from the blast thudded back to earth all around the ragged scar torn open by the MiG-23 as it flipped end over end and then completely disintegrated.

Abruptly, the ZU-23 fell silent, out of ammunition when it ran completely through the loaded belt of AP and HE rounds. McGill released his breath, feeling like he'd just run a marathon. His eyes were fixed on the burning wreck of the plane he'd just shot down. For just a moment, caught up in the madness of battle, he was tempted to hop down off the gunner's seat and wrestle in a new belt of ammunition. Using this 23mm cannon, he could gut buildings all along the southern edge of the runway. But then he came back to his senses.

Even if another Cuban combat plane made it intact out of its hardened shelter, it would no longer have anywhere to go. Not into the air, anyway. Until survivors from the base garrison could clear that wreckage-strewn runway, no aircraft would be able to safely take off.

No, McGill thought, it was past time that he got his people out of here. His team's casualties were already painfully high, with at least three killed. Fighting on longer would only add to their toll of dead and wounded—and without any chance of accomplishing more for the mission. They'd achieved their primary objective and crippled the military airfield at San Antonio de los Baños. Now he needed to get the survivors out safely and back to their ship.

"Gryphon Two Leader to Blue Team," he called. "Break contact with the hostiles and rally on your speeders. The job's done. Repeat, the job's done. We're finished here. It's time to head home."

Listening to the responses that rippled through his earphones acknowledging his recall order, McGill could only hope against hope that Flynn and his people had been able to finish their own mission. Because otherwise, he realized bleakly, all this carnage and death would be completely in vain.

FORTY-FOUR

MORA REMOTE OPERATIONS CENTER

THAT SAME TIME

Fyodor Maresyev looked up with a frown as tiny spurts of dust particles and insulation fibers erupted from the ceiling tiles overhead.

His deputy, Ilya Perskyi, suddenly spun toward him with a worried expression. "We've just lost our satellite links," he said sharply. "Every single one of them."

Ah, Maresyev thought. His momentary confusion cleared. That explained the dust drifting down from the ceiling. Apparently unable to break into this heavily fortified bunker, their enemies had opted to cut them off from the outside world instead—destroying the vulnerable satellite dishes located on the roof above them in order to stop his pilots from flying their Mora drones by remote control. He nodded. The raiders attacking them were not fools. But fortunately, neither were they. "Switch to our backup communications systems," he ordered Perskyi.

The other man nodded and entered a series of commands

on his keyboard. "Our backups are coming online," he reported, watching his screen closely. "They should be fully initialized in less than a minute."

Fiber-optic cables buried deep under the earth ran from this operations center to other, older satellite antennas sited around Cuba's University of Information Sciences. Left intact when the Lourdes Signals Intelligence facility closed down, those antennas had been discreetly restored to working order.

"Very good, Ilya," Maresyev said.

Perskyi looked up from his computer. "Being forced to use our own military communications satellites as relays means we'll experience more latency, up to six hundred milliseconds compared to the twenty to eighty milliseconds we hoped for," he warned. "Plus, we'll have to cope with slower data upload and download speeds."

Maresyev shrugged. "It can't be helped." Flying the UCAVs through conventional geosynchronous links would certainly be somewhat more difficult for his pilots, but they'd trained for all contingencies. In the larger scheme of things, losing access to the Starlink satellites was a minor hiccup, not a catastrophe. "Inform Moscow that we are under attack but proceeding as planned," he told the other man. "Tell them the first Moras will take off on schedule in minutes."

"Yes, sir," Perskyi acknowledged. He hesitated. "If they ask for details about the situation outside, what should I say?" It was a fair question. Sealed securely inside this bunker, they had no way of estimating the strength of the attackers. Nor did they have any information on how the battle was really going. After the first frantic warning that the garrison was under fire, there had been no further word from Hidalgo or any of his subordinates. And now the direct telephone line to the Cuban colonel's command post was dead, probably knocked out by enemy action.

Maresyev considered that. Much as he hated being blind like this, he saw little point in worrying the higher-ups in Moscow. Or his own men, for that matter. "Assure them that the situation is under control," he said with a bit more confidence than he actually felt. "If the Americans or whoever's attacking could actually breach our defenses, they'd already be inside by now. Instead, they're just pissing around blowing up a few satellite dishes on our roof. Whether they know it or not, they've already failed."

GRYPHON ASSAULT FORCE
THAT SAME TIME

Perched awkwardly in the crook of a tree about fifty yards south of the Russian-controlled bunker, Nick Flynn scanned the rooftop through his binoculars. From what he could see, the grenades they'd lobbed up there had more than done the necessary job of destruction. All twelve domes sheltering the satellite internet dishes were blackened and shredded, and smoke curled away from the large metal junction box at one end of the building. Something inside must have shorted out.

"*Sir!*" Hynes radioed from the other side of this southernmost stretch of woods, where he'd been posted to keep his eyes open for signs of renewed enemy activity. "*That fucking PT-76 tank is coming back just like you said. And it's got a bunch of infantry types along this time. They're coming straight up the road from the south.*"

Flynn's head whipped around. He could hear the tracked vehicle now, grinding and rattling along the pavement as it drew closer. Damn. He'd hoped it would take the Cubans a lot longer to mount another counterattack. Now it was going to be that much harder to break contact and retrieve their parked hover-bikes without being spotted. Not wasting any more time, he swung down off the branch and dropped lightly to the ground.

Laura Van Horn was at the foot of the tree waiting for him. She handed him his rifle. "We should bail out of here, Nick!" she warned. "We've blown their satellite links to hell. And Br'er Fox sure isn't paying us enough to go toe to toe with the whole fricking Cuban army for fun."

Flynn nodded. "Yeah," he agreed. He glanced back at the silent operations center. Breaking inside and grabbing intelligence on where Voronin's unmanned stealth aircraft were hidden would have been a much better outcome, but they'd have to settle for having wrecked the Syndicate's ability to fly those planes remotely. And at least he could take some comfort imagining all the hotshot Russian pilots locked inside that bunker staring at blank computer screens and cursing . . .

Suddenly, his mind went into overdrive. How could he assume those screens were really blank? he realized, feeling sick. "Ah, crap," Flynn muttered, finally putting two and two together and knowing that was something he should have done a lot earlier. "This was way too easy."

Van Horn stared at him. "You gone loco, compadre?" She waved a hand at the bodies and burning vehicles littering the woods around them. "There wasn't *anything* easy about this."

Flynn shook his head impatiently. "Think it through, Laura. Would *you* build an operations center without backup com links?"

She sighed, seeing what he was driving at. "No, because I'm not an idiot. And we definitely know Voronin's not one either." She scowled. "Damn. That means the ops center has an alternate satellite com system. So what do we do now?"

Flynn jabbed a finger at the bunker not far away. "We get in there and finish this mission," he said firmly.

Van Horn shrugged her shoulders. "Yeah, good plan. Too bad it isn't feasible. That place is built like Fort Knox, remember? Without Andy Cavada and those demolition charges he was carrying, we're fresh out of options."

He shot her a tight grin, hearing the clanking rumble of the Cuban PT-76 light tank getting even louder. By now, it must be only a few hundred yards away. "Oh, ye of little faith. We might not have any explosives left, but the bad guys sure as shit do." Quickly, he outlined what he had in mind.

Van Horn's eyebrows went up, and her head turned toward the sound of the enemy armored vehicle moving off in the darkness. "You're serious?"

Flynn nodded. "Dead serious."

She snorted. "The dead part seems pretty likely, anyway."

He shrugged. "Not if we're lucky. Besides, you said it yourself. We're fresh out of other options."

"So I did," Van Horn admitted. She laid a hand on his shoulder. Her expression was grave. "All right, you're the boss. But you have to promise me one thing first, Nick."

Flynn nodded. "If I can."

"Make sure you're lucky," she told him softly. "Because I look like crap wearing black."

"Roger that," he assured her. "I'll do my very best." Then he turned and sprinted across the woods, radioing for Hynes to join him and ordering the rest of his people to disperse among the Cuban trenches and dugouts and go to ground.

Van Horn watched him go without saying anything more. Then, with a determined look on her face, she slid a fresh magazine into her own rifle and headed for the edge of the woods.

Several minutes later, Flynn and Hynes were inside the hull of a wrecked BTR-50. It had been knocked out in the earlier battle by a grenade that killed its crew and passengers. The squat tracked vehicle sat slewed at an angle, with only its front half nosed out of the woods. Bodies still sprawled across the deck, with some hanging limply, heads down, over the armored sides.

Flynn sat slumped in the commander's position. He wore a steel helmet taken from one of the dead Cuban soldiers inside. From there, he could see out across the cleared ground around the Russian remote operations center. He breathed shallowly, doing his best to look like just another corpse among several. Hynes crouched next to him, out of sight on the BTR's blood-slick deck and just below the pintle mount of its 14.5mm KPV heavy machine gun.

Through eyes narrowed to mere slits, Flynn watched an eight-man squad of Cuban infantry advance cautiously across the open ground. They were moving by bounds, leapfrogging forward in four-man teams. Half of them were always ready to provide a base of covering fire for those in motion. It wasn't a particularly fast way to move, but it was tactically sound—especially since their commander must half expect to be ambushed at any moment.

The PT-76 light tank clanked slowly along about a hundred yards behind them. Its bright searchlight beam darted here and there, probing the terrain ahead and the two wooded areas on either side for any sign of hidden enemies. Another squad of Cuban troops patrolled alongside the armored vehicle, four on each flank.

Flynn shut his eyes entirely as the searchlight beam slid across the wrecked BTR-50. Even through his closed eyelids, the blinding glare was a deep-red glow. *Do not breathe*, he told himself. He was under no illusions. As jumpy as they must be, those soldiers and that tank crew would react to even the slightest sign of movement by shooting the hell out of whatever spooked them.

The searchlight moved on. He breathed out and reopened his eyes a crack.

That first group of Cuban troops had just advanced past the motionless BTR. The nearest soldiers were only yards away. "Holy God, Sergeant," one of them hissed to his squad leader. "What the hell's going on?"

"Zip it, Gonzales," the sergeant snapped back. "Keep your eyes open. Unless you want to end up like one of those poor bastards." He nodded his chin in Flynn's direction. "Now, get moving!"

The soldiers pushed on, fanning out a little as they got closer to the side of the bunker.

Flynn held himself absolutely still. The PT-76 rumbled closer, still following its infantry scouts.

"Sir?" Hynes hissed softly from his hiding place.

"Wait one, Cole," Flynn muttered.

The Soviet-made light tank kept going. Its treads squealed and rattled as it ground forward along the narrow access road. Slowly, the PT-76 advanced across his field of vision until it was broadside on and only twenty or so yards away.

Flynn's hands tightened on the AKM assault rifle laid out of sight across his lap. "Now, Cole!" he snapped. And over his mike, he radioed, "Leader to Gryphons. Let's go! Put these guys down!"

Instantly, rifles opened up from out of the woods on either side of the stunned Cuban infantrymen. Rounds tore into them, knocking men down or spinning them around to lie in crumpled heaps. Shooting from the protection offered by trenches or from behind solid tree trunks, Van Horn, Cooke, and the rest took full advantage of the surprise they'd achieved. Within seconds, all sixteen of the enemy soldiers were dead or dying. It was a massacre, not a battle.

Hynes jumped to his feet and grabbed the handles of the big 14.5mm machine gun. Without hesitating, he held the trigger down and traversed the weapon from left to right—drawing a line of fire along the entire length of the PT-76's hull. Large armor-piercing rounds a half inch in diameter punched holes right through its thin side armor. Hit repeatedly, the tank's 240-horsepower V6 diesel engine coughed and died in a haze of blue-gray smoke. More bullets slammed into the welded-steel crew compartment forward of the long, low rear deck. Both the turret and driver's hatches clanged open as the three men in its crew tried frantically to bail out.

Flynn shot them one by one as they appeared. Their bodies flopped over and tumbled off the tank as it ground slowly to a halt.

Beside him, Hynes stopped firing. He looked across at Flynn. "Scratch one fucking enemy tank, sir," he reported.

"I sure hope not, Cole," Flynn said dryly. "Remember, we need that thing in at least partially working order."

FORTY-FIVE

MORA REMOTE OPERATIONS CENTER

THAT SAME TIME

Unable to bear just sitting at his desk any longer, Maresyev jumped back to his feet. His impatient gaze slid across the two ex-Spetsnaz soldiers guarding the bunker's massive outer door. They stiffened to attention. Ignoring them, he whipped around to face Perskyi. "Is there any new word from Hidalgo's garrison? Or from the Cuban army's high command in Havana?"

His deputy shook his head. "None. We can't seem to raise anyone. Not by phone or by radio. All the lines are down, and our radio antenna must have been destroyed by whatever knocked out our Starlink dishes. There's nothing but static on every channel."

This situation, Maresyev thought, had elements of the absurd. Right now, his pilots had almost finished establishing the satellite links that would enable them to fly aircraft based more than 2,400 kilometers away. And yet, at the same time, he couldn't make contact with the men supposedly on guard right outside this locked-down operations center. Or with their senior officers located just a few kilometers away in Cuba's capital city.

"Sir!" Sergei Andrianov, one of the lead Mora pilots, flagged him over.

"Problems?" Maresyev snapped.

"No problems at all," the younger man assured him with a wolfish smile. "I thought you'd like to know that I've established a firm connection with Mora Zero-One, and I'm go for engine start. Next stop, the American submarine base in Washington State."

Maresyev clapped him on the shoulder. "Excellent work, Sergei." With a pleased nod, he walked back to Perskyi. "Get through to Moscow, Ilya. Maybe somebody there can rattle a few cages in Havana for us. I want those raiders outside eliminated before they come up with something clever—"

WHAAAMM.

Hit by a HEAT (high-explosive antitank) shaped-charge warhead, the bunker's inches-thick steel door bulged inward and then ruptured. An incandescent geyser of molten metal erupted from the impact point, along with a widening hail of razor-edged splinters. Maresyev, Perskyi, and the two submachine-gun-armed guards were hurled aside and ripped to pieces by the powerful blast.

Lights flickered throughout the building as fixtures shattered. A choking, blinding pall of smoke and burning debris swirled everywhere. With blood pouring from his punctured eardrums, Sergei Andrianov struggled grimly out of his chair. He'd been thrown backward into his flight console with enormous force. Dazed, he clawed for his sidearm. Around him, the other Mora pilots were doing the same.

OUTSIDE THE OPERATIONS CENTER
THAT SAME TIME

Inside the turret of the Cuban PT-76 tank, Shannon Cooke peered through the telescopic sight for the rifled 76.2mm main gun. He whooped with excitement. "Oh yeah! Right on target!"

He pressed his right eye against the sight, waiting for the haze to clear a little. When it did, he frowned slightly. That solid steel door still looked mostly intact, except for a glowing, fist-sized hole near its center. He shook his head. "Fine. Then we'll huff, and we'll puff, and we'll *blow* that fucking door down."

Cooke turned his head to Cole Hynes, who was manning the loader's station inside the tight space of this cramped turret. "Load HE!" Seeing the other man's blank look, he pointed. "One of those, the ones with the white bands at the top."

Hynes nodded. He grabbed the fourteen-pound shell with both hands and tugged it out of the rack with a grunt. "How do you know all this stuff?"

"Courtesy of Uncle Sam," Cooke replied, putting his eye back to the telescopic sight. "I took an enemy-equipment-familiarization course while I was in the Army's Task Force Orange." He grinned. "Typical Army class, though. You get to learn exciting new things—"

"In the dullest damn way possible," Hynes finished for him. He slid the shell into the cannon's breech, slammed it shut, and hunched back against the turret wall, out of the way. "Up!" he reported.

"Firing!" Cooke yelled, squeezing the trigger. *WHAANGG.* The whole turret shuddered when the big gun fired. Through the scope, he saw a brilliant flash against the side of the building as the HE round impacted on the already badly damaged door, blowing it inward.

When the smoke cleared, he could see weirdly flickering light spilling out through the ragged opening his shell had just made. *Well, hell*, Cooke thought, *screw the idea of close-assaulting that place. We'll just stand off and pump it full of 76.2mm rounds of hot, splintering death.*

"Uh, Cooke?" Hynes said from below him.

Cooke looked down. "What?"

"I think the gun's busted," the other man said, pointing to where the cannon's breech block now dangled at an awkward angle. Acrid-smelling gunpowder fumes swirled back out of the open breech.

"Well, that sucks," Cooke said conversationally. He reached up and pulled himself through the open turret hatch. "Gryphon Four to Lead," he radioed Flynn as he clambered onto the deck. "I figure we're gonna have to do this the hard way after all. The darned tank is kaput."

Following him out through the hatch, Hynes grumbled, "What a piece of junk."

"Hey, man. Show some respect," Cooke said with a crooked smile. "This thing was probably built way before your mom was even born. We're lucky it lasted as long as it did, especially with all those brand-new holes you shot in it!"

With his right shoulder set against the bunker's concrete wall, just to the left side of the entrance, Flynn nodded sharply to Daina Perez. The ex-Navy helicopter pilot was crouched over on the other side. "Go!"

She rolled out and lobbed a flash-bang grenade in through the opening. It sailed past the heavy steel door blown aside by Cooke's tank shells and exploded with a deafening *WHAAM* and a dazzling shower of sparks.

Flynn spun in through the doorway and slid to the

right—aware peripherally that the others in his assault group, Van Horn, Martinez, and Perez, were right behind him and already moving to cover their own assigned sectors. But almost all of his focus was down the sights of his rifle. Through the swirling haze and eerie, flickering overhead light, he glimpsed a dim figure rising up from behind some kind of office partition with a pistol in his hand. Flynn fired twice and saw the man stumble backward and fall out of sight.

More HK417s cracked. The other Gryphons were engaging half-seen targets of their own. Russian pilots went down, hit by 7.62mm rounds at close range. Shouts and screams echoed above the gunfire.

Flynn kept sidling to the right. Too late, he spotted another Russian aiming a pistol in his direction. They both fired in the same moment. Hit in the chest, the pilot crumpled. Flynn rocked back under a jolting impact across his right side. Pain flared there. *Christ, I've been shot*, he thought. But he didn't look down to see how badly hurt he was. Allowing the slightest distraction in this chaotic close-quarters fight meant dying.

There was more movement up ahead of him, out in the middle of a group of cubicles. His sights settled on another Russian, also wearing a flight suit. Flynn's finger brushed against the trigger . . . and hesitated. This pilot had both hands high in the air. Face white with fear, he was yelling out, "*Ne strelyay!* Don't shoot! Don't shoot!"

The same cry was going up in other corners of the smashed operations center as more of the Russians tried to surrender. "*Lezhat'! Litsom vniz!*" Flynn shouted at the terrified man in front of him. "Lie down! Facedown!" He heard the order echoed by Van Horn and the rest.

Shaking almost uncontrollably, the Russian obeyed.

Flynn risked a glance down at his side and saw that the

9mm round that had hit him had torn away a couple of his equipment pouches, ripped through the ballistic-fiber overlay of his armor, and then obviously ricocheted off the hard plate underneath. He breathed out. One more bad bruise to go with his collection, he thought in relief, but no penetrating wound.

The next minutes were a frenzied blur of activity for Flynn and his assault group. Twelve of the Russian drone pilots had survived. Most of them had been injured by steel splinters and fragments from the two 76.2mm tank shells that had blown through the ops center's armored door. They were hauled back to their feet, herded outside, ordered facedown on the ground again, and then roughly bound with plastic flex-cuffs.

Back inside the bunker, Flynn stared around at the jumble of toppled cubicles and smashed computers. Had any of the information they needed survived the fighting? Perez and the others went to work immediately, gathering up any documents they could find, plus any portable electronic components that appeared undamaged.

"Nick!" Van Horn called from the far end of the low-ceilinged room. "Jackpot!"

He hurried over to her. The last two flight control stations were still active, with computer monitors open on navigation displays. Glowing lines showed two separate flight paths, one for a drone apparently earmarked for Barksdale Air Force Base in Louisiana. The second computer showed the course planned for an aircraft aimed at Minot Air Force Base in North Dakota. Flynn nodded grimly. Those were the two bases for America's heavy B-52 bombers. Voronin had been planning a decapitation strike against major US military and political targets.

Most important of all, Flynn knew, was that the origin point for both flights was the same. Somewhere in the middle of Kansas. He leaned closer, memorizing the coordinates shown.

Then he turned to Van Horn. "I'm calling this in. Round up the others and get them started back to the hoverbikes. We need to head for the ship before the rest of the Cuban armed forces—all fifty-odd thousand of them—wake up and figure out what's going on."

"What about the Russians?" she asked.

Flynn shrugged. "We're not exactly equipped to take prisoners with us. So leave 'em. Without this center operational, they're not an immediate threat."

She nodded and turned away to start relaying his orders to Martinez and the rest of the Gryphon Force.

Flynn went back outside to activate his palm-sized satellite phone. With a soft beep, it connected to a commercial communications satellite out in space, high overhead. Quickly, he scrolled through his message presets to the one that would report mission success: *pirate valuables retrieved.* The phrase *pirate valuables,* of course, was code for both Pavel Voronin and the priceless information Gryphon Force had been after from the beginning. A quick bit of mental math allowed Flynn to enter the necessary latitude and longitude figures suitably disguised to anyone who didn't know the formula he and Fox had agreed on earlier. The NSA's supercomputers might flag this text for examination, he supposed, but he doubted any of its analysts would be able to make head or tail out of it.

A green indicator lit near one side of the small phone, confirming that his message had been sent. Flynn sighed. Now it was up to Fox to do what he could—and as quickly as possible. According to the navigation displays he'd just seen, those Russian stealth drones were still on the ground in Kansas. But that might not be the case for much longer. He turned back to where Van Horn and the others were gathering. They had some fast moving of their own to do.

FORTY-SIX

KOSVINSKY KAMEN NUCLEAR COMMAND
BUNKER, IN THE NORTHERN URALS, RUSSIA

THAT SAME TIME

President Piotr Zhdanov waited in icy silence while one of Lieutenant General Rogozin's top aides whispered urgently in the older man's ear. He saw Rogozin blanch. When the aide, a full colonel, straightened up and stepped back, Zhdanov barked, "Well?"

Rogozin looked him squarely in the eye. "We've lost contact with the Raven Syndicate control center outside Havana, Mr. President," he said formally.

Zhdanov stared at him. "Lost contact? How?"

The air force commander shrugged. "We don't know," he admitted. Then his shoulders straightened. "But we are also getting frantic messages from the Cuban government asking for our immediate assistance. One of their most important military airfields—the one closest to the control center for those Mora drones, as it happens—has been the target of a major commando assault. The Cubans report they've suffered dozens of casualties and that the air base is in flames. Their estimate is that the attackers numbered at least a hundred elite special forces troops, together with significant combat air and cruise missile support."

Like a striking snake, Zhdanov's head whipped toward where Pavel Voronin sat quietly, apparently as cool and composed as ever. "The Americans know!" he grated out through clenched teeth. "They know what we are planning!"

Around the table, the heads of his other advisers nodded in agreement. It was the only rational explanation for this powerful American special forces raid aimed so precisely and carried out with such ruthless force. Given the current US president's dithering on so many other diplomatic and military fronts, only a clear understanding of the existential threat posed by CASTLE KEEP could have persuaded the Americans to take so many risks.

Voronin shook his head. "The Americans may have penetrated some of our security measures, but they cannot possibly know everything about our plans," he argued forcefully. At this point, he knew very well that showing the slightest sign of weakness or uncertainty could be fatal. Zhdanov was looking for a scapegoat, for someone else to blame for what now appeared to be turning into another catastrophe—one that could easily be fatal for Russia itself if the Americans overreacted.

"Explain that," Zhdanov demanded.

Voronin met his gaze without flinching. Despite his lack of precise knowledge regarding how events were unfolding, he would not alter course. The menace in the president's voice was plain, like the warning hiss made by an angry cobra swaying slowly in front of its intended victim. "There is still no sign of any interference at our Mora hangar in Kansas," he pointed out. "If the Americans knew everything, the aircraft based there would have been their first target." He watched Zhdanov seize on that fact, like a drowning man snatching at a rope.

Carefully, Voronin continued, "This is no time to give in to panic. Or to make critical decisions based on unjustified, unproven assertions, Mr. President. Our attack plan remains viable."

"Viable? Without your pilots?" Zhdanov retorted, not hiding his skepticism. "How is that possible?"

Voronin shrugged. "Pilots can be replaced. So can equipment," he said. "With just a few more weeks of preparation, we can be ready to launch CASTLE KEEP as originally planned."

"Wait a few more weeks? Not a chance in hell! The risks are too high," Zhdanov shot back. "Perhaps the Americans don't have all the pieces of this puzzle yet. But they have more than enough to realize the danger they're in. And every moment of delay only gives them more time to find your hidden aircraft."

Voronin gritted his teeth. He could feel the tide of power in this room shifting against him. Faces that had once watched him with hatred and loathing now studied him with avid hunger and growing confidence—like members of a rival wolf pack pacing slowly around a weakened foe, their eyes glowing as they readied themselves to lunge for the throat and rip and tear. "Then let me offer an alternative," he said tightly. "Give my UCAV handling team at the Kansas site enough time to reconfigure the Moras for fully autonomous flight. They may not be as effective without humans in the command loop, but we can modify our plans, dropping some of the peripheral sites from our list—the American bomber bases, for example—in order to allocate more aircraft to the truly vital targets, like the Pentagon and the White House and their various strategic command headquarters." It was essential, he knew, that he demonstrate his continued control over matters. He shrugged. "After all, considering the power of the nuclear weapons they carry, not every Mora needs to reach its allotted objective for us to succeed in inflicting massive damage on the United States and its command and control nodes."

Zhdanov sat back, scowling. It was obvious that he was tempted by this option. Reducing the target list for CASTLE KEEP was less than ideal, but given the stakes involved, the hope that he might still be able to achieve a victory out of this spiraling mess was definitely alluring.

Rogozin chose that moment to strike. He leaned forward with his gaze fixed firmly on Voronin. "Exactly what do you mean by 'not as effective'?" he asked pointedly. "Do you expect to lose ten percent of your planes if they fly without real pilots guiding them to their targets? Or twenty percent, perhaps?"

Voronin fought for control over his expression. Inside, he felt a wave of rage rising. But it would do him no good to reveal his fury. Or to lie, he realized suddenly. Rogozin had been given access to all the Mora design specifications, including its flight control software. And it was clear that the air force commander had had them carefully evaluated by his own technical experts. For a long, painful moment, he said nothing—rapidly evaluating alternative replies and just as rapidly discarding them.

"Answer Rogozin's question, Pavel," Zhdanov growled. Now he too scented weakness.

Speaking carefully, Voronin admitted, "In some circumstances, the loss rate might be as high as one in two."

"Fifty percent?" Zhdanov said in surprise.

"The task is a difficult one," Rogozin explained, with a quick, triumphant glance at Voronin. "Even the most advanced autonomous-flight software has a hard time handling so many variables—weather, other air traffic, terrain features, and the rest. This difficulty is compounded by the requirement that our Moras

fly at very low altitudes to reduce the chances of radar detection."
He shook his head. "Frankly, in the conditions we face, I consider this estimate of fifty percent losses to our strike aircraft to
be far too low. In fact, I believe we would be lucky if even one
out of every three of the Moras survived to hit its chosen target."

Hard eyed now as reality came crashing in, shattering any
remaining hopes of retrieving some measure of success from
this failure, Zhdanov firmly shook his head. "No, you're right,
General," he said. "The risks are far too high." His gaze shifted
back to Voronin. "And any possible gains are now far too speculative. I will not gamble with the fate of our nation—not when
the cards are stacked against us." He rapped on the table. "Your
operation is canceled, Pavel! Effective immediately."

Voronin held himself rigid. Couldn't these fools see the real
situation? Did they seriously believe it was still possible to turn
and scuttle away in fear? "It will be difficult, *very* difficult, to
safely extract the Mora drones and their nuclear payloads," he
warned softly.

But then, to his immense surprise, Zhdanov only shook his
head. "And there, as so often lately, you are wrong, Pavel," he
said dismissively. He turned to Rogozin's aide. "Have the communications center transmit Code Omega over our very low
frequency radio array," he ordered.

OFFICE OF THE DIRECTOR, OPERATIONS (J3) DIRECTORATE OF THE JOINT CHIEFS OF STAFF, THE PENTAGON, WASHINGTON, DC
THAT SAME TIME

US Air Force Major General Douglas McKinnon sat at his desk,
studying another readiness report from one of the military's eleven

combatant commands. He was working well beyond midnight, as was his custom whenever he actually wanted to accomplish anything. Several different assignments in the Pentagon over the years had taught him that days were reserved for an endless procession of bureaucratic wrangling and time-wasting meetings. Fortunately, he thought, turning another page, he didn't need much sleep compared to most people. Although he wasn't supposed to be in on the secret, he knew his subordinates privately referred to him as "the Cyborg of E Ring"—E Ring being the outermost of the Pentagon's concentric rings of offices and corridors, the only one with windows to the outer world . . . which made it the province of senior officers and their planning staffs.

He looked up when his smartphone rang twice. Then it fell silent for a few seconds. And rang again.

Surprised, McKinnon answered it. "Yes?"

The voice on the other end belonged to an old friend, Carleton Frederick Fox. As far as the outside world was concerned, Fox was a managing director of Sykes-Fairbairn Strategic Investments. McKinnon was among the very few people who knew that the other man was much, much more than a financial executive.

"It's a little late for stock tips, isn't it?" the general suggested cautiously.

"It is indeed, Doug," Fox agreed. His tone was even, with only the faintest hint of strain. "But the US *markets* are going to go *hot* in the morning, and I thought you might want to be prepared."

McKinnon froze. Those were the code words used by Four to indicate a grave and imminent threat to national security. He hesitated. His relationship with the Quartet Directorate was, out of necessity, distant—mostly limited to keeping an eye out for individual officers with the kinds of unusual talents, skill sets, and independent, sometimes reckless attitudes needed by the secret private intelligence organization. Being asked by Fox to involve himself in something more . . . operational . . . was extremely unusual. Which meant this situation was serious indeed.

He tightened his grip on the phone. "Do you have any details on this upcoming market shift?" he asked quietly.

"Keep your eyes on a company called Kansas Meat Packing," Fox told him. "I expect its shares to begin fluctuating significantly very soon, somewhere in the following range of values—"

McKinnon jotted down the numbers the other man rattled off, knowing they were map coordinates. Still holding the phone in one hand, he pulled up a digital map on his computer and entered them. They indicated a spot deep in the middle of rural Kansas, miles and miles away from anything but country roads and farmland. He stared at the map. What the hell could be so important and urgent out there?

He turned his attention back to Fox. "And you didn't want to keep this news in house?"

"Unfortunately, my best people are a bit tied up at the moment," Fox said. "But they're the ones who brought this opportunity to my attention."

Before McKinnon could ask any more questions, a FLASH "Most Immediate Priority" alert popped onto his computer display, along with a new map. He stared in disbelief at the symbol blinking at its center. He swallowed hard. "That hot tip of yours?" he said to Fox. "It's no longer a secret. Not to anyone in the entire world."

CASTLE KEEP MORA UCAV HANGAR, RURAL KANSAS
THAT SAME TIME

The very low frequency radio signal transmitted from the Kosvinsky Kamen Nuclear Command Bunker set a very specific chain of events into inexorable progression—with each event following its precursor only scant milliseconds later.

First, the signal was relayed into the facility's enormous interior by the repeater Major Leonid Kazmin had wired into place up near the roof. Next, the coded message reached the nuclear warhead carried by a Mora drone still parked inside the warehouse. Inside that weapon, the replacement circuit board Kazmin had secretly installed in its permissive action link activated—comparing the Omega transmission to the code hardwired into it. They were a perfect match. In response, relays closed . . . and the 150-kiloton fusion bomb detonated.

In its place, a fireball blossomed—turning the pitch-dark Kansas night sky to daylight in far less than the blink of an eye. Hotter than the sun itself, it expanded outward at two-thirds of the speed of light, consuming everything within a three-hundred-yard radius. The giant distribution center, all twenty-three Mora aircraft, the Pemex fuel tanker, other trucks and cars, and Ivan Strelkov and most of his men vanished utterly. Plasma temperatures that peaked close to two hundred million degrees Fahrenheit left nothing but a swirling brew of subatomic particles.

Two seconds after the weapon exploded, the fireball faded away. But the damage it did rippled outward from the core of the blast. Over a two-mile-wide area, every telephone pole and fence railing burst into flame—only to be ripped loose and sent flying by the accompanying shock wave milliseconds later. Howling, tornado-force winds shrieked in every direction, smashing the lone nearby farmhouse and its outbuildings into kindling as though a giant's huge, open hand had swept them away.

The four men Strelkov had stationed as guards along the highway to the north and south of the improvised hangar lived approximately three seconds longer than their comrades. Hit first by a lethal dose of hard radiation sleeting out from the detonation point, they didn't actually even have time to realize they were already dead—because the roaring pressure wave that slammed into them immediately afterward was powerful enough to crush the cars they were in, squash their lungs and other vital organs to gelatinous gunk, and then send the wrecked vehicles that were now their coffins skittering and tumbling end over end across the scorched earth.

As the shattering noise slowly faded, a huge pall of dirt and dust—now highly radioactive—drifted slowly southwest on the wind across farmland and toward distant small towns. The fallout pattern, those areas where radiation levels would require civilian evacuations for days and weeks and even months, would eventually form a sixteen-mile-wide elongated oval extending nearly a hundred miles outward from the original blast point.

EPILOGUE

SOME DAYS LATER

Hiding his anger with difficulty, Pavel Voronin submitted to a thorough pat-down by one of Zhdanov's hard-eyed bodyguards. This intrusive search for concealed weapons was a pointed reminder that he no longer enjoyed the Russian president's full trust—just one more slap in the face among so many others inflicted on him in the wake of CASTLE KEEP's ignominious end.

The guard stepped back and nodded to one of Zhdanov's civilian aides. "He's clean."

"You can go in now, Mr. Voronin," the aide said, pointing to the half-open door to the president's private office. "You're expected."

Voronin's mouth tightened when he walked in and found Zhdanov seated behind his ornate desk, apparently studying a report of some sort. This time, there was no chair for him. *Yet another humiliation to be endured*, he thought bitterly. Apparently, he was expected to stand nervously before the president, like a frightened schoolboy summoned before an angry headmaster.

Finally, Zhdanov finished reading. With a grunt, he scrawled his signature across the bottom of the report and slid it aside. He turned his gaze on Voronin. "Well?" he demanded.

Stiff lipped, Voronin handed over a folder containing the special presidential authorizations he'd been granted to move CASTLE KEEP ahead. He was being treated like a file clerk or a messenger boy, he realized, instead of an important adviser. He waited in silence while Zhdanov paged through the documents, obviously determined to make sure that none were missing.

Apparently satisfied, Zhdanov tossed them into a metal bin beside his desk—one marked SHRED AND BURN. "A fitting end to a foolish waste of resources," he commented darkly. He looked back at Voronin. "You are fortunate that I am a forgiving man, Pavel," the president continued. "You understand that I gave serious consideration to simply having you shot, like Kokorin or the officers you corrupted in the Twelfth Main Directorate."

Intensely aware that his life still hung by a thread, Voronin only nodded.

"Instead, I've decided to give you one more chance to make amends for your failures so far," Zhdanov told him.

For a brief moment, Voronin allowed himself to relax. Evidently, Russia's leader still understood his desperate need for someone with Voronin's strategic vision and sheer ruthlessness. After all, without the Raven Syndicate and its skilled operatives, Zhdanov would be forced to rely on the same institutions— Russia's military and intelligence services—whose records were marked more by incompetence and corruption than by any real successes.

Zhdanov must have seen his relief, because his mouth turned downward. "But the terms of our association will be different going forward," he snapped. "Your days of operating with a blank check are finished."

"Mr. President?" Voronin murmured.

Zhdanov crooked a finger at a man who had been waiting in the corner of the office—a man who had been standing there so quietly and unobtrusively that Voronin hadn't even realized he was there until this moment. This man, lean and long faced, with short-cropped gray hair, now moved forward to join him in front of the president's desk. "This is Kiril Rodin. He will be joining your Raven Syndicate as its new chief of special operations."

And also as Zhdanov's personal spy, Voronin understood quite clearly. He glanced sharply at the other man, who met his gaze without any discernible expression. "Welcome to the Syndicate, Rodin," Voronin forced out through gritted teeth. He raised an eyebrow. "I assume you have experience in this sort of work?"

"Some."

Voronin caught a flicker of amusement in Zhdanov's eyes. "Some?" he repeated.

"Rodin has acted for a number of other organizations over the years," the president told him. "The SVR and GRU among them. His record is . . . remarkable."

Voronin frowned. "I don't recall hearing your name," he told Rodin bluntly.

The gray-haired man shrugged. "We haven't moved in the same circles." He smiled. "Until now."

And then Voronin understood. Rodin was not only Zhdanov's spy; he was also an assassin. Voronin shivered suddenly. From now on, he knew, he would be working with a pistol cocked permanently at the back of his skull. The president had meant what he said. Voronin would be given one more chance to succeed in pulling down the United States. But only one. His next failure would be his last.

SAINT JAMES CATHEDRAL, ORLANDO, FLORIDA
THAT SAME TIME

As the strains of the recessional hymn echoed through the cathedral's high, brightly painted interior, Nick Flynn and Laura Van Horn stood together in the last pew. Along with the hundreds of family members, friends, and other close acquaintances of Andy Cavada, Cristina Ros, and Javier Torres, they'd come here to participate in the memorial Mass for the three members of the Navarro Regiment who'd been killed during their desperate mission to Cuba. Officially, the three had died in a boating accident somewhere off the Florida coast, their bodies never recovered. Judging by the somber but pride-filled expressions he'd seen on quite a few of the mourners, Flynn was willing to bet that the real story—at least as far as the fact that Cavada and the others had actually been killed fighting in the service of their country—was somewhat more widely known than the Quartet Directorate might ideally have preferred.

Holding Van Horn's hand, he turned to watch the priest and altar servers, bright in their all-white vestments, depart. The closest family members and friends came next, walking two by two in ritual solemnity. Alex Zayas, Daina Perez, and Bill Martinez carried large, framed color photographs of their three dead comrades, each taken during their service with the US Army, Air Force, and Marines respectively.

Flynn and Van Horn stiffened to attention and nodded slightly.

Zayas and the others returned their nods. Deeply sad though this occasion might be, it was also a moment for pride—pride in the heroism, self-sacrifice, and undying devotion to duty displayed by their friends and comrades-in-arms.

Pew by pew, the cathedral emptied. Flynn sat back down

with Van Horn, waiting while the other mourners filed slowly out. When they were gone, he sighed. "Well, I guess we'd better be on our way," he said at last. Some part of him wanted to stay here in this silent oasis of peace and gentleness—so far removed from the harsh realities of the outside world.

"No rest for the good?" she suggested softly.

Almost unwillingly, he smiled. "Or at least the not-so-bad."

Together, they walked outside and down a short flight of steps to the stretch of pavement in front of the white stucco-and-marble facade of the Romanesque Revival cathedral. A dark-blue late-model Jeep Grand Cherokee pulled up to the curb and flashed its lights four times.

"Subtle. Oh, so very subtle," Van Horn murmured in his ear.

This time, Flynn laughed.

They got into the back seat of the SUV to find Fox waiting. He looked them over with a raised eyebrow. "You both still look a bit worse for wear," he commented.

"I wouldn't claim otherwise," Flynn admitted. "Together with Piero Lucente, we suffered four dead and another three wounded to one degree or another. That's more than a third of the people we took into Cuba." His mouth tightened into a thin, hard line. "And that's not counting the civilians we lost when the Russians set off that goddamned bomb."

"Our civilian casualties in Kansas were mercifully low, with no more than a handful of fatalities in all," Fox pointed out carefully. "Thanks both to the region being very thinly populated and to the prevalence of tornado shelters to protect our people there from the worst of the resulting fallout."

"Dead's dead," Flynn said in response. "And I signed on with Four to prevent innocent people from getting killed. Not to be glad their numbers were relatively small." From beside him, Van Horn nodded her own agreement.

Fox looked out the window next to him for a moment, obviously gathering his thoughts. At last, he turned back to face them. "Your regrets do you credit," he said gently. "But you'd be making a mistake to ignore the magnitude of what you—and your whole team—have achieved. Now that we know for sure Voronin's aircraft *were* armed with nuclear weapons," he pointed out, "your courage and determination have saved millions upon millions of other lives. Because there's absolutely no doubt that whatever the Russians really intended could only have ended in an unimaginable holocaust if you hadn't stopped them cold."

Slowly, Flynn nodded. That much was true, he supposed. Some small measure of the evil intended by Voronin and his backers at the highest levels of the Russian government could be seen in the fact that Moscow was willing to detonate a nuclear warhead on American soil—just to erase the evidence of its larger plan. He sighed. "Well, at least this time the CIA and our other intelligence agencies can't turn a blind eye to what's happened. Or pretend they were the ones responsible for saving the nation."

Van Horn snorted. "Uh-huh. And I bet that sad fact has generated a lot of wailing and gnashing of teeth inside Langley's sacred halls."

"Don't be too sure of that," Fox told them dryly. "My sources tell me that Washington, Havana, and Moscow, each for their own separate purposes, are already spinning very different tales. The Cuban government, for example, apparently desperate to avoid any overt connection to what Voronin was doing, has censored all news about our commando raids on its territory. Officially, there was only a chain of unfortunate ordnance storage accidents at the San Antonio de los Baños base, which resulted in serious damage and tragic casualties."

"Gee, how very . . . convenient," Van Horn commented.

Fox nodded.

"And the Russians?" Flynn asked. "What's their story?"

Fox shrugged his shoulders. "Zhdanov's government is blaming the nuclear explosion in our territory on a cabal of rogue officers—officers who were apparently seduced by bribes from unknown Middle Eastern terrorists."

Flynn stared at him. "Please tell me no one important is buying that line of crap, Br'er Fox."

The other man shook his head. "Unfortunately, I can't. The story, fictional though it is, fits the prejudices of Langley's analysts—and its senior executives, too. Which is perhaps more important." He sighed. "Besides, the Russians have offered up to a billion dollars in reparations for any damage caused by these so-called rogue officers. And they've informed our government that those responsible—a major general in their Twelfth Main Directorate named Krylov and two other officers, a Colonel Yakemenko and a Major Kazmin—have already been arrested, tried by a special military tribunal, and executed for what are termed 'crimes against the state and against humanity.'"

"In that order?" Van Horn asked, with a cynical look. "Or was it sentence first, trial afterward?"

"The Queen of Hearts' justice?" Fox said with an equally cynical nod. "My guess falls in that direction."

Flynn frowned. "What about Pavel Voronin?" he asked. "Is that psychopathic bastard heading for his own unmarked grave, along with this Krylov and the others?"

Fox sighed, with evident regret. "I strongly suspect not." He looked out the window a moment before turning back to them. "Oh, I doubt Voronin will get off scot-free. In fact, I'd bet that any financial reparations ultimately paid by Moscow will come out of his Raven Syndicate's corporate coffers. But I very much doubt that Zhdanov will take any permanent measures against him. Voronin is entirely too useful . . . and too clever. After all, this most recent plan of his nearly came to fruition, with what would have been horrific consequences for us and the whole free world. Piotr Zhdanov will not easily cast him aside, even as a scapegoat for this most recent disaster."

Flynn nodded. "Yeah, that's kind of what I figured." His eyes hardened. "Which puts the ball back in our court, doesn't it?"

Fox looked at him with a quizzical expression. Van Horn nodded encouragingly.

"We've been playing defense against Voronin," Flynn pointed out. "We detect a threat to our security. Or to the free world as a whole. And then we do our damnedest to stop that threat."

Fox nodded. Fundamentally, that was the task the Quartet Directorate had set for itself decades ago, a mission that it upheld to the current day.

"And there's the problem, Br'er Fox," Flynn continued urgently. "Playing only defense against someone like Voronin is a sucker's game. One way or another, sometime or another, we're bound to lose."

Van Horn leaned across him. "Nick's right," she said. "We have to take the fight directly to these Russian sons of bitches before it's too late. Somehow and soon, we need to wipe Voronin and his Raven Syndicate off the map."

"Or die trying?" Fox suggested softly.

This time, Flynn shot him a crooked grin of his own. "Not hardly, sir. Dying's not exactly in my vocabulary."

Van Horn offered a wry smile of her own. "And don't bother buying Nick a dictionary, Br'er Fox," she told the older man. "Because when he's got his mind fixed on a job that needs doing, he's not so easily distracted."

ACKNOWLEDGMENTS

As always, many thanks to Patrick Larkin for his hard work, expertise, and talent.